# KISSING THE HEIRESS

"Don't you dare come near me!" she cried.

"I have to come near you," he said reasonably. "It's a very small room."

"I have a toasting fork!" she said, fumbling for her leather reticule. "I will use it!"

With shaking hands, she brought it out.

Julian tried not to laugh. "I have nothing to say to you, madam, that your toasting fork cannot hear," he assured her, wrapping her up in his arms.

"What do you think you are doing?" she squeaked.

He didn't bother to answer. Instead, he kissed her on the mouth, leaning her so far back over the desk that she was afraid of falling. Startled, Viola grasped the desk to keep her balance, and the fork clattered to the desktop as his mouth moved freely over hers. His lips felt strange and warm as he tasted her. The sensation sent a shock of awareness through her entire body.

"Brute!" she gasped in absolute disbelief.

"I have been wanting to do that since the first moment I saw you," he murmured. "And, just so you know, it was everything I imagined it would be. . . ."

**Books by Tamara Lejeune**

SIMPLY SCANDALOUS

SURRENDER TO SIN

RULES FOR BEING A MISTRESS

THE HEIRESS IN HIS BED

Published by Zebra Books

# THE
# *H*EIRESS
# IN HIS
# *B*ED

## TAMARA
## LEJEUNE

## ZEBRA BOOKS
## Kensington Publishing Corp.
http://www.kensingtonbooks.com

ZEBRA BOOKS are published by

Kensington Publishing Corp.
119 West 40th Street
New York, NY 10018

All Kensington titles, imprints, and distributed lines are available at special quantity discounts for bulk purchases for sales promotion, premiums, fund-raising, educational, or institutional use.

Special book excerpts or customized printings can also be created to fit specific needs. For details, write or phone the office of the Kensington Special Sales Manager: Attn. Special Sales Department. Kensington Publishing Corp., 119 West 40th Street, New York, NY 10018. Phone: 1-800-221-2647.

ISBN-13: 978-1-4201-0130-0
ISBN-10: 1-4201-0130-7

First Printing: July 2009
10 9 8 7 6 5 4 3 2 1

Printed in the United States of America

# Chapter One

The engagement between Lady Viola Gambol and the Marquis of Bamph was of long standing, having been arranged by their respective parents when the lady was cooing in her cradle and the gentleman was galloping to St Ives on his rocking horse. By the time Viola could walk and talk, the matter was so widely understood amongst her acquaintances that no one thought it necessary to tell her. Consequently, she learned of her good fortune no sooner than her twenty-first birthday, when all the provisions of her father's will came fully into effect.

Being of excessively gentle birth, she flew at once into a towering rage. Her elder half brother, the Duke of Fanshawe, remained at home to weather the storm, and was not, as everyone expected, called away on urgent business. When Viola entered the breakfast parlor the next morning, he was seated at the table engulfing his steak and eggs as usual, a motley assortment of dogs whining greedily at his feet.

The duke—known to his friends as Dickon—was short in stature, but he wisely made up for it in bulk. Froglike, his bald head sat squarely on his shoulders without the assistance of a neck. His clothes, though not inexpensive, did little more than reflect his love of food and country life, being stuck all over with burrs and splashed with gravy. His mother had been married for her money, and it showed to a painful degree in the son's cheerfully ugly face.

Viola's mother, on the other hand, had been married for her beauty, and that beauty had been passed on to her daughter with scarcely any interference from the father. Her skin was flawless, if a little too olive for a well-bred English girl. Her bold eyes were a very dark blue, and her black hair grew in natural ringlets. She had an arrogant little nose and a stubborn little chin. When she smiled, nothing could stand against her. She was not smiling now, her brother could not help but notice, but at least she was no longer shouting.

"There you are," he said brightly.

"Here I am," Viola agreed, sounding as if she wished it might be possible to deny it.

As she went unsmiling to the sideboard, the palace dogs scrambled after the skirts of her expertly tailored riding costume. Viola dutifully tossed bacon to the dogs, but Dickon could tell her heart wasn't in it. Her heart wasn't in the chafing dishes, either; all she took for herself was a mean little slice of fish, hardly enough to keep body and soul together.

"Aren't you going to eat?" he asked her anxiously. "You'll need your strength for your wedding night. Men are beasts, you know."

Viola frowned at him, her dark brows drawn together in a straight line. When she frowned, she looked like a brooding young queen plotting wars and assassinations. "I'm not hungry," she said coldly.

"Not hungry?" he repeated in blank amazement. "No breakfast? And you didn't eat your dinner last night, either. Too busy throwing it at my head, as I recall."

The soup tureen had missed its intended target, but the memory was still unpleasant.

"It isn't fair," said Viola, pushing her plate away.

"No, it isn't fair," the duke agreed. "*I* had nothing to do with this engagement, after all. You had no reason to throw your soup at *me*. If you must throw your soup, you should throw it at our father. He arranged the marriage, not I."

"I can't," said Viola. "He's dead."

"And that should be enough for you, young Viola," he scolded her. "You needn't run about the place flinging soup just because you are engaged."

"I am not engaged!" she flashed. "I don't want to be married. I'm perfectly happy living here with you and the dogs."

"You don't look happy," Dickon observed.

"That's because I'm miserable," Viola explained. "I am not accustomed to the yoke of tyranny. Fathers should not be allowed to dictate to their children from beyond the grave."

"But he's nabbed you a marquis!" Dickon exclaimed in astonishment.

"Who asked him to?" she demanded in a rather surly tone.

"But why not marry Bamph?" Dickon wanted to know. "You'll have to marry somebody someday, young Viola. It might as well be a marquis."

"Why?" she demanded, her frown deepening.

Dickon gaped at her. "Why? Be sensible! There ain't any dukes out at the moment, and you wouldn't want to lower yourself with an earl."

"But why must I marry at all?" she demanded. "I have a home here with you. I'm not poor. I'm not bored. I'm not lonely. I don't need or want a husband."

"It's to do with the succession," he answered evasively. "You wouldn't understand."

"You mean *you* need an heir," she said scornfully. "Why can't you do it yourself?"

Dickon blushed hotly. "Because I can't, that's why," he snapped. "Cheeky madam! Now eat your fish like a good girl. There are babies starving in Ireland."

"What happens if I refuse to marry Lord Bamph?" Viola inquired haughtily.

Dickon was shocked. "Viola! You are bound by a father's promise. I know it's a cursed, shabby trick and all that, but you'll just have to make the best of it. If it's too beastly for you, you can always come home—after my nephew is born, of course. It's the only way to get your money, I'm afraid," he added.

"What about my money?" Viola said sharply.

"You should have listened to the attorneys before you lost your temper," he admonished her. "It's ironclad. If you don't marry Lord Bamph, you don't get your money."

There followed a long silence, in which Viola tried to imagine a life without money. To her, such a life hardly seemed worth living. "What sort of man is he?" she asked presently.

"Who?" Dickon asked blankly.

"Bamph, of course," she said impatiently. "Is he handsome at least?"

Dickon shrugged. "How should I know? I've never met the man."

"You mean you know *nothing* of him?" she cried.

Dickon bristled. "I know he's a marquis. That's not nothing. We'll know more when we meet him," he predicted. "You might even like him."

"No, I won't," she said crossly. "I shall make it a particular point *not* to like him."

"Come, now," he cajoled her. "Don't be so gloomy. He's sent you a letter. Wasn't that good of him? Wasn't that thoughtful?"

"That would depend on the letter," she replied. "What does he have to say for himself?"

"I hope you don't think I read your letters, young Viola," Dickon said indignantly. "I didn't even read the letter he sent *me*. Fetch the letters, Jem," he commanded the footman.

The footman quickly returned with two letters on his silver

tray. Viola's was only a page folded in half and sealed with a wafer, but the duke had been honored with a large envelope.

"I can find no fault in his handwriting," Viola murmured, placing her letter on the table and lifting the wax seal with her knife. "But his spelling—! Someone should tell him there's no *E* in my name."

"There is so an *E* in 'my name,'" Dickon pointed out. "It's silent, that's all."

"Well, there's not an *E* in Viola Gambol," she snapped. "We're in *DeBrett's*. He could look us up! Or can't this person read?"

"Bah," said Dickon. "It was probably his secretary. None of them can spell."

"And listen to this!" Viola said, her eyes fixed on her letter, her cheeks growing pink with indignation. "'For many years now, dear madam, I have lived in breathless anticipation of the happy event which is upon us at last.'"

She stopped reading to give an exclamation of disgust.

"He can't really have gone without breath for years," Dickon scoffed. "He'd have died."

"He admits that he has known of this ridiculous, medieval arrangement for—and I quote—'many years'! And yet," Viola went on angrily, "this is his first letter. He has never deigned to visit me. He's never sent me a present. As a gentleman, he should have come to Yorkshire in person and applied for my hand. He is a man without courtesy," she decided. "I can't marry a man without courtesy! I shall have to be poor! I don't want to be poor!"

Shoving back his chair, Dickon ambled over to the sideboard and helped himself to the ham, bacon, and kippers that always came after his steak and eggs. "I don't see why a man should apply for something he's already been given free of charge," he said reasonably as he waded back to the table through a sea of Great Danes, Dalmatians, Pomeranians, and pugs.

"Don't you?" Viola said, shocked.

"No," he said simply, licking his fingers. "Do you suppose

that Adam asked for Eve's hand in marriage after God gave her to him? No, of course not. The same principle applies here. Now, don't be angry, young Viola," he went on soothingly. "Read your letter. Ten to one it's chock-full of red-hot lovemaking, all the way from London."

"You're mistaken," she said coldly. "There is no lovemaking, thank God. His lordship merely writes to summon me. I'm to go to London *at once!* He seems to think I'm some sort of traveling exhibit! Oh, and he will condescend to marry me the first week of June at St George's Church, Hanover Square, London—by special license, no less!"

"The first week of June? But that's our holidays," the duke objected. "Then there's the grouse shooting when we get back. You couldn't possibly marry him until October at least."

"If then," said Viola, tossing her letter to the dogs. "As for St George, stuff and nonsense! I shall be married at York Minster, where I was baptized, and there will be no need *whatever* for such a vulgar, unnatural thing as a special license. I'd sooner elope! It's as if his design is to humiliate me—and we're not even married yet!"

Calming herself, she picked up her cup of chocolate and asked, with forced pleasantry, "And what, pray tell, has Lord Bamph to say to you?"

Dickon obligingly cracked the seal on his envelope. Inside was a thick sheaf of papers covered with tiny writing, precisely what he most disliked to find inside envelopes. But, for his sister's sake, he took up the top page, the frontispiece, as it were, and squinted at it.

"Oh ho!" he said presently. "*I* am summonsed to London, too, by God! To discuss *the enclosed document.*" He glared at the enclosed document almost savagely. "Behold your marriage settlement, young Viola. Thirty beastly articles! I pity the lawyer who must read it."

Viola was on her feet. "How much money does he want?"

"Rather a lot, by the look of it," said Dickon. "But you're worth it, my dear."

"I suppose he thinks *he's* worth it!" said Viola, running down the room to him. "Don't sign it, Dickon, whatever you do!"

"I'm not such a fool as you seem to think, young Viola," he said indignantly. "I don't sign anything without a solicitor's advice, not since . . . Well, never mind about *that*," he added hurriedly as Viola pored over the document. "The less said about *that*, the better. Now, don't worry, my dear. The lawyers will sort everything."

"That mumbling old fool!" Viola muttered, thinking very unkindly of their family solicitor. "Mr Peabody, Esquire, couldn't sort his own socks. This isn't a marriage settlement," she complained. "It's unconditional surrender! It's slavery. He wants everything I possess or ever will possess. I do *not* accept his lordship's terms."

"He doesn't want *Lyons*, does he?" cried Dickon, becoming alarmed. Lyons, pronounced simply "lions," was the lone piece of property Viola had inherited from her mother, and Dickon was very attached to it.

Viola stalked over to the fire and tossed Lord Bamph's proposal into the flames, stabbing it with the poker for good measure. "I told you I wouldn't like him."

The duke was almost as fired up as Lord Bamph's proposal. "He's not getting your hunting lodge, I can tell you that! Lyons has the best shooting in all Scotland. I may have to give him my sister, but I'll be damned if I let him shoot your birds, Viola!"

"No, he won't get Lyons," Viola assured him. "I will *not* become one of those pathetic, pitiful little women who must go to their husbands once a week and beg for their pathetic, pitiful little allowances. I may have to marry this cretin to get my fortune, but it is *my* fortune, and I mean to keep it! I'll just have to hide it somehow. He doesn't know how much I have.

I could give him, say, ten thousand pounds, and keep the rest for myself."

"Perhaps he doesn't know about Lyons," said Dickon hopefully. "Maybe we could tell him it don't exist."

Viola walked up and down the room restlessly, following her own thoughts. "These old lawyers are too soft to be of any use," she complained. "I need a ruthless man. For my sake, let him be entirely without scruples. Let him be cold, hard, and hungry. Dirty, too, if at all possible. Have we got anybody like that in our pay?" she asked her brother doubtfully.

Dickon thought for a moment while chewing. "There's Dev."

Viola stopped pacing. "Dev?" she repeated cautiously.

"Dev," he clarified. "Devize. I don't know if he's hungry, but I've heard him called all those other things. In fact, I've heard him called a lot worse."

"Well, don't tease me," said Viola, taking a chair. "Tell me all about this paragon."

"Not much to tell." Dickon shrugged. "Dev's our man in London. He's a stockjobber. He manages our money."

Viola groaned in disgust. "Dickon, this is *war*," she protested. "One doesn't bring a blunt instrument to a war. I need a man so sharp he cuts himself getting out of bed."

"What sort of an idiot cuts himself getting out of bed?" Dickon wanted to know.

"The point is, a stockjobber knows nothing of the law. Bamph will have many clever lawyers on the case."

"What do *you* want a lawyer for?" Dickon retorted. "Everyone knows the law hates women. The law won't help you cheat your husband. A wife is a man's property, you know, and a wife's property belongs to her husband. That's the law."

"You're right," Viola conceded. "But what do you suppose Mr Devize can do about it?"

Dickon shrugged. "Something underhanded and clever, I should imagine."

"Oh, undoubtedly! But would he willing to, say, bend the law?"

"He'll do better than that—he'll break it," Dickon said proudly. "I told you he was a stockjobber, didn't I? The authorities keep trying to put him in gaol, but they can never prove anything. The law can't touch him, you see. He's too clever."

"Really?" said Viola, suitably impressed.

"It takes a toll, however," Dickon said sadly. "It takes a toll. When I met Dev, he was fat and brown. I thought him a handsome fellow. However, he's grown so pale of late, I hardly know him. A shadow of his former! Skin like library paste!"

"I don't care what he *looks* like," Viola interrupted. "Do you trust him? If I'm going to embark on a campaign of unlawful deception with this person, I must be assured of his integrity."

"Integrity!" Dickon spluttered. "I'll have you know his father's a baron!"

"Mr Devize, your stockjobber, is a gentleman?" she said incredulously.

"I just told you his father's a peer of the realm."

Viola sighed. "A *gentleman* won't help me, Dickon! A gentleman is bound by a code of honor. Your Mr Devize would be far more likely to help *Bamph.*"

"Not Dev," Dickon insisted. "You wrong him, Viola. He ain't bound by a code of honor. He hates Society, and Society hates him. They say he's sold his soul to the devil, but that's probably just superstitious nonsense. *I* think they're all afraid of him."

Viola was intrigued. She had a low opinion of her brother's intelligence in general, but he did occasionally stumble across a good idea. "Very well. Send for him," she decided. "If he can help me, I'll make it worth his while. Will he care to bring his wife and children with him to Fanshawe, do you think?"

Dickon shook his head. "It's no good. He won't come. I've invited him to Fanshawe heaps of times, but he's always too busy to leave London. As for a wife, he can't afford one."

She smiled incredulously. "Can't afford a wife? What? In spite of all his shady, unlawful dealings? Where does his money go?"

"It goes to *us*, of course," Dickon answered. "Well, I suppose he takes what he needs to live on, and I don't begrudge him that. He told me once, he does it for the excitement, although what he finds exciting about speculating on the Royal Exchange, I can't tell you. To each his own. He gets all the excitement, and we get all the profits. Everyone's happy, except, of course, the poor fools who get in his way, but that's their lookout."

"Dickon," Viola said sternly, "if Mr Devize is dependent on us for his livelihood, he is ours to command. *Command* him to come to Yorkshire at once."

Dickon stirred uncomfortably.

"Would it be an act of courage?" Viola asked, amused. "Are *you* afraid of him?"

"No! But you don't understand, Viola," he protested. "Dev can't leave London."

"Why not?"

"Dev is a man of genius," he explained indignantly, "and genius is as delicate as the wing of a butterfly. There is a process, a method, to his success. It's very intricate—there's mathematics involved. I'd tell you all about it, but you wouldn't understand. But we interfere with the man's process at our own peril."

"I see," Viola sniffed. "Well, if your delicate genius is too important to come to us, you'll just have to go to *him*, won't you? You can leave tomorrow."

"Go to London!" he exclaimed. "At the height of the Season? Viola, if I went to London now, I'd be hunted down like an animal. I'm not just your elder brother, you know. I'm the only unmarried duke left in Great Britain! I'd be in constant danger. There would be invitations!"

Viola's dark eyes could be damp and imploring when it suited her purposes, as she now demonstrated. "This is my marriage settlement, Dickon. If it isn't done properly, I shall be little more than my husband's chattel. Do you want your only sister to be treated like chattel?"

Dickon thought about it. "I suppose not," he said reluctantly. "But why can't *you* go?"

"I shall be in York ordering my wedding clothes," she explained.

"Buy your wedding clothes in London," he urged. "Don't make me go to London on my own, I implore you! The women there are so fierce. I get such headaches."

Viola held firm. "York would be hurt and insulted if I bought my wedding clothes in London. Besides, if I go to London *now,* Lord Bamph will think I'm obeying his ridiculous summons. He must learn that Lady Viola Gambol is not at his beck and call."

"But *I* am, I suppose!" the duke said resentfully.

Viola started for the door. "I'm depending on you, Dickon," she said, pausing in the doorway. "Don't bungle it."

"When did I ever bungle anything?" he said indignantly.

In the wake of her departure, the duke looked down at his plate. "This is dreadful, Jem," he exclaimed unhappily. "Something must be done!"

"Her ladyship does seem a wee bit upset, Your Grace," the footman agreed.

"What?" The duke blinked in momentary confusion. "I'm talking about the *ham,* Jem. Remember the ham? I think it's turned. You'd better take it away."

"Certainly, Your Grace. Shall I bring out another?"

The duke looked at him incredulously. "Of course, dear fellow," he said. "I wouldn't have mentioned it otherwise."

# Chapter Two

Situated on the highest ground in Green Park, Lord Bamph's London mansion seemed more like a gentleman's country estate than a town house. The drive from the gate to the gleaming white facade of the house was long, giving Lady Belinda Belphrey ample time to observe that the Duke of Fanshawe's carriage was not very clever.

"Oh, Mama! It looks like a fat, brown goose waddling up a country lane."

Swathed in black lace, the dowager Marchioness of Bamph was seated at the escritoire in her boudoir, her handsome face completely innocent of rouge. Lady Bamph loathed black almost as much as she had loathed her dead husband, but she had made herself as plain as possible for the occasion, not wanting to spoil her daughter's chance to become a duchess by accidentally attracting the duke herself.

"When I am Duchess of Fanshawe, I shall put all my footmen in pink," sighed Belinda, smoothing down her pink skirts and patting the pink silk roses woven into her red-gold curls.

"Yes, my love," Lady Bamph murmured absently.

The duke's carriage, meanwhile, had arrived at the house. "Mama, he's getting out," Belinda reported, pressing her pert nose against the window. "Mama! He's wearing *trousers!*"

The dowager's hand jerked, causing an ink blot on the page. "Trousers!" she exclaimed. "You must be mistaken, child. Only shopkeepers and bank clerks wear trousers."

"Hurry, Mama!" cried Belinda, jumping up. "He's coming inside!"

Lady Bamph signed her letter with a flourish, and mother and daughter went down to the drawing room to greet their visitor.

They discovered the duke consulting his pocket watch. Upon seeing the ladies, however, he instantly pocketed his watch. Unlike the many dukes of Belinda's acquaintance, this one was a very good-looking man, with patrician features, a strong, square chin, and the most breathtaking blue eyes she had ever seen. According to Belinda's information, the duke was hideously old—six and forty!—but, in the flesh, he did not look a day over twenty-five. Incredibly, he was not fat.

Even more incredibly, he was tall, the perfect height and build for a dance partner, she decided. His spiky chestnut hair had been cut too short, and he was much too plainly dressed for Belinda's taste, but these were minor defects, easily corrected, and quite overruled by his beautiful eyes. Overall, Belinda was delighted with her prize.

"Oh, you're handsome!" she cried, almost before the requisite bows and curtseys had been exchanged. "I'm so relieved! That is to say, so glad!"

Although not immune to the young man's eyes, Lady Bamph had a cooler head. "I must apologize for my daughter's exuberance," she said, smiling. "She is young and impetuous. What a pity *we* cannot follow her example and say exactly what pops into our heads at any given moment," she boldly added, fingering the pearls at her throat and staring directly into his eyes.

Unaware that he had been mistaken for his employer, Julian Devize smiled faintly at Lady Belinda's exuberance, but her mother's subtlety seemed to leave him cold. "Is Lord Bamph not at home?" he asked, addressing the mother with an air of courtesy rather than preference. "As your ladyship may know, I have come on behalf of Lady Viola Gambol to negotiate her marriage settlement."

Lady Bamph felt the sting of rejection, but Julian was so handsome, she could not resist trying again. "Perhaps, when you have concluded your business with my son, you will allow me to show you the grounds," she suggested archly. "There are many beauty spots in my garden."

Julian smiled thinly. "When I am done, I don't doubt you will all wish me in Hades."

"No, indeed!" said Belinda, taking him quite seriously.

Lady Bamph laughed lightly. "A man like you must be welcome wherever he goes," she said, looking at him hungrily. "Now do stop teasing me and sit down."

Her fingers released the pearls at her neck and trailed down to rearrange the black lace draped across her bosom. How vexing that her maternal instincts had led her, on today of all days, to disguise herself as a grieving old widow!

"Your ladyship is very kind," Julian said firmly. "But I am come to deal with Lord Bamph. If his lordship is not here, it would be better if I went away again."

"Oh, no!" cried Belinda, seizing him by the arm. "Please don't go. We have so much to talk about before the wedding."

"Her brother's wedding, she means," Lady Bamph said quickly. "Please stay, Your Grace. My son has been a little delayed," she went on quickly, as his eyes flickered, "but he will join us presently. I apologize for the inconvenience. Won't you join us in a cup of tea?"

"Your ladyship has made a mistake," Julian said gravely.

The dowager blinked at him. "Mistake, Your Grace?"

"I'm not his grace," Julian said bluntly. "My name is Mr Devize. I'm the duke's . . . er, financial advisor."

Lady Bamph's voice was shrill. *"You are not the Duke of Fanshawe?"*

"No, indeed, my lady."

All the joy went out of Belinda's pretty face, and she sank down onto the sofa. "You look like a duke," she accused him petulantly. "That is to say, you look like they *ought* to look, but somehow never do," she corrected herself. "How vexing!"

"I'm very sorry to disappoint you, Lady Belinda," Julian said gently.

"I was prepared for disappointment," she said glumly, "but *you* got my hopes up."

"Indeed, it was very wrong of you to deceive us, sir," said Lady Bamph, embarrassed that she had fingered her pearls at a good-looking nobody. "You should have exposed yourself the instant you came into the house!"

"I apologize for my reticence," Julian said dryly.

"Where is his grace?" she demanded.

"His grace stepped out into the garden to attend a call of

nature," he replied. With the barest movement of his head, he indicated the French windows.

The dowager recoiled. "What do you mean? Do you mean he's . . . ? *On my terrace?*"

"In your shrubbery, I think," Julian answered calmly.

"My rhododendrons!" she gasped, darting toward the French windows as a rotund silhouette appeared at one of them.

"Oh no," Lady Belinda said sadly as the real duke came in through the French windows rubbing his hands together. "He's fat and bald, as usual. Is that *blood* on his stock?"

"Gravy, I should think," Julian said reassuringly.

Belinda's eyes filled with tears. "Oh fie! Nothing ever works out the way it should!"

"That is the tragedy of life," Julian agreed, offering her a clean handkerchief. "It always leaves us wanting more."

Lady Bamph, meanwhile, had gone forth to meet the duke with plenty of daggers concealed in her dazzling smile. "My lord duke! How did you find my rhododendrons?"

"It wasn't easy, but I managed," he answered, averting his gaze from her voluptuous black-clad form. "You should speak to the gardener about those bushes, madam. At Fanshawe, we always remove the thorns."

"My roses!" she gasped, turning gray. "How could you? You vile little gargoyle!"

"Ah, Dev," the duke said, hurtling quickly past this overwrought, emotionally incontinent female. "Where's Bamph, then? I haven't got all day."

"Lord Bamph is not yet arrived, Duke," said Julian.

"You're so ugly," Belinda whined, briefly claiming his grace's attention.

"Who are you?" he demanded.

She blinked in surprise. "I'm Belinda, of course."

"I'm not ugly, young Belinda," he corrected her sternly. "I have a unique manly beauty that few can appreciate."

"Oh," said Belinda. "I thought you were just ugly. What a

pity I'm not one of the few who can appreciate your unique manly beauty," she added glumly.

Tired of conversing with young Belinda, the duke turned to Julian. "What do you mean he's not yet arrived, Dev? It's nearly ten o'clock. I'm bloody hungry!"

By this time, Lady Bamph had decided to wrest back control of her drawing room, and it was she who answered. "My son has been delayed, Your Grace. He will be with us very soon."

"Oh, he's your son, is he?" Dickon snorted. "Why are you dressed like that? I thought you was the housekeeper."

Her ladyship's smile stretched taut but did not break. "While we wait for Rupert, shall we have tea, Your Grace? Belinda, touch the bell."

"And cake?" the duke said eagerly. "I like cake."

Almost before Belinda had touched the bell, two footmen entered the room, one to carry the heavy silver service and one to set up the collapsible tiger maple tea table in front of the dowager's chair. "Do take your place with Belinda on the sofa, Your Grace," Lady Bamph implored, choosing a delicate French chair for herself.

While the duke gorged himself on cake, Julian conversed easily with Belinda. Very properly, he remarked on the beauties of the house and grounds, the felicity of losing one's self in the wilderness of Green Park while remaining within a stone's throw of Piccadilly, and so forth, but Lady Bamph was not deceived. It was obvious to her that Mr Devize was a devious fortune hunter intent on seducing her child, his object being, of course, Belinda's well-publicized dowry of fifty thousand pounds.

"I hate Green Park," Belinda pouted. "One feels so cut off from everything. I want a proper town house. I want to be in the middle of everything, not hidden away in Green Park. Mama, can we not break our lease?"

"Lease? His lordship does not own the house, then?" Julian murmured. "Interesting." Taking a pencil and a small writing tablet from his pocket, he made a quick note. His memory required no such aid; he did it merely to annoy Lady Bamph.

And annoy her it did. "My son is looking for a suitable purchase," she snapped. "Where do *you* live, Mr Devize?" she asked him waspishly.

"In Lombard Street, ma'am," he replied, strangely unashamed of his humble address.

"I've never heard of it," she sniffed. "In which part of London is Lombard Street?"

"The City, ma'am."

"The City! How quaint. I thought only Jews and shopkeepers lived in that part of town."

"It's nothing like the West End," Julian answered with annoying complacency.

"Do *all* City men wear trousers, Mr Devize?" Lady Belinda asked eagerly.

"Yes, all, my lady," came the shocking reply. "However gentlemanlike, white silk stockings are not practical for a man who must earn his living in the dirt and coal dust of the City. And, for myself, I dislike the affectation of wearing riding boots in the metropolis. I've not been near a horse since I sold out of the army."

Belinda sighed happily. "Oh! Were you in the army, Mr Devize? You must have so many wonderful stories to tell."

"No, not one."

Belinda was taken aback, until she noticed that his blue eyes were twinkling again. "Oh, you are teasing me! But how splendid you must have looked in your regimentals! Was yours a cavalry regiment?" she asked hopefully.

"No, but I did ride a horse."

This riddle flummoxed Lady Belinda, but her mother understood. "An officer?" she sneered. "In my day, only gentlemen could be officers."

The duke handed Belinda his empty plate and licked his

fingers. "Madam, I'll have you know that Dev *is* a gentleman," he said angrily. "His father's a baron."

Lady Bamph's eyes widened. "You are *that* Mr Devize?" she gasped. "The son of Lord Devize?"

Julian smiled faintly. "I have that honor, yes."

"You are the odious wretch who broke Child's Bank!" she accused him, rising to her feet majestically. "Infamous cur! How dare you show your face among civilized people? You, sir, have been the means of ruining some of my dearest friends! I know your mother," she went on, her eyes gleaming with malice. "Odious, grasping female! She must be *so* proud of you."

"Of course she's proud of him," said the duke. "Aren't you proud of *your* son? Speaking of which, where *is* he? The sooner he marries my sister, the sooner I get my nephew."

Forcing a smile, Lady Bamph sat down again. "I'm sure Rupert is on his way, Your Grace," she said pleasantly. "He is most eager to meet you . . . and Lady Viola, too, of course. What a pity her ladyship could not come to London."

"No, Dev," the duke said firmly as Julian opened his mouth to speak. "I'll handle this. My sister is not a traveling exhibit," he announced as he sponged cake crumbs from his waistcoat with his fingers. "She flatly refuses to come to London. If your son wants her, he must go to Yorkshire and do the pretty. Now, don't ask me why a man should go all the way to Yorkshire to make love to a girl he's already engaged to. I couldn't tell you if you *did* ask. But Viola is not a man, and we can't expect her to behave like a rational human being."

Concluding his speech, he licked his fingers.

"It was I who suggested Rupert invite Lady Viola to London," Lady Bamph answered. "I thought her ladyship might enjoy the delights of the Season with us. I see now my interference has led to infelicity all around. I see no reason why Rupert, Belinda, and I could not go to Yorkshire with you for an extended visit, if that is Lady Viola's preference."

"But Mama!" Belinda protested. "Rupert said if Lady Viola didn't obey him, he'd make her very sorry indeed when they married. Rupert has a very bad temper when he is crossed," she confided to Julian, who was taking notes again. "And besides, Mama, it is the height of the Season! We shall miss some very important plays and assemblies. I do not suppose there are plays and assemblies in Yorkshire. Rupert says that Yorkshire is the back end of beyond."

Lady Bamph watched anxiously as Julian scribbled in his notebook. "Nonsense!" she snapped. "Rupert would never dream of saying anything so offensive. For myself, I long to see my future daughter. We will gladly go to Yorkshire as soon as it can be arranged."

Resigned to exile, Belinda asked hopefully if Mr Devize would be accompanying them.

"I'm afraid my work keeps me in London, Lady Belinda," Julian replied gently.

Belinda pouted. "Work! Haven't you made your fortune already?"

"I'm afraid not," he said, putting his notebook away.

"But you broke that silly old bank!" she protested.

"I make fortunes for other people, not myself," he explained. "It's how I earn my living."

"Oh, how sad," she sighed, full of pity. "I think you must be very brave, Mr Devize. Why, if *I* had to earn my living, I think I should die, or else starve."

"So that's settled," said Lady Bamph, smiling at the duke. "We shall pass the spring in Yorkshire, then travel back to London for the wedding."

The duke spoke up. "Viola wants to be married from York Minster. Is that a problem?"

"Not at all," said her ladyship agreeably. "I'm sure York Minster is very nice."

"And the first week in June is out of the question," said the duke, rather surprised that he was having such an easy time of it. "That's our holidays. Then there's the shooting, of course."

"Oh, yes," said the dowager. "There's a hunting lodge in Scotland, isn't there?"

"No, there isn't," said the duke, growing red in the face.

"I believe it's called Lyons," the dowager insisted. "Lady Viola inherited it from her mother, Louisa Lyon, the famous beauty."

"I tell you, you're mad!" the duke barked at her. Abruptly, he got up and went over to the window, beckoning for Julian to join him. "Lyons, Dev!" he whispered urgently. "The she-Bamph has found out about it somehow."

"She's just trying to rattle you," his advisor explained. "Leave everything to me, Duke."

But the duke could not be calmed. Indeed, he was on the verge of leaving the house when the doors of the drawing room were flung open suddenly.

"My son!" Lady Bamph announced proudly as Rupert Belphrey, the 3rd Marquis of Bamph, strode into the room tapping his thigh with a pair of yellow kid gloves. A proud, pretty fellow, he wore with distinction a garnet-colored coat and a pair of clinging buckskin breeches. His cravat was algebraic in its complexity, and his waistcoat was loudly figured in scarlet and gold. His sideburns were as carefully arranged as the red-gold curls on his brow, and he was as handsome as his mother, though a little less masculine. Gleaming black Hessian boots with long silver tassels and high heels completed the picture of a fashionable London dandy.

The duke's eyes were dazzled, and he dug his elbow into Julian's ribs. "Not bad, eh?"

"Isn't it wonderful, Rupert?" said Lady Bamph. "His grace has invited us all to Yorkshire for a nice, long visit."

"By all means, take Belinda to Yorkshire," the marquis said haughtily. Consulting the mirror hung beside the door, he painstakingly adjusted one of the red-gold crescents that made up his left sideburn. "If you think she has a chance of landing him. *I* shall stay in Town, of course. This Season is the best ever, and I am in great demand."

Lady Bamph fixed on her brightest smile. "But, Rupert, dearest, this trip will give you the opportunity to know Lady Viola better before the wedding takes place at York Minster in the fall. Surely that is more important than a few parties and balls."

"If my future wife wants to know me better," he replied petulantly, "she must come to London as I command. I can't be bothered to go to Yorkshire. Why, the society there must be primitive! And the wedding will take place at St George's in June," he added obstinately.

The Duke of Fanshawe suddenly remembered that he had a part to play in the scene unfolding before him. "But Viola was baptized at York Minster," he interjected. "And she ain't a traveling exhibit, you know."

The marquis turned to stare at the duke. "Who the devil are you?" he asked coldly.

"I'm the Duke of Fanshawe, but you can call me Dickon, if you like."

"No!" said Lord Bamph, now staring through his quizzing glass. "I don't believe it."

"Yes," said Lady Bamph. "It's quite true, Rupert."

"You really *can* call me Dickon," the duke assured him.

Lord Bamph stared at his prospective brother-in-law in dismay. There was nothing about the stout, bald duke to suggest that his sister was one of the loveliest young ladies in the kingdom, and everything to suggest that she was not. While perfectly willing to marry a female version of the duke in order to obtain her handsome fortune, the exquisite young marquis did not want his London friends to witness the happy event; they would be sure to mock him mercilessly, as only London friends can. "Perhaps it would be best if I *did* marry her at York Minster," he conceded. "At such a distance, my friends could not be expected to attend the wedding."

"I like this negotiating, Dev," cried the duke. "Everything seems to be coming our way."

The marquis caught sight of Julian, or more precisely, Julian's black trousers. He applied his quizzing glass to them with an air of disbelief, but they really were trousers. "And who are you, sir?" he sneered.

"This is Mr Devize," Belinda eagerly explained. "He lives in the City, and he works for the duke—because he must earn his living even though he's a baron's son. *And* he dislikes the affectation of wearing riding boots in town."

The marquis bristled. "These are not ordinary riding boots. They are Hessians."

"I beg your pardon," said Mr Devize. "I should have said I dislike the affectation of Englishmen rigging themselves out like German mercenaries."

Lord Bamph turned beet red. "I should call you out for such impudence!" he spluttered.

"That would do you no honor, my love," his mother cried in alarm. "Mr Devize is merely the duke's stockjobber. Pray, do not upset yourself over a trifle."

Lord Bamph's lip curled with scorn. "I do not shoot stock-jobbers," he sniffed. "Nor am I in the habit of receiving them in the drawing room. Why is this man here?"

"The duke has asked me to handle the negotiations for his sister," Julian explained.

"There will be no vulgar negotiating," Lord Bamph declared. "The marriage contract is a simple, straightforward agreement between gentlemen. I will never consent to allow any part of my wife's fortune to remain outside of my control. She will have an allowance, if she behaves."

Dickon's pale gray eyes bulged. "You think women are chattel, then?" he asked.

"You wrong me," replied the marquis. "I don't think women

are chattel. I think they should be *treated* like chattel, that's all. You see the difference."

"*I* do, of course," said the duke, "but you may depend upon it—Viola won't."

"Lady Viola will learn to submit to my will," the marquis sniffed.

"Of course Lady Viola will be *guided* by her husband," his mother said quickly, "but first she must learn to love and trust you, Rupert. When she understands that you only have her best interest at heart, she will obey you without question and submit to your wishes joyfully."

The duke shook his head sadly. "I only wish it could be so, ma'am. But I'm afraid my headstrong sister has made up her mind to dislike your son."

"She will not dislike Rupert," Lady Bamph laughed. "Women find him irresistible."

"It's true," Bamph said modestly. "I'm the most popular man in London."

"I'm not surprised!" the duke said with enthusiasm. "He's a splendid-looking fellow, isn't he, Dev? The hair! The clothes! He's got it all. I daresay he'd give a peacock a run for his money, eh? But I feel I must warn you, young Rupert," he said, with more gravity. "Viola's not a sophisticated man about town like you and I. She's grown up in Yorkshire, completely innocent of the ways of the world. She knows nothing of men—all she knows are dogs and servants and horses. She won't like being told what to do."

"She sounds like a wild animal!" the marquis complained.

"True," the duke admitted ruefully. "She's had voice lessons, of course, but I fear she's not much of a singer. I'd rather hear the dogs bark, to be honest."

"Perhaps it would be better if Lady Viola remains in Yorkshire, even *after* the wedding," Lady Bamph suggested. "Your sister might feel woefully out of place in London."

"There's no question of her coming *here*!" cried Bamph,

now determined that his friends never see his bride. "I am for Yorkshire! We leave at once."

"But, my dear," his mother protested, "you must give us poor females time to pack."

"Very well," he sniffed. "We leave for Yorkshire at dawn."

"Dawn, my love?" said his mama. "So early? I have just one or two little things that I must do before I leave town, a number of engagements I must cancel. The Duchess of Berkshire would never forgive me if I left town without taking leave of her."

"Very well!" he snapped. "We leave tomorrow afternoon, if that suits you."

"Yes, my love," the dowager said pleasantly. "Whatever you command."

The Duke of Fanshawe left Green Park in excellent spirits. Blinded by the marquis' elegance, he seemed to have forgotten all about the threat to his beloved Lyons. "Dev," he said, "I've got such a good feeling about that fine young man! I'm going to go out on a limb and say that I think Viola will like him."

Julian smiled faintly. "I daresay she might, Duke. Women are often taken in by brainless, mincing fops with brutish tendencies, I've noticed."

Dickon stared at him in amazement. "I'm talking about Lord Bamph, Dev. I would never describe his lordship as a brainless, mincing fop with brutish tendencies."

"No, Your Grace is too clever for that," Julian conceded. "It was a stroke of genius, pretending to like him the way you did. The man's vanity is unbelievable. What an ass!"

"You mean I don't really like him?" said Dickon, catching on.

"No, Duke. You only pretended to. He's your adversary. He'll fleece you, if he can."

"I had no idea," Dickon murmured in dismay. "I was completely taken in! I had no idea he was my adversary. I thought he was rather splendid. Now, his mother . . . !"

"Yes, his mother," Julian agreed. "How quickly she gave in about York Minster, and the first of June!"

"Was that not nobly done?" cried the duke. "Now you mention it, she did seem a little *too* eager to go to Yorkshire. And she knew all about Lyons, too! Don't forget that."

As the carriage ambled out of Green Park in the direction of the Mall, Julian felt obliged to remind the duke that the Mall was closed to traffic. "There are the gates now, with a guard posted. We'd better turn back."

"But it's the quickest way to get to the Strand," Dickon protested. "Can't I just show them my ivory pass? They always let me through before."

Julian stared. "You have an ivory pass?"

The duke looked innocent. "Doesn't everyone?"

"Actually, no," Julian said dryly. "Apart from the Royal Family, hardly anyone is allowed inside the Mall these days for security reasons."

"That can't be too convenient," observed the duke as they came up to the gates topped with gilded spikes. The duke got his pass from underneath the seat cushion and showed it to the Coldstream Guard on duty. "See how easy it is when one has an ivory pass?" he remarked smugly as the brown carriage passed on into the broad avenue of the Mall.

Julian easily agreed that it was very pleasant as they drove past the royal residences set like jewels in St James's Park. "I must warn you, Duke," he said presently. "You should be on your guard at all times during this journey to Yorkshire."

Dickon gave a start. "Good God, why?"

"I'd be very much surprised if Lady Bamph didn't try to make a match between you and her daughter," Julian replied. "You must take great care never to be alone with Lady Belinda."

The duke paled. "You mean *marriage?* Not me, Dev! They may have caught young Viola like a rat in a trap, but they won't catch *me*. Alone with young Belinda? I'd rather go hungry. If that's what they want, we'd better cancel this trip to Yorkshire."

"No, Duke. You must take the Bamphs to Yorkshire, as planned," Julian said calmly. "I don't want them breathing down my neck while I'm busy shuffling things around on this end."

"This is no time for card games, Dev!" the duke scolded. "They are trying to force me into a marriage with a complete stranger! I won't stand for it!"

"Remember what I told you about marriage, Duke, and you'll be quite safe."

Dickon took deep, fortifying breaths. "Hasty pudding good, hasty marriage bad."

"You've managed to stay a bachelor all this time, haven't you?" Julian reminded him. "This is no different."

Gradually, the duke calmed down. "What I can't understand," he confessed, "is why I must get them out of London so that *you* can shuffle cards."

"I won't be shuffling cards," Mr Devize patiently explained. "I shall be reorganizing Lady Viola's finances so that her assets can never be traced by her future husband. But I needn't explain all that to *you,* Duke."

Dickon lived in fear that someone would discover that he was not quite as intelligent as he made himself out to be. "It's all pretty self-explanatory, isn't it?" he hastily agreed. "I suppose you need me to sign some papers?"

"No, Duke. I've had power of attorney for quite some time, so you needn't worry about anything at all. Of course, I'll keep meticulous records of all my transactions."

Dickon was appalled. "Dear boy! There's no need of *that.* I trust you completely."

"Thank you, Duke. I take that trust very seriously, you know."

Dickon blushed, and quickly changed the subject. "But Dev! What if Viola really likes this ghastly Rupert person? What if she *wants* to give him everything?"

"Some women *do* like their husbands at first," Julian

admitted. "But what about two years from now, when the novelty wears thin? Your sister's affections may change in time, and, if her husband has all her money, that doesn't leave her with many options, now does it?"

"I forgot about the novelty wearing thin," cried Dickon.

The duke's carriage rolled on, traveling east into the Strand. There Gambol House, the palatial London mansion of the Duke of Fanshawe, had stood for nearly two centuries. On the night of a ball, its vast cobbled plaza would be filled to capacity with jostling carriages, merrymaking servants, and barking dogs, but in the cold light of day it was something of a wasteland. In architecture, in size, and, above all, in inconvenience, the house rivaled the royal palaces of Buckingham and St James, but its location was now far less fashionable than it had been in the early seventeenth century, when the 1st Duke of Fanshawe had begun to build his London residence. Its overgrown south gardens bordered on the Thames, which had been silvery and teeming with salmon in the previous century; now the river was brown and redolent with waste and rubbish. The northern facade, which faced the Strand, had been remodeled in gothic splendor by Christopher Wren, but the original baroque southern facade, by Inigo Jones, remained untouched, although these days it could only be seen by bargemen plying their crafts up and down the river.

"You can set me down here, Duke," said Julian, knocking on the hatch. "I'll walk back to the City."

"You're staying to lunch, surely," Dickon exclaimed in surprise as the carriage stopped. "You must eat, Dev. You're wasting away before my eyes! I insist that you stay to lunch."

Julian only smiled. "There's a perfectly good tavern just around the corner from the Exchange. They make excellent sandwiches, and the ale's not bad, either."

The duke's belly rumbled ominously. He was too hungry to press the young man.

"Suit yourself," he said gruffly.

Julian put on his hat and walked east toward Fleet Street and the City.

# Chapter Three

Viola sat in the private parlor of the King's Head Inn, York, surrounded by her most recent purchases as she fortified her tissues with afternoon tea. Never in her life had a shopping excursion failed to restore her to good spirits, but, without question, she was as unhappy after a week in York as she had been at the start.

"Perhaps," she said doubtfully, "I should have gone to London with my brother."

Viola's maid was busily applying her ladyship's labels to the parcels with a little pot of rabbit glue, but at the mention of London, she abandoned the task. London, the grandest city in all the world, packed to the rafters with beautifully dressed lords and ladies, both foreign and domestic, had filled Dobbins's dreams for years. "I've always wanted to go to London, my lady!" she cried eagerly.

"Yes, I know you have," Viola said dryly. "And I promised your mother I would never take you. You'd only fall victim to some silver-tongued London man and never be seen or heard from again. I could go alone, and hire a new maid when I get there."

"My lady!" Dobbins protested. "You can't go to London alone."

"I wouldn't really be alone, Dobbins. I'd be in my carriage, with my driver, my footmen, and my postboys." She grimaced suddenly in annoyance. "And I might as well hire a brass band, flambeaux, and jugglers! I can't very well blazon the fact that I'm taking my business to London! York would be so hurt."

"We could go on the stagecoach," Dobbins said eagerly. "You'd have to take me with you then, for there's highwaymen and bold kidnapping rakes all along the Great North Road! Now, where's that pretty little toasting fork your ladyship found at the silversmith's . . . ?"

To Viola's amusement, Dobbins hunted through the open boxes on the table until she found the toasting fork. "See how sharp it is?" she cried, extending the telescoping handle and testing the tines with a finger. "I'd stab anyone who got near your ladyship."

"Give me that," Viola said, disarming her maid. "You are incorrigible, Dobbins," she went on, collapsing the silver handle. "No, I couldn't go on the stagecoach. Ladies don't travel by stagecoach, and besides, York would know I was on it. My people would feel abandoned."

"They'd get over it," grumbled Dobbins. "Everyone goes to London, my lady. It's not a crime. We could take the Night Mail!" she said suddenly, lighting up. "It stops here in the dead of night, so no one would see us."

"*Ladies*, Dobbins, do not avail themselves of such vulgar modes of travel," Viola said severely. "We do not depart in the dead of night like criminals."

"There's a young lady in the taproom right now with a ticket on the Night Mail," Dobbins argued. "I heard Mrs Reynolds talking about it."

"Nonsense," Viola said stoutly. "Gentlewomen do not sit in common taprooms, and they certainly don't travel on the Night Mail. You are mistaken, Dobbins."

Dobbins looked mulish.

Viola sighed impatiently. "I can see I shall have to get to the bottom of this," she said crisply. "Let Mrs Reynolds come before me. I'm sure you must have misunderstood what you

heard, Dobbins. As sometimes happens when one eavesdrops,"
she added severely.

The landlady appeared in all haste, smelling of onions and
trembling in fear. "My lady!" she cried, curtseying madly. "I
trust that everything is to your ladyship's satisfaction?"

"Ah, Mrs Reynolds. My maid tells me there is a *lady* in the
taproom," Viola said, chuckling at the absurdity, "but I am
certain this cannot be so."

Mrs Reynolds's face turned as red as a beef heart.

Viola frowned. "*Is* there a lady in the taproom?" she demanded.

Mrs Reynolds began a fresh round of curtseying. "I beg
your pardon, my lady! I had nowhere else to put Miss Andrews, your ladyship having taken both the private parlors."

"You make it sound as if I burgled them," Viola complained.
"I would have given up the other parlor before I let you put a
gentlewoman in a common taproom. In any case, no gentlewoman I know would *allow* herself to be put in a taproom."

"It's poor little Mary Andrews," said Mrs Reynolds.

"I know Mary Andrews!" Viola exclaimed. "My brother
gave her father the living at Gambolthwaite upon my advice."

"The vicar's been dead six months," said Mrs Reynolds.

"Yes, I know," Viola replied dryly. "I just found a replacement
for him. I am not so out of touch with my people, Mrs
Reynolds, that they can die without my knowing of it. "

"No, my lady," said Mrs Reynolds, chastened.

"And so you put Miss Andrews in the taproom!" Viola
shook her head. "That will not do, Mrs Reynolds. Desire her
to come up to me at once, and bring us a fresh pot of tea—she
will need it after her ordeal. And what's all this nonsense
about her traveling on the Night Mail?"

The last question was asked too late to receive any reply
from Mrs Reynolds, who had bolted from the room almost in
advance of her orders.

Presently, Miss Andrews appeared. She was a thin, little

person with a scrubbed face that might have been pretty if its eyes and nose had not been so red from crying. Her bonnet looked like an upside-down coal scuttle, and her black bombazine dress was uncommonly ugly. Viola, who believed in being well-dressed, even in times of the greatest adversity, was offended by this poor showing, but, remembering the sylphlike young girl in sprigged muslin that Miss Andrews once had been, she said kindly, "Come in, child. Don't be afraid. It is I, Lady Viola."

"I'm sorry to be such a bother, my lady," the girl whispered, choking back a sob.

"You couldn't bother me if you tried, dear," Viola said briskly. "I can't believe you were in the taproom. Indeed, I am ashamed of Mrs Reynolds for putting you there."

"But Mrs Reynolds has been so kind to me," protested the girl, taking a few courageous steps into the room. "I'm sure I don't deserve it. You see, I have no money." As she spoke, she kept her enormous brown eyes fixed on her shoes. Viola found all this cringing highly insulting. Anyone would have thought the child expected Lady Viola to eat her!

"Do sit down," said Viola with determined kindness. "Help her, Dobbins," she added, as Miss Andrews showed no signs of knowing how to operate a chair. "Now, then," Viola said brightly when the unhappy girl was seated. "It's Mary, isn't it? Mary Andrews?"

The brown eyes flew up in amazement, then crashed down again. "Indeed, your ladyship is *very* k-kind to remember me," she stuttered, her eyes streaming. "I never dreamed you would."

"A good memory is hardly an indicator of kindness," Viola said dryly, drawing a look of sheer terror from the brown eyes. "However, I am not an ogre, I hope," Viola added quickly. "Now, then, my dear, what's all this about you going to London on the Night Mail?"

Miss Andrews's story emerged in a veritable flood of tears.

The gist was that she was being sent to London to live with an aunt whom she had never met. "To own the truth, there was a rift between my father and my aunt some years before I was born. Papa did not approve of the man she married, and even after he died—my Uncle Dean, I mean—Papa could not forgive her. I fear my aunt is not quite respectable, but I have nowhere else to go!"

"If she isn't respectable, you cannot live with her, my dear," Viola said instantly.

"No, my lady," Mary agreed, her eyes and nose overflowing again. "But my mother—my stepmother, I mean—says that I am too stupid to be a governess, and what else can I do?"

"*Are* you too stupid to be a governess?" Viola asked politely.

"I don't think I am, my lady," Mary answered. "My father educated me himself in all the classical subjects. Perhaps," she went on, plucking up her courage, "if your ladyship could recommend me to a good family . . ."

Viola spoke bluntly. "My dear girl, all the Latin in Sweden could not save you from the scorn of high-spirited English children if you cannot keep your waterworks under good regulation. You have no natural authority, and authority is a quality essential in a governess. I could not, in good conscience, recommend you to anyone as a governess."

The courage Mary had just plucked up vanished as if it had never been plucked up at all, and a fresh waterfall of tears began to flow down her soggy, red face.

"Why can't you remain with your stepmother?" Viola asked impatiently.

"She has a place to live with her cousin in Gloucester, but she cannot take me. Her cousin is not a wealthy man, and I am no relation to him."

"I see. Well, perhaps your Aunt Dean is not so bad," Viola suggested. "Your father did not like her, but clergymen always *do* seem to think the worst of people, I have noticed. Perhaps your aunt is no worse than the *average* sinner. I will know more when I meet her."

Mary blinked at her in amazement. "When you meet her, my lady?"

"Of course," said Viola. "I have been thinking of going to London myself, but, for reasons of my own, I would prefer to travel incognito. Your dilemma comes at a perfect time for me. I shall go to London on the Night Mail in your place. I will meet your aunt. She will think that I am you, and I will allow her to think so. In that way, I will be able to determine whether or not she is a fit guardian for you pretty quickly. If she is, I will send for you. In the meantime, you will go home with Dobbins, where you will be safe."

"I have no home, my lady," Mary said pathetically.

"I meant *my* home," said Viola. "Fanshawe. Dobbins will dress you in my clothes for the journey, and no one in York will ever suspect that Lady Viola is on her way to London. They will assume I'm in my carriage with Dobbins."

"What am I to do at Fanshawe, madam?" cried Mary, quivering with fresh panic.

"You'll be my guest, dear," Viola explained. "You needn't do a thing. Dobbins will look after you. It will give her something to do while I'm away."


Three days and four nights later, a little after three on a very foggy morning, the Night Mail from York rolled into the yard of the Bell Savage Inn, Ludgate Hill, London. "Within an inch of time," the big, beefy landlord told the postmaster as the two met in the yard.

"On the nose, Mr Jennings, on the nose," the postmaster replied as the armed guards who had accompanied the Mail on its journey repaired to the inn for breakfast.

Half-asleep and bone-weary, Viola stumbled down the steps, blinking in the sudden glare of torches. For the first time in her life, she was not pristine. The Night Mail's grueling schedule scarcely allowed its passengers time to visit the convenience on its brief stops, let alone bathe or change clothes. Underneath her unwashed garments, Viola's skin itched. Although she had kept her bonnet on at all times, she was desperately worried that she might have picked up lice or something worse from her fellow travelers. Her head ached.

"Perfectly respectable," the postmaster was saying. "Parson's daughter . . . Poor as a church mouse. . . . 'Tis a shame. . . ."

The landlord's eyes touched on her doubtfully, but she could not blame him for that. Respectable females did not travel on the Night Mail, after all.

No one had come to meet Mary Andrews, not even a manservant, Viola realized with a shock. To be left standing in the yard of a busy London coaching house, two hundred miles from one's home, in the darkest hours before dawn, was decidedly an unhappy experience. At least, on the Night Mail, Viola had been under the protection of the guards. Here she had no one to defend her. *This* was the reception that Mrs Dean had planned for her young niece?

Fuming, Viola stood in the yard for what seemed like an age before the busy landlord made his way to her. He smelled strongly of onions. "Miss Andrews?" He greeted her uncertainly, as if not quite sure he had received good information from the postmaster.

"Good morning, landlord," Viola said crisply. "I would like a private chamber, if you please. A hot bath, and a hot breakfast, too, if that's not too much to ask."

To Mr Jennings she was a puzzle. Her superior accent proclaimed her to be a gentlewoman accustomed to good service. Her clothing, however travel-stained, was of the best quality, too. Miss Mary Andrews didn't look poor to him, but the postmaster had said she was. If she *wasn't* poor, why had she come to London on the Night Mail? And if she *was* poor, how could she expect to afford the hospitality of the Bell Savage Inn? Something was not quite right here, he decided. Because she was young and fine-looking, he suspected that she was meeting a man, probably running away from home.

Viola impatiently took her purse from her reticule and gave the man a shilling. "A room, landlord," she repeated firmly.

"I've a snug room for you with a lovely little sitting room, miss," he said, instantly pocketing the silver coin, and with it his scruples.

While Viola would never have described the tiny sitting room he led her to as "lovely," it was adequate. "Which would you like first, miss?" he asked her as the porter brought up her trunk. "Bath or breakfast?"

Viola's stomach lurched. She had eaten nothing but hard cheese and even harder tack biscuits over the last three days, but she couldn't even think about food until she was clean.

"Bath, I think, and I shall need a maid, too, of course. Just a girl to help me," she explained when the landlord hesitated. "Anyone will do."

When she was alone, Viola removed her bonnet. The mirror over the washstand presented a shocking sight. Her face was greasy and pale, her fine, dark eyes were puffy from exhaustion, and her curly black hair was flat and dull. She noticed an offensive odor, and had wondered what it was. With a start, she realized that it was herself. "I stink," she confessed, red-faced, to the mirror. "I, Lady Viola Gambol, *stink.*"

After her bath, Viola felt almost human again. Bundled in her quilted dressing gown of blue satin, she curled up in front of the fire in the sitting room to dry her hair while the maid-servant emptied the tub. When instructed to get rid of the pile of clothing in the corner, the girl looked incredulous, but silently obeyed.

Breakfast arrived, and Viola ate lustily, washing burnt sausages down with cool buttermilk. After eating, she felt sleepy, but a sudden, violent knocking on the door of the sitting room put an end to all thoughts of rest. She scarcely had time to open the door before the landlord came in, dragging the unfortunate maidservant by the ear. As Viola watched in shock, he threw the girl bodily across the room. She landed in a broken heap at Viola's feet.

"There's your thief, miss," he roared while the girl whimpered. "I caught her red-handed with your clothes!"

Viola was an aristocrat, but she did not care to see servants mistreated. "I gave her those things, landlord," she said angrily, helping the girl to her feet.

The landlord stared at Viola, confused. "What do you mean?"

Ignoring him, Viola examined the servant. "Your ear is very red, my dear," she said gently, "but there does not appear to be any permanent damage. You'd better sit down," she added, leading her to the fireside.

The landlord scowled. "There's nothing wrong with her, miss. Her ears are always red. Get back to work, you!" he added menacingly. "I'm not paying you to sit on your arse, crying."

"There's no question of her returning to work, I'm afraid," said Viola, taking another shilling from her purse. "This young woman is under my protection now."

"You're mighty high-handed for a parson's brat, I must say," he said, pocketing her coin.

Viola was tempted to tell the odious man that he was addressing Lady Viola Gambol. However, she decided that the damage to her reputation would not be worth the pleasure of watching him cower. Besides, she was perfectly capable of getting her way without using her rank to bully people. "Thank you," she said simply. "You may go now."

"You'll regret any kindness you show that worthless bonetail," he predicted. "I never had a decent day's work out of her."

Viola opened the door for him. "What a relief to you to be rid of her," she remarked pleasantly. Then, closing the door on him, she turned to look at the thin young woman. "You must allow me to apologize, my dear," she said quietly. "I did not mean to cause you trouble."

The girl looked at her in amazement. No one, let alone a fine lady dressed in satin, had ever apologized to her before in her life.

"I had meant to hire a lady's maid when I got to London," Viola told her. "You will do. My name is . . ." Here she paused. While she had no intention of taking the girl into her confidence, she did not like to tell a direct lie if it could be avoided. "You may call me 'madam.'"

"Lady's maid!" the girl exclaimed. *"Me?"*

"What is your name, dear?" Viola asked.

"Pansy Cork, miss—er, madam."

"Very good, Cork. I expect you know nothing about the care of clothes?"

"I've only worked in the kitchen my whole life, madam," Cork confessed.

"Perfect," said Viola. "I like a blank slate. That way I needn't waste any time purging you of bad habits. The only decent maids I've ever had are the ones I've trained myself."

Without further ado, Viola brought the girl clean clothes. She had chosen her plainest dress, a walking dress of soft gray wool, but to Cork it looked like the raiment of a princess. There were also clean silk petticoats, drawers of soft white lawn, and a pair of silk stockings.

Cork stared, afraid to touch them. "Don't ask me to iron them, madam," she pleaded. "I'd be sure to ruin them." She flew into a panic when Viola told her they were for her to wear.

"If you're going to be a lady's maid, you must look the part," Viola said firmly. "Later, I will cut your hair and show you how to clean your teeth, but I'm far too tired at present. I'm going to bed."

In fact, Viola fell asleep the moment her head hit the pillow.

\* \* \*

East London was heavily invested with bells, and Ludgate Hill, with its proximity to St Paul's Cathedral, as well as dozens of other smaller churches, had more than its fair share of the daily bombardment. Promptly at six AM, they all began to ring at once, though not, of course, in unison. It was as if hell itself had broken loose and this cacophony was London's way of beating it back, or else joining it.

At the first toll, Viola awoke with a violent start and sat up, her heart pounding, her hands clapped over her ears. The clanging was so loud she might as well have been inside a bell tower, with the peals breaking directly over her head. She jumped out of bed, and was astonished to find Pansy Cork peacefully asleep in a chair in the next room.

"Wake up," she screamed, shaking the girl. "The inn is on fire!"

Cork jumped up. The dress Viola had given her was too long, and she stumbled over the skirts. "Six of the clock! I'm late! I'll be skinned alive!"

All at once, Cork remembered that she was no longer employed in the kitchen. "It's only the church bells, madam," she assured Viola.

"Oh," said Viola, feeling a little foolish. Gradually, her pulse returned to normal. "Well, we may as well have breakfast now we are awake," she said, recovering. "Ring the bell, and let's hope someone hears us over the din."

Everyone in the inn seemed to have had the same idea at once, and breakfast was very long in arriving. In the meantime, Cork stood atop the table while Viola pinned up the hem of her dress. "These silk drawers is tickling me, madam," Cork complained.

"These silk drawers *are* tickling me," Viola corrected. "And they are not silk. They are made of lawn. Lawn is a very fine, sheer linen that is lighter than cambric. Originally, it came from a place called Laon, in France. For that reason, it is sometimes called French cambric."

"Blimey!" Cork breathed, intimidated by the young lady's expert knowledge.

When breakfast arrived, Cork sat down with her mistress at the table near the window.

"You will not be eating with me, of course, when we are at home," Viola explained, looking out the window. "You will eat with the other servants. But when I'm traveling, I enjoy the company. What can you tell me about the shop across the street? Difficult to tell in this beastly fog, but I think I see hats. Hats are very important, Cork. I must teach you all about hats. I'm very particular—"

Viola's dissertation on hats was interrupted by a sudden loud banging on the door.

"Mary Andrews! Mary Andrews, I know you're in there! Open this door at once!"

The woman on the other side of the door was screaming furiously.

Cork jumped to her feet, but Viola motioned her to be seated. Going to the door herself, she flung it open, disclosing an ample woman with a red face. The woman wore a short pelisse of rabbit fur over a day dress of puce wool. Ostrich feathers curled over the high poke of her straw bonnet. Her small, wet mouth fell open as she stared in surprise at Viola. Arrayed in an impeccably tailored walking dress of coral pink cambric, with ribbons threaded through her now clean and glossy black ringlets, Viola obviously was not what she had expected.

"My good woman," said Viola, with unfounded optimism, "what do you want?"

"I beg your p-pardon, ma'am," she stammered, curtseying. "I was looking for my niece."

"Oh? You are Mrs Dean, I collect? I have been here, madam, for nearly four hours!"

The woman gaped at her. "You mean that *you* are my niece?" she cried. "You naughty girl! You are not in mourning for your father, I see. And what do you mean by hiring a room—with a parlor, no less! Who do you think is going to pay for all this? You may think because I live in London that I am rich, but, I assure you, I am no such thing!"

Viola looked at her coldly. "I am quite able to pay for my room, madam."

"Oh!" said Mrs Dean, pleased. "You have some money about you? Excellent. But you mustn't waste it, Mary," she cautioned. "There was no need to hire a room, not when I have gone to the trouble of coming all this way to fetch you."

"Was I meant to stand in the yard for four hours? I didn't realize," Viola said tartly. "And what do you mean when you talk of coming all this way? Do you not reside in London?"

Mrs Dean chuckled at her ignorance. "London is a great big place, Mary. York is nothing compared to it." She sailed into the room and went directly to the breakfast table. "And you are?" she inquired of Cork as she picked up the teapot.

"This is my maid, Cork," Viola said coldly.

"A servant! Off you go, then," cried Mrs Dean, taking Cork's place at the table and helping herself to the remains of Cork's breakfast. "I must say, my dear Mary," she cried, almost choking on her bacon, "that you are far better looking than I had dared to hope. Having seen you in your infancy, I was expecting a rather common little miss, but you have grown into a beauty. You will do very well on the London market. Who knows? You might attract a rich gentleman, possibly even a handsome young lord."

Viola was skeptical. A husband, of course, was just what little Mary Andrews needed, but what sort of husband could the teary-eyed niece of this vulgar, blowsy female expect to attract? That was the material question. "I am obliged to you, madam," she said, looking away from the disgusting spectacle of Mrs Dean consuming her appropriated breakfast.

"What are you now—sixteen, seventeen?" Her greedy eyes went over Viola's twenty-one-year-old figure, settling on the well-developed bosom. "You seem very poised and grown-up for such a young girl! But gentlemen like that."

Viola's eyebrows went up. "Do they?" she asked politely.

Mrs Dean smiled on, even as she picked her teeth. "Are you packed and ready to go, Mary? I have a hack waiting."

Viola recoiled. "Don't you keep a carriage?"

"My dear, it's too expensive! None but the very rich can afford to keep a carriage in London. Owning a carriage . . . Why, that's almost like owning one's own town house!"

"You don't own your home?" Viola exclaimed.

"Don't worry, love," said Mrs Dean with a sly wink. "I've a strong, steady lease as long as Mr Pettigrew has got a pulse."

Viola made no attempt to determine the meaning of this cryptic remark.

By the time Mrs Dean and Viola emerged from the inn, followed by Cork carrying her own small bundle, and the porter carrying Viola's luggage, the fog had dissipated, and the sun was shining. The big shop windows sparkled up and down the length of Ludgate Hill. Viola caught sight of a large domed edifice at the end of the street, and her opinion of London was elevated. While it was hardly as grand as her beloved Fanshawe, the structure was impressive in its own small way. "Who lives there?" she asked brightly, cheered by the sunshine.

Cork giggled. "God lives there, madam. 'Tis St Paul's Cathedral."

"Oh," said Viola, disappointed. "I thought it would be bigger."

As the hackney carriage rolled west, Viola pushed her head out of the window, staring in awe at the endless manmade scenery. She could scarcely believe she was still in England. London was surely the biggest, busiest place on earth. People were everywhere, loud and alive, both men and women, rich and poor. Horses, vehicles, dogs, even children, thronged the streets. And everyone, it seemed, was in a devil of a hurry.

Viola was terrified. "Do they mean to attack us?"

Mrs Dean looked at her in surprise. "Who, Mary?"

"That angry mob out there," Viola cried. "It looks very ugly. Are there no soldiers to subdue them?"

Mrs Dean laughed heartily. "You call that a mob, Miss Mary?" she jeered.

"Is it always so busy?" Viola cried in amazement.

"I told you, York is nothing to London," Mrs Dean said smugly. "And close your mouth, Miss Mary—you look like a bumpkin."

Viola closed her mouth with a snap.

Ludgate Hill flowed into Fleet Street, which seemed to go on for miles and miles and miles, with no end in sight. Then, just past the Law Courts, Fleet Street became the Strand, and Viola instantly recognized Gambol House; she had seen dozens of artists' views of the place, and was inclined to think it the finest house in all London. "Beautiful!" she exclaimed, grateful for any landmark in this strange, frightening city.

"That old heap!" scoffed Mrs Dean. "No one lives in the Strand these days," she informed Viola. "It ain't considered fashionable."

"I shouldn't call the Duke of Fanshawe 'no one,'" Viola said coldly.

"Did you never meet the duke?" Mrs Dean asked her curiously. "His grace gave your father the living at Gambolthwaite, I think."

"I know the duke," Viola replied. "I know his grace very well."

"Oh ho! Did he try anything?" Mrs Dean asked eagerly, jostling Viola with an elbow. "A beautiful young girl like you! I wouldn't be a bit surprised. He'd be used to getting what he wants, being a duke and all. If he's been at you, girl, we'll make him pay."

Cork stared at the woman, goggle-eyed.

"I'm sure I don't know what you mean," Viola said icily. "The Duke of Fanshawe enjoys a spotless reputation in Yorkshire. And no one has been 'at me.' Ever."

"Pity," said Mrs Dean. She then reverted to the previous topic. "Nowadays, all the fashionable set take houses in the West End. In Pall Mall, in Mayfair, in Green Park, in Grosvenor Square. Piccadilly. Park Lane." She closed her eyes dreamily.

"And where do you live, Mrs Dean?" said Viola, unable to bring herself to call this indelicate stranger "aunt." "In the West End, I suppose?"

"Almost!" Mrs Dean answered proudly. "*Very* nearly. I'm in Portland Place. It's very new and coming. Just down from the Regent's Park. It *does* pay to have influential friends," she added smugly, preening and petting her rabbit pelisse.

As the hackney carriage turned north, the smell of coal dust and horse dung mingled in the air even more strongly, causing Viola's eyes to water. "Is Portland Place much farther?" she asked, taking out her handkerchief and pressing it to her nostrils.

"We're not even to Regent Street," Mrs Dean replied.

Regent Street was so choked with vehicles and pedestrians that the hack could advance only inches at a time. Viola was so cross and so tired that not even the luxurious wares displayed in the many shop windows could divert her. "Is no one in London where they are supposed to be?" she said irritably. "Must everyone be in motion at once?"

"Regent Street is quite impossible this time of morning," said Mrs Dean complacently.

At last, they turned into Portland Place. Mrs Dean's house was at the bottom of the handsome street, farthest from Regent's Park. The three females alighted from the vehicle. Mrs Dean, preoccupied with her pelisse, inadvertently left it to Viola to pay the driver.

The house, tall and slender and semidetached, with iron railings and a pretty green door, seemed respectable enough; at least it did until the door opened and a portly middle-aged man darted out, pulling on his coat as he barreled down the steps. His horsehair wig was askew, and his nose was so bulbous and red it seemed to be crying out for a physician. To Viola's astonishment, Mrs Dean greeted the coarse-looking man with familiar jocularity.

"Not now, Dolly," he answered, hopping down the steps on surprisingly dainty feet in buckled shoes. "I'm shockingly late for breakfast. Mrs Pettigrew don't like it when I'm late."

Late or not, the sight of Viola seemed to affect him strongly. He came to a sudden stop and stared at her, his rheumy eyes moving rapidly from this part to that, rather like a colony of ants. Never in Viola's life had any man looked at her so lecherously. She was too surprised even to speak. Then, just when she thought it couldn't get any worse, the scoundrel had the temerity to speak to her. "Hello, pretty!" he said. "Present me, Dolly!"

"Mr Pettigrew, behave yourself," Mrs Dean implored him giddily as Viola struggled to keep her breakfast from coming up. "This is my shy little niece from Yorkshire! The parson's daughter, you know. She's far too good for the likes of you. I've a gentleman in mind for her, if not a lord."

Undeterred, the ocular rapist completed his violation of Viola's personal dignity by winking at her. Viola felt around in her reticule, her fingers closing over her trusty toasting fork as he smacked his lips repulsively.

"You saucy little minx," he said. "I wouldn't put it past you!"

Then, grinning like an ape, he jumped into the hack the women had just quitted and departed.

# Chapter Four

With one gloved finger, Baroness Devize held the dimity curtains of her carriage window slightly apart, just enough to observe her youngest offspring as he sauntered down Lombard

Street. Born and bred a gentleman, Julian, the handsomest of her three children, was dressed like a common clerk, in black trousers, black coat, and a truly unforgivable hat. Naturally, he wore no gloves. As he sauntered, he alternately ate of the hot cross bun he held in one hand and drank from the small amber-colored bottle he held with the other.

Unaware that his primitive habits were being remarked, Julian ran briskly up the steps of No. 32, a ramshackle, semi-detached house immediately next to a storefront window emblazoned with the pawnbroker's device of three golden balls. The young man licked his fingers, knocked on the door, and was admitted, bottle in hand.

Paralyzed by strong disgust, his mother could only stare.

"Hurry, Mama!" said the other lady seated in the closed carriage. "He's getting away!"

"Really, Perdita," Lady Devize murmured repressively, removing her index finger from the divide in the curtains. "Was that remark intended to be humorous?"

She spoke to her only daughter as if the latter were still a girl of sixteen fresh from the schoolroom. In fact, Perdita, Lady Cheviot, was thirty-six years of age, married, with seven children. Unlike her mother, Perdita had allowed herself to grow a trifle plump over the years, but she was still a handsome woman, with the rich, chestnut hair and brilliant blue eyes she had inherited from her rail-thin mother. "What if he won't come out, Mama?" she suggested mischievously. "Will *you* go in and get him, or shall I?"

Life had dealt Lady Devize too many cruel blows for her to see anything humorous in life, her youngest son being the cruelest blow of all. With his good looks and razor-sharp intellect (both inherited from the baroness, of course), Julian might have made a brilliant marriage, but, instead, at twenty-five, he was content to turn his back on Society and eke out an existence among the middle classes. The baroness rounded on her daughter with a vengeance.

"Don't be ridiculous, Perdita," she snapped. "His man will give him my note, and your brother will join us presently."

The baroness proved correct. In just a few moments, the young man who had gone into No. 32 came out again. He had lost his amber bottle, but he was still wearing the unforgivable hat. Perdita recklessly threw open the window. "Julian! Over here!"

"For heaven's sake, Perdita!" the baroness hissed. "Someone might see you!"

"No one knows us in this part of London, Mama," Perdita answered. "No one we know would be caught dead in the City. Apart from Julian, of course."

"Quite," said the baroness coldly as a knock sounded on the door. "Enter!"

Julian opened the door, climbed inside the carriage, and sat next to Perdita. His hat—and Lady Devize had an excellent view of it as he leaned forward to close the door—was even worse than she had thought. In fact, it was execrable.

"Where on earth did you get that hat?" Perdita exclaimed.

"I bought it," Julian replied. His brilliant blue eyes, rendered breathtaking by the sunlight, were fixed on his mother, and her brilliant blue eyes were fixed on him. Although there was no love lost between them, the family resemblance could not be denied. "If it offends you, I will remove it." So saying, he took off his hat and balanced it on his knee.

The baroness closed her eyes in shame. Her son had one of those horrible close-cropped haircuts that men who do not keep creditable valets are forced to get from barbers.

"It doesn't look like you bought it," Perdita said frankly. "It rather looks like you stole it from the family of mice that were nesting in it. What did you do with the poor mice?"

"It's not as bad as that," said Julian, smiling faintly.

"I was trying to be kind," said Perdita.

"Aren't you going to greet your mother?" Lady Devize demanded, exasperated.

"My lady," he said politely. "What brings you to the City?"

The baroness did not reply. "Portland Place," she called sharply to the driver, and the closed carriage began to move, traveling northwest along Lombard Street.

Julian frowned. "I'm afraid I don't have time to go for a drive with you just now, madam. I work for a living, as you know."

"My son, the stockjobber," said the baroness, drenching those four simple words in oceans of icy contempt.

"At your ladyship's service," Julian replied. "Are you buying or selling?"

As the baroness choked on her own fury, Perdita caught Julian's arm. "It's Papa," she said quietly. "He's very ill, Julian. They don't seem to expect him to live much longer."

All traces of mockery disappeared from the young man's face.

"I see," he said quietly. "Of course I'll come."

His mother sniffed. "By all means! Visit your father on his deathbed—*if* you wish to hasten his demise, that is. The sight of *you* would surely kill him on the spot."

"Mama! No!" Perdita cried, horrified.

"Naturally, I have no wish to commit patricide," Julian said stiffly. "I will, of course, absent myself from the touching family scene. But why take me to Portland Place?"

"Your father wants to see your brother, his heir, before he dies," Lady Devize explained.

Perdita said quickly, "Alex is in a—a *house*, Julian, and we need you to get him out."

"Have you tried knocking on the door?" Julian inquired politely.

"Your brother is in a bawdyhouse," said the baroness impatiently. "We couldn't possibly knock on *that* door."

"And we can't send a servant, either," said Perdita, anticipating Julian's next suggestion. "What if he's drunk? What if he won't come out? What if he creates a disturbance? There would be a dreadful scandal! And how would it look if Papa actually *died* while his heir was creating a disturbance in a *brothel?*"

Julian sighed. "Where is the house?"

"Portland Place!" the baroness said indignantly.

"Portland Place?" Julian repeated, chuckling. "Isn't that where *you* live, madam?"

Lady Devize drew herself up. "I am at the *top* of Portland Place," she informed him icily. "Mrs Dean's . . . *establishment* . . . is at the *bottom* of Portland Place. Thus far, she has managed to elude detection. To coin a phrase: The law is an ass."

"So you left your house at the *top* of Portland Place. You drove all the way out to Lombard Street to fetch me. And now we are on our way to the *bottom* of Portland Place?"

Julian was almost smiling; it was so ridiculous.

"I'm sorry to have taken you away from your labors on the Exchange," Lady Devize said nastily, "but the matter could not be delayed if we are to reach Sussex by nightfall."

Julian frowned. "Sussex? Is my father not in London?"

"I was forced to come to London without him this Season," said his mother. "After what you did to Child's Bank, sir, your father could not face his friends in the House of Lords. Some people of very high rank were affected by your underhanded dealings."

"There is nothing underhanded about my dealings," Julian said hotly. "Believe me, the matter has been very thoroughly investigated. If I had done wrong, I would be in prison."

"You *should* be in prison," the baroness said flatly. "It is not enough that you disgrace your family by going into Trade. No, indeed! You must *break* Child's Bank, and make Lady Jersey look a perfect fool! Her ladyship won't even speak to me now. I am having to fight my way back into Society tooth and claw because of *your* conduct. A *gentleman* does not break a lady's bank, Julian!"

"Lady Jersey has no business running her grandfather's bank

or any other bank," Julian replied harshly. "You'd be better off keeping your money in a china pig than in Child's Bank."

"All's well that ends well," Perdita interrupted in an attempt to make peace. "Parliament has voted to bail out Child's Bank, so it's all right, Mama. The *on dit* is that Lady Jersey called in favors from all her former lovers—a majority in the House of Lords, from what I hear," she added, laughing. "Lady Bamph said that Lady Jersey must have a stomach lined with copper to have abased herself with so many Members, to which the Duchess of Berkshire replied, 'My dear, I think you mean *quite another part* of her ladyship's anatomy!'"

The baroness's blue eyes gleamed. "Fortunately, there *are* some who take pleasure in poor Sally's troubles. Now, if I could just find a way to *cultivate* the Duchess of Berkshire, I might regain my position in Society."

"Ah, the cultivation of duchesses," Julian murmured. "I understand they require inordinate amounts of strong fertilizer if they are to bloom by season's end. And should your duchess chance to have aphids—"

"I understand Doctor Weston's Elixir is very good for that!" Perdita finished gaily.

The baroness glared at them, her eldest and youngest in league against her.

"I'm sure you will find a way back into Society, Mama," Perdita said contritely.

"It certainly doesn't help matters that my son has insinuated himself into the marriage settlement of Lord Bamph and Lady Viola Gambol," said the baroness. "His mother is seriously displeased. Are there no depths to which you will not sink, Julian? No—don't answer that!" she pleaded angrily. "Having seen you consume your breakfast in Lombard Street, in full view of the public, I fear I know the answer already."

"Are you cultivating Lady Bamph, too?" Julian asked coolly.

"The marchioness condescended to visit me before she left

Town," Lady Devize said proudly. "She begged me to put an end to your shocking interference, Julian. She also gave me to understand that you had been making love to her daughter!"

"Shame on you, Julian!" cried Perdita. "You randy little stockjobber, you."

"Belinda Belphrey is a mere child," Julian said repressively.

"Lady Bamph has threatened to give me the Cut Direct if your interference continues," the baroness complained. "With the Jerseyites against me, I would never recover. The doors of Society would be closed to me forever. Julian, you must make sure that Lord Bamph gets every penny of Lady Viola's fortune when he marries her, or else I am ruined. Do you understand?"

"Madam, I am employed by the Duke of Fanshawe. I am bound to serve *his* interests."

"You are *my* son," snapped Lady Devize. "You ought to serve *my* interests. What do you care about Lady Viola? Lord Cheviot has met her on several occasions. Apparently, she is something of a grotesque."

"Now, Mama," Perdita chided her. "We don't know that she is precisely ugly. My husband is far too chivalrous to call a lady ugly."

"Of *course* she's hideously ugly," the baroness insisted. "Why else has she never been presented at Court? Depend upon it—she has a hunchback, a squint, a clubfoot, a harelip, leprosy! I don't know *what* exactly, but there's definitely *something* wrong with her."

"She cannot be physically deformed," Perdita protested. "She couldn't shoot with a squint, and she couldn't ride with a clubfoot or a hump. And Tony has told me she does both very well. He's been to several shooting parties at their place in Scotland, and she always goes out with the gentlemen. She plays billiards, too. She's just like one of the men, he says."

"I don't approve of women who shoot," sniffed the baroness.

"Birds or billiards?" Julian asked her.

"Neither, sir!" flashed the baroness. "It is unwomanly. However, she is very rich," she went on in a more complacent tone, "and we must make allowances for the very rich."

"Of course," said Julian.

"Just how rich is she, Julian?" Perdita asked. "Strictly *entre nous*, of course."

"I am not at liberty to divulge any information about my clients."

"Please, Julian! We won't tell a soul, will we, Mama?" said Perdita.

"No, indeed," promised the baroness. "We will be silent as the grave."

"You'll have to be," Julian said dryly, "because I'm not telling you anything."

"I hear she has millions," Perdita said provocatively.

"What a bunch of arse," Julian scoffed.

"A gentleman does not use such language in front of ladies," the baroness said coldly.

"You ladies say whatever you please, I've noticed," he retorted.

The carriage jogged on, its occupants falling silent as Lombard Street became Newgate Street, and Newgate Street became Oxford Street. Finally, the carriage turned north into Portland Place. They had arrived in good time, having missed the early morning tradesmen's traffic on Oxford Street. It was just nine o'clock, and the gentry were not yet stirring. Portland Place looked deserted.

"You must knock three times on the door and give the password." The baroness took her writing tablet from her reticule to check her information. "Today's password is 'Whistlejacket.' The woman who runs the place is called Dean. She is a poor widow, very deeply in debt, of course, but that is no excuse. Ask for Alexander Pope. That is your brother's alias."

"My compliments to your spies, madam," said Julian, half-impressed, half-dismayed.

"Make your brother presentable, then send him to me at the top of Portland Place. And don't dawdle," she added as Julian opened the carriage door. "It's a long way to Sussex. Drive on," she commanded her coachman almost before Julian's feet had touched the ground.

As instructed, Julian gave the password to the manservant who answered the door. He was admitted into a hall dominated by a round divan upholstered in crimson velvet. The walls were bright pink. The carpet had been worn thin by constant traffic. On the walls were lurid pictures. Julian recognized the usual subject matter. Leda and the Swan. Danae and the shower of gold. A truly bad copy of Rubens's *Rape of the Sabine Women*. The cumulative effect of all this naked female flesh was about as erotic to him as a pile of old doorknobs.

"I'm looking for Mr Alexander Pope," he politely explained to the manservant, who looked like a former prizefighter, complete with crooked nose and cauliflower ear.

"Wait 'ere," the man mumbled, indicating the round divan.

"I'd rather not," Julian said quickly, eyeing the divan with suspicion. "Wait here, that is. Is there a room—an empty room, I mean—where I might wait?"

The servant opened the door beside the staircase then trudged up the stairs. The room revealed was as garishly furnished as the hall, albeit in shades of purple rather than pink and scarlet. A cloying perfume hung in the air, mixed noxiously with smoke and stale tobacco. Painted satyrs leered from the walls while nymphs writhed in what appeared to be pain but was probably meant to be ecstasy.

On the positive side, the curtains were open, admitting bright, cleansing sunshine through reasonably clean windows. As Julian entered the room, he noticed a well-fed fluffy white puppy stretched out on the rug. She lifted her head briefly and silently, looking at him with curious, almond-shaped black eyes before returning to the glove upon which she was cutting her teeth.

Completely disarmed, Julian dropped his hat on a table and knelt down beside her on the rug. He had grown up with mastiffs, but he was not disdainful of lapdogs. She looked well cared for, he was pleased to see, and there was a big bow around her neck. One side of the ribbon was deep purple, while the other side was striped lavender and white.

"What's that you have there, miss?" he scolded her gently. A minor struggle ensued, but, in the end, Julian came away with a woman's kid glove, dyed lavender. The puppy had chewed off all the buttons, and she was not at all apologetic.

"There you are, you naughty thing!" a girl's voice scolded from the doorway.

Jumping to his feet, Julian turned to feast his eyes on at a tall, dark-eyed young beauty. Her skin had almost an olive cast to it, which gave her an exotic look, but her English was perfectly refined. She wore her jet-black hair in a braided crown that allowed not even the tiniest ringlet to escape, but the severity of the style suited her. He liked her arrogant little nose and her stubborn little chin. Her red lips also interested him. While knowing nothing of ladies' fashions, he very much approved of the way her purple and white striped gown fitted her full breasts and slender waist before flaring over what promised to be slim, athletic haunches. Everything about her tempted him, and yet she did not look at all like a prostitute. Quite the opposite, in fact. She looked as if she had been kept all her life in a locked glass case, clearly marked: FOR DISPLAY ONLY. She was quite as unexpected as the puppy, and, again, Julian was completely disarmed.

"I protest," he said, smiling at her. "I am not a naughty thing. Well, not *very* naughty."

"Come, Bijou!" she said to the puppy; she couldn't even be bothered to frown at Julian.

In response, the little dog wagged her tail politely and tilted her head to one side.

"I don't think she knows how to come yet," Julian said cheekily. "I don't think she knows her name, either."

Still ignoring him, the beauty went to the dog and picked her up. With her arrogant little nose in the air, she headed for the door, her skirts hissing at Julian as she went by.

Julian was irritated. A very superior girl she might be, but she was still a girl in a brothel, and, even if he was not rich enough to afford her favors, he was not dirt under her feet. "Don't you walk away from me, girl," he said sharply. "I'm talking to you."

She turned to look at him incredulously, and he got between her and the door.

"That's better," he said, pleased to have her attention. For a moment, she looked as if she wanted to strike him, but then she decided to proceed as if he wasn't there. She walked straight at him, expecting him to stand aside. When he did not, she was obliged to stop inches from him. In her high-heeled slippers, she was tall enough to look him in the eye as they stood nose to nose. At this proximity, he could tell that, incredible as it seemed, neither her soft, olive skin nor her red lips bore any trace of cosmetic enhancement. Her eyes, which looked black from a distance, were actually a very dark blue. Every instinct he possessed told him that she was much too good for her surroundings, and his curiosity and desire were aroused equally.

"Now, then," he said softly as she glared at him. "Let us begin again."

"Sir!" she said, frowning severely. "I took you for a gentleman. Was I mistaken?"

"I apologize," Julian said instantly, standing aside to allow her to pass. "I did not realize you had mistaken me for a gentleman," he went on as she opened the door to walk out. "You seemed to have mistaken me for a speck of dirt, unworthy of even the most commonplace civility!"

It was her turn to flinch. "I do not mean to be uncivil," she said, her color rising. "I daresay, you must think me very rude—"

"I do, miss! I only wanted to return this to you," he said, producing the lavender glove he had rescued from the puppy. "It *is* yours, I believe?"

The trap was sprung. She could not avoid conversing with him now.

"Yes," she admitted, reaching for the glove. "It is mine."

He would not let her have it. "You must kiss me first," he said huskily.

She frowned, not exactly the response he was hoping for. "You must excuse me, sir," she said haughtily.

Julian stopped smiling. "Why must I excuse you?"

"Because, sir, I am new to London. I am not accustomed to London manners!"

He smiled slowly. "Are manners so different in your own part of the country?"

"Indeed they are, sir," she answered. "In Yorkshire, people do not go on in this ramshackle way. I would never be prevailed upon to speak to a young man without a formal introduction. And, in Yorkshire, a gentleman does not prevent a lady from leaving a room. Nor does he demand kisses. Such behavior is inexcusable."

Julian stared at her, astonished. *Lady?* Either she was in the wrong place, or he was. "I must be in the wrong house," he said, mortified. "I beg your pardon, Miss . . . er . . . Miss . . . ?"

"I certainly have no intention of introducing myself!" she informed him.

"Of course not," he murmured. "I'm very sorry to have offended you. Is this Mrs Dean's . . . er . . . establishment?"

"It is, sir," she admitted, petting the dog in her arms to cover her embarrassment. "But I have nothing to do with the running of this house, and I have *less* than nothing to say to the lodgers! Am I obliged, in London, to talk to a man just because he happens to be standing in a room when I walk in?" she demanded, her color rising. "To *kiss* him, just because he has taken my glove?"

"Certainly not," he answered. "I have apologized. What more can I do?"

"Well, at least you do not *wink* at me," she said, somewhat mollified. "*That* insolence I cannot bear. I have begun to call it the London squint! The lodgers all have it."

Julian was more at a loss than ever. "May I ask you a question?"

Her eyes flashed. "No, I will not sit on your knee," she said. "No, you may not see my ankles. And no, I most certainly do not want to know what you have in your pocket."

"It's nothing like that," he hastened to assure her. "It's just . . . Did you say . . . *lodgers?*"

"Yes." She paused, taken aback. "Are you . . . ? Aren't one of the lodgers?"

"No. I've never been here before in my life. I'm just looking for my brother."

"I should not be talking to you at all," she murmured in dismay. "This is most irregular. Mrs Dean should show more care for her niece. I don't like it."

"Neither do I," he said stoutly. "However, it's very important that I speak to my brother at once. The name is Alexander Pope. My mother told me I could find him here."

"Well, I'm sorry, Mr Pope," she said, shaking her head. "I cannot help you. You will have to wait for Mrs Dean, the proprietress."

Momentarily startled to be called by a name other than his own, Julian was tempted to correct her. But how could he explain to her that "Pope" was his brother's alias? She already thought him rude; he did not want her to think him sinister.

"But I must see him now," he said, letting the assumption

stand. "The matter is urgent. Will you help me, please? If you were looking for your brother, I would certainly help you."

"I suppose I could ask which is his room," she said reluctantly. "I will have to wake Mrs Dean. She keeps London hours, I'm afraid. Will you please wait here, Mr Pope?" she requested, stopping him in the hall. "In Yorkshire, a gentleman does not follow a lady up the stairs unless she asks him to. I'll be as quick as I can."

"Thank you," he said, but she was already running lightly up the steps, the little white dog tucked under one arm. He tried not to look at her slim ankles, but he could not help himself.

# Chapter Five

To Julian's disappointment, the black-haired girl did not return. Instead, it was the big, ugly manservant who led him upstairs to his brother's room. Although exceedingly untidy, the room was comfortable, with plenty of coals glowing in the fireplace and a window that overlooked the street. Unconscious and unshaven, the Honorable Mr Alexander Devize lay supine on the bed, naked but for a bunched-up sheet. One arm hung over the side of the bed.

Going over to the bed, Julian struck the sleeper with his hat none too gently. When there was no response, he picked up the pitcher of water next to the bed and poured its contents onto his brother's face.

Alexander Devize sputtered to life. "Bloody hell!" he roared, sitting up and blinking as water ran into his bloodshot brown eyes. His thick, dark hair was standing on end in pomaded clumps, surely not what his valet had intended. He reeked of brandy. Stubble rasped against his palm as he wiped the water from his face. He looked around him blearily. He was only thirty-four, but, at the moment, he looked almost fifty.

"Julian," he croaked. "What the devil?"

Julian was brief. "Get dressed. It's the governor. He wants to see you."

"Well, I don't want to see *him*," Alex said sullenly. "He keeps trying to arrange marriages for me. He threatens to cut off my allowance."

"He's very seriously ill, Alex," Julian said quietly.

"No, he isn't," Alex said bitterly. "He's never ill. It's only a ploy to get me to marry Miss Molly Peacock."

"You could be right, of course," said Julian. "I hope you are. But our mother is waiting for you at the top of Portland Place. Perdita's with her. Now, where are your clothes?"

Groaning, Alex swung his legs out of the bed and began fumbling for his shirt.

Julian walked over to the window and looked out on the street as his brother dressed.

Alex spoke to Julian's back. "Are *you* going to Sussex?"

"No," Julian replied. "I'm still disowned."

"Lucky devil!" Alex grumbled. "Of course, if he were *really* ill, he'd want you at his side, Julian. You were always his favorite. How I hate living under his thumb. He holds the purse strings like an old maid guards her virginity! I'll go to Sussex, but I'll be damned if I let him choose me a wife. There's only one girl I ever wanted to marry, and she's dead now."

The revelation caught Julian by surprise, and made him feel excessively awkward, as if he had accidentally overheard something intensely private. "I'm sorry," he murmured.

"She married someone else," Alex went on, to his brother's acute dismay. "She died in childbirth. If she were not dead, I think I would hate her. She was such a plain little thing, too," Alex said, his eyes suddenly filling with tears. "I still remember how she felt in my arms when we danced together."

"All the same," said Julian. "Life goes on."

Alex glared at him. "How can you be so callous? Life goes on? No, it doesn't."

"Obviously, it does," Julian said dryly. "Would you be *here* if it didn't?"

"You think I come here to feel alive?" Alex demanded indignantly. "Do you think I enjoy passing out every night in the arms of a strange woman who doesn't give a tinker's damn for me?"

"You could do that with Molly Peacock," Julian said. "At considerably less expense."

"That's right," Alex said grimly. "Make your jokes. *You've* never been in love."

"No," Julian agreed cheerfully, "but I can't wait. You make it sound so pleasant."

Alex went into the closet to wash, leaving the door ajar.

Julian was looking out of the window, watching as a man exited the house. With his collar turned up and his hat low over his eyes, he scurried into Oxford Street to be swallowed up by the traffic.

"Sorry about all that," Alex said presently. "I didn't mean to be so maudlin. I hope I didn't embarrass you?"

"It's quite all right," Julian assured him. "I wasn't listening anyway."

"Good." Alex sounded relieved. Half-dressed now, he began to shave.

"Alex," Julian said thoughtfully, still observing the street, "this *is* a brothel, isn't it?"

Alex laughed shortly. "If it isn't, I want my money back," he said. "Why do you ask?"

"I met a girl downstairs who seems to think this is some sort of boarding house," Julian replied. "A very pretty, genteel sort of girl, nothing like what you'd expect to find in a place like this. She seemed like a carefully brought up young lady," he added. "She refused to talk to me because we hadn't been introduced. Just like the girls back home."

"Ah, yes," Alex said, yawning. "The tragic little niece from Yorkshire. I've heard all about *her*. Supposedly, her father was a vicar. He left his daughter on the aunt's hands, penniless. To recoup her losses, Mrs Dean is auctioning her off on Friday. She tried to sell me a ticket, but I'm afraid primitive country virgins are not at all to my taste. I hear she's pretty, though. She should fetch a pretty price."

"I don't think I understand you," Julian said indignantly. "What do you mean Mrs Dean is *auctioning her off?*"

Alex looked at him in surprise. "You're shocked," he said. "I do believe you're blushing. My dear boy, the girl has no money, no connections. Her aunt's in debt. What else are they to do with her? This *is* a brothel, after all."

"It's barbaric," said Julian. "Not to mention immoral and illegal."

Alex shrugged. "That's London for you."

"Alex, this girl thinks she's in a boarding house."

"Then she's either a fool or a liar," Alex said heartlessly. "Chances are, your genteel, pretty girl knows exactly what she's doing. She's just reeling you in with her innocent eyes."

"Then she should be treading the boards," said Julian. "She's a remarkable actress."

"I wouldn't worry about her too much," Alex said dryly. "If she plays her cards right, she'll be the mistress of a very rich man who will dote on her and buy her anything she wants."

"But for God's sake," said Julian. "She's a clergyman's daughter."

Alex snorted. "That's the story, anyway. Who knows if it's true? I don't want to disillusion you, Julian, but, occasionally one finds that lies are told in brothels. Your genteel, pretty girl mightn't even be a virgin."

"And what if she *is* innocent?" Julian demanded. "We have to help her."

Alex wiped his now clean-shaven face with a towel. "We?"

"This girl you were in love with," Julian said impatiently. "What if *she* were in trouble? Wouldn't you want someone to help her?"

Alex's face darkened with anger. "Obviously, a *lady* would never be in such a situation," he snapped. "Never think with your privates, brother, or didn't they teach you that in the army?"

"I'm concerned about her welfare," Julian said stiffly. "It has nothing to do with my privates."

"You're too poor to be concerned about her welfare," Alex retorted, "and it has everything to do with your privates. Would you be quite so concerned about her welfare if she weren't quite so pretty?"

"You're a cynic," Julian accused him.

Alex laughed grimly. "So will you be in ten years."

"Perhaps," said Julian, "but I hope the idea of young women being bought and sold like chattel will always be disgusting to me. I'm going to help her, even if you won't."

"Don't be a bloody fool," said Alex, but he was talking to himself; Julian had already left the room.

"I wish to speak to Mrs Dean at once," Julian told the manservant downstairs.

Alex joined him in the hall a few minutes later. Never as handsome as his brother, and pockmarked from a childhood illness, he at least looked respectable now: clean-shaven and wearing a tailored coat of blue superfine. "Would you call me a hack?" he asked Julian.

"You are a hack," Julian said obligingly.

"Ha, ha. My legs are still a bit wobbly, and my purse seems to be empty," Alex said. "It has been suggested to me that I drink too much. Please summon a hack for me."

"The hack is waiting outside," Julian said. "It's only half a mile to our mother's house, but I didn't think you'd care to walk in your condition."

"Thank you," Alex said ruefully.

Glancing up, Julian saw a middle-aged woman coming down the stairs, presumably Mrs Dean herself. Alex saw Mrs Dean at about the same time. "Look here, Julian," he said quietly. "Don't get yourself mixed up in this dirty business. Even if the girl *is* innocent—which I rather doubt—you have no money. There's nothing you can do about it."

Mrs Dean reached them, and Alex was obliged to hold his tongue. "Do come again, Mr Pope," she said warmly to Alex. "The girls are so fond of you."

Julian shook his brother's hand. "Will you keep me informed? I am still in Lombard Street. If my father wants me, of course I'll come," he offered.

Alex promised to send word. Giving his brother one last warning look, he then departed, leaving Julian alone with the mistress of the house.

Mrs Dean bore no resemblance to her lovely niece; indeed, Julian could scarcely credit the notion that the two were related. Her yellow satin gown fitted her too tightly in the bosom, so that unsightly mounds of freckled flesh spilled over the lace edge of the bodice. Kohl lined the lids of her small, greedy eyes. While not quite realistic, her ivory teeth were well-carved.

"Mr Pope!" she purred. "How may I please you?"

"I'm interested in your niece," he said bluntly. "I want an introduction."

Mrs Dean looked amused. "I'm afraid, Mr Pope, that my niece is quite beyond your touch. She is—"

"What do you know of my touch?" he interrupted sharply.

Mrs Dean blinked at him. The handsome young man had a commanding air, quite at odds with his youth and his unfashionably plain clothes. Perhaps he was a man of greater wealth and importance than his elder brother; in her lifetime, Mrs Dean had seen stranger things.

"I meant no offense," she said quickly. "I should warn you, Mr Pope, that Miss Andrews has generated a great deal of interest already. It will not be easy to obtain her favors."

"Is that her name? Andrews?"

"Mary Andrews," Mrs Dean affirmed. "Why, only yesterday, Lord Barrowbridge offered me five thousand pounds for her." Her flesh quivered as she recalled the lucrative offer. "He was very disappointed when I sent him away."

Julian was disgusted. "Lord Barrowbridge is ninety if he's a day!"

"And he couldn't pop a cherry if his life depended on it, poor man," Mrs Dean agreed. "But what do I care? It's his lordship's money. He can spend it as he likes."

"This is your niece we're talking about," Julian reminded her severely.

"And who should profit from Mary's beauty but her own aunt?" she returned harshly. "God knows my brother, the saintly vicar, never lifted a finger to help me when he was alive! It is only right that Mary help me now. Sooner or later, she will be bedded, Mr Pope. You know it, and I know it. She'll be better off with a rich man than a poor man, and you know that, too."

"But the girl is very pretty," Julian argued. "She speaks well—almost like a lady. Surely you could find her a husband."

Mrs Dean laughed. "A husband? With Dolly Dean for an aunt? I'm afraid she'd be tainted by association. And, of course, she has no dowry, poor thing. Who will marry her? Some middling tradesman? Some adventurous rogue? I made *that* mistake in my youth, Mr Pope. Mary will benefit from my experience. As the mistress of a rich gentleman, she will want for nothing. It's no use looking at me like that, Mr Pope! You know I'm right. No gentleman is going to marry her, and she likes her fine clothes and pretty things, does Mary."

Julian saw that it was pointless to argue with the old witch. "I'll attend the auction."

"Will you, now?" Mrs Dean said craftily. "You must first buy a ticket, and I'm afraid they're quite expensive. I mean to keep out the riffraff, you understand."

"How much?"

"Fifty pounds, sir, and not a penny less," she said defiantly.

Julian did not flinch. "Will you accept my I.O.U.?"

She smiled. "I'm afraid I can only accept hard currency. You *do* understand, Mr Pope."

"That won't be a problem," said Julian curtly.

Mrs Dean licked her lips. "The cost of the ticket is nonrefundable," she said quickly, "and, of course, it only entitles you to participate in the auction tomorrow evening. I expect to open the bidding at five thousand pounds."

"Then I shall return this afternoon for my ticket," Julian said, starting for the door. "Naturally, I expect an interview with the young lady at that time. Perhaps I might walk with her in Regent's Park early this evening?"

"I'm afraid my niece is engaged to go driving in the park this evening," Mrs Dean replied, "but you might come to tea, Mr Pope. I shall be here to chaperone, of course. I could not risk putting damaged goods on the block, you understand. The man who gets her might feel cheated."

Julian favored her with a pained smile.

"However, you must not speak to Mary of the auction. She's quite shy about it."

Julian looked at her sharply. "You mean she doesn't know she's being auctioned off," he said contemptuously.

Mrs Dean blinked rapidly. "Of course she knows," she cried, just a little too late to be credible. "Mary is a practical young lady, sir, and nothing better guards a girl's virginity than self-interest, don't you agree?" She laughed. "After all, virtue can be penetrated by seduction. Self-interest cannot. Do you doubt, sir, that she is a virgin?"

Julian glared at her. "No."

"Of course, if *you* won't buy Mary, someone else will," Mrs Dean went on pleasantly. "I only hope he is kind to her. My first time was *very* painful, and Mr Dean *would* do it again and again, no matter how I begged him to spare me. I was only sixteen, Mr Pope, but he was my husband, and I had no hope in law. My brother the vicar wouldn't help me, either. What God hath joined, and all that rot. He said it was my Christian duty to submit. Mary, at least, will be free to find another protector, if she wishes. I was not free until Mr Dean died, and then I was left penniless. Poverty, I soon discovered, is a worse prison than marriage."

"How much would it take to stop the auction?" Julian demanded.

Mrs Dean shook her head sadly. "It is beyond my power, Mr Pope. I couldn't cancel now, even if you should offer me the moon and the stars. I have sold nearly twenty tickets."

"Then I had better go and see my banker," Julian said grimly.


Mrs Dean was all politeness when he returned that afternoon. The young man parted with his money so easily that Mrs Dean never suspected that he had pawned everything of value he owned in order to raise the sum. Inclining her head graciously, she brought her guest into the sitting room, where she locked his money in her desk and brought him a large card in return.

"Your ticket, Mr Pope."

Julian looked at it in surprise. Handsomely printed in gold letters on a card about the size of a playbill, it announced the auction of one Bijou, a superior purebred bitch donated by Her Royal Highness, the Princess Charlotte. All proceeds were to go to an unspecified charity.

"There must be some mistake," Julian said irritably. "I don't want a dog."

"A little subterfuge, Mr Pope . . . for the law's sake," Mrs Dean explained. "They can be so inquisitive about things that do not concern them. If anyone asks, the auction is for that stupid little dog someone left here as a present for one of my girls."

Julian affected surprise. "Then she is not one of Princess Charlotte's prize pups?"

"Don't be silly, Mr Pope," Mrs Dean laughed. "Everyone knows Her Royal Highness keeps Pomeranians." Still laughing, she took the chair next to the fire. The tea table was already set up between the chair and the sofa, and a pot of tea was steeping under a quilted cozy.

Having pawned his watch, among other things, Julian checked the little French clock on the mantel. "Will Miss Andrews be joining us soon?" he asked.

"You must be patient, Mr Pope. Mary will join us presently."

While they waited, Mrs Dean beguiled the time by counting her chickens before they were hatched. "With that face and that figure, there's no telling how much she'll go for in the end," she sighed happily. "I shall be able to pay off all my creditors, I shouldn't wonder. Ah, Mary! There you are!" she said as the girl came into the room. "Come and meet Mr Pope."

Julian stood up, pleased and relieved to see that Miss Andrews appeared undamaged. Not a hair on her head was out of place. Her purple and white striped dress looked freshly ironed, and she was holding the white puppy in her arms. Bijou wagged her tail at the sight of Julian.

Viola had not expected to see the impudent young man again. "You!" she exclaimed.

"You know this young man?" Mrs Dean asked sharply.

Julian smiled at Viola, but his words were intended for Mrs

Dean. "I have met your niece already. But she would not speak to me because we had not been introduced."

"Mary!" Mrs Dean scolded. "How could you be so rude to Mr Pope?"

"Indeed, Miss Andrews was the soul of propriety," Julian said quickly. "*I* was rude. But do not judge me too harshly, Miss Andrews. I have come to make amends, as you see."

Viola found she could not hold a grudge against him. He had a certain audacious charm, and, of course, he was young and good-looking, a rarity amongst Mrs Dean's acquaintances. She certainly preferred his company to that of Mrs Dean, and she was in no hurry to be rid of him. "By London standards, I think you were only a little presumptuous," she said primly. "Of course, you *were* anxious to see your brother."

"I was, but that is no excuse for bad manners. Shall we begin again? How do you do, Miss Andrews?" he said, presenting her with a formal bow.

"Very well, Mr Pope," Viola answered, curtseying. "What a pleasure it is to make your acquaintance at last."

"Indeed the pleasure is all mine, Miss Andrews."

"Oh, don't let's argue, Mr Pope," she said, taking her seat on the sofa and arranging the bichon in her lap. "Shall we say half the pleasure is mine, and the other half yours?"

"That certainly seems fair," he agreed, a little taken aback by her confidence. Apparently now that they had been introduced, flirting was in order. Just like the girls back home, he thought, hiding a nostalgic smile.

Viola was already pouring the tea. "How do you like it, Mr Pope? Sugar? Milk? Lemon?" Without seeming in any way coy or vulgar, she managed to make the simple offer of tea sound seductive. And Julian didn't even like tea.

"Black, thank you," he said, accepting his cup.

"Macaroon?" she inquired, holding out a plate of unassuming biscuits.

"Thank you," he said.

"Of course, if you were *chivalrous,* Mr Pope," Viola said, returning to their "argument" as she poured out Mrs Dean's cup, "you would give me *all* the pleasure, and keep none for yourself. But, I daresay, there's no chivalry in London. You London men are too modern for all that."

Julian was provoked to defend himself.

"Actually, I'm from Sussex," he said, tasting his macaroon. "But I believe it was you ladies who put an end to chivalry. You simply don't want to be rescued nowadays. You seem to prefer the company of rogues and scoundrels, and, as ever, we men must conform to your taste or die of loneliness."

"What do you mean?" she protested, laughing. "Rogues and scoundrels have no appeal for me, I assure you."

"But you will allow, Miss Andrews, that a Knight of the Round Table would be accounted a pernicious bore in today's society."

"And so very hard on the furniture, too," Viola solemnly agreed. "But, in all seriousness, Mr Pope, you know perfectly well that it is *women* who rescue *men*. Indeed, without the civilizing influence of my sex, you men would be no better than wild beasts. Do you not agree?"

"I certainly do not," he protested, laughing in spite of himself at her preposterous assertion. "If men were barbarous by nature, Miss Andrews, you ladies would have a very bad time of it, and never mind your civilizing influence!"

"This from the man who said to me not five hours ago, 'Don't you walk away from me when I'm talking to you, girl!' If that is not proof of a barbarous nature, Mr Pope, then I don't know what is. Your behavior was infamous. Admit it."

"That was very wrong of me, to be sure," he promptly admitted.

"Oh! But look at you now," she teased him. "Here you sit beside me on the sofa, perfectly tame, with your cup in one hand and your macaroon in the other. And all this I accomplished in just two minutes! Imagine what I might make of you in five. Now be a good gentleman and drink your tea."

Julian discovered, to his chagrin, that he could think of no clever reply. Miss Andrews was too fast for him, which only proved her inexperience. A more accomplished flirt would stoop to conquer, and allow her prey the illusion that *he* was wittier than *she.*

Unable to comprehend that the young people were merely talking in jest, Mrs Dean had become alarmed by Viola's banter. "My dear Mary," she said breathlessly. "Mind how you talk to Mr Pope! He is a rich man. You must not go on so wildly! Mr Pope, I do apologize! My niece has a lively sense of humor, but she means no disrespect, I'm sure."

"My aunt seems to think you need rescuing, sir," Viola laughed. "Are you afraid of me?"

"Terrified," he replied, chuckling. "See? I'm drinking my tea for fear of you."

"Yes, all men hate tea," she said, growing more pleased with him by the moment.

"Here I thought it was just me."

"No. All," she insisted. "Only think . . . if men did not despise tea so much, there would be no glory in forcing them to drink it every afternoon! Would you like another cup, Mr Pope?"

"Have I not been punished enough?" he wanted to know.

"I'm not punishing you, Mr Pope. I'm making you better," she explained, filling his cup.

"I see. And tea will perfect me?"

"Oh, I hope not," she said softly. "Perfection in a man is an unforgivable fault! It leaves a woman with nothing to do. On the other hand, *you* are terrible—with so much to do, a girl doesn't know where to begin. What a dilemma! I almost wish Mrs Dean had not introduced us. Then you would be some other girl's problem."

"But I particularly wish to be *your* problem, Miss Andrews."

"And something must be done about you—you're practically

feral. Perhaps I'd better take you on, after all. You might be too much of a trial for the next girl."

"But will I be too much for *you,* Miss Andrews?"

"It is possible," Viola admitted. "You *are* the worst case I have ever seen. But *someone* must take charge of you, Mr Pope. You're an absolute menace."

Julian did not want to talk anymore. It was only the presence of her aunt that prevented him from acting on the desire to take her in his arms and kiss her until they were both exhausted.

For her part, she seemed pleased to have rendered him speechless yet again. It was short-lived, however, and, when he recovered, they spoke at length on a variety of subjects. Julian found her to be wholly ignorant of economics, which was his chief interest in life, and surprisingly well-informed about politics, which he despised with all his heart.

"And so you have bought your ticket to the auction," Viola remarked presently, sensing that he did not care a straw about the latest shakeup in the Cabinet. "To own the truth, Mr Pope, I have entered into a dark conspiracy with the other bidders," she confessed. "They have all promised to give her to me, should they win the auction. Will you promise the same?"

"I will make you no promise of the kind, young woman," Julian said sternly. "That sort of chicanery may be all well and good in *Yorkshire,* but where I come from, we frown upon all trickery and deceit."

Her smile threatened to take his breath away. "And where are you from, sir?" she asked playfully. "Suffolk, did you say?"

"Sussex."

"Sussex. How strange that we should meet in London."

"Not very strange. My business is in London, and so is your aunt."

"Even so, it is a very big place, is it not? Two people could live here a hundred years and never meet."

"My dear Mary," interrupted Mrs Dean. "The time!"

Viola looked at the clock. Leaving the dog on the sofa, she extended her hand to Julian. "I'm so glad you came to tea, Mr Pope. It has definitely made you a better man."

Julian looked at the clock, too. "Has it been twenty minutes?" he asked in surprise. Twenty minutes, as all the world knew, was the proscribed length of a social visit. Even in London, to go beyond that was considered bad form.

"I'm afraid it has, Mr Pope. But we will meet again tomorrow at the auction," Viola added as the front doorbell rang. Julian got to his feet.

"That will be Lord Simon," Mrs Dean trilled excitedly, jumping up. "Hurry, child! You mustn't keep his lordship waiting. Go upstairs and put on your bonnet, there's a good girl. Lord Simon Ascot," Mrs Dean clarified for Julian's benefit. "The younger son of the Duke of Berkshire. He's taking Mary for a drive in his high-perch phaeton. Of all your admirers, Mary, I believe I like his lordship the best." She flung open the doors and ran out.

"Shall I envy him for being Auntie's favorite?" Julian murmured.

"By all means," Viola answered, laughing. Then, almost before she knew what was happening, he had slipped his arm around her waist and pulled her close to him. His voice was deep in her ear, saying urgently, "You're in grave danger, Yorkshire. Meet me tonight at nine o'clock at the lamppost across the street. I'll explain everything then. Yes?"

Viola drew back, scoffing. "Danger! What on earth can you mean?"

"Please, you must trust me," he urged. "I am concerned for your welfare."

"I was born in Yorkshire, Mr Pope," she said coldly, "but it was not a recent event. You must think me a fool! Will I meet you? I'll meet you in China in twenty years, if you like."

She flung his arm from her, saying, "Good day to you, sir!"

"But I just got here," said Lord Simon Ascot, striding into the room. Attired in the full dress uniform of a Horse Guard, he looked like some strange cross between a medieval knight and a special messenger. Being wholly preoccupied with Viola, he took no notice of the other man. "As you can see, I come to you straight from the parade ground, Mary. Am I not a fine fellow, and a credit to the Blues?"

Viola had to concede that he was indeed a fine fellow. His face was, perhaps, a little too harshly featured to be handsome, but it was a strong, attractive face nonetheless. Tall and broad-shouldered, he wore his uniform with distinction. His steel cuirass gleamed like a mirror. His white leather riding breeches clung to him like a second skin. His thigh-high black boots, complete with jingling spurs, had been polished to such a high sheen that when Viola drew near him, they reflected her striped dress as truly as a mirror. His sword was buckled at his side, and he carried his tall silver and brass helmet under one arm. The helmet's crest, composed of a horse's long tail which had been dyed blood red, trailed almost to the floor.

Viola cleared her throat. "Lord Simon, may I present Mr Pope?"

The big Guardsman whirled around to see Julian for the first time. "I beg your pardon, sir!" he said angrily. "I did not see you there."

"It's this cursed invisibility," Julian kindly explained. "It comes and goes."

"Mr Pope!" Viola rebuked him. "Have some respect for your betters. This gentleman is Lieutenant-Colonel Lord Simon Ascot of the Royal Horse Guards Blue."

Lord Simon smiled at her warmly. "That's very good, Miss Andrews," he congratulated her. "Most females get my ranks and titles hopelessly muddled. Just the other day, a viscountess introduced me as 'My Lord-Lieutenant Ascot.'"

When he looked at Julian, Lord Simon's smile grew colder

and did not extend to his eyes, which were pale green, in contrast with his bronzed skin and dark hair. "You should have made your presence known, sir," he said crisply.

"Mr Pope was just leaving," Viola said firmly. "Weren't you, Mr Pope?"

"On the contrary," said Julian. Parting the tails of his plain black coat, he sat down again on the purple sofa. "You were just about to ring for more tea, weren't you, Miss Andrews?" Viola glared at the smiling young man. Audacity, she was discovering, was a quality best admired in theory. In real life, it was vastly annoying when men did not do as they were told. "You are confused, Mr Pope," she said angrily. "I was *not* about to ring for more tea. I was about to go for a drive in the park with Lord Simon, and you were on your way to– to China, was it not? I understand there's plenty of tea there!"

"Oh, I'm afraid I can't leave England just yet," Julian replied smoothly. "Not until I know the Mall is quite secure," he added, turning to Lord Simon with mocking concern. "No fatalities in today's exercises, I trust, my lord? No one injured on parade?"

"Injured? Don't be ridiculous," Lord Simon sniffed. "Go and put on your bonnet, my dear," he told Viola. "Wait until you see the cunning little ponies I have just bought."

With infinite care, Julian selected a macaroon from the plate. "I'm glad no one was hurt," he said. "It's almost impossible to replace a Guardsman, you know. *Real* soldiers just aren't pretty enough to put on parade."

Viola gasped at the brazen insult, and Lord Simon saw at once that could no longer ignore the other man if he meant to keep the young woman's esteem. Anger flashed in his green eyes. "And what was your regiment, sir?" he sneered.

Julian told him.

"Ah, yes. Infantry," Lord Simon sniffed. "Out of Sussex, I believe."

"That's right. Nothing succeeds like Sussex."

Viola could not help but smile at such an arrogant motto.

Lord Simon's eyes narrowed as he studied his opponent. His lips curved in a thin smile. "I know you, don't I?" he said suddenly.

"No," said Julian, frowning.

"Yes, I do," said Lord Simon, still smiling his thin smile. "Someone pointed you out to me in White's Club. You were dining with the Duke of Fanshawe. You're the blackguard who broke Lady Jersey's bank. Can you deny it?"

For the first time, the young man seemed discomfited. Lord Simon smiled triumphantly. "You are no better than a thief, sir. If there were any justice, Miss Andrews, this upstart would be in prison, but there is a loophole in the law, or so I understand."

Viola had larger concerns than justice. "Are you acquainted with the Duke of Fanshawe, Mr Pope?" she demanded.

"His name is not Pope," said Lord Simon. "It's something like 'Devilish' or 'Devious.'"

"Devize!" Viola exclaimed in dismay. Her legs felt unsteady, and she was forced to sit down. "*You* are Mr Devize? You told me your name was Pope!" she accused him angrily.

"No, I didn't," said Julian. "I told you my brother's name was Pope."

Her dark eyes blazed. "And from that I should have inferred that *your* name was, in fact, Devize?" she cried, outraged. "Oh! How stupid of me!"

Julian had the grace to look ashamed. "Miss Andrews, I can explain," he began.

"No, don't, please," she said quickly. "Don't explain."

Viola did not believe in coincidence, or even in fate. There could only be one reason for Mr Devize's presence here: Dickon must have sent him to find her.

Viola blushed hotly as she recalled Mr Devize's voice in

her ear, urging her to meet him later that night. She had thought he was attempting to seduce her, when, of course, all he had in mind was restoring her to her brother's custody. She had protested just like the heroine of a melodrama. What a conceited little fool he must think her!

"I understand perfectly, Mr Devize," she said as calmly as she could. "There's no need to explain. Please don't say anything more."

To her grateful relief, Mr Devize did not expose her true identity.

"All the world knows of your crimes, sir," said Lord Simon, his lip curled in scorn. "Even Miss Andrews, who has not been in London a week, has heard of your infamy. Indeed, Miss Andrews, this cad has imposed on you most grievously. Mr Devize is not a gentleman. You've got a bloody cheek, man, imposing on this young lady."

Julian frowned. "Miss Andrews will not be accustomed to such language as this."

"I beg your pardon, Miss Andrews," Lord Simon muttered. "I did not mean to swear. I was provoked."

"Mary!" cried Mrs Dean, bustling into the room. "Don't just stand there gawping! Go and put on your bonnet! All the fashionable people are about, taking their exercise in the park. Hurry, child! You are in excellent looks, is she not, gentlemen?" She beamed at the two men happily. In her view, having two or more interested parties locking horns was good for business.

"I was not *gawping*," Viola said, scowling. "I wouldn't know how."

"Madam," said Lord Simon. "I must inform you that this man is an impostor. He is not Mr Pope. He is, in fact, the infamous Mr Devize. He's not even a gentleman. He's nothing more than the Duke of Fanshawe's stockjobber. He should be ejected from this house at once."

The effect on Mrs Dean of Lord Simon's revelation was not

what he had hoped. Mary's aunt seemed strangely pleased. "Oh?" she said, wriggling with pleasure. "The Duke of Fanshawe! Why, Mary, you sly thing! You said you only knew his grace a little! It would seem you have made a conquest of him, after all."

"I wish you wouldn't say such foolish things, Mrs Dean," Viola murmured, not daring to look at Mr Devize.

"I beg your pardon!" Lord Simon said sharply. "How, exactly, is Miss Andrews acquainted with the Duke of Fanshawe?"

"'Twas the duke who gave Mary's father the living at Gambolthwaite," Mrs Dean explained proudly. "His grace was her father's patron."

"I see," Lord Simon said, glowering at Mr Devize. "Then you will be attending the auction on his grace's behalf, and bidding, too, on his behalf?"

"How else could I afford to do so?" said Julian.

"But why lie about your identity?" Lord Simon pressed him.

"I daresay, the duke values his privacy, milord," Mrs Dean answered. "Rest assured, Mr Devize, not a word about the duke's interest will cross my lips."

"But how did the duke know that I was here, Mr Devize?" Viola asked. "That part I can't understand. I certainly did not inform him of my plans."

Julian smiled at her. "It is my duty to keep the duke informed, Miss Andrews."

Her dark eyes widened. "But how did *you* know I was here? I told no one in London. How did you even know I'd left Yorkshire?"

"I keep myself informed," he arrogantly explained. "As your father's patron, the duke is, of course, most concerned about your welfare, Miss Andrews. As am I."

"That is very good of his grace," said Mrs Dean dreamily. "But now, Mr Pope—or Devize or whatever your name is— it is Lord Simon's turn to enjoy Mary's company. You are most welcome to attend the auction on the duke's behalf, of course, but now you must go." She held out her hand, and Julian had no choice but to take his leave. Before going, he strolled over to the sofa and ruffled the bichon's ear.

Viola extended her hand to him. "Good afternoon, Mr Devize. Indeed, the duke is very fortunate to have such a capable young man working for him. You may be certain that I—"

"Nine o'clock, Mary," he murmured for her ears alone as he kissed her hand.

"Impossible," she breathed.

Viola was not in the habit of blushing, but a blush crept into her cheeks as he lifted his impossibly blue eyes to hers. The shock of attraction startled and embarrassed her, and, as he left the room, she felt a sense of loss quite out of proportion to the relationship. *What a pity he is not Lord Bamph,* she thought as he went out.

As if pulled by a string, she moved to the window, hoping for another glimpse of him. Oblivious to everything else, she heard the front door close, and Mr Devize came into view as he stepped into the street. He had no walking stick or gloves, and he had not yet put on his hat. The wind ruffled his short hair into spikes, then smoothed it down again like an invisible hand.

As he turned into Oxford Street, Viola had the most ridiculous impulse to leave the house and run after him. And then he was gone.

Lord Simon was beside her, glowering. "Come away from the window, my dear," he urged, taking her arm. "Are we to have our drive or not?"

Viola went to the sofa to collect the puppy. "You must forgive me, Lord Simon," she said absently. "I have the headache. I'm going upstairs to lie down. I look forward to seeing your lordship tomorrow at the auction," she added, extending her hand to him.

Anger flashed in his green eyes, but he bent over her hand like a gentleman. "Good afternoon, then, Miss Andrews."

"Good afternoon, Lord Simon," she replied with well-bred politeness, but it was clear to him that her thoughts were elsewhere.

# Chapter Six

Despite regular improvements, Castle Devize in Sussex had maintained through the centuries the appearance of an ancient, neglected Norman ruin. Upon close examination, one was surprised to find all its ivy-covered stone walls in good repair, its roof sound, its staircases sturdy enough to support a stampede of elephants. And yet one was left with the feeling that a sudden storm might blow it all down into an ignominious heap of rubble. Thus it had appeared since the days of William the Conqueror, when the first Devizes had roasted oxen in the enormous fireplace of the Great Hall.

George, Lord Devize, was sitting comfortably before this same fireplace playing chess with his physician when he heard the rumble and squeal of the drawbridge being let down. Still vigorous at sixty-one, he jumped nimbly to his feet, clapped his big hands together, and barked, "Standish! It has begun."

Dr Standish, who suffered from rheumatism in his old age, was not so quick on his feet.

"I am going to bed," Lord Devize informed his butler. "Remember, I have been in bed dying for the past three days. Give me ten minutes to get into my nightshirt, then let Madam come in to me alone. And get someone to help Standish up the stairs. He should be taking my pulse and shaking his head very sadly when Madam comes in."

With that, the baron sprinted up the nearest staircase like a man half his age. He scarcely needed ten minutes to run to his chamber, strip off his clothes, put on his nightshirt, and jump into his big, lonely, four-poster bed.

"Splash a little water on my face to make me look feverish," he instructed his valet as Dr Standish, still seated in his chair, was carried into the room by two big footmen.

The baron and his physician might have continued their chess game, so long did Madam keep them waiting. By the time the baroness put in an appearance, Dr Standish was sound asleep, and so could not be caught in the act of taking the patient's pulse. The baron wheezed piteously as his immaculate wife approached the bed. Unfortunately, his lordship looked excessively brown and healthy against the whiteness of his pillowcase, and her ladyship had already scared the truth out of the butler. "George, you old fraud," she greeted him. "I know you're awake."

Dr Standish was now awake, too, thanks to the cold penetration of her ladyship's voice. He hobbled over to the bed and began to take the baron's pulse.

The baron lifted his leonine head from the pillow an inch, then let it fall again, as if it were too heavy for him. "Madam?" he said weakly.

"Don't you madam me," snapped his wife. "You're not dying, more's the pity. You're not even sick. How *dare* you take me away from London at the height of the social Season? How could you be so selfish? I was *this close* to gaining an invitation to Berkshire House! Now I shall have to begin all over again. If one is gone even a day, one is forgotten!"

Lord Devize retaliated with the agonized moan he had been practicing.

"I'll give you something to cry about, you selfish old man. I wish you *would* die," the baroness added, gritting her teeth. "As your widow, I might get on in Society. As it is, people don't invite me for fear *you* might come along."

"Alexa!" Startled by her venom, the baron stopped pretending. "You don't mean it."

The baroness opted to glare at her husband rather than confirm or deny. "My name is Alexandra," she informed him coldly. "'Madam' to you."

Abruptly, the baron slapped away Dr Standish's hands. Punching his pillow into shape, he sat up. "I wonder you bothered to come at all," he grumbled.

"I was obliged to come, and you know it!" she snarled. "How would it look if I didn't? People would say I was cold and unfeeling."

With a look from her glittering blue eyes, she sent Dr Standish limping from the room. "Well, George?" she demanded. "What do you want this time?"

The baron looked shifty and furtive. "Perdita's not with you?" he inquired.

"Yes. Pregnant again," the baroness sniffed. "Now she'll never get her waist back."

The baron grunted. "And my son?"

"Alexander is here, too, of course," she said. "Shall I bring them in? They are so delighted that you've recovered from your recent brush with death, I don't doubt they wish to share their delight with you before they leave."

The baron scratched one ear for a moment. Then he scratched the other. He moved around in the bed uncomfortably. Finally, he said what was on his mind. "Julian?"

The baroness sniffed. "I'm afraid he couldn't be bothered to come. He's very busy, you know. Why, he could scarcely give his own mother five minutes."

The baron's eyes were the eyes of a hurt child. "He's not here? Did you tell him I was dying?" he demanded plaintively.

"Of course I did. He did not seem to care. I'm sorry, George," she said evenly. "I know you had hopes for the boy, but he's a selfish, disobedient wretch. He went into the army against your wishes, and he didn't even have the decency to distinguish himself during the war."

"He was mentioned in the dispatches," the baron protested weakly.

Her eyes blazed. "But was he *knighted,* George? No, he was not! After the war, he still would not apologize to you. He would not take holy orders as you wished, and—"

"I wanted him to have the living here at Devizes," the baron erupted in anguish, "and be close to me always. Why would he not come home to me? Miss Grant would have made him an amiable wife. As Vicar of Devizes, he would have had three thousand a year. All he had to do was come home and beg my forgiveness. It was his for the asking. I would have killed the fatted calf for that boy."

The baroness smiled thinly. "Instead, he sold out of the army and began speculating on the Exchange like a common I-know-not-what. Your son is no longer a gentleman, George. He is dead to us. You must try to forget him."

"Some gentlemen do speculate," the baron protested.

"For *themselves,*" she retorted. "It's no good trying to defend what is indefensible. He takes a *percentage* of the profits as payment, for heaven's sake! It is Trade, George. Trade."

The baron shuddered helplessly at the thought of his own flesh and blood sinking to such depths. "Julian, my boy," he moaned with genuine grief.

Lady Devize fired up. "He has broken all our hearts, destroyed our place in Society. He lives in the City, you know. His neighbors are Jews, tradesmen, pawnbrokers! He eats his breakfast in the street like a gypsy. And if you had but seen his hat!" With difficulty, she reined in her fury. "And I have it on good authority that, just the other day, he visited a brothel!"

"What!" the baron cried, starting up in alarm. "Julian

shouldn't go to brothels! He'll catch the French disease. He should keep a mistress."

"I shouldn't think he could afford to keep a mistress," his wife replied. "He can't even afford a decent hat. The point is," she went on quickly. "Julian is lost to us forever. You must concentrate on your eldest son, your heir, and forget your foolish partiality for a young man who wouldn't even come to you on your deathbed! Alexander is well-liked and respected everywhere he goes. He is considered one of the best young men in London."

"His debts are excessive."

The baroness shrugged. "All gentlemen gamble."

"I wish he were better at it," the baron grumbled. "He never seems to win! He should marry and settle down. I want to see the line secured before I die. The barony has passed from father to eldest son in an unbroken line for a thousand years. Why won't he marry?"

"How can he afford a wife," she countered, "when you cut his allowance to the bone? You have made him a laughing-stock before his friends. People think we are *poor!*"

"I thought you said he was well-liked and respected," her husband snorted. "Rest assured, Madam, when my son marries, I'll give him a very handsome allowance—provided he marries to please *me*, of course."

"Would you like to see him now? He's waiting outside."

The baron looked mutinous.

"Julian isn't coming," she said firmly. "Alexander and Perdita, on the other hand, have proved their love for you. They are here. Let them come in."

He nodded grudgingly.

Perdita rushed to the bed and kissed her father. "What a mean trick!" she reproached him. "If you wanted to see us, you had only to ask. There was no need to resort to deception."

The baron squeezed his daughter's hand. "Not in your case, my beauty, but, as for some others I could name . . . ! I knew

I could rely on *you*, Perdy. Your sex was a disappointment to your mother because it meant she had to return to the marriage bed, which she hated, but *I* never minded that you were a girl."

"Be quiet, George," Lady Devize said angrily.

"Madam tells me you're breeding again," said the baron, wagging his finger at Perdita. "Tell Cheviot I said to leave you alone. Tell him to get a mistress. You're getting too old for such exercise. You must think of your health."

"I'm not breeding, Papa," Perdita exclaimed in surprise.

"Are you not?" asked the baroness. "You have grown so plump of late that I naturally assumed—"

"I'm not pregnant, Mama!" Perdita snapped, her cheeks flaming.

"I'm glad to hear it. It's embarrassing enough that you have *seven* children. And five of them male!" Lady Devize shook her head in disgust. "You might reasonably have stopped after William was born. Why, if Alexander had not contracted the pox when he was eight, *I* should never have returned to the marriage bed at all, and there would be no troublesome Julian. But, at the time, we thought we might need a spare boy."

The baron turned to his heir. "Nothing to say to me, Alex?" he demanded.

"Only that you look remarkably well, sir," Alex replied, bowing to his parent.

The bland response enraged the baron. "I trust I did not take you away from the card table, sir!" he roared.

"No, indeed, Father. I was nowhere near a card table."

"Hmmmph! Something I wish to say to you, now you are here."

"Very well, my lord," said Alex. "I attend your words with the greatest pleasure."

"It's high time you married, boy. Your mother and I were just discussing it. You will marry Miss Peacock. She's a sweet girl, and her father has no heir. It's perfect. When old Peacock dies, the neighboring estate will come to us through Molly. In the meantime, if you marry her, I will double your allowance. What do you say? Her father's very eager."

"I say no, sir," said Alex.

"No!" the baron repeated in amazement. "That's an extra five hundred pounds a year. Are you in love with someone else? You want more money, is that it?"

"Not everything is about money, my lord."

The baron scowled. "This is what I have come to expect from my sons," he said bitterly. "Brazen, foolhardy disobedience! The least you can do is marry where I tell you."

Alex shook his head. "You're living in the past, my lord. No one arranges marriages anymore. I will choose my own wife."

"You refuse to marry Miss Peacock?"

"I do, sir."

"Very well, then! I know how to proceed. The title is entailed upon you, of course, as well as the castle and lands and the incomes. But my fortune, boy, is my own." The baron rubbed his hands together. "You shall have no allowance, none at all, until you come to your senses and marry Miss Peacock. I'll put notices in all the papers to whit that I, Lord Devize, am no more responsible for your debts. Perdita, my dear . . ."

"Yes, Papa?"

"You shall have twenty thousand pounds. I'll give it to you outright. I had meant to divide it equally among my three children, but now I see my sons are both equally unworthy."

"Papa, how thoughtful!" Perdita exclaimed in delight, but, after an awkward moment, she smiled ruefully at Alex. "I'm sorry, Alex, but with *seven* children . . . And all the boys, except Henry, at school! I'm afraid I cannot be too proud to take it."

"I'm happy for you." Alex shrugged.

Perdita kissed her father's brow. "Thank you, sir."

"I wish you had been a boy, Perdy," the baron said fondly. "You are the only one of my children conceived in love. At least there was love on my part, eh, Madam? *Her* heart was ever cold to me. What a fool I was to think otherwise. She only wanted my title."

"Much good it did me," the baroness snapped. "I should have held out for an earl."

"Ha! You were lucky to get a baron, Miss Alexandra Lyndon, and you know it!"

"Really, George. You will burst a vein." The baroness turned to her eldest son. "You will return with me to London. I will find you a suitable wife with a handsome fortune."

"Madam!" cried the baron. "I want him to marry Miss Peacock!"

She smiled thinly. "Who is Molly Peacock? Her father is merely a country booby squire. . . . And her mother! A *farmer's* daughter! Who are her uncles and aunts? Alexander is the heir to a barony. When word gets out that he is looking for a wife, he will be showered with invitations from all the best people. How popular I shall be for the rest of the Season! We'll leave at once. Come, Alexander. Come, Perdita."

She started for the door.

Perdita cleared her throat delicately. "Actually, Mama . . . I don't think I shall be going back to London with you. I've left Tony in Hampshire with the children too long as it is. Thank you so much for the money, Papa, but I must go home."

"You're leaving me, too?" the baron protested.

"Of course if you were *dying,* I would stay, Papa," said Perdita, kissing him good-bye. "But my children do need me, after all."

"The children need me, too," Alex said quickly. "I think I'll just biff off to Hants with Perdita and give them a bit of the old uncle treatment."

"Nonsense," said the baroness. "Perdita may do what she

likes, but *you* are coming to London with me. You won't find a wife in Hampshire."

"Not with the London Season in full swing," Perdita agreed.

The baron threw off his coverlet and stood up in his night-shirt. "He's going to stay right here and marry Molly Peacock!" he roared, jutting out his jaw.

"London!" said the baroness. "Debutante!"

"Peacock! Land!"

Alex and Perdita crept out of the room as the argument blazed on.

"You're not really thinking of rusticating with us in Hants?" Perdita asked her brother.

"Why not?" he answered. "You're rich now. The least you can do is put me up."

"You'll be bored to screams," she warned as they made their way back downstairs. "The only society in Hampshire this time of year are those who can't afford to go to London."

"Some very nice people can't afford to go to London," he pointed out. "I certainly can't."

"Oh, Mama will give you an allowance, if—"

Alex cut her off. "It's the *if* that kills."

Downstairs, the servants were still carrying in the luggage.

"Shall we hire a carriage, do you think?" Perdita asked her brother.

Alex shook his head. "No. We'll abscond with Mama's carriage and fresh horses from the governor. That's fair, I think, after all they've put me through. Put Lady Cheviot's trunk back in the boot," he instructed the servants. "We wish to leave immediately. Time, as they say, is of the essence."

"I must write to Julian," Perdita protested. "He thinks Papa is ill."

"At the absolute first inn where we stop, we'll dash him off a few lines," Alex promised. "I don't intend to be here when our mother comes out of our father's room."

"Quite!" she hastily agreed.

"Who do you think will win the argument?" she asked him some time later, as the carriage sped away into the night. "Mama or Papa? Peacock or debutante?"

Alex snorted. "Neither! I'm not marrying Miss Peacock so the governor can grab some land, and I'm not marrying some inbred heiress so that Mama can secure her place in Society."

Perdita sighed. "I wish we had some pretty girls for you in Hampshire, but, of course, all the good ones are in London for the season. Only the vicar's daughters are left, all five of them."

"You'd better give a ball," he said, yawning. "Or else I shall have to meet them one at a time. I'd much rather dispose of them all at once. Come now, Perdita. You mustn't begrudge your neighbors a little amusement, now that you are twenty thousand pounds the richer."

"Very well," she said, laughing. "I'll give a ball, but you must promise to be charming and dance every dance."

"What? All five of the vicar's daughters?"

"Worse than that, I'm afraid," said Perdita, her blue eyes dancing. "There's the Chisholm girl. And Colonel Markham's horse-faced niece, Miss Eccles—whom I strongly suggest is no better than she should be. And Miss Rampling, of course." She sighed heavily. "I hate giving balls! There are never enough gentlemen to go around."

Alex scowled. "Who the devil is Miss Rampling?" he demanded almost violently.

Perdita gave a scream of laughter. "Don't say you've forgotten her! She *is* a poor mousy little thing, to be sure, and I daresay, it has been years since you met. However, it is very bad manners of you to forget her so completely. I am sure you cannot have forgotten her mother, Lady Caroline Rampling? Dreadful woman—always foxed."

"How could I forget?"

"Well, they have become our neighbors in Hampshire. About five months ago, the neighborhood was atwitter because Gambol Hall was let at last, but it was only Lady

Caroline and her spinster daughter. We are obliged to see something of them. If I could be sure Lady Caroline would decline, I would invite them."

"Did Lady Caroline have *two* daughters?" Alex asked, looking white around the mouth.

"No, just poor Lucy, whom you have forgotten," laughed Perdita.

"I did not forget her," Alex replied. "I didn't know she was alive."

Perdita howled. "Alex! That is too cruel," she reproved him amidst her hilarity. "She is lacking in personality, to be sure, but I cannot allow that she is *lifeless*. Henry and Eliza adore her. Why, in the last five months, she has become like a second governess to them. Indeed, they like her better than Miss Shipley. She plays badminton and croquet with them, which Miss Shipley won't do. She even takes tea with them in the tree house."

Color had begun to creep back into Alex's face. "I thought Miss Rampling had married her cousin, Lord Southwood, some five years ago," he said, puzzled.

"Oh, no," Perdita assured him. "Southwood is far too sensible a man to marry a girl with no money."

"No money? Miss Rampling had a fortune of thirty thousand pounds."

"Her father gambled it all away," Perdita explained. "That is why he committed suicide. Lord Southwood married Lord Wembley's daughter. She died in childbirth, poor thing."

"I know," said Alex. "I sent her a wreath. I sent a wreath for a woman I never knew."

"Really? I didn't know you and Southwood were such good friends."

"How do the Ramplings get on without any money?" he asked abruptly.

"Tolerable," said Perdita. "I believe Lord Southwood has granted them a small annuity, and the Duke of Fanshawe let them have the house for next to nothing. The son is in Parliament, you know—one of the duke's pocket boroughs, I shouldn't wonder—but Lucy and her Mama are too poor to go to London for the Season, like the rest of the people you will meet at my ball." She sighed. "For propriety's sake, I shall have to invite them. I do hope Lady Caroline has the good sense to decline."

"I'll open the ball with Miss Rampling, if you like," Alex offered.

"She isn't likely to attend without her mother," said Perdita. "Or want to! She's quite thirty, you know, and a confirmed spinster. An old maid! An ape-leader!"

"Yes, thirty is a very awkward age for a female," Alex agreed. "That's when the crow's-feet start. From there, it's all downhill."

"Some women are handsomer at thirty than they are at twenty," Perdita said indignantly. "Unfortunately, Lucy Rampling is not one of them. She's so thin, and so plain, and so dull. She's no conversation at all! I do believe her only friend in the world is our governess."

Alex's lips twitched. "Miss Trent? Is she still kicking?"

"Not *our* governess," Perdita said crossly. "My children's governess. I don't think Miss Shipley could manage the twins without poor Lucy's help. I feel so sorry for her."

"Why should you feel sorry for Miss Shipley?" Alex asked, pretending to misunderstand her. "Surely my niece and nephew are not as bad as that."

"To be sure, they are angels," Perdita said. "I meant Miss Rampling. She never complains, of course, but it must be hell living under the same roof with Lady Caroline. She hasn't a penny, nothing to tempt a man."

"How sordid," said Alex, closing his eyes again. "I wish you hadn't told me."

* * *

They arrived at Cross Mere well after dark. Lord Cheviot was pleased to see his wife; even more pleased to learn that her time away from him had enriched them both; and, if he thought it odd that his brother-in-law was to be encamped at Cross Mere for some duration, he was at least not unwelcoming.

At breakfast, Alex announced his intention of riding over to Gambol Hall to pay his respects to the Ramplings. Perdita saw no need for such solicitude; Miss Rampling visited them nearly every morning, and it would be a punishment to visit Gambol Hall only to find Lady Caroline its sole occupant. Lord Cheviot was completely indifferent to the matter, and shut himself up in his library as soon as he possibly could. The six-year-old twins, Henry and Eliza, confirmed that Lucy was expected at Cross Mere, and so the matter was settled.

"May we go out to the Folly and meet Lucy?" Eliza begged her mother. Like many pretty, well-behaved young ladies, Elizabeth Cheviot had few ideas of her own. Fortunately, her twin was there to put her up to all sorts of mischief. Today, Henry planned to let the bull out of the pasture. It would be fun to see Lucy run while they watched from the safety of the Folly.

Perdita frowned at her children severely. "Should you not be in the schoolroom by this hour? Miss Shipley will be wondering where you are."

"No, she won't," said precocious young Henry. Like many naughty boys, he was unduly attractive, with his mother's bright blue eyes and thick chestnut hair. His angelic appearance enabled him to get away with all sorts of high crimes and misdemeanors. "She is in bed today with a sick headache."

Perdita sighed. "How tiresome," she complained. "But I daresay Lucy will give you your lessons. Very well. You may go out to meet her, but do not go any farther than the Folly," she called after them as they ran from the room, Henry in the lead. "It's only three miles to Gambol Hall, but the park there is excessively woodsy. It won't do for them to get lost."

"Do the Ramplings keep a carriage?" Alex asked, with a slight frown.

"Dear me, no," said Perdita. "If they were to accept my invitation to the ball—heaven forbid—I should have to send my carriage for them. So tiresome!"

Alex's frown deepened. "Does Miss Rampling come on horseback?"

"I daresay the duke keeps a few saddle horses at Gambol Hall, but they are wasted entirely on the Ramplings, I assure you. Lucy doesn't ride. Well, she rides, but she doesn't jump, which amounts to the same thing when one is in the country."

"She *walks* here?" Alex said sharply. "Three miles here and back, nearly every day?"

"Yes, but you must not tease her if there is mud on her petticoat," Perdita told him sternly. "There is mud in the country, you know. It cannot be avoided. You should take a walk yourself," she urged him. "The fresh air would do you good. You remember the way to the Folly, of course?"

Alex did, but when he reached the place, there was no sign of the twins. Miss Rampling, however, was just coming across the field. She had removed her bonnet, but, as soon as she saw a male figure awaiting her at the Folly, she put it back on. It was a plain straw bonnet. Her dress was gray and plain. Alex was struck all over again by how physically insignificant she was, how easily overlooked. Her eyes were gray. Her hair was brown. She had neither beauty nor fortune. She wasn't even clever, or, at any rate, she lacked the quick wit so prized by Society. Plain good sense and sweetness of temper were all the qualities she possessed, and these were of no value in the fashionable world.

"Mr Devize!" she exclaimed. Recognition was immediate, her surprise at seeing him evident, but try as he might he could detect no signs of any deeper feeling on her part. His own heart was pounding so loudly he was afraid she might hear it. At times such as these, etiquette was a most welcome crutch.

"Good morning, Miss Rampling," he said, giving her a bow.

"Good morning. I did not know you were expected in Hampshire," she said, her smile open, warm, and friendly. "You are visiting your sister, I collect?"

"Yes," he replied. "May I suggest we go into the Folly?"

Lucy blinked at him in surprise. "What? Why?"

"Because the bull has got out of the pasture," Alex replied, taking her firmly by the arm, "and it's coming toward us now."

This Folly had been built in the form of two towers with a parapet joining them. Like a miniature castle, it straddled the lane between the Cross Mere and Gambol Hall properties. Alex pushed in the wall of the nearest tower and a door opened, a single large slab of stone operating on a pivot. Inside, there was nothing but a set of stairs leading up to the parapet. Moss grew on the walls, and there was a smell of damp.

"I am obliged to you, Mr Devize," Lucy said when they were safe.

The twins appeared at the top of the stairs. "Hullo, Uncle Alex. Hullo, Lucy. You should come up and watch the fun. Toby and John are trying to catch the bull."

"Presently," said Alex. "Let us catch our breath."

The darkness and closeness of the space made Alex feel less inhibited. "Miss Rampling," he began a little shakily. "You must forgive me for not coming to see you sooner."

"There is nothing to forgive," she said gently. "We were foolish to think we could remain friends after so much had passed between us. I fully comprehend your feelings, sir. I only hope my presence in Hampshire will not prevent you from visiting your sister as often as you like."

"You do not understand my feelings at all," he replied bluntly. "I did not visit you because I thought you were dead."

"Dead?" she repeated blankly.

"Well, first I thought you were married. Then I learned you had died."

Bewildered, Lucy could only shake her head.

"Did you not tell me your family expected you to marry your cousin, Lord Southwood?" he demanded.

"My mother desired the match very much," Lucy admitted. "However, Cousin Alfred had very different ideas. I am sorry you thought I was dead. I confess I thought I had lost all claim to your friendship and regard when I . . . When the matter ended."

"You mean when you refused my offer of marriage."

"Yes," she said.

"Do you ever regret that you did so?" he asked sharply.

"No, of course not," she said softly. "My only regret was the loss of your friendship."

"You have not lost my friendship," he assured her. "Indeed, my feelings for you are unchanged. I never cared for anyone else. I never wished to marry anyone else."

"Please don't," she said quickly. "To renew your addresses to me would only cause pain to us both. I can no more accept you now than I could then."

"Then I shall be silent on the subject forever," he threatened.

"Thank you," she said, so gratefully that it provoked him to retaliate.

"You realize, however, that I must marry someone else," he said coolly.

"Of course," said Lucy. "It is your duty, Mr Devize. You are the heir."

"Then it would not pain you to see me marry?"

"To be sure it would not," she said stoutly. "To see my good friend secure a lasting happiness could only give me the greatest of pleasure."

"Then there is no reason to delay the matter," he said angrily.

"No, indeed," Lucy agreed.

Abruptly, he offered her his arm. "Shall we go up to the parapet to watch the fun?"

# Chapter Seven

Having glided into Portland Place with relative ease the morning before, Julian was astounded by the horrendous traffic on Oxford Street Friday afternoon. Without the pocket watch he had pawned, he could only guess at the time, but he was reasonably certain that he was late for the opening bid. The hackney in which he was traveling had been at a full stop for what seemed like an eternity. Abruptly, he flung open the door and jumped out. Tossing a coin up to the driver, he sprinted off toward Portland Place.

In the City, he walked everywhere, and so was reasonably fit; all the same, he was heaving for air when he burst into the sitting room of Mrs Dean's house. Chairs had been set up for about two dozen bidders, but Julian did not look at them. He saw only the tall, black-haired girl brushing out the little white dog that stood on the tea table before her. She was wearing a blue dress, translucent muslin over white satin. Blue ribbons were threaded through her black hair. He thought he had never seen anything so beautiful in all his life.

"Five thousand guineas!" he gasped. Falling forward, he clutched his knees and struggled to catch his breath.

"You're late, Mr Devize," Viola informed him. "The bidding stands at *fifteen* thousand pounds."

"Fifteen thousand, five hundred," Lord Simon Ascot drawled,

turning in his seat to glance at Julian. No longer in uniform, the Guardsman was attired in correct evening dress, as if he had just come from a ball or the theater. Julian dearly wanted to kick him.

"Very generous, Lord Simon!" Mrs Dean called from her place at the back of the room. "Lord Barrowbridge?" she lilted, calling to an elderly gentleman seated in the front row. "You are outbid, sir!"

"Sixteen thousand pounds," said the Earl of Barrowbridge, clutching the silver knob of his walking stick. He was not only old, but old-fashioned, too. His was the only powdered wig in the room. In his pink velvet coat heavily adorned with braid, he looked rather like a footman.

Some of the other gentlemen, evidently out of the bidding, shook their heads in amazement. "For God's sake, Simon, 'tis only a female," said a slim, red-haired man seated next to Lord Simon Ascot.

"She's worth it, Sir Myron," Viola said.

Sir Myron laughed. "You almost make me believe it, you little vixen."

Lord Simon flashed Sir Myron a warning look. "Seventeen thousand pounds!"

"Seventeen thousand," Julian said, almost at the same time.

Lord Simon looked annoyed. "You cannot bid the same, stockjobber," he snapped.

"My bid is in guineas," Julian answered coldly.

Sir Myron chuckled. "What say you, Lord Simon? If the bitch is worth a pound, she must be worth a guinea."

"Lord Barrowbridge?" Viola smiled kindly at the old man. "Are you out, my lord?"

"I can't do it," said the old man, hanging his head. "I'd like to, my dear, but I can't."

"Could you ever?" Sir Myron wondered aloud.

Lord Barrowbridge planted his malacca cane in the carpet and pulled his soft, pudgy body up onto his bony legs. "I would have adopted you," he told Viola sadly. As he bent to kiss her hand, his backbone cracked loudly, eliciting laughter from Sir Myron. "So beautiful . . . What a terrible waste. I cannot bear to watch this spectacle a moment longer."

So saying, his lordship hobbled past Julian and out the door.

Viola stared after him in confusion. "Poor old thing," she said softly. "Why, it's almost as if he believes that *I'm* the one being auctioned off instead of Bijou!"

There was a startled silence. Then Sir Myron began to laugh. No one seemed inclined to join in his hilarity, however. Julian looked down at his feet, unable to look at the girl as the humiliating truth dawned on her. This was exactly the scene he had hoped to avoid.

"She doesn't know?" Lord Simon's curt voice cut through the air like a knife. His cold green eyes sought out Mrs Dean, who was seated at her desk at the back of the room. Her rapture had climbed with every bid, and she was scarcely aware that she was being addressed until Lord Simon stood up and repeated his question.

The look of wrath on his harsh features brought her to her feet. In her lace cap and shawl, she looked almost respectable. "My lord? What is the matter?"

"You did not tell Miss Andrews the truth," Lord Simon accused her. "She believes this auction is for that ridiculous little dog! You told me that was just to confuse the law."

Viola clutched Bijou protectively. "What *is* the truth?" she demanded.

Sir Myron laughed, Mrs Dean dithered, and Lord Simon looked furious, but no one answered her. "This is infamous!" Lord Simon said after a moment.

Mrs Dean began to make excuses. "I have debts, my lord! Crippling debts! How else am I to pay them?"

"You were selling *me*?" Viola gasped. "To these gentlemen? For what purpose?"

"For pleasure, of course," Sir Myron drawled. "It's what you were made for, my girl. Didn't your mother ever tell you that?"

"My mother!" cried Viola. "How dare you!"

"And now we shall have tears," Sir Myron predicted. "Tears and hysterics."

If he had not said that, Viola might indeed have burst into tears, but, fortunately, his contempt reminded her of who she was. She drew herself to her full height. "I don't suppose," she said coldly, "it would do a bit of good to tell you how ashamed I am of you all. And *you,* Mrs Dean! I knew you were a vulgar woman, but I never thought anyone could be as bad as this. Your own niece! How could you? Mr Devize!"

"I am here," said Julian, on his feet.

Mrs Dean strode to the front of the room. "I did you a favor, you parson's prig," she snapped. "I could have sold your quim a hundred times these last three days! Oh, you wouldn't have liked that, Miss Mary! You should be on your knees thanking me."

"I will see you in the dock for this!" Viola replied.

Mrs Dean lifted her hand to slap her face, but several gentlemen intervened. Lord Simon got there first and caught her arm. "There will be none of that, Mrs Dean," he said harshly. "Miss Andrews, please believe me when I tell you I had no idea you had not been told the truth. I thought you knew. I believed you to be a willing participant. I would never—"

"Willing participant? In my own slavery and humiliation?" Viola's eyes raked over him. "I see! You thought I was . . . You thought I was . . ."

"A whore?" Sir Myron helpfully supplied the word she could not bring herself to say.

Unable to contain her fury any longer, Viola struck Lord Simon across the face as hard as she could. "You are not a gentleman," she said, wincing as pain shot through her hand.

"You are no better than an animal. *You* are a disgrace to your regiment, sir!"

"Are you going to let the bitch get away with that, milord?" cried Sir Myron. "The bidding stands at seventeen thousand guineas. Bid again. Come, Lord Simon, I'll lend you some money, if you like."

Lord Simon pressed his hand to his cheek and worked his jaw. His mouth tasted of blood. "I don't think Miss Andrews wants me to bid again," he said ruefully.

"Never mind what *she* wants," Sir Myron said comfortably. "I find the struggles of a virgin stimulating in the extreme, especially when the girl pretends not to like it. Come, let us pool our resources. Together we can outbid Fanshawe. We'll toss a coin for first rights."

"Sir Myron, I do believe you are drunk," Lord Simon said stiffly.

"What sterling company you keep, my lord," Viola said coldly. "This auction is at an end. I shall go with Mr Devize."

"You will?" Julian said, startled.

"Miss Andrews! Are you sure?" Lord Simon asked, almost as surprised as Julian.

"I am quite sure, Lord Simon," Viola answered. "I certainly shan't be staying here with Mrs Dean! No, I shall be quite safe with the Duke of Fanshawe, for, unlike yourself, Lord Simon, *he* is a gentleman!" She turned to Julian. "I'm going upstairs to pack my trunk, Mr Devize. Immediately I come down, I shall want to quit this house forever."

Head high, she swept from the room, carrying the bichon in her arms.

When she returned some forty-five minutes later wearing her coat and hat, only Julian remained with Mrs Dean in the sitting room. Julian was pacing the floor. "Here she is," said Mrs Dean, rising from her desk. "Now give me my money, Mr Devize."

"One moment, madam," said Julian, holding the banknote

out of reach. "You were very long in coming, Miss Andrews. I trust you encountered no difficulties?"

"I shouldn't call it a difficulty," she answered, fussing over one of the Persian lamb cuffs of her white leather coat. "One must expect delays when one is training a new girl. My maid had never packed a trunk before in her life! We had to do it several times over, but it's all sorted now," she added with a smile.

"Is this really the time to be fastidious, Miss Andrews?" Julian wondered.

Viola frowned at the implied criticism. "I suppose I *am* fastidious, Mr Devize, but I don't care to see my gowns crushed. In any case, I'm ready to go now."

"Give me my money, young man," said Mrs Dean, licking her lips. "That's the bargain."

"Yes! Pay her and be done with it, Mr Devize," Viola said coldly.

Julian's expression was pained as he handed over the cheque.

"Anyone would think it was *your* money, Mr Devize," said Mrs Dean.

Julian laughed humorlessly.

"Good-bye, Mary," Mrs Dean went on, her eyes sparkling. "I knew you could not be so beautiful for nothing! Seventeen thousand guineas!" Kissing her cheque repeatedly, she cackled with glee.

Revolted, Viola took Julian's arm firmly. "Get me out of here, Mr Devize, I beg you."

"Of course," he murmured. "I have engaged a hackney."

Cork and Bijou were waiting for their mistress in the hall. Viola gave the manservant a threepenny piece to bring their luggage to the hackney carriage outside. It was quite dark when they left the house. Cork sat beside Viola in the carriage with Viola's hatbox on her knee.

Julian entered the carriage after seeing to the rest of the luggage. He signaled to the driver, and they were off. The carriage turned onto Oxford Street, traveling east. The traffic had lightened considerably, and they were able to travel at almost a country pace. They went along in silence, the two women seated opposite the gentleman.

Viola, with Bijou snoozing contentedly in her lap, gazed steadfastly out of the dark window. She could feel Mr Devize's eyes on her, but she could not look at him. Humiliated, she dreaded having to face her brother, too. Dickon did not often have the opportunity to lecture his clever sister on the foolishness of her behavior, and he was sure to make the most of the occasion. She would rather have gone straight back to Yorkshire to hide her shame.

*Now what?* Julian thought. He had rescued Miss Andrews, but now what? He hadn't given much thought to what might come after the auction. Now he had two women and a dog and no money to keep them. Worse than that, he had stolen seventeen thousand guineas from the Duke of Fanshawe, and if his crime were ever discovered, he might very well hang for it.

Setting aside his own worries, he thought of Mary. Her chin was trembling as she looked out of the window. Obviously, she was too ashamed to look at him. How frightened and dejected she must be feeling right about now, he thought. He longed to comfort her, but he wasn't sure how to go about it without frightening her.

"You won't believe me," he said, breaking the silence, "but when I left the City this afternoon, the traffic was so bad, I had to get out of my hack in Oxford Street and *run* to Portland Place. That's why I was so late. Is the light too bright for your eyes?" he asked, concerned, as Viola cringed in her seat. "Shall I lower the lamp?"

She shook her head. She looked utterly miserable.

"It's going to be all right, you know," he said gently.

She stole a glance at him. "He didn't send his carriage for me?"

"The duke? Er . . . no."

Julian bit his lip. Of course she thought he was taking her

to her father's patron, the Duke of Fanshawe. He hated to deceive her, even for a moment, but he could scarcely make a full confession in front of her servant.

"I suppose he was afraid his crest would be recognized," she sighed, still unable to meet Julian's eyes. "Oh, Mr Devize! You must think me the biggest fool who ever lived!"

"Not at all," he answered. "You could not have known."

"Charity auction, indeed! How could I have been so stupid?" She shivered violently. "Those horrid, horrid men! And Mrs Dean! I never dreamed there were such people in the world, not even in London!"

"You mustn't blame yourself," Julian said firmly. "You're certainly not the first pretty girl to be taken in. I'm sorry I could not get you out sooner."

"If I had been sensible to the danger . . . !" Viola bit her lip in mortification. "If I had been *sensible* at all, I should never have been there. I should have stayed in Yorkshire with my fellow bumpkins! Mr Devize, it pains me to admit it, but *I* am a bumpkin!"

He leaned across the seat and took her hand. "You are not a bumpkin. You could not have known, and—forgive me—I could not bring myself to tell you."

His warm, gentle voice and the touch of his hand comforted her more than anything he said. Although she was startled that he had dared to touch her, Viola did not withdraw her hand. The sudden urge to throw herself in his arms and cry like a baby startled her briefly, but she managed to suppress it.

"I would not have believed you anyway," she said. "I thought that *you* were the danger. Forgive me, Mr Devize. I ought to have trusted you."

"I had hoped to get you away from that place without your ever knowing the truth. I did not consider how my abrupt proposal must have seemed to you. I hope you trust me now?"

"Oh, yes," she said instantly, actually clinging to his hand.

"Completely. And I will make sure that the duke knows it was not your fault I didn't get away sooner. Indeed, I could not have gotten away to meet you last night, even if I *had* been sensible to the danger. My room was in the attic, and, after dark, Mrs Dean always locked me in."

"Thank God!"

"Yes," Viola agreed. "The lodgers made *such* noises! I'm sure they were drinking. Mr Devize, no one must ever find out that I was in a common boarding house."

The sudden change in his expression caused Viola fresh embarrassment. "It was not a boarding house at all, was it?" she groaned. "They were not lodgers. They were . . . Mr Devize, was I in a . . . a . . . ?" Her courage failed her.

"Yes," he said quietly. "I'm sorry."

She drew her hands away from him as if they had suddenly burned her. "Oh, Mr Devize, I shall die if anyone finds out!" she moaned. "I don't suppose it would do any good to bring charges against Mrs Dean?"

"It would be worse for you than for her, I'm afraid. You would have to testify."

Viola shuddered. "Could you take me back to Yorkshire now?" she asked bleakly.

He smiled. "That would not be possible, I'm afraid. Come now! You mustn't let London get the better of you. You mustn't give it the satisfaction. You must rally."

"London *has* gotten the better of me," she said bitterly. "How they must have been laughing at me the whole time. 'Look at the little Yorkshire bumpkin! Let's tell her another whopping big lie and see how stupid she is!'"

"This may surprise you, but I myself was cozened when I first came to London."

Viola stared at him in amazement. "You, Mr Devize? Oh, I don't believe you. You're just saying that to make me feel better."

"It's true," he insisted. "When the war ended, I sold out of the army. My father wanted me to become a clergymen, but I knew better. *I* decided to take my money and give it to a London stockjobber. He promised to make me a fortune overnight. I never saw him—or my money—again. I know what you're feeling right now, because I have felt it, too. But I rallied, and so will you. Look at me now," he added, grinning. "Financial advisor to the Duke of Fanshawe. Dizzying heights!"

Viola found herself smiling back at him. True or not, his confession had cheered her flagging spirits. "Is that how you became interested in stock trading, Mr Devize?" she asked.

"I suppose so. Having no money of my own, I began to invest for others in a small way. Profits were laughable, my percentage minuscule, but I soon became addicted to the excitement."

"Oh, yes," she said politely, unable to guess what he might find exciting about speculating with other people's money. He didn't even get to keep what he earned, poor man.

"Then, one day, I met the Duke of Fanshawe at the Bank of England. He was being assaulted by the Bank Nun. I rescued him, and he became a client. I soon found that I could use large sums of money—his money—to manipulate the market, rather than be swept along in its wake. I've been having great fun ever since."

"Bank Nun?" she asked, intrigued.

"London is full of odd characters, and Miss Whitehead may be one of the oddest. Her brother once worked in the Bank as a cashier, but he was hanged a few years back for forgery. Since then, she has haunted the place, importuning passersby for money."

Viola hid a smile. "Oh, Dickon wouldn't like that."

Julian frowned. "Dickon?"

"The duke," Viola explained. "Did you never hear him called that?"

"No," Julian said, a little stiffly. "You must be on terms of some intimacy with his grace."

Viola giggled. "Well, of course I am!"

"Oh, yes? I can't help but wonder, Miss Andrews . . . How can it be that the daughter of a simple country vicar is on such terms with the Duke of Fanshawe?"

"What?" Viola looked at him in confusion. Could it be possible that Mr Devize did not know she was really Lady Viola Gambol, the duke's sister?

"I realize that his grace gave your father the living at . . . at Gambolthwaite, was it? However, it seems excessive that you should address your father's patron as 'Dickon.'"

Viola hid a smile. It appeared that handsome, clever Mr Devize did indeed think she was Miss Andrews. How surprised he would be when they got to Gambol House!

"I'm not accusing you of any impropriety, Miss Andrews," Julian went on, unable to guess her thoughts. "Not at all. And, as for the duke, he has never given me any reason to think ill of him. I'm only curious. It *is* a little strange."

"I have known the duke all my life," Viola said, sticking scrupulously to the truth. "He knew my mother and father quite well. I have always regarded him as an elder brother, in fact. It seemed natural enough to call him Dickon."

"I see," said Julian thoughtfully. "Your parents are both dead, then? And I have met your lovely aunt. Have you no other family? Is there no one else who can offer you a home?"

"I have a home with the duke," she pointed out mildly.

"Besides the duke," he said impatiently. "Forget about the duke for a moment. Have you any friends or acquaintance here in London?"

"Besides the duke? And yourself?" Viola had to think. "Well, let's see . . . Parliament is in session, is it not? Of course I know all the Yorkshire M.P.s. I write them each a letter once a week when Parliament is in session. They find my advice very helpful."

"I'm sure they do, Mary," Julian said, barely concealing his amusement. "But that is not quite what I meant. I mean someone you know personally, someone respectable, someone who might be willing to, say, adopt you."

"Adopt me!" she laughed. "I'm twenty-one, Mr Devize. You will agree, that is a little old to be adopted."

His face became unreadable. "Twenty-one? Are you sure? Mrs Dean gave me to understand that you were a mere child of seventeen."

Her dark eyes twinkled. "Do I look like a child to you, Mr Devize? I am twenty-one."

"Then she lied. Shocking, isn't it?" he said dryly. "But your father *was* the Vicar of Gambolthwaite? That is not a lie?"

With a little ingenuity, Viola was able to answer truthfully. "I can assure you that Reverend Andrews was indeed the Vicar of Gambolthwaite, and a very respectable gentleman, despite his unfortunate sister."

"We're just coming up on St Paul's Cathedral now," Cork suddenly exclaimed in surprise.

Julian glanced out of the window. "Yes, we're nearly there."

Viola frowned. She knew little of London geography, but she did know that St Paul's was situated much farther to the east than the Strand. "This can not be the way to Gambol House, Mr Devize."

"We're taking the long way, Mary," Julian said. "To avoid the traffic. It's a little farther, perhaps, but it will save time in the end."

Viola could easily accept his explanation, having had some experience of London traffic already. "I was set down very near to St Paul's when I first arrived in London," she told him presently. "At the Bell Savage Inn. Do you know it?"

Julian frowned. "Busy place! I'm glad you had your maid with you, at least."

"Oh, no," said Viola. "I left my maid in Yorkshire. I found Cork at the inn."

Julian's eyes scanned the thin, young woman on the seat

across from him. Unimpressed, he said, "What do you mean, you *found* her there? Was she lost?"

Viola was certain that Mr Devize would think her a heroine when he learned she had rescued Cork from the horrible landlord of the Bell Savage Inn, but the young man saw the matter very differently. "You should have left her where you found her," he said brutally. "How do you know you can trust her? I know you meant well, Mary, but, for God's sake, how do you know this girl's not a thief, or even a murderess?" He looked very stern.

"A murderess! Cork?" Viola laughed.

"No, I'm sure you're not a murderess, Miss Cork," Julian said quickly. "The point is, Mary, you can't afford to go about taking in strays. Not in London. There are more bad people in London per square inch than anywhere else on earth. You're not in Yorkshire anymore."

"I know I'm not in Yorkshire," she said indignantly.

"You're surrounded by people who will cheat you and take advantage of you, given half a chance. My dear girl, I couldn't bear it if you were harmed."

Viola hid a smile. "Oh, but I have *you* to look after me now, Mr Devize."

"True," he said. "But I can't be everywhere at once, you know."

"I shall be very careful," Viola promised. "Indeed, I've learned my lesson. From now on, I shall trust no one but you, and suspect everyone else. I shall be on my guard at all times, and never go anywhere without a servant. Furthermore, I promise to keep my toasting fork with me at all times." To his amusement, she took a silver fork out of her reticule and showed it to him, opening the telescoping handle. "See how sharp the tines are?"

"Very handy, I'm sure," he complimented her.

Viola was pleased. "I thought so, when I was on the Night Mail. Oh, I never had to use it," she added quickly. "I simply introduced it into the conversation, and all went quiet. I'm not completely helpless, you see, Mr Devize. You needn't worry about me quite so much."

"You came to London on the Night Mail?" he said incredulously. "Poor darling! You must have been shaken to bits."

No one had ever called Lady Viola a poor darling before, but he sounded so tender and concerned, so sincere when he called her darling, that she felt uplifted rather than degraded.

"It was a little tiring," she said quickly, putting away her toasting fork. "But I managed. I must say, some of the creatures I encountered on the Night Mail were more gentleman-like than the *gentlemen* I met in Portland Place! Oh, I don't mean you, Mr Devize! I'm sorry I ever doubted you. Can you forgive me?"

"You're safe now," he said quietly. "That is all that matters."

He spoke as if it were the end. Soon they would be at Gambol House and it *would* be the end, she realized. Her rank must separate them forever. "Could we not drive around a bit more?" she asked. "I don't want to go to Gambol House just yet. I don't know what I shall say to Dickon when I see him. Was he very shocked when you told him where you found me?"

"I didn't tell him," Julian admitted. "The duke knows nothing about it whatsoever. He's not even in Town at the moment."

Viola sat up straight. If true, this was the most amazing stroke of luck. "Not in Town!"

"He *was* in London," said Julian, "briefly, but now he's gone back to Yorkshire with his future in-laws. His sister's to be married, you know."

"Nothing is settled," Viola said quickly.

"Oh? Are you acquainted with Lady Viola as well her brother?"

"Oh, yes. I've known her ladyship for years and years. She's one of those *wonderful* people that everyone loves. She's one of the few people I really admire."

Julian was surprised. "Indeed? I hear she's a bit of an oddity."

"Oddity!" Viola said angrily. "Who told you that?"

"I gleaned as much from the duke's description. She sounds like an ill-mannered brute. She throws soup at his head."

"Once," Viola protested. "Mr Devize, would you say that *I* am an ill-mannered brute?"

"I would say you are charming, Miss Andrews."

Viola felt her skin grow warm as he looked at her with appraising eyes. "So is Lady Viola charming," she said sulkily. "She's been slandered."

"She has been spoiled," Julian argued. "I imagine her as an immense lady with several chins, too fat to get up from the sofa."

Viola gasped. "I'll have you know, Mr Devize, that I wear Lady Viola's clothes without alteration! As a matter of fact, *this* is one of her dresses!"

"I daresay it looks better on you than it does on her," he said.

"Thank you, Mr Devize," she said dryly. "But, you know, you must not take seriously everything the duke says. He has a big heart, but he's not terribly clever. He needs a minder. Do you live with him at Gambol House?"

Julian loosened his cravat with a finger. "Live at Gambol House? Oh, no. I live in the City, in Lombard Street. It's a modest house, but convenient to the Exchange."

Viola looked down at the dog in her lap. "Too bad. I shall feel very lonely rattling around that great house by myself, Mr Devize," she said slowly. "Since the duke is not in London, perhaps you should stay with me . . . as my guest. I do need looking after, as you know. And you *are* responsible for me until he gets back. At least, stay and dine with me," she added persuasively as the hackney came to a sudden stop. "I hate to eat alone."

At that moment, the driver opened the hatch above their heads. "'Ere we are, guv. Number Thirty-two Lombard Street. That's half a crown you owe me."

"Lombard Street!" Viola exclaimed. "Mr Devize?"

"Not now, Mary," Julian told her harshly. "We'll discuss this when we are alone."

Startled by his sudden change in manner, Viola could only fume at his abrupt command. She decided to give him the benefit of the doubt, for the moment, and wait for his explanation, but she glowered at him as he fished in his pocket for the fare.

"I seem to be short," he muttered in dismay.

A loud click echoed in the cab.

"What was that?" Viola demanded, her nerves on edge.

"He's locked us in," Julian explained. "Look here, Mary, I hate to ask . . . but I saw you tip the porter at Portland Place. Could you lend us tuppence?"

"Certainly not," she said coldly. "You gave the man the wrong address, not I. Tell him to take us to Gambol House at once!"

"I can't do that, Mary," he said tightly.

Viola paled. "You never meant to take me to Gambol House at all, did you?"

"Quiet," Julian commanded, frowning at her. "My good fellow," he called up to the driver, who was threatening to fetch the Watch if they didn't pay the fare. "If you would just knock on the door of the house, my man will pay you."

"Drive on!" Viola said at the same time. "To Gambol House, the Strand."

"I'm not going anywhere until somebody pays me," retorted the driver.

"I am not paying you until you take me home!" declared Viola.

Julian lowered the window and shouted, "HUDSON!"

Presently a tall, thin man in a bottle green coat came out of No. 32. Moments later, the fare was paid, and the doors were unlocked. Julian jumped out. Cork, who was nearest the door, would have followed him, but Viola prevented her. "I am not getting out," she declared, even as the driver was throwing her trunk down in the street. "I don't like the look of this place," she added, bending her head to survey the long row of semidetached houses.

The driver appeared before her, blocking the view.

"Never mind what you like, madam," he said gruffly, hauling Cork out by the wrist. Viola's hatbox flew and landed on the cobbles.

"How dare you!" said Viola, clutching Bijou.

"I've another fare waiting on me," he protested angrily as Julian pushed him aside.

Viola looked at the young man mistrustfully as he held out his hand. "What are you *doing,* Mr Devize?" she asked desperately. "Why have you brought me here?"

His face was strained, but he spoke very gently. "Mary," he said. "I know how nervous you must be, but you cannot stay in the hack. You must trust me. Everything will be all right, I promise. Now give me your hand."

His plea for trust had the opposite effect. "Mr Devize, I insist that you take me to Gambol House at once! Have you gone mad? This is . . . this is abduction!" she accused.

Her lovely face and fine clothes lent credence to the assertion, Julian knew. The hackney driver was already firing up in the young lady's defense.

"'Ere now, guv! What's she on about? Abduction?"

"Nothing," Julian hastily explained. "Nothing to see here! My wife is just a tiny bit nervous, that's all. It's our wedding night, you understand."

He held out his hand to Viola. "Give me your hand, Mary," he commanded.

# Chapter Eight

Viola's mouth worked helplessly. In vain she tried to think of some innocent explanation as to why he had taken her to his home, and not the dukes's, and why he was now claiming to be her husband. There was none, of course. She had been hoodwinked *again*. She had never felt so foolish in her life.

"Madam, are you married?" cried Cork. "You never said a word!"

The hackney driver winked broadly at Julian. "Oh, so that's how it is!" he said, chuckling. "Congratulations to the pair of you. She's a fine-looking, healthy girl, if you don't mind me saying so, guv. And you'll find, you know, that two can live as cheaply as one."

"I hope you're right," Julian said uneasily.

"Mr Devize!" Viola was so angry her voice shook. "I demand to know—!"

The driver wagged his finger at her. "Now, don't be such a shrew," he admonished her. "Go easy on the man. He seems like a nice young fellow."

"He is not my husband!" said Viola.

"Not yet, missus," chuckled the driver. "You've got your work cut out for you!"

"Ugh!" said Viola.

"Come, Mary," Julian said firmly, half-climbing into the cab. "We've kept this fellow from his livelihood long enough. You must get out. Get out, or I shall drag you out!"

"I want to go to Gambol House," she shrieked as he dragged her out. As she emerged, Viola bumped her head on the door, and the bichon squirmed loose. "This is not my husband! I'm not married! Please! You must believe me!"

She screamed again as Julian put her over his shoulder and picked her up. "Put me down!" she cried, pummeling him with her fists.

"Why, if you were my wife, I'd beat you!" the driver said sternly, climbing back up to his perch. "Good luck to you, guv," he called as he drove off.

"Hudson," Julian said as calmly as he could while he continued to support Viola's not-inconsiderable weight. "Bring Mrs Devize's trunk. This is Cork, her maid, and Bijou, her dog. This," he added, swinging around so that Viola faced his manservant, "is Mrs Devize. Oh, and fetch her hatbox, please."

Viola lifted her head. Although plainly shocked, Julian's manservant was trying hard not to show it. "Very good, sir," he said. "Welcome home, madam. I hope you will be happy here."

"I am not staying here!" Viola screamed at him. "Help me!"

Julian had not anticipated that the genteel young lady would make so much noise. Quickly, he opened the door to No. 32, and started up the stairs.

"Put me down, Mr Devize," Viola commanded him.

"It's traditional for the groom to carry the bride across the threshold," Julian replied, panting from the exertion. "Hudson will think it very strange if I don't."

He set her down on the landing. Viola straightened her clothes angrily, as, in the hall below, Hudson closed the door. "I shall make you sorry you were ever born, Mr Devize!"

"A wife's prerogative, I believe," he said cheerfully.

Cork came up the narrow staircase carrying Bijou, and Julian went down to help his manservant with Viola's trunk. "He's so handsome, madam," Cork whispered. "His eyes are like sapphires, they are. Not that I've ever seen a sapphire," she added as Viola glared at her.

"You live over a shop?" Viola called down to Julian scornfully.

"Yes," he replied, heaving her trunk up the stairs by main strength. "And, now, so do you, my dearest love."

"Don't you *dare* call me that!"

Hudson joined the women on the landing while his master struggled with Viola's trunk. Taking out his handkerchief, Hudson mopped his forehead. Viola could see that Mr Devize's servant was old, past fifty, and hardly strong enough to carry a loaf of bread up the stairs, let alone her trunk.

"Hudson, will you please show Miss Cork to her room?"

said Julian as Viola's trunk landed with a thud on the landing. Viola began to sputter angrily, but Julian quieted her by holding up a finger. The gesture was so infuriating it robbed her of speech.

"Room, sir?" Hudson looked at his master with reproach. "If I had known you were getting married, Captain, I would have made arrangements, but as it is . . . I hardly think . . . !"

"I'm sorry to spring it on you like this, old man, but it was rather sudden, you see."

"It was *immensely* sudden," Viola said darkly.

"I suppose Miss Cork could take *my* room," Hudson said reluctantly.

"Just so," Julian agreed pleasantly. "Well, off you go, then. I'll look after Mrs Devize," he added, pushing Viola into a tiny, dark room off the landing. He closed the door.

Viola pulled away from him, bumping successively into a wooden desk, a wooden chair, and the corner of the brick fireplace. There was no fire. The room was chilly, and the only light came from the street lamp outside, shining through a tiny curtainless window above the desk. Viola had been in privy closets bigger than this room.

"I demand to know what you think you're doing!" she raged. "How dare you tell your man that I am your *wife?*"

"Hudson is very old-fashioned," Julian explained. "He'd be shocked if I brought home a young lady who is *not* my wife. Frankly, I didn't know what else to tell him. I can hardly tell him that I purchased you in a brothel. He'd have an apoplexy."

He moved away from the door.

"Don't you dare come near me!" she cried.

"I have to come near you," he said reasonably. "It's a very small room."

"I have a toasting fork!" she said, fumbling for her leather reticule. "I will use it!"

With shaking hands, she brought it out.

Julian tried not to laugh. "I have nothing to say to you,

madam, that your toasting fork cannot hear," he assured her, wrapping her up in his arms.

"What do you think you are doing?" she squeaked.

He didn't bother to answer. Instead, he kissed her on the mouth, leaning her so far back over the desk that she was afraid of falling. Startled, Viola grasped the desk to keep her balance, and the fork clattered to the desktop as his mouth moved freely over hers. His lips felt strange and warm as he tasted her. The sensation sent a shock of awareness through her entire body.

"Brute!" she gasped in absolute disbelief.

"I have been wanting to do that since the first moment I saw you," he murmured. "And, just so you know, it was everything I imagined it would be."

Viola caught her breath. While she was free of his hands and mouth, he still had her more or less pinned against the desk. "And I have been wanting to do *this*," she panted, leaning back to strike him across the face. "You, sir, have just made the worst mistake of your life!"

"You're right," he said, laughing. "I must try to do better."

He pulled her back into his arms and kissed her again. Viola was at a loss to explain her own acquiescence. He used only the gentlest force to pull her to him, and yet she felt quite helpless to resist. The feel of his mouth on hers again startled her, and she grasped the corners of the desk with white fingers. The strange sensation of his kiss fascinated more than it pleased, but as he continued to warm her lips, she began to like it. Dimly, she was aware that he was pushing her lips apart with his tongue. He brought his hands up to her face, skimming his fingers along her skin. Nerves jumped randomly throughout her body, and she could not bear it.

"There now," he said softly, his mouth brushing against her cheek. "Was it everything you thought it would be?"

Viola drew back from him, staring and trembling. Suddenly, she felt weak and helpless and confused; she had never felt any of those things before. It was as if she were suddenly a stranger to herself. It frightened her.

He stared back at her with his unfairly blue eyes. "Damn me," he said, his voice shaking. "I didn't think your eyes could get any bigger."

"You, sir, are not a gentleman," she complained, mortified by her own response.

"You were hysterical," he protested. "You needed a shock to return you to your senses."

"I am not hysterical," she argued. "I am justifiably perturbed."

"You do seem calmer now," he said smugly. "Were you never kissed before, Mary?"

"Certainly not!" she said, shivering.

With his finger he traced the line of her jaw. It was mortifying how, even now, she wanted to rest her cheek against his hand. She just managed to turn her face away. "Are there no red-blooded men in Yorkshire?" he chuckled.

"I don't know," she retorted. "I never had to *stab* a Yorkshireman."

"You'd never get away with it in Sussex, I can tell you that."

"Get away with what?" she asked crossly, slapping his hand away.

"Being so bloody beautiful."

Lips that no longer felt like her own parted in anticipation of a third kiss, and that strange feeling of passionate attachment, quite out of keeping with who he was and who she was, overwhelmed her senses again.

But he did not claim her lips a third time.

Instead, he picked up her toasting fork and restored it to her. "It's a very good thing you had your fork with you," he said cheekily. "Poor thing looks hungry. I'll try to find it a little bread and cheese before I leave."

"Leave!" cried Viola, forgetting everything else. "Where are you going?"

Julian calmly struck a match and lit the candle on the desk. The desk was shoved under the tiny window, leaving just room enough for a chair, a small bookshelf, and a few boxes. The desk itself was covered with ledgers and newspapers. Putting her in the chair, Julian sat on the corner of the desk.

"I won't be gone long," he assured her. "I want to talk to you before I go. I want to explain. Will you let me do that? Will you listen?"

Viola pressed her lips together, ashamed that she had sounded so forlorn at the prospect of his leaving her and determined to show him that she was made of sterner stuff.

"That," he began, "was quite a tantrum you threw out there on the street."

Viola stuck out her chin. "I'm so sorry I embarrassed you, Mr Devize! But, really, what did you expect me to do? *Let* you kidnap me?"

"I thought perhaps you might give me the benefit of the doubt," he said, shrugging. "I've earned that much, I think. You might trust me a little, after all I've done for you. You might allow me to explain before you begin hurling accusations at me."

"You should have explained quicker," she said remorselessly.

"I will explain now. I wasn't bidding on the duke's behalf."

"I beg your pardon?" said Viola.

"I only said that to be assured of a place at the auction. I was bidding for you on my own behalf, Mary. I can't take you to Gambol House, because the duke doesn't know anything about it. I brought you here because I have nowhere else to take you. I've no money for a hotel."

Viola stared at him. "I d-don't understand," she stammered. "What *do* you mean?"

"Which part don't you understand?" he asked her gently.

His gentle tone was beginning to rankle. He seemed to think she was some overwrought child that needed soothing.

"I understand that you are a liar!" she said. "Of *course* you were bidding on the duke's behalf! Where would *you* get seventeen thousand pounds, after all?"

"Guineas," he corrected her. "I . . . I borrowed the money from the duke."

"You borrowed it?" she repeated, frowning. "How? You said the duke isn't even *in* London. Perhaps you've told so many lies, *Mr Pope,* that you cannot keep them all in order!"

"I borrowed it," he repeated, "without his knowledge or consent. Very well! I stole it!" he confessed, bringing up his hands and letting them fall onto his knees. "I've stolen seventeen thousand guineas from the Duke of Fanshawe."

He laughed weakly.

Viola was still incredulous. "Impossible! How? The duke keeps his money in his bank, does he not? Do you mean to tell me you robbed *the Bank of England?* "

"I have power of attorney," he explained. "I can draw from his grace's accounts—with the understanding that I will act for *his* benefit, of course, and not my own."

"And do you often steal from the duke?" she asked politely.

"No, of course not. But what's the good of having access to an enormous fortune if one doesn't occasionally use it to rescue beautiful girls?" He smiled crookedly.

"I don't believe you," she snapped. "Why, if this were true, you could hang for it!"

"I know perfectly well I could hang!" he snapped back. "I don't need *you* to tell me that I could hang. Believe me, that little possibility has been large in my mind all day."

"But why would a sensible man like yourself risk his neck for a total stranger?"

"Obviously, I couldn't let you be sold."

"But I *have* been sold," she pointed out. "I have been sold to *you,* Mr Devize."

"You look a tiny bit hyster—perturbed. Would you like another kiss?" he offered.

Viola snapped open her toasting fork. "May I ask what you intend to do with me?" she said coldly. "Has *that* little possibility been large in your mind all day? It seems to me, I've gone from the frying pan into the fire!"

"No," he protested. "It isn't like that at all."

"Isn't it? Tell me, Mr Devize. How exactly am I better off with you than I would have been with, say, Lord Simon? It seems to me that with *him,* I would be in a much nicer room with a fire and servants and, possibly, a cup of chocolate. But that is the only difference!"

"You would be his mistress," said Julian. "*That* is the difference."

Viola jumped to her feet, bumping into his knee. "I would never consent to any such thing," she said hotly. "Such an arrangement would be disgusting to me."

"I doubt he'd think it necessary to obtain your consent," Julian answered plainly. "When a man pays for a woman, Miss Andrews, he doesn't tend to take no for an answer!"

"Indeed? Is this the voice of experience, Mr Devize?" she said, glaring at him. "What shall I call you now that you have bought me? Master?"

"Julian will suffice."

Viola held her toasting fork to his nose. "You will take me to Gambol House at once, Mr Devize. If, *as you claim,* the duke is not at home, his servants will look after me."

"Be reasonable, Mary," he told her. "They don't know you at Gambol House. They won't let you in. Your connection to the duke is slim at best. His servants won't have orders to take in strays."

"You refuse to take me to Gambol House?"

"I do."

"Then I shall go on my own."

"You will find London quite unfriendly after dark," he said, stepping in front of her.

"I will take a hackney," she said. "Be so good as to summon one for me."

"I have not the slightest wish to identify your body at the morgue," he replied. "Young women have been known to get into hackney carriages after dark, never to be seen alive again. I can offer you a bed for the night. You'll be quite safe here, you know."

"You expect me to spend the night with you?" she cried in disbelief.

"You have nowhere else to go," he pointed out. "You'll stay the night, and tomorrow we'll . . . we'll think of something."

"Such as?"

Julian shrugged. "My man already thinks we are man and wife. He would probably think it curious if you simply disappeared. We *could* be married, I suppose. Marriage, as they say, covers a multitude of sins."

"Is that a proposal?" she asked in disbelief.

"My dear Mary, what else can we do?" he said gently. "You needn't decide anything now, of course. We'll talk about it in the morning. Come, I'll show you to your room. You must be exhausted."

"You mean to compromise me," she accused him, "to force me to marry you."

"You read too many novels," he laughed. "Besides, I don't have to compromise you. You were pretty damn well compromised the moment you set foot in your aunt's house. If you're really frightened of me, take your toasting fork to bed with you," he offered, walking out of the room. After a moment, she followed him, toasting fork in hand.

The hall was empty. Quickly, she ran down the stairs and opened the door. The street was almost blanketed in fog. She could make out the moving shapes of people. She heard men's voices, laughter. If this had been York, she would not have hesitated to walk out, but this was not York. It might as well have been Calcutta.

"Well?" said Julian. He was standing at the top of the stairs.

Silently, she closed the door and walked slowly up the stairs to him.

While Julian's bedroom was larger than the closet off the landing, it was still a close, dismal chamber by Viola's standards. The bed was narrow and covered with a thin, drab quilt, the floor was bare, and the chimney smoked. Viola's bichon was curled up on a worn, upholstered armchair next to the fire. Viola collected her immediately.

"I'll leave you to it," Julian said cheerfully as Cork came from the adjourning dressing room. "Shall I bring you back something to eat?"

"Where are you going?" Viola demanded again.

"The Stock Exchange, of course," he answered. "That's where I spend most of my time."

"On your wedding night?" Cork exclaimed indignantly. Immediately, a look from her mistress sent her scuttling back into the closet.

Julian stood in the doorway. "The closing bell is at nine o'-clock," he informed Viola. "You will hear it, if you're still awake. If you need anything while I'm gone, just ask Hudson."

In disbelief, Viola followed him to the landing. Julian was still wearing his coat, but Hudson was waiting at the foot of the stairs with his master's hat. "Lock up," Julian instructed him. "I have my latchkey. If Mrs Devize doesn't need you, you may go to bed."

"On the floor in the kitchen," Hudson said expression-lessly. Having given Cork his own room, it was the only place left for him. "Very good, Captain."

Viola watched the manservant lock the door and pocket the key. "Is there anything I can get you, madam?" Hudson asked her, coming up the stairs, his old bones creaking mournfully. If he thought it strange that his master should go out on his wedding night, he gave no sign of it.

"Have you been with Mr Devize long?" she asked him.

"I have been with the captain for many years," Hudson replied. "I knew him as a boy."

"Captain? Oh, yes, of course—he was in the army," Viola murmured. "Did your captain give you orders to hold me prisoner?" she inquired.

"No, madam," Hudson replied. "Is there anything I can get you before I retire?"

"Yes—dinner. I'd like a white soup, half a roast chicken with a side of asparagus, and a meringue for my sweet. Oh, and a cup of chocolate, for afters."

Hudson frowned at her. "What do you think this is?" he demanded. "Roast chicken indeed! There's a bit of cheese, and some hardtack biscuits, if you like."

"Hardtack biscuits!" Viola said, horrified. "Oh, very well!"

Hudson muttered something under his breath.

"What was that?" Viola said sharply.

"Nothing, madam."

In the bedroom, Cork had laid out Viola's nightgown on the bed. "There's a kettle of hot water," she said, coming out of the closet. "Shall I fill the hip bath?"

"No, Cork," Viola said firmly. "You may go." Still wearing her coat and bonnet, she went over to Bijou and took the little dog onto her lap.

"Don't you want me to help you undress at least?" Cork asked, surprised.

"Certainly not!" Viola said sharply.

"There's naught to be nervous about, madam," Cork said kindly. "From what I hear, 'tis over in a flash."

With an unpleasant jolt, Viola realized her maid was talking about the consummation of her "marriage." "Perhaps even quicker than that," she said dryly.

"Aye," Cork said seriously. "The younger the fellow, the faster it goes. So I hear."

"Yes. Thank you, Cork."

Alone in the room, Viola sat down beside the fire and untied the strings of her bonnet. Outside bells were ringing, but, unlike the natives, she could not tell one set of bells from another. Suddenly, she was very tired.

Just after nine o'clock, Julian crept silently up the stairs in his stockinged feet. Cautiously, he set his shoes out in the hall. As quietly as he could, he entered the room and moved stealthily over to the bed.

"What are you doing, Mr Devize?" Viola demanded from her seat beside the fire.

Julian started at the sound of her voice. "Hello!" he said, spinning around to face her. Silently, he absorbed the fact that, other than her hat, she had not removed a stitch of her clothing. She had not even taken off her shoes. "Are you hungry? I've brought sandwiches."

Viola could not feign disinterest. "Considering I have had nothing but hardtack biscuits to eat—!" she began bitterly, breaking off abruptly as he handed her a hunk of something wrapped in brown paper. Unwrapping it, she discovered thick slices of ham and cheese surrounded by thick, crusty bread. Toasted, it would have been delectable, but she was far too hungry to bother with all that.

As she was occupying the only chair, Julian sat down on the cracked leather fender in front of the fireplace to eat his own sandwich. He took two small amber bottles from his inside coat pocket. "Ale or lemonade?" he asked her.

"What, no claret?" she grumbled, but she took the lemonade to wash down her food. Her hunger assuaged, she fed the last tidbits of her sandwich to the puppy.

"Why aren't you in bed?" he asked her as he finished his ale. "I told you, you needn't be afraid of me."

"Oh, I'm not frightened," she assured him. "It's freezing on that side of the room. Do you know there's nothing but greased paper in your window?"

"I'll speak to the landlord, if it bothers you," he said. Going over to the bed, Julian crouched down and gave it a manly shove. The bed did not budge.

"What are you doing?" she asked him scornfully.

He was shoving again, his muscles straining, his face growing red with embarrassment. "I'm going to move the bed closer to the fire so you will not be cold," he explained.

"Oh." She let him shove a bit longer, changing positions, then relented. "I think you'll find that the bed is nailed to the floor. I tried to move it while you were gone."

"Ah," he said, desisting. "You might have said so."

"You don't really live here, do you?" she said.

Julian flashed her a look of surprise. "What do you mean?"

"There's no furniture. No clothes. Apparently no food."

"You're sitting in a chair," he pointed out. "And my clothes are in the wardrobe in my dressing room, if you would care to see them."

"I have already done so. *Two* shirts and *one* waistcoat. Where are the rest of your clothes? Do you expect me to believe that you have only two shirts and one waistcoat?"

Julian laughed ruefully. "I suppose I *do* live a somewhat Spartan existence," he admitted. "Of course, I don't spend much time here."

"Clearly."

"I must be on the Exchange ten or twelve hours a day. I eat in taverns mostly. I come home at night to sleep, but that's about it." Grasping the mattress, he pulled it off the bed and flung it on the floor at her feet, startling Bijou, who yapped in alarm.

"You expect me to sleep on the floor?" Viola asked him incredulously.

"You'll be warm," he pointed out, fetching the pillow and blanket for her.

"Where are *you* going to sleep?" she asked him suspiciously.

"What are you suggesting?" Julian asked. "I shall sleep in the chair, of course."

"Mr Devize, do you actually think I'm going to let you sleep in this room with me?"

Julian frowned at her. "The servants will think it very odd if I don't," he pointed out, with forced patience. "It *is* supposed to be our wedding night, after all."

"But it's *not* our wedding night," Viola said sharply.

"Thusly, I will sleep in the chair."

Viola felt strangely annoyed with him. After a moment, she rose from the chair, carrying Bijou close to her body. He instantly took possession of the chair.

"How do I know you'll stay there?" Viola demanded.

"My dear girl," Julian said wearily. "If I intended to ravish you, I would have done so already. Besides, you have your toasting fork, haven't you?"

"Yes, I do," she told him fiercely. "It's in my pocket."

Julian put his feet up on the leather fender in front of the fire. He closed his eyes. "Good night, Miss Andrews," he said, settling in.

He looked quite content. Keeping her eyes on him, Viola sat down on the mattress and took off her shoes. The mattress was lumpy. She could not bring herself to lie down.

"I want the chair," Viola said suddenly.

Julian opened his eyes. "No, you don't. It's quite uncomfortable, I promise you."

The lady insisted, however, and soon Viola was curled up again in the chair with Bijou, while the gentleman stretched out on the mattress on the floor. "Good night, Miss Andrews," he said pleasantly, closing his eyes.

Viola twisted and turned in the chair, upsetting the puppy. Mr Devize looked quite content stretched out on the mattress, his head on the pillow, his feet sticking out from under the quilt. In fact, his lack of interest in her was downright insulting.

Perhaps he had not enjoyed kissing her. Perhaps she was not as attractive as she thought.

"This chair is uncomfortable," she announced abruptly. "I want to change places."

Julian sat up and eyed her with dislike. "I'd forgotten why I gave up on women," he muttered. "This brings it all roaring back. Are you quite sure you want the bed, sweeting?"

"Get out of my bed, if you please," she said imperiously.

Julian stood up and, with an ironic sweep of his arm, invited her to lie down while he reclaimed the chair.

Viola lay down on the mattress, punched the feather pillow into shape, and pulled the rough quilt up to her chin. She felt wide awake.

"Are we done?" he asked her curtly. "Are you satisfied with the arrangements?"

"Did you really give up on women?" she asked him.

"Yes," he answered emphatically.

"Why?"

"Because they keep me up at night," he said sternly. "Go to sleep, Mary."

"Good night, Mr Devize."

They both closed their eyes and pretended to sleep. Presently, Viola heard the chair creak as he moved about. It creaked again. Sitting up, she opened her eyes and glared at him.

"I can't get comfortable," he protested.

"It *is* a very uncomfortable chair," she agreed pleasantly.

"But *you're* comfortable, are you? That's all that really matters."

"For your information, I'm not at all comfortable," said Viola, disliking his sarcasm. "The fire is only warming one side of me. I'm quite cold on the other."

"I'm sorry to hear it," he said. "You could take turns, warming one side, then the other."

"Or . . . *you* might warm the other side of me, Mr Devize," she suggested. "It's your fault I'm cold, after all."

In a trice, he was beside her on the mattress.

"No, Mr Devize," she complained, as he grabbed one side of the quilt. "This pitiful blanket is not big enough for us both. *You* must do without."

In the next instant, he had her turned on her side, facing the fire. His body was fitted to hers. With one arm, he held her snug to him. "I think you'll find," he said in her ear, "it's quite big enough for both of us."

"So it is," she said faintly.

"Warm enough?"

"Yes, I think so," she breathed, her heart pounding.

"Good," he said roughly. "Now go to sleep, damn it."

# Chapter Nine

With a strange man at such close proximity, Viola did not expect to sleep at all, but, within moments, she was so warm and comfortable that she drifted off. Some time later, her eyes popped open. The fire was flickering low in the grate. The bichon was whimpering softly in her chair. *His hand,* she thought wildly. It was not a dream. It was really happening. He had actually slipped his hand inside her coat. Even as she lay frozen in disbelief, his hand seemed to be reconnoitering for a way inside her dress.

"Mr Devize!" she said sharply. "What—!"

Julian grunted in his sleep, pulling her even closer to him, his damp mouth nuzzling the side of her neck, sending ripples of shock through her body. At the same time, his hold on her breast became even more possessive. Needless to say, Viola was not used to such treatment. "Mr Devize!" she cried indignantly, sitting up and giving his hand back to him.

"What?" Julian sat bolt upright, his handsome face creased in four places by the pillowcase. His short hair was sticking up in spikes. His heart was pounding. In the firelight, he looked so disoriented that she almost giggled. "What's the matter? You all right?" he slurred, still half-asleep. "C'mere," he mumbled, hauling her back into his arms. "You're all right. Go to sleep."

Viola found herself lying half across his body, her breasts crushed against his chest. She pulled away, but he only wrapped his arms around her more tightly, and threw a leg over her for good measure. "Hush, you," he muttered irritably, then went back to sleep.

Almost immediately his grip on her loosened and an indignant Viola was able to extricate herself without the least difficulty. The arms that had clasped her so fiercely now dropped like rubber. Free, yet somehow bound, she propped herself up on her elbows and looked down at his sleeping face. Even without the shocking intensity of his blue eyes, it was a handsome face, boyishly softened in sleep. He looked quite innocent, in fact. Probably, he didn't even know he had been holding her breast. Her fingers longed to smooth down his badly behaved hair.

Instead, she poked him hard in the chest. "Wake up!"

He opened his eyes and frowned up at her. "What's the matter?" he mumbled drowsily.

Viola stood up and collected the bichon from the chair. "You were snoring," she lied primly, looking down at him. "And I think Bijou needs to go out."

Julian rubbed his eyes, yawning as he sat up. "What time is it?"

"It's four o'clock," said Viola. "In the morning," she added helpfully.

"How do you know?" he asked, yawning.

Viola pointed at the little clock on the mantel.

"What's that?" Julian demanded, squinting at it. He hadn't seen it before; it certainly wasn't his.

"That's my little travel clock," she explained.

He smiled faintly. "You have a travel clock?"

"Doesn't everyone?" Viola asked coolly. Her travel clock was a particularly nice travel clock set in a frame of pink diamonds. She was not so insulated that she believed that everyone had such a nice travel clock, but surely every lady who traveled needed a travel clock! Men, of course, had their pocket watches, so they did not count. "All ladies, I mean," she clarified.

Julian stumbled to the chair and sat down to put on his shoes. Pulling on his coat, he stood to take the puppy from her. "Good God," he said softly, looking at Viola as if seeing her for the first time. "Is that really you, then?"

"I beg your pardon?" she said crossly.

He smiled at her. "You're really that beautiful, is that it? It's not a trick?"

"Trick!"

"Your skin, your lips . . . That's not paint?"

Viola glared at him. "Paint!"

"And your hair," he went on pleasantly. "Your raven tresses, I should say. It just sort of curls like that, all on its own, does it? Without any curl papers?"

Viola was absolutely not charmed by this string of compliments. "I have a glass eye, and a wooden leg, if that helps," she said sullenly, dumping the dog into his arms. "Take Bijou out, and make sure she does her business. And *don't* let her get hit by a cart."

Viola heard his key turn in the lock. Fifteen minutes passed before he returned. A blast of cold air entered the room with him. Bijou was trembling. "Did she do her business?" Viola demanded.

"Of course," he said, setting Bijou down on the floor.

Instantly, the little dog eliminated on the floor. "Perhaps not," Julian said solemnly.

"She doesn't like the cold," said Viola.

"I'll clean it up." Julian went for the closet as Viola picked up the dog and returned her to the chair. "Unless you're absolutely certainly she's done her business outside, don't put her on the floor," Viola instructed. "She's too small to hop down from the chair, and she won't go where she sleeps."

"That's good to know," said Julian, finishing the cleanup. He glanced at Viola's travel clock. "Fancy a cup of coffee?" he yawned.

"It's four in the morning," she protested. "Aren't you coming back to bed?"

He shook his head. "I'm wide awake now," he said ruefully. "Must have been the bracing air! I think I'll try to do a little work. I'll just be in the next room, if you need anything. I won't disturb you."

And to her astonishment, he left her. Again, Viola felt insulted, almost cheated.

Angrily, she punched her pillow and lay down.

For his part, Julian found it difficult to concentrate on Lady Viola's marriage settlement in the next room. Having to hide a fortune for a spoiled aristocratic lady while eaten up with worry for his own future put him in a thoroughly bad humor. Adding to his worries was a painful erection that he had no hope of satisfying without Mary's help, help she did not seem at all inclined to give him. Not even walking that bloody dog up and down the cold, dark street for twenty minutes had cooled his ardor.

Angrily, he opened Lady Viola's portfolio.


Much later in the morning, Hudson made the mistress's tea and toast personally, plunking it all down on a tray for Cork to carry upstairs. The kitchen was now his de facto bedroom, and he would sooner have taken to dancing the hornpipe in church than allow a lady's maid access to his bedroom. "About time she woke up," he said irritably.

"You let her alone," Cork said angrily. "A lady's allowed to sleep late after her wedding night. She'll be all done in, I shouldn't wonder." Taking the tray, she swept off.

Viola had bathed and changed her clothes in Julian's dressing room.

"Is that my breakfast?" she asked, returning to the bedroom. "Put it on the fender—there doesn't appear to be anything like a table. Where's the bacon?" she asked, puzzled, as she surveyed the tray. "The eggs? The marmalade?"

Having relieved herself of the tray, Cork picked up the dog. "I think that's all there is, madam," she said. "I think Mr Devize is poor."

Rather grimly, Viola poured thin brown tea from the brown teapot into a chipped enamel cup. "Where is he?"

"Captain Devize? Oh, he's gone to 'Change, madam."

"Change?" Viola said crossly. "Change what?"

"The Stock Exchange, madam."

"I see," said Viola, glancing up at her little pink clock. It was half past ten. She was amazed that she had slept so long; she was used to rising with the dawn in Yorkshire.

"Shall I unpack your trunk now, madam?" Cork asked eagerly.

"No," said Viola, going to the bedroom door. Opening it, she listened intently. "Where is that manservant of his, do you know?" she asked, hearing nothing.

"In the kitchen, I think. He doesn't like you very much, madam."

"How tragic," said Viola, stealing out into the hall. Quick as a cat, she ran lightly down the steps and tried the front door. It was locked. Viola looked around impatiently. There must be a spare key somewhere. If she could find it, and hail a hackney carriage, she could be breakfasting at Gambol House within the hour; she was not at all afraid of London by day.


Summoned up from the kitchen by the bell, Hudson stood in the doorway of the tiny study, his long face a mask of disapproval. Why, the impertinent female had quite torn apart his master's study! Books, ledgers, and newspapers had been tossed about with reckless abandon. Hudson felt a burst of anger toward his master.

*It serves him right,* he thought, *for marrying so far beneath him!* Why, there had been no engagement at all. Not even a notice in the *Post.* It was all highly irregular. Hudson hated all irregularity, but he particularly despised irregular females.

"You rang, madam?" he coldly intoned.

In her search for a key to the front door, Viola had discovered a desk drawer that she could not open. At present, she was more interested in the contents of this drawer than in her freedom. "Why is this drawer locked?" she demanded angrily. "Where is the key?"

"There is no key, madam."

"I see." Viola found a letter opener in another drawer. Ignoring his protests, she plunged the thin blade of the letter opener into the lock and twisted it viciously. Hudson could only watch, trembling with impotent rage.

"Captain Devize will not be pleased, madam!"

"Give me the key!" said Viola, struggling with the lock.

Hudson's temper gave way. "If the captain had wanted you to have the key to that drawer, he would have given it to you himself!" he said indignantly.

Viola only redoubled her efforts to force the lock, and succeeded at last in breaking off the tip of the letter opener.

"Now you've done it!" said Hudson.

"No," said Viola, tossing aside the broken letter opener. "But I shall." Pulling herself up, she slowly removed her toasting fork from her pocket. It looked quite insignificant until she extended the handle. Hudson's eyes widened. "This," Viola said proudly, "is Sheffield steel."

Eschewing the lock, she inserted the tines between the drawer and the frame of the desk. The front of the drawer broke in two with a violent crack, sending a stack of papers on the desk flying. Unperturbed, Viola reached inside the drawer. They both heard a metallic snap, and then Viola felt a sharp pain in her fingers as a mousetrap clamped down on her hand.

"Is anything the matter, madam?" Hudson asked sweetly.

"No," Viola choked, her eyes smarting with tears as she pried her hand free of the trap. She pulled her hand out of the drawer and inspected her fingers. "I'm perfectly all right. Thank you for your . . . concern."

They both heard Julian opening the front door at the same time. Hudson hurried downstairs to take his master's hat. Viola froze, surrounded by the wreckage of the room. She felt oddly guilty, almost as if she had done something wrong. She looked around furtively, as if to hide, but there was nowhere.

"What's the matter, Hudson?" she heard Mr Devize say quite cheerfully.

Hudson could scarcely contain his glee. "Good morning, Captain. Mrs Devize seems to be having some difficulty with a drawer."

Julian went up the stairs, frowning. "Why didn't you help her?" he demanded.

Hudson blinked at him. "It was your desk drawer, Captain," he explained. "She broke it! I–I tried to stop her, but what could I do?"

Viola stood up defiantly, braced for an unpleasant scene.

"Hullo," said Julian, entering the room. He was carrying a parcel wrapped in brown paper. He placed it on the desk. Most of his papers were on the floor, but if he was annoyed, he gave no sign. "I see you've cleared a space for our luncheon," he noted wryly. "Good. Ham or tongue?"

Viola stared at him. "I beg your pardon?"

"The sandwiches," he explained, drawing a chair up to the desk and seating himself. "I've got ham and I've got tongue. What is your preference?" Opening his coat, he pulled out two amber bottles. "Lemonade for you, and ale for me. Ham or tongue?" he repeated, unwrapping the sandwiches.

Viola's stomach lurched. She was quite hungry, she realized. Seizing the nearest sandwich, she tore into it ravenously, hardly tasting it.

"Good lord," Julian said mildly. "Didn't Hudson give you breakfast?"

Viola finished chewing and swallowed. "Toast!"

"He's not much of a cook, I'm afraid. You're dressed to go out," he noted.

Viola was wearing her white leather coat over a deceptively simple gown of lemon-yellow muslin. She had changed the black lamb cuffs and collar for ermine. At her neck was clasped a string of pearls. "Yes, I was going out. Am I a prisoner?" she asked defiantly.

"Not at all. Where did you want to go?"

"Well, I was hungry," she said. "Then I thought I'd see the sights."

"The sights. Yes, of course." He looked amused. "I have some free time this afternoon, as it happens. I could show you the sights. What would you like to see first?"

Viola had just discovered that she had chosen the tongue sandwich. She looked longingly at his ham sandwich. "I don't know," she said irritably. "The Tower, or something. Westminster Abbey."

He chuckled. "All in one day? They're on completely opposite sides of Town."

"I was going to buy a guidebook."

"No need. You have me."

Viola pushed her sandwich away.

"Were you looking for something?" he asked, looking

about the room she had torn apart. "Or just having another tantrum?"

"The key."

An amused smile curved his mouth as he surveyed the broken drawer. "You obviously didn't need a key," he observed.

"Why do you keep that drawer locked anyway?" she demanded. "There was nothing in it but an old mousetrap."

"A mousetrap? Really? I never use that drawer because it sticks."

Viola felt like an idiot. Her fingers throbbed from the mousetrap. "What are you doing here anyway?" she asked him rudely. "You said you only came home to sleep."

"I left something here," he said. "Besides you, I mean. A ledger I needed. I don't suppose you saw anything like that while you were . . . ahem . . . tidying up?"

"What sort of ledger?" she wanted to know.

"Actually, it's Lady Viola's portfolio. I'm working on a little project for her ladyship."

"Are you indeed?" she said suspiciously. "What sort of project?"

"The lady is soon to be married, as you know. I'm hiding her money so that her future husband can't get his hands on it. The more I hide, the less Lord Bamph can claim in the marriage settlement." He smiled at her. "You want the ham, don't you?" he asked gently, pushing his sandwich toward her.

"Thank you," Viola said gratefully. "I was so hungry I forgot I don't like tongue."

Julian uncorked her lemonade for her. "I'll try to remember that. No tongue."

"Do you not think it's wrong for a wife to hide her money from her husband?" she asked him presently. "You would not want *your* wife to keep secrets from you, I am sure."

Julian shrugged. "If Lord Bamph gains control of all Lady Viola's money, it's a safe bet I won't be kept on as her ladyship's broker. His lordship and I not the best of friends, you see."

Viola's eyes flickered. "You are acquainted with Lord Bamph?"

"I've met him. Lucky me."

Viola smiled to herself. "Didn't you like him?"

"Well, let's see," said Julian between bites of his sandwich. "The man's an idiot, a snob, a coxcomb, and an ass of epic proportion. I tried to like him. I just couldn't. Lady Viola is to be pitied, I think."

"Perhaps she will take a lover when she marries," Viola said lightly. "It's often the case, is it not, in these Society marriages? Theirs is not a love match, after all. One cannot expect the lady to be faithful under such trying circumstances."

"I see," he said, his eyes darkening. "You approve of adultery, do you?"

"N-no, of course not," Viola stammered. "But where the gentleman and the lady have not been given a choice in the matter . . ." She faltered beneath his brooding gaze. "Surely they should be given *some* latitude. One must have love, after all."

"I'm sorry I can't join you in your enthusiasm for adultery! Frankly, I'm shocked that a clergyman's daughter should take such a lenient view of the matter. Shocked and grieved."

"But Lady Viola's position is unique," Viola protested. "She won't get her money if she doesn't marry Lord Bamph. Do you expect her to choose a life of poverty?"

Julian chuckled drily. "Her fortune! It would simply revert to the estate; and, since her brother's one of the richest men in Britain—thanks in great part to me—I seriously doubt she would suffer anything like poverty. The duke dotes on her, from what I can tell. He'll give her anything she wants."

Viola frowned; this aspect of the matter had not occurred to her. "But it was her father's wish that she marry Lord Bamph," she argued. "Is she not bound by a father's promise? You would not disobey your own father, I am persuaded."

"I'm no example of a dutiful son," he replied. "I joined the army against my father's wishes, and I have yet to beg his pardon."

"Did your father's wishes mean so little to you?" she asked.

"There was a war on, Mary," Julian explained. "I'm a younger son. I had to go. Family honor was at stake. My father allowed his affection for me to interfere with his judgment. It was unthinkable that Lord Devize's son should cling to safety while the rest of Sussex sent their sons off to war. My father would not listen to reason, so I had no choice but to disobey him."

"He must be very proud of you," said Viola.

Julian laughed shortly. "Not at all, I assure you. Shall we talk about something else?" he went on quickly. "Something more pleasant? I've half taken a house for us in Gracechurch Street. If you like it, I'll close on it directly."

"What?" she said, astonished.

"Well, I can't keep my wife in rooms over a pawnbroker's."

"But I'm not your wife," she pointed out.

"You will be," he said confidently. "There really is nothing else to be done. You can't go on living with me, unless we marry—I'm not that sort of man. And, if you don't live with me, what will become of you? Where will you go? What have you decided to do instead of marry me and bear my children?"

Viola's cheeks were burning. "Children! Are you mad?"

"It has been known to happen following marriage."

"Madness?"

"Children."

"You *are* mad. I've no intention of marrying a madman."

"What will you do otherwise? You could be a governess, I daresay," he went on before she could answer. "My sister has a numerous family, as it happens. She always seems to be looking for a new governess. You play and sing, of course?"

Viola stared at him, rigid with indignation. "Are you suggesting that I *work?*"

Julian burst out laughing. "It's just as I feared. You're fit only to be married. And, since we've already spent one glorious night together, you're fit only to marry me."

"It was hardly glorious!" she protested.

"It was for me," he quietly insisted, and even though she did not take him seriously, a tingle went down her spine.

"You snore," she lied.

"You smell nice," he retorted.

Neither of them heard Hudson open the door, and he was obliged to clear his throat.

"I'm sorry to interrupt, Captain. Mr Parsley is here to see you. He says the matter is quite urgent."

"I'll say it's bloody urgent!"

The booming, angry voice was accompanied by the violent pounding of feet on the stairs, but, to Viola's relief, the man who pushed his way into the room was plump and harmless-looking. "Dev!" he bawled, catching sight of his quarry. "Dev, you lying, thieving bastard! I ought to cut your throat, same as you've cut mine!"

"Is anything wrong, Tom?" Julian asked politely.

"Wrong! How can you sit there chewing, you bastard, when you know damn well that you've ruined me!" Here the caller lapsed into a string of gutter talk that brought Viola into the fray.

"I beg your pardon!" she said coldly.

The Cit could only stare at her with his mouth open. Belatedly, he snatched his hat from his head. He was bald in the middle, but well-endowed with thick brown hair over both ears.

"What my wife means," said Julian calmly, "is that you should beg her pardon for your unseemly language. If you don't, Tom, I'll kick you down the stairs."

Mr Parsley's mouth worked helplessly to form words. "Beg pardon, ma'am!" he finally exclaimed in a high-pitched voice. "I didn't see you there! I didn't even know Dev had a wife!"

"It was immensely sudden," Viola explained graciously.

"You seemed to be upset about something when you came in," she prompted him. "Perhaps you should tell us about it, now that you've calmed down."

Mr Parsley glanced at Julian. "It's business, Mrs Devize. I think it would be best if I talk to your husband alone."

"You come into my home," Julian said idly. "You browbeat my servant. You swear at my adored one, and now you expect me to send her from the room so that you can go on swearing? Think again, Parsley."

"I would very much like to hear what you have to say, Mr Parsley," Viola chimed in.

"Well, missus," said Parsley, gripping the brim of his hat. "I don't want to shock your delicate female sensibilities, but your husband is a lying scoundrel!"

"Please, go on," Viola invited him politely.

"What the devil do you mean by selling off all your shares in Australian wool?" Mr Parsley demanded, turning to Julian. "You told me I'd triple my investment! You said I couldn't fail with Australian wool! You said it would go up."

"It *is* going up," said Julian. "I was loath to sell at two and six, but I needed the money."

"But it's *not* going up," Parsley protested angrily. "Since you sold off, it's gone down, and nothing but! Everyone thinks you know something they don't. I'm ruined! What am I going to tell my wife? How am I going to feed my children?"

Julian did not seem overly concerned. "I'm sorry, Tom, but I needed the money. I have a wife now. I daresay you've noticed that Mrs Devize is a gentlewoman? I can't keep a gentlewoman in rooms over a shop in Lombard Street."

"No, of course not," Mr Parsley agreed. "But, dash it all, you *swore* to me it would go up! It's the only reason I bought in. Australian wool, indeed!"

"It *will* go up," Julian assured him. "You've just got to hang on. Be patient."

"That's it?" Viola said. "You ruin this poor man, condemn his entire family to penury, and all you can say is 'Hang on'?"

Julian looked at her in surprise. "You seem to have acquired a champion, Tom," he observed. "What do you propose I do, Mrs Devize?"

"You must think of something," she replied airily. "There must be some way to undo all the damage you've caused."

"Possibly."

"There, Mr Parsley," said Viola. "You see, my husband is not a complete scoundrel, after all. He got you into this trouble, and he will get you out of it."

Julian's eyes gleamed with amusement. "My dear wife, if I help Mr Parsley, it will mean that you and I won't be able to afford the house in Gracechurch Street."

"I could never be comfortable in Gracechurch Street knowing that you ruined Mr Parsley to get me there," Viola declared. She looked around the small, dark room thoughtfully. "I could make this place nice for you."

"I'm sure you could," Julian agreed. "But we'd have to tighten our belts and pinch our pennies, I'm afraid. Do you think you can manage with a budget of, say, twenty pounds?"

"I don't see why not," she answered with a shrug.

Julian crumpled the brown paper in which the sandwiches had been wrapped and tossed it into the fire. "In that case, I'd better get down to 'Change and sort out this mess."

Viola jumped up. "I'm going with you! What do ladies wear on the Exchange?"

Julian chuckled. "There are no ladies on the Exchange."

Viola was disappointed. "How long will you be gone?" she demanded.

"I'm afraid I shall be there until the closing bell again," he said apologetically. "You'll have to have your tea without me."

"Nine o'clock!" Viola objected. "So late!"

Sensing a marital dispute, Mr Parsley discreetly withdrew.

"The time goes by quickly enough," Julian said cheerfully. "I like keeping busy."

"I was thinking of myself, Mr Devize," she informed him coldly.

"Of course you were," said Julian.

Viola bristled. "Meaning that I am selfish, I suppose!"

"I didn't say that. It's perfectly natural that you should think of yourself."

"Nine hours is a very long time. What am I supposed to do for nine hours?"

"Housekeeping," he suggested. "A little cleaning, a little cooking. You could iron my spare shirts, all two of them."

"Cleaning! Cooking! Ironing! Who do you think you're talking to? Your man?"

"You *did* say you would make the place nice for me," he reminded her. "And you did make a mess breaking into my desk." Taking out his purse, he gave her a coin. "Here's a shilling. I'm not at all particular. I'll eat anything. A bit of boiled mutton will do me. Take Cork with you when you go to the market," he advised her. "You'll be safe enough. Just be home before dark," he added ominously.

"Mr Parsley seems to be growing impatient, Captain," said Hudson from the doorway.

"Hang Parsley," Julian muttered. "Can't a man kiss his wife good-bye in peace?"

Viola gasped in surprise as he caught her in his arms, lifting her inches off the floor.

"Good-bye, Wife," he said, kissing her chastely on the mouth. "If you need anything, my love, just ask Hudson. He'll be more than happy to help you." Setting Viola down, he moved to the door.

Viola went out to the landing to watch him join Mr Parsley on the street outside. Hudson quietly closed the door. "I'd like to go out, Hudson," Viola called down to him in her haughtiest voice. "Would you be good enough to summon me a hackney carriage?"

Hudson smiled coldly. "Of course, madam."

Viola blinked in surprise. "You mean you'll do it?"

"Nothing," he said, "dear madam, could please me more."

# Chapter Ten

The first footman at Gambol House had nothing but contempt for hackney carriages and the people who rode in them. "Bloody tourists," he muttered grumpily as he shoved his stockinged feet into his high-heeled shoes. "Always after a free peek at our treasures."

Waving his arms to the driver of the hack, he trotted briskly down the steps. "Drive on!" he bellowed. "The family are all away, and the house ain't open to the public!"

Viola let down the window and called out to him, "Jem! Jem, is that you?"

Jem gawped at her. "My lady!" he cried in astonishment. "Run and tell Mr Lover that her ladyship has come to London," he growled over his shoulder to the second footman before sprinting down the steps to hold the carriage door and let down the steps.

Viola emerged from the hack carrying a fluffy little white puppy. Jem knew all the ducal dogs, but he didn't recognize this one. "That's a new one, ain't it?" he said brightly.

"This is Bijou," said Viola, handing the dog to him. "She needs a bath and a trim. And this is my new maid, Cork," she added as her maid in training alighted from the vehicle.

Cork's eyes were big and round as she stared up at the facade of Gambol House. The duke's London residence was bigger than Mansion House, where the Mayor of London lived, and grander than St Paul's Cathedral. The thought of going inside turned her knees to water.

"Jem is our footman, a lower servant," Viola explained to Cork. "As my maid, you are an upper servant. You needn't talk to him at all, if you don't wish to. He's a very bad, cheeky fellow, but the men in his family have worked for us for so many generations, I'm afraid we're stuck with him. Is my brother at home?" she asked Jem as she started up the steps.

Jem trotted after her. "His grace left for Yorkshire last week. I daresay, milord duke is back at Fanshawe by now and wondering where the devil his sister's got to!" he added, laughing.

Viola came to a stop. "My brother left last week? Jem, are you sure?"

"Yes, milady."

"Why did *you* not go to Yorkshire with him?" she asked Jem.

"It was my brother's turn," Jem explained. "Whenever the duke comes to London, we trade off. That's the only fair way to go about it. Besides, I can't abide them snooty Bamphs."

"I didn't know you had a brother," said Viola, starting up the stairs again.

"No reason you should, milady," he replied cheerfully. "We're twins, and we're both called Jem. Easier that way."

The front door opened, claiming Viola's attention, and a tall, austere man, the picture of dignity, came out. "Welcome to Gambol House, my lady. I am Lover, the butler here."

Lover tried to hide it, but the unexpected arrival of the duke's sister had sent him almost into a panic. "Good afternoon, Lover," said Viola. "I must apologize for not giving you proper notice of my intention to visit London. Indeed, it was very thoughtless of me."

"My lady, this is your home," Lover said fervently as he ushered her into the immense entrance hall. "We are all at your ladyship's disposal. Would you care for some refreshment?"

Viola's stomach fairly snarled. "Actually, I'm famished," she confessed. "I've had nothing but a bit of sandwich all day. I'd love a proper luncheon, if you can manage it."

"Of course." Lover watched her ladyship nervously as her beautiful dark eyes scanned the room. "I trust everything is to your satisfaction, my lady?"

"Oh, yes," Viola replied, her attention coming to rest on a life-sized portrait of a dark-haired lady wearing a white dress and a black velvet picture hat. Apart from her clothes, which were in the style of perhaps twenty years before, the lady looked quite a bit like Viola herself. "I don't recall posing for that," she said, puzzled.

"That is a portrait of the late duchess, my lady," Lover told her awkwardly. He didn't want Lady Viola to think he was correcting her.

"Oh! I thought my father had destroyed all pictures of my mother," Viola said, devouring the portrait with her eyes. "Beastly jealous old fool that he was."

"I managed to save that one, my lady," Lover answered, winning a smile from her. "It has graced the entrance hall since your father's death. I would have known you anywhere."

Viola frowned suddenly. "I daresay Mr Devize has seen that portrait many times!" she exclaimed, her temper flaring. "He must have recognized me instantly!"

"Mr Devize?" Lover repeated with some puzzlement. "Is your ladyship referring to the young stockjobber employed by his grace? To my certain knowledge, that young man has never set foot inside this house. The duke often invites him, of course, but he always declines. He seems to be a young man who knows his place, unlike so many these days."

Viola was appeased. "It is very important to know one's place," she agreed.

Cork, in the meantime, had drawn Lover's attention. She was dressed well enough to be an acquaintance of Lady Viola's, but she was obviously dazzled almost to the point of terror by the opulence of her surroundings. With her head as far back on her neck as it would go, she was revolving in a circle as she gazed up at the painted ceiling of the dome, half-blinded by the glittering crystal drops of the chandelier that hung from the center. Lover was far too polite to inquire as to the young person's identity, and it was left to Viola to explain.

"This is my maid, Cork. I would like to keep her in an adjoining room, if such an arrangement can be made. A room adjoining mine, I mean."

"Of course, my lady," Lover assured her, leading her up the grand staircase. "Your late mother's room has been kept exactly as she left it. Her grace's maid always slept in the dressing room, which adjoins her grace's bedchamber."

Viola's eyes sparkled. "My mother's room? Take me to it!"

The duchess's apartment consisted of several well-appointed rooms, but the jewel in the crown was certainly the blue and gold bedchamber. The walls were paneled in pale gold brocade, and the bed was hung with curtains of pale blue velvet. A vast Aubusson carpet of cream, gold, and blue covered most of the floor. The furnishings were in the rococo style, which would have been old-fashioned even in Viola's mother's day, but were quite in keeping with the style of the house. The wainscoting was painted cream. A delicate bowfront desk had been placed before a wall of French windows overlooking the Thames. In another part of the room, on a round work table, were leather-bound copies of *La Belle Assemblee* and *Le Journal des Dames*. Going over to her mother's desk, Viola discovered fresh ink in the standish.

Cork stood just within the door, not daring to touch anything, hardly daring to look around, terrified that her feet would leave a mark on the beautiful rug. Rather unwisely, Viola flung open the French doors to the terrace. Immediately, she recoiled. "What is that smell?" she asked, tears pricking her eyes.

Lover rushed forth to make sure the doors were securely closed. "I'm so sorry, my lady. I should have warned your ladyship. It's the river, I'm afraid. The Thames is having a particularly trying week. It seems to be getting worse every year."

Viola pressed her scented handkerchief to her nose. "Can't you clean it?" she pleaded.

"I'm afraid not, my lady." After closing the window, Lover burnt a pastille. Soon the agreeable scent of roses filled the air.

"Thank you, Lover," said Viola as the smell of the river dissipated. "It really is a lovely room, and you've kept it beautifully. It really feels like Mama has just stepped out for a moment." She sat down at her mother's desk and began to write, talking at the same time. "I need to see the Governor of the Bank of England as soon as possible. I want you to send Jem for him with the carriage. I am writing a note for Mr Harman just now," she added, scratching away on the page. "I hope it won't take Jem away from his other duties?"

In the duke's absence, Jem's duties consisted mainly of lounging on the front steps when he wasn't eating his head off in the kitchen. "No, indeed, my lady," Lover assured her. "We are all at your ladyship's disposal."

Viola finished her note and gave it to him. "That will be all for now, Lover."

"Very good, my lady." Withdrawing, he closed the double doors firmly.

Viola turned to Cork. "Don't look so frightened, my dear," she said. "I won't eat you."

Cork giggled nervously. "No, madam."

"Let us see what Mama has in her closet," Viola suggested, jumping up from the desk.

The duchess's dressing room featured a huge garden tub of rose-colored marble and two enormous closets stuffed with clothes. Viola could not resist indulging in a hot, scented bath. While she bathed, Cork brought out a number of dresses for her mistress to look at. The fashions of a quarter of a century ago were new and interesting to Viola. After some consideration, she chose a tailored gown of Nile green silk. The gown fitted her beautifully, the waist being cut just above the natural waist, rather than under the breasts, as current fashions dictated. The bodice was lightly boned, leaving nothing to chance. Viola recognized at once that the nipped-in waist suited her full figure better than the flowing gowns that left her curves unsupported. She vowed never to wear a short-waisted gown again.

After dressing, there was just enough time to show Cork how to do a creditable chignon, and then it was time for luncheon. An elegant meal, quite without sandwiches, was served to Lady Viola in a charming Oriental-style parlor guarded by four enormous Foo dogs of celadon green porcelain. The walls of the chamber were paneled in turquoise silk embroidered with scarlet orchids, and the doorways were trimmed in lacquered bamboo. The octagonal table was of black lacquer painted with gold chrysanthemums. For Gambol House, it was a small room. Bijou, fluffed and perfumed, joined her mistress at the table. Lover waited on Viola personally, and seemed gratified by her ladyship's appetite.

After lunching, Viola passed the time writing letters at the big mahogany desk in the duke's study. She wrote first to her brother to explain her sudden decision to go to London, and to consign Miss Andrews to his care forever, if need be. Under no circumstances was that young lady ever to be sent to her aunt, Mrs Dean. Viola could not underscore that point enough, and, in fact, tore the page as she repeatedly drew thick black lines under the words. On the subject of the Bamphs, she conveyed nothing. In her view, there was nothing to convey. She advised her brother that she meant to stay in London for quite some time and included a separate page of detailed instructions for her maid Dobbins.

Having sent this letter off to Yorkshire by special messenger, she then began penning the usual long letters of encouragement and instruction to her Parliamentarians. This task kept her peacefully occupied until Lover came in to announce that Mr Harman, the Governor of the Bank of England, had arrived.

Mr Harman was a stout man with a sensitive face and unappealing side whiskers. Like all City men, he was pale as library paste. He wore the Cit's uniform of black coat, white stock, and black trousers. Viola received him impassively in her brother's study. At her request, Lover remained in the room. "You seem nervous, Mr Harman," she observed, setting down her pen.

In fact, Mr Harman was trembling. There were two perfectly comfortable oxblood leather chairs opposite the desk, but, as the lady had not asked him to be seated, he was obliged to remain standing. His discomfiture became more and more apparent as Viola waited expectantly.

"My lady," he finally burst out. "I can explain everything!"

Viola leaned back comfortably in her chair. "What an extraordinary claim," she said dryly. "I'm not sure I believe you can explain *everything*, Mr Harman, but I'm happy to see you try. Go on, then. Explain away."

"He made me do it!" Mr Harman exclaimed, clutching his hat to his breast.

"Who made you do it?" she asked pleasantly.

"That scoundrel Devize! I was most unwilling, my lady, but he made me issue a blank cheque on your brother's account. It's completely against policy, of course, to issue a blank cheque, but, I swear to you, my lady, the blackguard gave me no choice."

"Has the cheque been cashed?" Viola inquired.

Mr Harman looked gray. "Yes, my lady. The . . . er . . . party . . . was in the bank first thing this morning. I cashed it myself, though my heart was very troubled. Very troubled, indeed!"

"Surely there was enough in the account to cover the cheque," said Viola.

"Yes, my lady," he assured her. "But it was a very large payout."

"Of course it was. You say Mr Devize forced you to issue the blank cheque? How?"

"With threats, my lady. With threats and intimidations! I was terrified."

Viola was astonished. "He threatened you? With violence?"

"Oh, no, my lady. He's too clever and insidious for that! He threatened to close all the duke's accounts. If he were to do so, the Bank of England would be besieged by masses of people all wanting to close their accounts at once. Panic would set in. We should be obliged to close our doors to the public. It would take years, decades, to restore the public confidence."

"Do sit down, Mr Harman," she said impatiently. "You're giving me a pain in the neck. Could he break the Bank of England as he did Child's Bank? Is that what you're telling me?"

Mr Harman sank gratefully into a chair. "I'm afraid he *could* do it, my lady. What's more, when I looked into those cold, inhuman blue eyes of his, I knew he *would* do it. The man is a cold-hearted snake! I'm a patriot, my lady. I couldn't let him bring the Bank of England to its knees." He put his valise on his knee and opened it. "I have brought your ladyship his file, so that you can see for yourself what a dangerous man he is."

Viola's eyebrows rose. "You have a file on him?"

"Yes, my lady," he replied, handing Viola the bundle tied up with string. "Ever since he broke Child's Bank, the government has been forced to take an extraordinary interest in that young man's activities."

Viola accepted the file curiously. "I thought these little banks collapsed all the time."

"Child's Bank is not a small bank," he informed her.

"Some very important people lost a great deal of money. It was a terrible scandal. Parliament was obliged to intervene. There is even some fear that Mr Devize may be working for a foreign government."

Viola scoffed.

"Why, just this morning, he created a crash on the Stock Exchange when he sold off all his shares in Australian wool," Mr Harman told her. "Fortunately, the Bank of England keeps a richly varied portfolio, but, I understand, some people have been ruined."

"In life there must be winners and losers, Mr Harman. What cause have you to accuse Mr Devize of working for a foreign government?"

"It is most alarming, my lady," said Mr Harman. "But he seems to have a terrible weakness for foreign women!" Encouraged by the lady's sudden frown, he went on eagerly. "Three that we know of. He kept a Spanish lady during the war, but he was obliged to pass her on to his colonel, owing to the financial strain."

"What do you mean *pass her on?*" Viola demanded, revolted by such an idea.

"He was then only a lieutenant," Mr Harman explained. "He could not afford to keep her, so he gave her to his colonel. That's the sort of man he is, you see. Shortly thereafter, he was elevated to the rank of captain."

"Are you implying that Mr—that Captain Devize *traded* this lady for a promotion?"

"That I cannot say," Mr Harman said discreetly.

"You said there were three," Viola prompted him.

"Yes, my lady. After the war, Mr Devize became enamored of a Miss Schwartz, the daughter of a Prussian emigre, a watchmaker. He courted her for some time, but, in the end, she married her father's apprentice. They have since returned to their native land."

"Then she is firmly in his past," Viola murmured. "And the third lady?"

"*She* is not in his past," Mr Harman said gleefully. "We have not yet established her identity, but she's obviously foreign. Mr Devize purchased her from a house of disrepute. In fact, my lady, the money he stole from your brother went to the mistress of this house."

"Mrs Dean," Viola exclaimed.

Mr Harman blinked, startled. "Your ladyship knows of her?"

"I know a great deal, Mr Harman. What makes you think the lady is foreign?"

"She made a very noisy scene on the street last night," replied Mr Harman. "Mr Devize must be besotted with her. Otherwise, he would not risk so much in stealing from the duke. You see the danger, of course?"

"Danger?"

"In the throes of lust, there is no telling what he will do to please his bit of stuff. If she is merely a strumpet, we need not worry, perhaps. But if she is a foreign agent . . . He might be persuaded to betray his country. If you love England, my lady, you will persuade your brother to bring charges against this thief."

"You would see him hanged? As you hanged that clerk, Mr . . . Whitehead, was it?"

Mr Harman looked uncomfortable. "Mr Devize's crime is the same as Mr Whitehead's, if on a grander scale. Why should he not meet the same fate? My lady, a strike against the integrity of the Bank of England is a strike against England itself."

"I know that, Mr Harman."

"At least persuade your brother to dismiss him. If he no longer has access to the duke's accounts, he will not find it so easy to make mischief."

"I will consider the matter very carefully, I assure you. You may go."

Mr Harman jumped to his feet, startled by the abrupt dismissal. "What about . . . What about me, my lady?" he asked breathlessly.

"I'm sure you are blameless in this matter," Viola answered. "I will see that you do not suffer. As far as I am concerned, you do not exist."

"Thank you, my lady!" Mr Harman bowed and scraped and fled the room.

"Well, Lover?" Viola said, as she opened the file. "What do you make of Mr Harman's assertions? Self-serving twaddle? Or gospel truth?"

The butler was not accustomed to being asked his opinion. He was flattered. "Both, I would imagine, my lady. Will that be all?"

"Yes," said Viola. "Take the letters on your way out, please. And send me a cup of chocolate. I've some reading to do."

By the time she had finished reading the file on Julian, it was already close to three o'clock. "I'm afraid I won't have time to go over the whole house with you, Lover," she said apologetically, when he answered the bell. "But will you show me the guest bedrooms?"

Of all the many richly appointed rooms he showed her, only one seemed to meet with her approval. "Yes," she said, walking into the Blue Room. "This will do. This will do very well indeed. I'll take the bed, all the hangings, too. This small sofa, I think. Those two chairs. The game table. The carpet. The curtains. The clock . . ." She looked around, frowning in concentration.

Lover was bewildered. "My lady?"

"I'm furnishing a home for a friend," Viola explained. "I shall need a coffee service, as well. Tea service, table linen, china, silver, crystal—but only for two. That should make it easier for you. Would you care to write all this down?" she asked him gently.

Lover instantly took out a pencil and a tablet of paper.

"As for dinner," said Viola. "I won't tax you with that. I'll get it myself."

"Move your bleeding arse!" Jem roared some time later. The footman was furious as he stood on the running board of Lady Viola's barouche. Traffic was at a standstill. Viola's driver had edged the open carriage through the crowd of vehicles almost to the entrance to the Mall. If the landau directly ahead of them would only move a foot or two to the right, Viola's barouche would be able to squeeze through. Polite appeals had produced no joy, however, and Jem had been forced to turn nasty. His vulgarity was rewarded; Lady Arbogast, the grandam in the landau, turned with an icy stare while the young lady with her, evidently her daughter, cringed under the carriage rug.

"*Madam,*" the grandam called to Viola in an awful voice, "your barouche is encroaching upon my landau."

Viola, naturally, did not respond; she was far too engrossed in the latest issue of *La Belle Assemblee* to give anything else her attention.

"You heard me," bawled Jem at his colleague on the running board of the landau. "Move your arse. There's a lady coming through, and you're blocking the way."

Not to be outdone, Lady Arbogast's footman snarled, "Move yourself! You've got to get here early, if you want to see the parade."

"Bloody hell!" Jem groaned. "Not another parade! Ram through, Judd! Ram it! Maybe we can dash across the street before the ruddy thing starts."

Throughout all this, Viola remained serenely deaf.

Unable to ram, the coachman crept forward, the wheels of the barouche coming perilously close to the landau. "Desist!" shrieked Lady Arbogast, becoming quite alarmed. "You will scratch my vehicle, madam! If you do so much as an *atom* of damage to my beautiful landau, I will take you to court! Madam? Madam, I am talking to you!"

Viola looked up from her magazine. "Jem, is that lady addressing me?" she asked.

Jem angrily apprised his mistress of the situation. Now it *was* Viola's place to interfere. "Madam," she said, leaning forward and speaking quite conversationally, "my footman informs me that, if you were to move your excellent landau just eighteen inches to the right, we might get through, and avoid the parade altogether. Be an angel and squash over, won't you?"

"Avoid the parade?" cried Miss Amelia Arbogast, leaning forward to look incredulously at Viola. "Why should anyone want to avoid the parade? *We* have been waiting here this age so that we can be front and center."

"I assure you I have no intention of blocking your view," Viola answered. "I simply want to get through this crush to visit the shops in Piccadilly."

The young lady's eyes widened. "Oh, but you can't get to Piccadilly from here! You'll have to go around! Access to the Mall is strictly prohibited."

"Not to us, it ain't," Jem sneered. "*We've* got an ivory pass. Ha!"

It was as if an invisible iron smoothed out all the wrinkles on Lady Arbogast's face. "An ivory pass?" she repeated in astonishment and awe. "I beg your pardon! Had no idea! Roberts! Roberts!" she called to her driver, snapping her fingers frantically. "Move to the right *immediately,* and let this lady through. She has an ivory pass!"

"Thank you, madam," said Viola, returning with perfect contentment to her magazine.

Her thanks and, indeed, her contentment, proved to be premature, however, as Roberts, in his eagerness to comply with Lady Arbogast's command, lurched rather too suddenly to the right and succeeded in locking the back left wheel of the landau with the right front wheel of Lady Viola's barouche.

Jem cursed violently at the landau. Lady Arbogast apologized profusely to the lady with the ivory pass. The wheels of the two vehicles grinded together. By the time the landau and the barouche could be uncoupled, the parade was well under way.

"I *do* apologize, madam," cried Lady Arbogast, mortified. "I don't know *what* Roberts could have been thinking."

Viola stood up in the barouche and surveyed the crowd of vehicles and pedestrians behind her. There was no going back, and no going forward. She was marooned for the duration, and she had nothing but a few magazines to entertain her. "How long do these ghastly things last?" she inquired entirely without sweetness as she sat down again.

"Oh, aren't they splendid?" cried Amelia, bouncing up and down in her seat and waving her miniature Union Jack as ranks of red-coated Life Guards trotted by on matching black chargers, their swords gleaming in the April sunshine, the white plumes on their tall helmets dancing gracefully.

Viola was not inclined to think them splendid at all. They were between her and good shopping, and there could be nothing splendid about them. She felt decidedly unpatriotic.

"Let us hope it is a quick march," she murmured, returning to *La Belle Assemblee*. The "articles" and the fashion plates were complete rubbish, of course, but the advertisements were informative, beguiling, and, occasionally, brilliant. One particularly clever slogan caught her eye: "After what seems like a century, Fortnum & Mason is one hundred years old." It went on to promise "a cornucopia of fine food and drink, gifts and luxuries."

Viola was intrigued; she determined to go there as soon as the parade was over.

The red-coated Life Guards passed at last, only to be succeeded by Horse Guards in blue coats, steel cuirasses, and scarlet plumes. At the head of the Blues rode Lieutenant-Colonel Lord Simon Ascot. Viola felt a burst of cold fury as she looked at him.

Miss Arbogast had rather a different reaction to the spectacle.

"Isn't he splendid?" she breathed. She stood up in her mother's landau and began calling his name with enthusiasm.

"Amelia!" cried her mother. "Do sit down! You will embarrass Lord Simon!"

Lord Simon cut his eyes in the general direction of the unsubtle Amelia and encountered Viola. A grin spread across his harsh features as he recognized her, and he raised his sword in a mocking salute. The gesture was immediately copied by the rest of the Blues.

Viola rolled her eyes in disgust and picked up her magazine.

"There, Amelia!" cried Lady Arbogast, catching her daughter's excitement. "He has saluted you, my dear! He *does* mean to propose, after all. He must!"

"Oh, Mama!" Amelia cried, blushing.

The rest of the household guards plodded by in somber procession, but, Viola noticed, the attention of her neighbors waned considerably after the Horse Guards had passed. Viola herself was most interested in the Grenadiers, who brought up the rear. When it was all over, her barouche shot across the street toward the gates of the Mall, almost mowing down the last man. Behind her, bedlam broke out as everyone began trying to leave at once.

Within the palings of the Mall, however, all was peaceful. To Viola's left, St James's Park looked green and inviting as the barouche rolled southwest toward Buckingham Palace. To her right was Carlton House, the Prince Regent's residence, and, beyond Carlton House, stood Marlborough House and Clarence House. It was rather like a model village, except that it was composed entirely of palaces.

"Not a patch on Gambol House," Jem declared loyally.

"No, but the smell is much nicer," Viola replied absently, the greater part of her attention taken up by the not-unpredictable approach of a lone Horse Guard. Viola resigned herself to the unpleasant encounter with a sigh.

"Miss Andrews!" Lord Simon called.

"How *tiresome* it is to see you again, Lord Simon," she said as the latter drew alongside her barouche on his beautiful black charger. "And what a small place London is, as it turns out. Even in a crowd, one cannot seem to avoid the people one wishes to."

Lord Simon laughed easily.

"If you wished to avoid me, Miss Andrews," he said, his green eyes twinkling, "I wonder you would come to Horse Guards Parade! I myself *am* a Horse Guard, you know."

"I did *not* come to see you, my lord," Viola said coldly. "I did not come to see the parade. I am on a shopping expedition. It was my intention to cut through the Mall and avoid a great deal of traffic. Guess my joy when I found my path obstructed by a gaggle of fools on horseback."

Lord Simon smiled incredulously. "Did you not enjoy the parade?"

"No, I did not," Viola replied honestly. "I found it to be long, dull, and in my way."

"Indeed," said Lord Simon. "Is that why you were calling my name so urgently?"

Viola glared at him. "Again, my lord, I did not come to see you, and I certainly did not call your name. *That* was the young lady in the landau next to me. She had a twee little flag she was waving. Perhaps you noticed her?"

"I'm afraid I saw nothing but *you*, Miss Andrews," he replied gallantly.

"Ugh! Have you nothing better to do than follow me around?" she asked crossly.

"You're very cruel," he complained. "It is too unkind, when I have been up all night worrying about you. I must say you look well. You seem to have landed on your feet. I trust the duke has not been unkind to you?"

"I am quite well, Lord Simon," Viola said shortly.

"I'm glad. I imagined you were having a very bad time of it at Gambol House. But the duke was to your liking? I'm glad. Surprised, but glad."

Viola found his insinuations particularly rude in view of

the fact that the duke in question was actually her brother. "For your information, the Duke of Fanshawe is not in London at the moment, but his servants at Gambol House are looking after me quite beautifully, as you see."

Jem drew himself up proudly.

I see," Simon said gravely. "And the indispensable Mr Devize? I trust he is not making a nuisance of himself?"

"Unlike yourself, Lord Simon," Viola said coldly, "Mr Devize knows how to treat a lady. And he can tell a lady from a common strumpet, which helps, I think."

"Well, let us hope the Duke of Fanshawe bears the same hallmark!" said Lord Simon, drawing up his mount. "If not, you may find yourself in a very queer street, Miss Andrews. You may find you need a friend. If you do, you can always find me at the Albany, in Piccadilly," he called after her.

"I'll be sure to send assassins," Viola snapped. "Coachman! Drive on!"

# Chapter Eleven

"Good evening, Hudson," Viola greeted the servant.

Hudson stared. It was well after dark, and the new Mrs Devize was attired in a Nile green leather coat trimmed with mink. As she entered the hall carrying her white dog, she was pulling the strings of a Nile green bonnet lined in peacock blue satin with her free hand. Hudson was quite certain she had been wearing a white leather coat and matching bonnet when she had left No. 32 Lombard Street much earlier in the day. Her dog looked different, too: whiter and fluffier.

For a moment, Viola thought he might refuse to admit her

into the house, but he gave way to her, saying frostily, "Welcome home, madam."

"Is Mr Devize not back yet?" Viola asked anxiously, pausing in the hall as Cork carried the freshly groomed bichon upstairs. The City was flooded with the sound of bells, and she had to shout to be heard.

"No, madam."

"Oh, I do hate these bells," she added peevishly as she pulled off her gloves. "They make one feel one is late, even when one is not. I asked for some household things to be delivered, Hudson. Did they arrive?"

"Yes, madam," he said angrily. "You'll be the ruin of him," he muttered under his breath as she started up the stairs.

"What did you say?" Viola asked.

"Nothing, madam."

This time, Viola refused to let it go. "You did say something," she insisted. "You shouldn't bottle up your feelings, you know."

"Very well, then, madam," he said, drawing himself up to his full height. "You'll be the ruin of him. Running up debts in all the shops! Velvet curtains, eiderdown quilts, cushions, and featherbeds—"

"There should have been only one featherbed," Viola interrupted. Running lightly up the steps, she looked in the bedroom. Everything appeared to be in order; all the creature comforts she had appropriated from Gambol House had been placed according to her detailed instructions.

"China cups!" Hudson railed at her. "Crystal goblets! Silk carpets! Tables and chairs! Champagne and caviar! How's my poor captain to afford the likes of you? When he's already pawned everything he owns?"

"What do you mean, he's pawned things?" Viola asked curiously.

"His watch! His beautiful saber and all his regimentals!

Even his boots he pawned! Because of *you,* I shouldn't wonder!" he added, seeped in deep resentment.

"No, no," Viola said impatiently. "What does it mean to pawn things? I'm not familiar with the term."

Hudson was taken aback by her ignorance. "Why, it means he's given his treasures up to Mr Mordecai in the shop next door, in exchange for a small loan. If he can't pay back the money, he loses his property. And Mr Mordecai is the landlord, too! We're sure to be evicted."

"The landlord," said Viola, clapping her bonnet back on her head. "Next door, you say? I'd like to have a word with him about my bedroom window." She was out of the door before Hudson could even think to try to stop her.

Viola had never met a Jew before, but she had read *Ivanhoe,* and so she was not at all apprehensive. In fact, she thought Mr Mordecai quite picturesque with his long gray beard and tiny little black cap. His shop was picturesque, too, being full of almost every sort of thing Viola could imagine. Clocks seemed to be most abundant, but there were also coats, hats, and umbrellas, musical instruments of all sorts, tapestries, tea sets, dressing cases, writing desks, and marble and china figures. Paintings and frames were stacked against the wall.

"Good evening," she called to the proprietor as he came out of the back room. "You're open very late. Do you do much business this late in the evening?"

"Sometimes yes, sometimes no," answered Mr Mordecai, staring at the fashionable young lady almost in disbelief. She was not his usual clientele; when a lady wanted to pawn something, she usually sent a servant or a gentleman in her place. "Are you interested in a loan, madam?"

"No, thank you. I'm Mrs Devize. If you are Mr Mordecai, then I am your tenant."

"I am Mr Mordecai," he replied. "I did not know Captain Devize was married."

"It was immensely sudden," said Viola. A marble statuette of Daphne and Apollo caught her eye, and she nearly lost her train of thought. "I understand the captain recently pawned a few things. They are not on display in your shop, I hope?"

Mr Mordecai assured her that they were not. He went into the back room and emerged with a large box, which he placed on the counter. "You may inspect the contents, Mrs Devize," he invited her.

Opening the box, Viola found a silver pocket watch, a razor with an ivory handle, and a string of silver buttons, all stuffed into an enameled shako bearing the silver badge of Julian's regiment. At the bottom of the box, wrapped in tissue, was a scarlet coat with gold braid and orange facings. With it was the saber of an officer sheathed in a battered scabbard.

"How much did you lend him?" Viola asked, touching each of these interesting things in turn.

"Fifty pounds," he replied. "Oh, it isn't worth that much, I know, but he's a good sort, and he said he needed the money very badly. Now that I see you, I understand."

The compliment pleased Viola. "I can see you are looking after his property very well, Mr Mordecai," she said, closing the box. "He will pay you very soon, I'm sure."

His bushy brows went up. "You have not come to repay your husband's loan?" Judging by her clothes and jewels, she could have done so easily, in his estimation.

"Lord, no," said Viola, quite scandalized by the suggestion. "The captain wouldn't like that at all. He will pay you himself. I've come about our bedroom window. There's no glass in it, Mr Mordecai, only brown paper. Brown paper is not sufficient. We must have the glazier."

Mr Mordecai was surprised. "The captain has not complained."

"I daresay *he* is accustomed to cold rooms, but I am not."

"The window will be repaired, Mrs Devize, first thing in the morning," he promised her.

"Thank you," said Viola, looking around the shop.

He looked at her curiously. "Was there something else, madam?"

"No," said Viola. "Not really. I must say, you have quite an interesting shop. It reminds me of my grandmother's attic. That coat in the corner . . . Is it very old?"

Mr Mordecai instantly went to the coat rack she indicated. "This one, madam?"

"No, the spotted fur," Viola said eagerly, unbuttoning the coat she was wearing.

Mr Mordecai brought the leopard-skin coat to her. It was double-breasted with a long skirt, beautifully lined in black satin. Viola reached for it like an eager child, letting the coat she was wearing fall to the floor.

"This coat," he told her as he helped her into the sumptuous fur, "belonged to a Russian prince. He committed suicide over a woman, and never came back for it."

"He must have been a small man—it fits me perfectly," Viola said, going over to a tall mirror to admire herself. To her delight, the coat looked as delicious as it felt. "I'll take it, Mr Mordecai. Where do I sign?"

Mr Mordecai looked perplexed. "Sign, madam?" he echoed. "Oh, you mean the credit. I'm afraid I cannot offer you credit, Mrs Devize. The captain, your husband, is in debt to me."

Viola was aghast. "You mean I cannot have this coat, Mr Mordecai?" she cried.

"Perhaps we could come to an arrangement," he said, looking at her thoughtfully. "These earrings that you are wearing . . . They are pearls, yes?"

Viola's hand went to her ears. "These were my mother's," she said. His eyes widened in surprise as she opened the coat to unpin a brooch. "What about this? It's set with diamonds."

Mr Mordecai took out his loupe and examined the brooch carefully.

"Is it enough for the coat?" Viola asked anxiously.

"Yes," he said, almost breathlessly. "More than enough, I should think."

"I'll wear it out, Mr Mordecai," she said happily.


Julian was a little late returning home that night. His day had been tiring and unpleasant. Fortunes had been won and lost on the Stock Exchange that day. Julian found himself blamed for every loss, but never credited for any gains. He knew he had made a few enemies, but he was quite surprised when, at the sound of the closing bell, he was chased down the steps by a mob of angry stockjobbers hurling insults, accusations, and threats. Indeed, he was fortunate they hurled nothing worse. In Change Alley he managed to elude them by darting into Garraway's tavern and out the back door. Just in case his colleagues turned violent, he took the long way home.

All was quiet at No. 32, but Hudson pounced on him the moment he walked in the door.

"Captain! Thank God you're home."

Julian was instantly concerned; Hudson did not usually wait up for him. "What's the matter?" he demanded, his thoughts instantly going to Mary. In a second, he imagined all sorts of calamities. "Has something happened to Mrs Devize? She's not still out?"

"She's here," Hudson glowered. "Safe. But she's bought out all the shops," he complained. "She was out all day, Captain, and half the night, too. And when she came back, looking like butter wouldn't melt, she was wearing a different dress! I know it's not my place to say, Captain, but that female is no good."

"You're right, Hudson," Julian said sharply. "It's not your place."

"I cannot hold my tongue," Hudson said stubbornly. "I've watched over you for too many years to see you ruined—yes, ruined!—by the likes of her. I don't know how she prevailed upon you to marry her . . . Well, I suppose I *do* know," he added with loathing.

"Careful!" Julian interrupted. "You've said quite enough, Hudson. Another word on the subject, and I shall dismiss you," he warned.

"Good evening, Captain," Viola called down to him from the top of the stairs.

Julian looked at her, his eyes warm with approval. She was wearing a white dress that to him at least appeared very simple, just the sort of dress a country vicar's daughter ought to wear, if she had the figure for it. A single strand of pearls was clasped at her throat, her only ornament. Part of her black hair had been pinned up loosely; the rest was allowed to tumble down her back.

"Go to bed, Hudson," Julian said softly, his eyes glued to Viola.

"Yes," said Viola. "Go to bed. *I* will look after the captain this evening."

Hudson took one look at Julian's face and knew the young man was lost. He descended to the kitchen, shaking his head.

For a moment, the two young people only looked at each other, each taking pleasure in the physical beauty of the other. Viola broke the silence. "What a day this has been," she remarked lightly. "I feel as though I've gone around the world and back again!"

"You must have missed me terribly," he said, starting up the stairs.

Viola laughed. "I only came back to find out what happened to poor Mr Parsley."

"Parsley?" he growled. Joining her on the landing, he pulled her into his arms. When she made no objection, his hands traveled up her back to her shoulders, pulling her closer still.

"Don't tease me," she said, her lips scarcely an inch from his. Proximity made them both breathless. "I have been most anxious about the poor man all day."

"Have you?" he said softly, drinking in her fragrance. "Then let me put your mind at ease. Parsley is safe."

His breath on her neck made her shiver. "Hurrah," she said faintly.

"I bought back all his shares. Now *he* is rich, and *I* am poor."

"How poor?" she wanted to know.

"Very poor."

"That was not very clever of you," she observed.

"Oh, but in six months, I shall be very rich indeed. If you decide to marry me, you will be a very rich woman, my love," he added, his arms tightening around her.

"In six months?" she laughed. "Mr Devize, are you asking me to speculate?"

"In six months, I will be so rich, you will not be able to get near me," he warned her. "Every eligible maiden in the kingdom will be in hot pursuit of me. Now is your chance."

"Then I'd better take it," she said. She spoke lightly, but her dark eyes left him in no doubt of her acceptance.

"Dear girl," he said huskily.

"I have just condescended to throw myself away on you, sir," she chided him. "A Yorkshireman would be sufficiently moved to show a little gratitude, if not affection."

Julian instantly claimed her mouth. Viola, already in his arms, melted against him with a sigh of contentment. The silence was long and sweet, tinged with fire. He kissed her beyond decency, his hands brushing lightly against her breasts, his tongue exploring her mouth until her lips burned. Unschooled, she did little in response, but she did not stop him. He had to stop himself. "If you're not careful," he murmured shakily, "you'll get more than you bargained for."

"But it's so pleasant to get more than one bargains for," she said sensibly. "One hates to get less."

"I meant," he told her as sternly as he could, "we are not yet man and wife. You mustn't tempt me. It isn't kind. I am not made of stone, you know."

Very firmly, he put her away from him.

"I'm so glad," said Viola. "I wouldn't like a stone for a husband."

"This morning, you swore you wouldn't have me at all," he reminded her. "What changed your mind?"

Viola smiled. "Let's just say I put our time apart to good use."

"They do say that absence makes the heart grow fonder."

"And the fastest way to a man's heart is through his stomach. Are you hungry? Your dinner is on the table," she added proudly. "I'm practicing to be a wife, you see."

"I haven't got a table," he said.

"Of course you have a table," she told him. "It's in front of the fireplace. No, not that room," she said quickly as he started for his study. "I'm not finished in there. This one," she said, leading him by the hand into the bedroom.

Julian followed her into a room he didn't recognize, a room dominated by a huge four-poster bed, each of the posts being larger than himself. The hangings over this bed made it look rather like the battle pavilion of some medieval king. Deep blue velvet curtains covered the window, and most of the walls. A hunting scene in a magnificent gilt frame hung over the fireplace, almost dwarfing the chimneypiece. A huge ormolu clock ticked away on the mantel. An Aubusson rug covered the entire floor. A small table, covered in a fine white linen cloth and laden with covered dishes, had been set up in front of the fire. In lieu of chairs, a pale blue sofa, just big enough for two very intimate people, had been placed behind the table, its high back touching the foot of the bed.

For all the wrong reasons, he was breathless. Visions of

debtor's prison appeared before his eyes. He hardly noticed as she peeled the coat from his shoulders, leaving him in his waistcoat and shirt sleeves. "Woman, what have you done?" he whispered.

"Do you like it?" she asked behind him, sounding quite pleased with herself. "It is a sweet room now, is it not? All the creature comforts. The curtains quite keep out the cold. We can even close the curtains on the bed for additional . . . warmth."

Julian went to the table and picked up a bottle of wine: an antebellum Beaujolais, cripplingly expensive. Worse yet, it had already been opened, and so could not be sent back to the vintner. "I have but two questions," he said coldly, replacing the bottle on the table. "How much did all this cost? And how am I to afford it? The bed alone must have cost twenty pounds!"

"Nothing like!" she hastened to assure him. "It's not new, you know. None of it is new, except the food, of course."

Julian began to breathe again. "Secondhand? Good. All the same, it must have been very expensive," he insisted. "How much do I owe?"

"Nothing," Viola said proudly. "It's all paid for. I *pawn-broked* some of my jewelry."

Julian was thunderstruck. "You what?" he said, strong displeasure in his voice.

"Did I say it wrong?" she asked innocently.

"You pawned your jewelry? Mary!"

"I went to see Mr Mordecai about our window. One thing led to another, and, before I knew it, I was pawning things like a Londoner. I got all this, and the most smashing fur coat you ever set eyes on."

Julian sighed. "You should never have gone to see Mr Mordecai. The window is my responsibility." His masculine pride had been injured, and he lashed out at her. "You should not have pawned anything. I don't like it, Mary."

"Why not? *You* did it—he showed me your regimentals. Very pretty."

"You did *not* repay my loan," he said, firing up with real anger. "Tell me you didn't!"

"Well, of course I didn't," Viola snapped. "I felt instinctively that you would want to do it yourself with your own money. Besides, as you know, I'm very selfish. I couldn't be bothered!"

"I don't want you pawning things," Julian grumbled. "It unmans me."

"Does it really?" she asked curiously. "Why?"

"It implies you have no faith in me," he complained. "I've got something in the works, you know. I'll be able to look after you very well, very soon."

"In six months."

"Yes, six months!" he said angrily. "This will all have to go back. I will deal with Mr Mordecai in the morning."

"No!" said Viola. "I don't know your views on the subject, but I'd much rather have a comfortable bed than a diamond brooch—if one must choose, that is."

"That is my point. You should not *have* to choose. I will get your brooch back for you."

"I don't care three straws for that silly old brooch!" Viola said impatiently. "I want a comfortable bed. I want good food to eat. I've worked very hard on this dinner, and you're spoiling it," she accused him. "I think you're being very mean and petty. After all, it was *my* brooch, not yours. I can do with it what I like. You're not my lord and master."

Julian blinked at her. "You're right," he said presently. "I'm sorry. I should be thanking you instead of haranguing you. I'll go and wash up. When I return, I will be a different man."

Viola forgave him instantly. "There's hot water in the dressing room."

When he returned, Viola was removing the cover from the main dish. As she moved in front of the fire, parts of her dress became wholly transparent, and her body was outlined in red. Desire pealed in his body like alarm bells. Julian caught his breath as she looked up and smiled.

"Sit down," she invited him. "Will you pour the wine while I cut the pie? Men are the worst pie cutters in nature, I have noticed."

Julian sank mutely onto the sofa. It was covered in pale blue satin. It had been years since he had felt the icy smoothness of satin. The pleasure was absurdly keen. He stroked the fabric absently as he watched Viola cut the pie with unhurried grace. He no longer felt hungry in the least. Not for food, anyway.

He forced himself to speak. "What sort of pie is it?"

"Pheasant, topped with morello cherries and drenched in brandy."

Julian's stomach rumbled as she placed the dish before him.

"Shall I pour the wine, too?" she asked, laughing at him.

"Yes, please," he said almost meekly.

Viola cut a slice of pie for herself and sat down on the sofa to watch him eat. "How is it?" she asked as he paused to reach for his wine.

"Delicious!" Julian answered, gulping the Beaujolais. "You're an excellent cook, Mary."

Viola frowned at him. "I don't cook, Mr Devize," she said severely. "I'll have you know I was very carefully brought up. I should have thought that was obvious."

"I beg your pardon," he said contritely. "Was it Cork?"

Her frown deepened. "Cork? No, Mr Devize. I went all the way to Piccadilly and got your favorite meal for you, and this is the thanks I get?"

Julian paused to reevaluate his meal. "*Is* this my favorite meal?"

"It's what your grandmother sent you every month when the war was on," she told him.

"Good Lord! So it is. Did Hudson tell you?" he asked in disbelief.

"No, indeed," Viola said. "I found it out myself from the clerk at Fortnum and Mason's. They remembered your grandmother very well."

"We cannot eat like this every night, Mary."

"Of course not," she replied. "Sometimes we will have my favorite dinner."

"You know what I mean," he said quietly. "It is expensive."

"In that case, it should not go to waste," she said pointedly.

Julian couldn't argue the point. He ate. When he had taken the edge off his hunger, he set down his knife and fork. Wiping his mouth on his napkin, he turned a little on the sofa to face his beautiful companion. Plate in hand, Viola was sitting at her end of the sofa with one leg tucked under her, her satin slipper dangling from her foot. She was only toying with her food. As he watched, she plucked a brandy-soaked cherry from the top of her pie.

Julian watched it all the way to her mouth.

"This must remind you of the war," she said.

"Oh, my, yes," he said with a short laugh. "Beautiful girls were constantly feeding me pie. It's a wonder I got any fighting done."

Viola licked her fingers. "Oh? Did the Condesa de la Vega feed you pie?"

"Hudson has a big mouth," Julian said angrily, his face reddening.

"It's all right, Dev," Viola said mildly. "I didn't expect to marry a monk, you know. In fact, you're well under your limit. I would have forgiven you as many as . . . ten women, provided they were *very* firmly in your past. With Fraulein Schwartz safely married in Glockenspiegel or whatever, and the condesa having been *passed on* to your colonel, I am not in the least bit upset."

"I am going to murder Hudson," he said.

"Oh, you mustn't blame Hudson," she said easily. "I made it my business to find out all about you. If I am to be your wife, I have the right to know everything about you, do I not?"

"Perhaps," he said, finishing his wine, "when you are my wife."

"We're as good as married," she said, popping another cherry into her mouth.

"Are we, by God?"

His hand brushed against her knee. His fingers closed over her soft skirts instinctively. For a moment he was caught up in the sheer pleasure of touching the fine, filmy fabric, warmed by the girl who was wearing it. His body responded wildly to the sensation. He wanted to feel it next to his skin, to bury his face in her skirts. Instead, he tugged her skirts toward him, and Viola slipped farther down on the sofa, her dress sliding like water on the satin sofa.

Bemused, she watched him fondle her skirt. "Is this what husbands do in Sussex?" she asked. "Rumple their wives? I shall need ironing after this."

His eyes flashed up to her face. "If you're not careful, Mary," he warned her, "you will find out what husbands do." Reluctantly, but firmly, he smoothed down her skirts.

Viola caught his hand as it was withdrawing. "But I *want* to find out. I want to know what sort of husband you will make me."

Julian caught his breath. "You will find out soon enough," he assured her.

Viola plucked another cherry from her pie, eating it with relish. "I want to find out now," she said, reclining like a lazy queen. "I don't like surprises."

"You don't know what you're asking," he said.

"We're only talking," she replied with impish delight. "What will you do to me first? On our wedding night, I mean? Will you dismiss my maid and undress me yourself?

Or will you come to me in darkness like a thief? Will you be tender or cruel? Will I like it?"

"Don't be naughty," he pleaded softly, quite unable to remove his hand from her skirts.

"Why not?" she whispered, licking her fingers slowly. "We're completely private."

"Yes, where is the dog?" he said desperately. "Where's our little mop?"

"Bijou?" she said coolly. "She is with Cork in the attic. The food was driving her mad."

"You're driving me mad," he muttered. "Stop that," he said angrily as she picked yet another cherry from her dish.

"Oh, did you want it for yourself?" she asked, leaning forward. As she slid forward on the slippery satin, his hand slid higher even though he had not moved it. "Take it," she urged him. Sliding closer to him, she brazenly pushed the fruit between his lips. Julian closed his eyes, drawing the fruit and her finger into his mouth.

"Isn't it good?" she whispered. Tossing her plate onto the table, she took his hand and brought it to her breast. "Does it give you pleasure?"

"We're not married yet, miss," he chided her gently, even as his hands moved restlessly, one cupping her warm, full breast, the other slowly pushing up her skirts, caressing her stockings.

"Are we not?" she argued, tugging at the white stock wound tightly around his throat. "You have given me your promise, have you not? And you are a man of your word, are you not? You would not abandon me, surely."

"Never," he agreed as his neckcloth slowly slid away. With his eyes closed, he felt the tops of her stockings, the bits of satin that gartered them above her knees.

She was now unbuttoning his waistcoat. "Then for all intents and purposes, I am your wife already," she said silkily. "You are my husband. You may kiss the bride," she added, trying to claim his mouth. To her annoyance, he would not allow her to kiss him. "Do we really need some moldy old bishop saying grace over the union of our hearts, our souls, and our bodies?" she added impatiently. "What can he give us but a piece of paper? Kiss me, Julian. Kiss your bride."

Julian opened his eyes. "What about the blessing of the Church?" he asked, pulling away. "The sanction of Society? Are these things of no importance to you?"

"Not really," she admitted with a pretty pout.

Julian almost choked. "If I didn't know you were a vicar's daughter, I'd say you were a devil's daughter," he complained, smoothing down her skirts so that they showed no signs of ever having been rumpled.

"I'm only curious," she pouted. "It's perfectly natural."

Viola hardly listened as he recited all the reasons why they should wait until after the formal ceremony to satisfy her perfectly natural curiosity. When she wanted something, right and wrong had little meaning for her. He was not going to wriggle out of satisfying her immediately just because it was wrong in the eyes of the world. She cut him off with a kiss.

Julian stifled a groan. Encouraged, Viola redoubled her efforts, kissing him as hard as she could. But try as she might, she could force no response. In fact, he caught her hands in his so that she could not continue undressing him. "Good Lord," he said, when she had exhausted herself. "Is this what goes on in Yorkshire?"

"A Yorkshireman would have helped me," she complained. "A Yorkshireman would be done by now," she added, flushing angrily.

Julian could not help laughing. "I'm sorry," he said, bringing his mirth under control. "Are you insulting the men of *my* county or your own?"

"I hate you," she said, flinging his arms off and struggling to get up. "I've changed my mind. I don't want to marry you, after all."

Julian would not let her go. "I'm trying to protect you," he said, wrapping her up in his arms. "Be patient."

To his horror, she burst into tears.

Viola was equally horrified. Doubly humiliated, she broke free of him and ran into the dressing room, slamming the door. She did not feel protected. She felt foolish and rejected. Hurt and angry, she consulted with the mirror in Julian's dressing room. Try as she might, she could find no fault with her appearance. She had been blessed with good looks, but she took nothing for granted. Every night, after her bath, she polished her soft skin with beeswax until it glowed like a newborn's, and every morning she meticulously groomed her dark eyebrows with a tweezers. She washed her lustrous black curls with a frequency that alarmed her physician, who thought that wet hair led invariably to pneumonia. Her body was not neglected, either. Both her fingernails and toenails were manicured, and everything in between had to be perfect, too. She waged a constant war against unwanted body hair, plucking and trimming and shaving, so that all was perfection. She dressed, not according to fashion, but in consideration of what best suited her tall, voluptuous form. Even with tears (tears!) streaming down her face, she was a sight to behold.

And yet, incredible as it seemed, Julian Devize did not want her. He had not paid her a single compliment all evening! Not that she needed his compliments, of course; she dressed only to please herself. "I look good," she told herself, sniffling.

For a while, Viola sat on the upside-down bathtub, fantasizing that at any moment, Julian would appear to take her in his arms and assure her that his desire for her matched her own need for him. He did no such thing. Embittered by his coldness, Viola went back to the bedroom, determined to punish him.

He was gone. As she went out on the landing, she heard his latchkey turn in the lock.

Angry and hurt, she went back to the bedroom and folded the tablecloth up over the food. Then she poured herself a generous glass of wine, drank it too fast, and went to bed. At least now, thanks to her own efforts, she had a warm, comfortable bed in which to sleep. If it were up to *him*, she would be on a thin, lumpy mattress on the hard floor. And he hadn't even thanked her—not for the bed, the dinner, or for anything else!

She lay wide awake, feeling ill-used and plotting revenge. When they were married, obviously she would make him very sorry. Much later, she sensed rather than heard the door opening. Squeezing her eyes shut, she pretended to be lost in uncaring sleep.

The back of Viola's neck tingled as he slid into bed beside her. "Mary? Are you awake?"

Viola refused to answer, even when he put his hand on her shoulder and said, "I know you are awake. Don't be angry, love. Talk to me."

After a moment, he sighed and moved away from her to the other side of the bed. With the keenest of pleasure, Viola imagined him lying awake on his side of the bed, feeling hurt and rejected, his heart torn into a thousand tiny bits. The illusion was shattered when he began to snore.

Enraged and insulted, Viola sat up, her mouth opened to complain. Naked from the waist up, Julian lay flat on his back with his arms flung up over his head. A fascinating trail of fine, dark hair leading the eye from his chest down to the band of his trousers. Viola thought he was beautiful, and it hurt all over again that he did not want her. The urge to punish him dissolved into despair. She put out her hand cautiously and touched his shoulder. He stirred in his sleep and stopped snoring. His skin was warm, smooth and firm to the touch. Viola could not take her hand away. Spreading her palm over his chest, she fancied she could feel the hum of his heart vibrating through his flesh. She stroked him lightly, watching his face carefully in the firelight. It would be too embarrassing for words if he should wake up, of course, but touching him while he slept hardly counted as touching; he would never know.

She teased the light hairs on his chest, first with her fingers, then with her breath, then, finally, when she could no longer resist, with her mouth. She trailed her lips from his throat to his belly then back again, light as a butterfly. Julian stirred restlessly, rolling his hips. A sharp groan fell from his lips as she edged closer and closer to the buttons of his trousers.

Snatching her hands away, Viola held her breath and waited until she was certain he was asleep before touching him again. Afraid of waking him, yet quite unable to leave his body alone, Viola slid her hands up and down his torso, her eyes glued to his face. His belly tightened, and he stirred restlessly. In sleep, at least, he could not help but respond to her.

"Are you trying to drive me mad?" he inquired, his eyes still closed.

At the sound of his voice, Viola yelped in fright and threw herself down on the bed with her back to him. Her heart pounding, she closed her eyes as tightly as possible. She was asleep, and nothing on earth could induce her to admit otherwise.

He surged behind her, pulling her hips against his almost roughly, but the hand that swept her hair off of her neck was gentle. "I warned you," he said in a voice that did not sound like him at all. "I warned you not to tempt me." As he spoke, he tugged her gown from her shoulders. If Viola had not been sound asleep, she almost certainly would have stopped him.

He brushed his lips against her neck. "Is this what you want?" he murmured, his husky voice every bit as intoxicating as his mouth. Viola shivered in anticipation as he held her wedged tightly against him. Rocking her against him with a gentleness that surprised her, he ran his tongue lightly along the lines of her exposed neck while at the same time his hand found and caressed the rich curve of her breast. The lace of her gown seemed to displease him, and, impatiently, he pushed it aside. Viola whimpered softly as his bare hand touched the exquisitely sensitive bud that crowned her breast. Never in her life had she been touched so intimately. She seemed to feel the shock and thrill of it all the way down to her toes. Her entire body had a share in the pleasure as he stroked the very tip of her nipple. She felt an odd ache, almost a pain, deep in her belly, and, as if sensing it, he moved his hand lower, smoothing her lace gown down as he went. He found the full globes of her bottom and caressed her through her gown until she moved restlessly against his hand. He pushed his hand against her insistently until she gave way and opened herself to him, and then he could feel through her gown that she was wet. The ache in her belly spread into her untouched womanhood. She bit her lip to keep from crying out.

"I know you're awake," he panted, pulling up her gown until the bottom he now knew so intimately was fully exposed. The sight of her naked rump drove him into a frenzy. In a trice, he freed the member that had been straining against his trousers all evening. "Turn around and face me. Do you want me to take you from behind, like a mare?" he asked softly.

Viola gasped as she felt him opening her with his hand. In the next instant, he had tossed her onto her back and was kneeling over her, a dangerous light in his eyes. His strength surprised and excited her. She stared up at him, trembling from head to foot.

He was kneeling between her thighs, completely naked, his sex fully extended. "So you're awake, after all," he said, smiling down at her.

Viola could hardly deny it. Her gown bunched around her waist, and, absurdly, she tried to cover herself. One of his hands splayed against her belly, holding her down, and the other was between her legs, caressing her with absolute mastery. "This is what husbands do in the middle of the night," he said, still smiling. "How do you like it so far?"

Viola turned her face away in embarrassment as pleasure overtook over her senses.

"You're right, of course," he said, easing down beside her without breaking the caress. "Why should we deny ourselves? Why should you be unhappy? Why should I be in agony?"

"Are you in agony?" she murmured.

"Since the moment I saw you, I have been in agony."

"So have I," she said feebly.

He chuckled. "You don't know what agony is . . . not yet." Viola choked back a sob when he stopped caressing her. Her limbs were like water, and he could have done anything he liked with her. Using both hands, he undressed her, laying her bare. In the flickering firelight, he gazed at her with satisfaction. "What a sight you are," he murmured as she stared up at him, wide-eyed. "Every moment I am not inside you is a torment to me."

Pressing his hands onto her thighs, he opened her completely and looked at his prize. The innermost lips glistened like a shell in the firelight. Awakening to shame, Viola struggled weakly and again tried to cover herself. "What are you doing?" she breathed fearfully.

"I'd rather not say," he replied gently. "Sexual intercourse is rather like sausages. Everyone likes them, but no one really wants to know how they are made."

Viola frowned. She was in no humor for such ribaldry. This was supposed to be a beautiful, natural experience, and such remarks were distinctly unwelcome.

"Lost your nerve?" he taunted her, dipping his finger into her honey-filled recess.

Viola's cheeks flamed. "I have plenty of nerve, thank you,"

she said, her voice shaking only a little. "But then, I'm not from Sussex, am I?"

Julian chuckled softly as he lowered his body onto hers. "You'll pay for that," he said, placing his swollen member with slow deliberation between the glowing lips of her sex. The fit was unbelievably snug. The urge to break through her maidenhead and possess her fully almost overpowered him. It was all he could do to maintain his self-control.

Viola could scarcely breathe. It was done. He was inside her. She was no longer a virgin. For some reason, she had thought there must be some pain attached to the event. Instead, she felt quite content. The warmth of his body was pleasant and she scarcely noticed his weight pressing her into the mattress. She had won. He had tried to resist her, but, in the end, he could not. She was simply too desirable.

In that moment, she felt nothing but sweetness and security. In the next moment, she felt nothing but pain as he drove his full length into her soft, yielding flesh. Viola was so shocked, she could only gasp. Julian was gasping, too. He had controlled himself as long as he could, and he could control himself no longer. "How sweet you are," he gasped, riding her almost frantically. "Come with me, love. Come now."

Viola was in no position to struggle. Pinned underneath him, she was no longer the mistress of herself. He had possession of the tenderest part of her, which he was tearing apart with terrifying rapidity. Beating at his shoulders with her hands only seemed to encourage him. As for her cries of protest, he seemed to enjoy them. He threw back his head and made a terrible noise, a mad cross between a wolf's howl and a cock's crow, drowning her out.

It was crystal clear to her that she had made a terrible mistake. If this was the reality of married life, Viola wanted no part of it. After the howling and the crowing, he finished with loathsome gasps and weird cries. It was all very distasteful, but, apart from the very real pain in her belly and between her legs, she managed to remain above it all. He collapsed at her side with a dreamy smile on his lips.

"Was it good for you?" he asked smugly.

Viola was stunned. "You gave me a pain," she informed him angrily.

Julian laughed softly. "Wait until you give birth," he murmured.

Rolling over, he promptly went to sleep.

# Chapter Twelve

In the morning, Julian stumbled naked into his dressing room, only to be assailed by a chorus of feminine screams. Viola was having her bath with Cork in attendance. At once, she sank down in the water as far as she could without drowning herself, shrieking, "Get out!"

Cork shrieked as the master climbed bare-bottomed into the enameled tub with her mistress. Viola was forced to the opposite end of the tub with her knees under her chin as he wedged in behind her, his knees on either side. The fit was tight and not at all comfortable. "Are you mad?" she gasped in disbelief. "How *dare* you expose yourself to my servant!"

"Cork very wisely has left the room," Julian replied, splashing away. "I'm sorry to inconvenience you, my love, but I'm afraid I'm late for 'Change, and, after last night, I simply must have a bath."

Viola started violently as she felt his hands slipping past her thighs. Half turning her head, she snarled over her shoulder, "Stop that at once! *What* do you think you're doing?"

"Looking for the soap," he answered mildly.

Viola handed it to him angrily. To her annoyance, he began

lathering her back at once, his cool touch raising goose bumps. "Cork has already done my back," she snapped, squirming in an effort to throw his hands from her. "I want to get out," she added irritably.

"What's stopping you?" he inquired pleasantly.

"You are," she complained. "I'm wedged in. If I try to get out now—"

"I'll have a lovely view of your delightful bottom," he said. "I quite understand. Maidenly modesty is a beautiful thing. However, as we are to be married, I'm afraid you will have to accustom yourself to the idea of being gazed upon by your adoring husband."

"What are you looking for *now*?" she yelped as his hands again plunged under the water, questing around her bottom.

"Washcloth."

Viola flung it over her shoulder, slapping his face. She then wrapped her arms tightly around her knees, digging her heels into her thighs with her ankles clapped together. He began scrubbing himself with her washcloth.

"Did you sleep well?" he inquired presently.

"No," she said coldly.

He chuckled. "If you were restless, you had only to wake me up, and we might have been restless together."

Viola bristled. "I was not restless, Mr Devize," she informed him. "I was disgusted. I was disgusted by *you.*"

Julian flushed in embarrassment. "Well, my dear," he said. "I had a very good dinner, and, if I made a noise in my sleep, I can only apologize. I'm only human."

"Noise? You know perfectly what you did," she accused him. "You gave me a pain—you know you did—and I shall never forgive you for that."

Julian laughed. "Oh, that," he said.

"Yes, *that!*" Viola hissed at him. "You were like some stupid, rutting animal. It was the most horrendous, beastly, nightmarish experience of my entire life!"

"Strange," Julian said thoughtfully. "I've never had any complaint before."

Viola stiffened. She considered it quite ungallant for him to allude to his other liaisons, particularly when he knew she could not retaliate in kind. "Some girls have never learned to stand up for themselves," she informed him icily.

"Or perhaps they did not want to hurt my feelings," he suggested.

"After such treatment, I doubt any woman would care about your feelings!"

"Oh, come now," he said with a touch of impatience. "It was not all bad. I seem to recall you rather enjoyed it. And I *did* ask you if you were sure it was what you wanted."

"I was sure," she snapped, "until you gave me a pain! Had I known you meant to injure me, I would never have acquiesced to your mad desires."

Julian sighed. "Darling, it was your first time. Didn't your mother explain all this to you?"

"My mother died when I was very young."

Julian slipped his arms around her. "My poor darling," he murmured in her ear. "It will get better, I promise. Next time—"

"Next time! Do you imagine," she said, struggling furiously, "that I will ever permit you to do that to me again?"

Julian's laughter was ill-concealed. "My dear girl, I'm absolutely certain of it!"

"You are mistaken," she insisted angrily. "The thought is repugnant to me."

His arms tightened around her. "Forgive me, Mary. I was never with a virgin before. I did not realize how difficult it would be for you. For me, you see, it was heaven."

To her chagrin, Viola felt the forces of attraction again at work on her weak flesh. "It was not heaven for me, I assure you," she said peevishly, unable to summon righteous indignation.

"The good news is it only hurts the first time," he said, smoothing her hair with one hand. "You're not in pain now, are you?"

In truth, most of Viola's physical discomfort was long gone. There was only a dull ache in her loins now. "I am in pain," she declared. "You hurt me quite dreadfully."

"Oh dear, oh dear," he murmured. "Should we have the physician?"

"No!" Viola cried, blushing furiously.

"My dear girl, if you are truly injured we must not take chances," Julian said firmly. "Tell me if this hurts," he added, one hand slipping under the water.

Viola squirmed so violently that the tub overturned, spilling both of them in a wave of soapy water onto the floor. Viola scrambled to her feet, grabbed her dressing gown, and ran into the next room. Julian discovered her curled in a ball on the sofa. He knelt down beside her and gently pried her hands apart. "Let me see, sweetheart. Don't treat me like a stranger."

"I won't permit it," Viola said primly. "I'm perfectly all right."

Julian tugged at her legs. "Mary, don't be foolish. If you are still in pain, that could be a sign of some permanent injury. If, for example, there was blood—"

"There *was* blood!" Viola choked, panicking. "Heaps of it! Is that a bad sign?"

Julian knew perfectly well that there had been blood, but he doubted her assertion that there had been heaps of it. There had been a few streaks on his member, but none on the sheets. However, he was more interested in soothing her anxiety than in correcting her exaggerations. Her anxiety seemed real enough.

"It can be a *very* bad sign," he said very gravely. "Let me look," he added gently, applying pressure to her knees. "Let me in."

Overwrought, Viola gave up guarding her lower body, but she screwed both eyes shut and clutched her dressing gown around her shoulders as Julian gently spread her knees apart.

In order to get a better view of the lady's injury, Julian was obliged to arrange her with her bottom a little over the edge of the sofa. "I beg your pardon," he murmured courteously as he made the necessary adjustments. He spread her legs a little wider and blew gently on her sex, coaxing it to open like a rose.

Viola bit her lip and whimpered. The ache in her loins intensified almost to the point of pain. Her breasts, which, as far as she knew, were disinterested parties, were beginning to tingle too. "How does it look?" she ventured to ask. "Don't spare me."

To him, the sight was one of infinite fascination. The lips, scarlet and inflamed, to be sure, nonetheless seemed to be pouting most invitingly. "It's just as I feared," he said grimly. "You are very tender and swollen. I'd better bathe you with my handkerchief."

"I've had a bath already," she protested weakly as he went off in the direction of the dressing room.

"Yes, a hot bath. A hot bath is the very worst thing for a sore young lady."

Never in her life had Viola felt so ill-informed. Viola looked at him between her fingers as, still quite naked himself, he studiously dipped his handkerchief in a bowl of cold water. His manner was scientific and impersonal as he approached her.

At the first touch, the center of pleasure stiffened with such exquisite pain that she gasped.

"Too cold?" Julian asked solicitously—too solicitously. Viola suddenly had the sneaking suspicion that he knew precisely what effect his ministrations were having on her. And when he bent his head suddenly, his warm, moist mouth replacing the cold, wet handkerchief, she was certain of it. Outrage and need and pleasure all mingled together in sublime confusion as his soft tongue entered her swollen opening, soothing the tender flesh. Her body trembled with shock, and, even though she did not feel at all repelled, as any decent woman ought to have done, she felt obliged to protest.

"Please don't," she whispered. "It isn't nice."

He seemed not to hear her weak protests. He continued to stroke her gently with his lips and tongue. He had stroked her before in this intimate way, but only with his fingers. She had not thought anything could please her more, but she had been quite wrong. The pleasure of his driving tongue and clinging mouth was as keen as a knife's edge. Incoherently, she cried out for release, but, when he stopped suddenly, she cried out again. "No, don't stop," she pleaded humbly. "I didn't mean it."

Julian laughed softly. He had no intention of stopping until she achieved enough pleasure to erase the pain of the loss of her virginity. "You're strangling me, love," he chided her gently. Placing his hands firmly on the insides of her thighs, he loosened the hold her legs had on his neck.

The feel of his hands forcing her open, which had been so strange to Viola the night before, excited her now. It was but the work of a few seconds to drive her to the first shuddering climax of her life. Satisfaction of a kind unknown to her spread through her body, invading her from the roots of her hair to the ends of her toes. Her lover remained between her legs until the tumult subsided. Then he sat back on his heels with a very smug look on his face.

"Better?" he asked kindly.

Viola summoned her dignity. "Thank you. I think it is a little better."

"I'm afraid I am a little worse," he said apologetically. Rising to his knees, he presented her with his dark, straining member. "You *will* let me try again, won't you?"

Viola groaned. She was as weak as water, and he knew it. "You tricked me," she complained as he climbed over her. Her eyes widened as he filled her, but there was no pain, even when he had entered her completely and she swore she could feel him all the way to her navel. "Are you really inside me?" she whispered in disbelief.

Julian brought his mouth to hers as their bodies joined. "Yes, love, I really am."

"I can't believe it!"

"This is not a good beginning," he observed wryly. Slowly, he pulled his sex from its tight sheath. Then, in one hard thrust, he took her again. "Do you believe it now?"

"Oh, yes," she whispered, her head thrown back.

"And how is the pain?" he inquired, holding her haunches firmly with both hands as he thrust into her again. "Better?"

Viola flung her arms around him and hugged him tightly. "It's lovely," she confessed recklessly. "It's quite the loveliest pain I've ever had."

"You're bloody well right it is," he muttered through gritted teeth.

He was maddening her with slow, careful strokes. It took great self-control and concentration not to give in to the urge to take his own pleasure as quickly as possible, but he did not care to be likened again to an animal by his future bride. The pleasure of her snug passage was almost too much to bear. He groaned deep in his throat.

Viola was apologetic. "Was I very unkind to you this morning?" she asked, her head lolling in lazy pleasure from side to side.

"Yes, you were," he told her plainly, moving slowly between her thighs.

Viola smiled bewitchingly. "Oh, I am sorry," she purred. "I did not understand."

"And now you think you do?" he said harshly.

"Yes," Viola said happily.

Julian pulled out of her until only the very tip of his sex touched hers. "I think not," he said, and, this time, when he thrust, he pulled her sharply to him at the same time, so that he went deeper than he had before. Viola cried out as he struck her womb, but he was remorseless. "If you really understood, Mary, you would move your bottom. Like so," he added, guiding her into his stroke a little more gently. "I cannot do it for you all the time, you know."

Viola did her best. Her legs flailed over his hips; then they found a brace in the arm of the sofa. She arched against him awkwardly at first, but, as he wisely let her set the rhythm, the awkwardness soon vanished and they moved together.

Despite his best efforts to let the lady outrun him, Julian reached the end of the course before she did. Viola was perfectly content as he drew away from her, but Julian could not conceal his disappointment. "What's the matter, darling?" she cried tenderly.

"You didn't go off with me," he murmured, beginning to dress.

Viola sat up and pulled her dressing gown around her. She did not understand his dismay, but she was sorry for his disappointment. "I will try to go off with you next time," she said, in her most conciliatory tone.

"See that you do," he said sternly, but his eyes were twinkling. "And now I really must get ready for work. God knows what those fools are getting up to on the Exchange without me to lead them."

Viola laughed in disbelief. "You're not really going? Not now?"

"I must," he said, going into the dressing room. "I don't mean to keep you in shameful poverty for another day if I can help it. I must get to work."

"You worked yesterday," she complained, following him into the little room.

"I must work every day," he told her.

"Not today, surely. I thought, perhaps, you might marry me today."

Julian looked surprised. "I'm afraid that won't be possible, my love."

Viola went cold. "What?" The word fell from her lips.

"I shall marry you, of course," he told her quickly. "But, first, we must have money. One cannot buy a special license on credit, after all. Then I must find someone to marry us. That costs money, too."

"How much money?" Viola demanded.

"Let me worry about that," he said. "And, no, I don't want you pawning anything else—my pride couldn't take it. I shall have the money we need at month's end, and then we shall be able to . . . do all things we want to do," he finished awkwardly as Hudson came into the room to help his master dress.

"So long?" said Viola, oblivious to the fact that she was in Hudson's way.

"I'm afraid so, my love."

Hudson cleared his throat angrily, and Viola had no choice but to leave the room.

In a few moments, Julian emerged from the dressing room looking remarkably gentlemanlike in a brand-new suit of clothes: a dark gray, short-waisted coat with matching trousers, a peacock blue waistcoat, and a snowy white neckcloth. On his head was a curly brimmed beaver.

Viola smiled in delight. "Oh, they fit you like a glove. I was a little worried."

"Madam," he said coldly, "would you care to explain this?"

"You needed new clothes," she said. "How gentlemanlike you look," she purred, going over to him to make some minute adjustments.

"I look ridiculous."

"Not to me you don't," she said persuasively. "I've got butterflies."

"Where are my old clothes?" he demanded, refusing to be distracted. "Hudson can't find them."

"I'm afraid I had to get rid of those clothes, Dev," she told him without apology.

"What!"

"They were horrid, shocking clothes," she said defensively. "These are much better."

"The coat is too short," he complained. "And the waistcoat is garish."

"The coat is cut to show off your waistcoat and give you access to your watch," she helpfully explained. "The color of your waistcoat does wonderful things to your eyes. And your eyes do wonderful things to me," she added silkily.

"I don't even *have* a watch at the moment," he snorted. "And this putrid hat has got a curly brim! I look like a dandy!"

"Well, *I* think you look splendid," she said. "Your old hat wasn't even a true beaver! No wonder it couldn't hold its shape—or its color," she added scathingly.

"It kept my head dry."

"I doubt that very much," she drawled. "*This* hat will keep your head dry, and hold its shape in the rain. Most importantly, it will declare you to the world as a respectable gentleman."

"I'm surprised you don't put me in tall Hessian boots with twee tassels," he grumbled.

Viola frowned. "Why should I put you in Hessian boots? You are an English gentleman, I think, not a German mercenary. And I don't object to trousers. I think men should dress as sensibly as possible, and leave high fashion to the ladies."

"Thank you for that, at least," he muttered. "How much did all this *low fashion* cost?"

Viola shook her head. "It's my wedding present to you. You're not allowed to ask."

"I suppose I *could* get married in this getup," he said grudgingly. "A man shouldn't look his ordinary shabby self on his wedding day, after all."

"No, indeed," she agreed. "But I want you to be married in your uniform."

"Then what do I need *this* for?" he grumbled.

"I think you owe it to me to look the gentleman," she answered firmly. "Come to that, I think you owe it to the people you ruin. How do you think they feel being bested by a badly dressed young man? It must be humiliating."

Julian chuckled. "I'm sure you're right," he said merrily.

"Of course I'm right."

"I'll just go and put your theory to the test, shall I? Ruin a few people, and see if they like it better today than they did yesterday?"

Viola smiled. "Will you be home for luncheon?"

"I'll bring sandwiches," he promised, kissing her good-bye.

Viola spent the rest of her morning at Gambol House making her wedding plans. Lover, who simply assumed that the groom would be Lord Bamph, was only too happy to assist.

Returning to Lombard Street at noon, Viola was just in time to intercept the postman.

The London postal service was one of the marvels of the modern world. Mail was delivered six times a day with remarkable efficiency and economy. The letter Viola had sent out from Gambol House but two hours before had already made its way to Lombard Street.

"I'll take Mr Devize's mail," she said quickly, taking the letters from the postman.

As Hudson let her in, Julian appeared at the top of the stairs. "Mary! I told you to take your maid with you if you go out," he said angrily.

"It's broad daylight, Dev," she protested, taking off her gloves. "I only went out to post some letters. Didn't Hudson tell you?"

"You were gone quite some time," Julian complained.

"I couldn't resist looking in the shop windows," Viola said, walking up the stairs. "Is anything the matter?"

"Yes," he said. "My study. It's pink!"

"It's not pink," she said. "It's cerise."

"Cerise!" he said, dragging her to his study. "Madam, it is pink!" he snarled, his voice breaking from strong emotion.

The walls were undisputably, violently pink. "It will darken with age," she assured him. "Now, *this* is pink," she went on, holding up one of his letters. "The postman just delivered it."

Julian sat down at the table and began unwrapping the sandwiches he had bought. "*Two* letters," he remarked. "My cup runneth over."

"And one of them so positively pink!" Viola said coolly.

Julian chuckled. "Jealous?" He picked up his pink letter and studied it with great interest.

"Not at all," Viola replied. "I stopped using pink paper when I was ten."

Julian chuckled. "It's from my sister. I know her handwriting."

"You have a sister, do you?" she sniffed. "I don't recall reading anything about a sister."

He looked at her curiously. "Reading?"

Viola frowned slightly. She had been referring to Mr Harman's file on the young man, but, of course, it would never do for Julian to learn about that. "Hearing, I meant to say," she said quickly. "You never mentioned her. Only your brother, whose name I don't even know."

"My brother is Alexander. At one point, he tried to persuade us to call him Zander—didn't take, of course."

"I should think *not*," said Viola, joining him at the makeshift table.

"We call him Alex. As for my sister, her Christian name is Perdita, but other than that, she's perfectly charming. Upon her marriage, she became Lady Cheviot and, if her father-in-law ever dies, she will become Countess of Snowden."

"I know Cheviot!" Viola exclaimed.

"Do you, by God?" he said.

"A little," Viola said, becoming more circumspect. "He visited the duke in Yorkshire once or twice. I saw him in church. What does your sister write?"

"Perdita writes to tell me that my father is alive and well in Sussex. *She* has gone home to her husband, with my brother. She warns me, however, that my mother has returned to London."

"Was it necessary to write all this on *pink* paper?" Viola asked.

Julian laughed. "If you do not believe this is a letter from my sister, you may read it."

Viola sniffed. "Naturally, I take your word for it. And the other letter?"

Julian took up the heavy, cream-colored envelope. "I don't know the handwriting," he said curiously, breaking the seal. "Indeed, I can scarcely *read* the handwriting. I stand in awe of the postman who deciphered my direction."

"It is a very elegant, ladylike hand!" Viola objected.

"Indeed," he responded. "If by *elegant* you mean *illegible*. It appears to be from Lady Viola Gambol, but what her ladyship wishes to communicate to me remains shrouded in mystery."

"Give me that," Viola snapped, snatching it from him.

"Don't tell me you can read that chicken scratch."

Viola glared at him. "Dear Mr Devize," she said, reading her own words quite easily, "this is to advise you that I have decided not to marry Lord Bamph after all. It has come to my attention, through an unimpeachable source, that the man is an ass. Therefore, there will be no further need for your services in regard to my marriage settlement. However, I am most appreciative of your efforts and have enclosed a cheque for one hundred pounds to compensate you for your time.

And, if you have an ounce of decency, you will take your be-trothed to Gunter's for a well-deserved treat."

"She does *not* say that," Julian said, snatching it from her.

"No," Viola admitted. "But she should have."

"I see no banknote," Julian pointed out. "But I daresay her ladyship *forgot* to put it in. You'd be amazed at how often these aristocrats forget such details."

Viola frowned. "Lady Viola forgets nothing. Look in the envelope."

Julian drew out the banknote and gave a low whistle. "You did not see many of *these* in your father's almsbox, I'll war-rant."

Viola duly admired the banknote. "Not one!" she said, smiling. "Well, Dev? Does this mean we can be married sooner?"

Julian chuckled. "Yes, Mary."

"Dear Lady Viola!" Viola purred. "Is she not the soul of generosity and kindness?"

Julian snorted. "When it suits her, perhaps. The very rich are not like us, Mary," he added, touching her on the tip of her nose. "They feel no real connection to ordinary people. They have no responsibilities. They are like butterflies, flitting from one pleasure to the next."

"Lady Viola has been very kind to me over the years."

"By that you mean she has given her old clothes for many years," Julian scoffed. "She's made a charity case and a pet of you. Where was Lady Viola when you were in the clutches of Aunt Dean? At the very least, she ought to have made sure your guardian was a respectable woman. A simple inquiry would have revealed your aunt's character, which, I'm sorry to say, is well-known in London. Indeed, if her ladyship knew you had ever set foot in Mrs Dean's establishment, you would be dead to her."

"She's not like that," Viola insisted. "I know her. You don't."

"I know her kind, Mary," he replied. "These Society she-wolves are all alike."

Viola smiled faintly. "I should have thought that *you* were a great favorite of Society she-wolves," she said playfully. "I'll bet you got lots of pink letters—and *not* from your sister."

Julian snorted. "I was invited into my share of beds."

"And?" she said, scowling.

"I don't care to be a rich lady's toy," he replied. "I could have had my pick among the widows and the matrons, but, you see, I wasn't good enough to marry their daughters."

"Did you want to marry someone's daughter?" Viola asked seriously.

He shrugged. "I don't know. I was never allowed to find out. I'm a younger son, Mary. In Society, the younger son is commonly regarded as a highly useless article."

"If you take me to Gunter's this afternoon," she said seductively, "*I* shall not regard you as a highly useless article. Quite the opposite, in fact."

Julian chuckled. "Very well."

"Yes?" she said, as though fearing he was only teasing her.

"Yes," he said firmly. "Go and get your coat and bonnet. I'll get us a hack."

Twenty minutes later, Viola met him in the hall carrying Bijou. "What in God's name are you wearing?" Julian asked, his eyes wide with astonishment.

"My coat and hat," she said, pleased by his violent reaction. "The hat's an old one, but I got the coat from Mr Mordecai. It belonged to a Russian prince who committed suicide. Isn't it absolutely fabulous?" she added, preening in her leopard-skin coat.

"It's certainly eye-catching," he said grimly. "Shall we?"

The morning was sunny, but the wind was shockingly cold, and Viola was glad to have her fur coat as they ventured out. "I wonder what Lady Viola will say to that coat," he mused.

"Lady Viola will adore it," Viola laughed, before the import of his words fully registered with her. "What do you mean? Lady Viola is not likely to see my coat, is she?"

"Well, it's on our way," he replied, looking out of the window.

"What's on our way?" she asked sharply.

"Gambol House," he answered. "Naturally, I must pay my respects. I doubt her ladyship will condescend to see me, but I must pay my respects all the same. How would it look if I simply drove past her house, knowing she's in London?"

"What makes you think she's in London?" Viola scoffed. "Surely she is in Yorkshire."

"Her letter arrived in the twopenny post," he explained. "Ergo, she must be in London."

"How very clever of you," Viola murmured, a little sourly.

"You're not afraid of Lady Viola, are you?" he teased her. "You were so vigorous in your defense of her."

"Of course I am not afraid of her," Viola said, her mind racing. It was the servants' reactions that she feared. She did not trust the footmen in particular to keep their mouths shut. Any one of them might bawl out her name at her first appearance.

The doors of Gambol House opened as the hack came to a halt. To her relief, Lover himself walked out. "Don't mind that fellow," Julian said, patting her hand. "He looks like a duke, but I assure you he's only the butler."

Julian left the hack first, turning back to offer Viola his assistance.

"Good morning, Mr Devize," Lover said pleasantly. "We did not expect to see you this morning. His grace is still out of town."

Julian was a little surprised that the duke's butler remembered him by name. "My fiancée and I have come to pay my respects to Lady Viola," he said. "I understand she is in London," he added.

"Your fiancée?" Lover said politely.

"No, Lady Viola. This is my betrothed. May I present Miss Andrews?"

As Viola stepped out of the hackney carriage, she was able to warn the butler with a slight shake of her head. At the sight of Lover, the bichon in her arms began to squirm and wag her tail.

Lover's countenance betrayed not the slightest surprise. He favored her with an old-fashioned bow, sticking one leg out before him as he bent low from the waist. "Miss Andrews."

"Perhaps her ladyship is indisposed," Viola suggested.

"Her ladyship is indeed indisposed," Lover agreed.

"Oh, that's too bad," said Viola. "What a pity. I did so wish to see her ladyship. But if she is indisposed, we'll have to leave cards."

Lover accepted their visiting cards with great solemnity. "I will see that her ladyship gets them," he promised.

"Perhaps I'll call again tomorrow," said Viola. "You never know."

# Chapter Thirteen

Olivia, Duchess of Berkshire, was snoozing in her barouche in Berkeley Square when her paid companion, Miss Shrimpton, suddenly exclaimed, "Oh dear! Lord Edgerton just walked into a lamppost!"

Eager for any relief to boredom, the duchess fumbled for the lorgnette hung about her neck and opened her sharp green eyes. A tall girl in a leopard-skin coat was walking up the street toward Gunter's. She wore the exotic fur with perfect ease, and her hat was a fearsome affair: black, yet somehow sheer, with a sweeping brim and six peacock sword feathers arranged across the narrow brim like a cat's whiskers. The duchess knew hats, and this was one that made her tingle.

The duchess's eyes narrowed as she studied the newcomer. There was an alluring sway to her walk that was almost predatory. She made an unforgettable impression; it was as if a hungry leopard had suddenly appeared in Berkeley Square.

At the girl's side was a young man wearing an excellent beaver hat, a good coat, and trousers. Other than the trousers, there seemed to be nothing extraordinary about this young man. The duchess might not have noticed him at all had it not been for the fact that from time to time the girl tickled the side of his face with the sword feathers on her hat. Apart from the young man, the young woman's only other accessory was a fluffy little white dog with a diamond collar.

The duchess was perplexed; she was quite sure she knew everyone worth knowing. The girl in the leopard-skin coat obviously fell into that category, and, yet, the duchess did not know her. And that walk! "I know I've seen that walk before," she muttered angrily.

"Good heavens!" Miss Shrimpton shrieked. "Now *Lord Bromleigh* has walked into a lamppost! I've always said the lampposts in Berkeley Square are peculiarly placed. *Now*, perhaps, something will be done about it!"

The duchess couldn't be bothered to laugh at Lords Edgerton and Bromleigh. "Who is she?" she muttered in frustration. "Where did she get that ridiculous coat? No one offered it to *me*," she pouted. "And who the devil makes her hats? I pay a great deal of money to have the best hats in London, but it appears my money has been wasted! Who can she be? I must know!"

"Who, Your Grace?" Miss Shrimpton twittered.

The duchess spared her a withering look. Miss Shrimpton was slow-witted, respectable, and deadly dull. The duchess would have preferred a livelier, saucier companion, but she had never been able to find one; everyone was afraid of her. "Guess," she drawled.

Miss Shrimpton stared into every corner of Berkeley Square until she came across something unfamiliar. "The girl in the spotted coat?" she ventured timidly. "She must be foreign. Mercy me! Lord Bromleigh has walked into the lamppost *again*—the *same* lamppost!"

The duchess clucked her tongue unfeelingly. "That's going to leave a mark. Be a dear, Shrimpy—run and ask Princess Esterhazy who that girl is."

The wife of the Hungarian ambassador was parked in her own barouche a little farther down the green. Miss Shrimpton obediently scampered off.

At about the same time the duchess was noticing her, Viola was noticing another lady.

"Who," she said, elbowing her companion in the ribs, "is that horrid old dame in the barouche?"

Julian snorted. "You'll have to be more specific, I'm afraid."

Viola laughed. The green in the middle of Berkeley Square did indeed seem to be brimming with matronly grandams in barouches. "The one in the horrid purple bonnet. Everyone else has the good sense to stare at us. *She* is trying desperately to pretend we don't exist."

"Good Lord! It's my mother," said Julian, turning abruptly. "Come, Mary! I'll take you to Gunter's another day, I promise."

"Nonsense," said Viola, digging in her heels. "I want to meet my future mother-in-law."

"No, you don't," he said curtly.

"Dev!"

"I don't wish to overstate the matter," Julian said, "but my mother is a gorgon."

"Julian!"

"I'm quite serious. My mother will not scruple to treat you

with the utmost discourtesy. Let us take the hint, pretend not to see *her*, and slip quietly away. We'll do this another time."

Viola laughed. "Introduce me to your mother at once, sir, or I shall accidentally drop Bijou's leash!" she threatened. "You will look awfully silly trying to catch her on the green."

"You wouldn't!"

"Darling, you know I will," she replied. "I'm quite ruthless, you know. Your mother may be as rude as she likes. I shall be delightful. Then we will have our tea at Gunter's as planned."

Julian succumbed to her charm, if not to her threat to loose the dog, and reluctantly brought her over to his mother's barouche. The baroness turned a gimlet eye upon her son as he drew close to her vehicle. Julian tipped his hat to her and said quietly, "Good afternoon, my lady. May I present Miss Andrews to you? Miss Andrews and I are engaged to be married."

Viola sank into a graceful curtsey. The baroness did not look at Viola. Instead, she turned away deliberately and called out a greeting to Lady Arbogast, who was seated in the next vehicle with her charming daughter.

Julian was furious.

Viola's cheeks reddened. "Well!" she gasped.

"Do you still want to go to Gunter's?" Julian asked her quietly.

"Of course, my darling," she said brightly. "I'm dying to try one of their famous ices. Perhaps we will find your mama on the menu!" she laughed, leading him away.

Unless accompanied by a gentleman, the fashionable ladies of London preferred to remain in their carriages outside of Gunter's and have their treats brought out to them by a waiter. Consequently, the confectionary was more crowded outside than within. Viola was easily able to secure the table in the big window. From this vantage, she could see and be seen by the baroness, and the two ladies could ignore one another to their heart's content.

*Impudent strumpet,* thought the baroness.

*Insolent old hag,* thought Viola.

The Duchess of Berkshire, and, indeed, everyone in Berkeley Square, had witnessed the snub. "She must know them," cried the duchess as Miss Shrimpton returned from Princess Esterhazy. "She would not bother to give them the Cut Direct if she did not know them."

Plump Miss Shrimpton was quite out of breath. "But her highness does *not* know them!" she cried. "However, Lady Arbogast saw her yesterday in the Parade Grounds, and she is most *definitely* foreign! She was wearing a black silk picture hat with ostrich plumes!"

"The devil take the Arbogast!" snapped the duchess. "I am talking of the Baroness Devize. Go at once and give her my compliments, Shrimpy, and tell her I would be delighted if she would join me in Gunter's."

Miss Shrimpton blinked rapidly. "Lady Devize? But, Your Grace, you despise the baroness! You said she was worse than cold soup in winter."

The duchess snapped her fingers for her footman. "Go at once and tell Lady Devize that one desires her to join one in Gunter's," she commanded.

The footman could not quite believe his ears. In all his years of service, the duchess had never left her carriage to enter Gunter's establishment. "*Inside* Gunter's, Your Grace?"

"Quicker!" said the duchess impatiently, flinging open the door of her barouche with her own hands. Kicking down the steps before her footman knew what was happening, she jumped lightly to the ground. "Wait in the barouche," she instructed the bewildered Shrimpton.

As though afraid her quarry might escape, the duchess took up a position outside the window while she waited for the baroness. To the duchess's surprise and irritation, the young woman's face did not suffer from a closer inspection. She was a true beauty, not one of those everyday pretty girls that England produces every year like a crop of identical roses. Her face had character: flashing dark eyes, an arrogant little nose, and plump red lips. There was something familiar about that striking face, but the duchess still could not place her.

Viola glanced up from her menu and discovered a tiny, middle-aged woman with hawklike features, hungry green eyes, and iron gray hair staring back at her. The stranger's bonnet was lined in the same pale green satin of her afternoon dress and decorated with a stunning arrangement of feathers. Her gown was directly from the pages of *La Belle Assemblee*, Viola noted with amusement. "Do you know that woman?" she asked Julian.

Julian glanced at the Duchess of Berkshire. She looked like a scrap of a female in a weird hat to him. Immediately, he covered Viola's hand protectively with his own. "Inbred lunatic," he pronounced. "Sadly, the West End is full of them. Shall we change our table?"

"Oh, no," said Viola, giving the lunatic a polite nod. "That's the best hat I've seen in London, apart from my own. I would prefer it, however," she went on thoughtfully, "if the lining did not match her gown *quite* so perfectly."

"That troubles me as well," he said gravely, but she knew he was really laughing.

"Oh, you," she said fondly.

"No, you," he replied in kind.

They had both removed their gloves, and the simple act of holding hands thrilled them both, while shocking the other patrons. Alarmed by such risqué behavior, the waiter hurried over. "I'm afraid we're going to need a little more time," Julian told him apologetically.

"Would you mind awfully taking my bichon for a tiny, little walk?" Viola asked the waiter sweetly. Judging that her smile might not be enough to convince the young man, she slipped him a guinea along with the leash. *That*, certainly, did the trick.

Outside, the duchess barked at the baroness. "Hurry up, woman! I haven't got all day."

"You wished to see me, Your Grace?" Baroness Devize gasped in her eagerness. As always, she was astonished by the other woman's diminutive stature. The Duchess of Berkshire seemed so much bigger in one's thoughts, somehow.

The tiny duchess tapped on the window with her walking stick. "Well? Who are they?" she demanded in her deep, gravelly voice. "The girl in the spotted coat, and that rather good-looking young man? I want names, and I want them now."

"I have no idea, Your Grace," the baroness protested.

"Nonsense!" rasped the duchess. "You would not have given the Cut Direct to *strangers*. So who are they? Out with it, woman. I shall find out anyway, you know."

The baroness sighed. "That young man, I'm ashamed to say, is my younger son, the wretch who broke Lady Jersey's bank. His father and I have disowned him, of course," she added quickly. "I cannot think what possessed him to try to scrape an acquaintance with me."

The duchess snorted. She had a low opinion of people who disowned their children, especially for such a ridiculous reason. "Who is the girl?" she demanded.

"He had the temerity to introduce her to me," the baroness complained. "I'm afraid I wasn't paying close attention. I could tell at once she was a grasping hussy."

"Good! You can present her to me!" barked the duchess, barreling into Gunter's with one startled baroness in tow.

"Don't look now," said Viola. "But here comes your mama. And the well-hatted lunatic is with her," she added with a chuckle.

"Bloody hell," Julian muttered. "What do they want?"

"Be nice," Viola advised him, studying her menu. "What looks good to you, darling?" she asked as the two grandams drew up to their table, clearing their throats for immediate attention.

"Pineapple, I think," Julian replied, drawing Viola's free hand to his lips and nibbling at her fingertips. "What looks good to *you*, my sweet?"

"It all looks good to me. Now, where has that waiter got to?" Viola wondered, looking around the duchess and baroness without seeing either of them. "I do hope our little mop hasn't gotten away from him."

"Julian!" Baroness Devize shrilled, taking the young couple completely by surprise.

Julian leaped to his feet. "Mama!" he warmly exclaimed, giving his mother a smacking kiss. "What a pleasant surprise! What brings you to Gunter's?"

"The duchess and I have been standing here this age, Julian," the baroness admonished him. "Where are your manners?"

"I'm afraid I mistook you for someone else," Julian apologized. "Someone to whom I have never been introduced. Madam, you remember Miss Andrews, of course. Won't you join us? We were just about to have ice."

"*More* ice, you should say," Viola drawled. "We had some *lovely* ice standing alongside your barouche, Baroness. I shall never forget its unique flavor."

Julian's mother glared at them, helpless with rage. "Your Grace!" she said quickly, as the duchess cleared her throat. "Pray, allow me to present my younger son, Julian."

Julian obligingly bowed over the duchess's scrawny hand. "I confess I thought you were a lunatic, ma'am, but my beloved assures me that your hat is the best she's seen in London."

The baroness's face turned pink with indignation, but the duchess took it all in stride. She liked impudent young men, provided they were good-looking, as this one certainly was. "Yes, your beloved, Mr Devize," she said eagerly, her eyes darting all over Viola as if looking for a way into an impregnable fortress. "I know you, don't I?" she asked, addressing Viola directly. "You seem familiar to me, child."

"Not *overly* familiar, I trust," Viola replied coolly, proving that she was at least as impudent as Julian. "One hates to be overly familiar, particularly before one has been introduced."

The duchess bristled at the implied criticsim of her own behavior. However, the girl's coat and hat were far too important to let anything divert her from her purpose. "Be good enough to introduce your fiancée to me," she commanded Julian.

"With pleasure," said Julian. "This angelic creature is Miss Andrews. Mary, you have just been accosted by the Duchess of Berkshire."

"My attackers are not usually so charmingly attired," Viola remarked, eyeing the duchess's pale green ensemble with an experienced eye. "Plate Number thirty-six of the January edition of *La Belle Assemblee*, if I am not mistaken?"

Scowling, the duchess plunked her skinny bottom into the chair recently vacated by Julian. "I changed the fabric and tucked a lace," she said testily.

"I am glad to hear it," Viola said warmly. "It's so important to dress appropriately for one's time of life, don't you think, Duchess?"

The duchess's face was rigid. "What time of life are *you* dressing for, my dear?"

"Three o'clock," Viola replied, smiling. "It's the most difficult time of life, is it not? Too late for luncheon, yet too early for tea. My mother always said if one can dress for three o'clock, one can dress for anything, and I have found it to be perfectly true."

"Hmmph!" said the duchess. Angrily, she drew off her gloves and picked up her menu.

Julian, meanwhile, had brought two more chairs. His mother sat down next to the duchess, and he sat down next to Viola.

"You speak English rather well, Miss Andrews," she said, smiling nastily at Viola.

"I owe it all to my governess," Viola explained. "It took her

nearly two years to teach me the language, but, then, mine
was a difficult birth. I didn't walk for almost a year."

The duchess scowled at her menu as Julian tried un-
successfully to hide a smile.

"But I understand you are foreign, Miss Andrews," the
baroness accused. "Lady Arbogast was certain you are foreign, and your attire would seem to confirm it."

"Not at all, I assure you, Baroness."

The baroness's lip curled. "I see. It is an affectation, to
draw more attention to yourself."

"There *is* some Italian on my mother's side," Viola volunteered. "My great-great-great-great-great-great-grandfather
was a musician in the court of Mary, Queen of Scots. He was
murdered, of course."

"Naturally," said the duchess, glancing up from the menu.

The baroness closed her eyes in mortification. "Italian,"
she murmured in a stifled voice. "Musicians. Murder. Julian,
are you quite mad?"

Following the Duchess of Berkshire's lead, others of the
fashionable set had elected to descend from their carriages
and enter Gunter's as well. There was a veritable stampede for
the best tables. The best tables, of course, were those located
within earshot of the duchess's table. Preeminent amongst the
new arrivals was Lady Jersey. "Olivia," she greeted the
duchess coldly. "All alone, I see," she added in a cutting tone
just as Lady Devize opened her mouth to speak.

Julian, who had gotten to his feet at the lady's approach,
now decided not to bother and sat down again. Viola regarded
the famous Countess of Jersey with interest.

"Is this the lady whose bank you broke?" she asked Julian.

Even though she could not hear or see Viola, Lady Jersey
stiffened. "Would you not care to join *my* party, Olivia? I *do*
hate to see you sitting at an empty table like this."

"Go away, Sally," the duchess said impatiently. "I'm form-
ing a new acquaintance."

With her head high, Lady Jersey retired to the next table. Dressed in one of the more daring, low-cut, high-waisted gowns of the Season, the countess steadfastly refused to see anything beyond her own little fiefdom, while the more curious members of her entourage stared at the enemy through their quizzing glasses and filed regular reports.

Mindful of her audience, the baroness bared her teeth at Julian.

"You will be glad to know that your father has made a miraculous recovery while you have been romping in London with your . . . friend." Her blue eyes touched Viola coldly.

"Recovery from what?" Julian replied, placing a protective hand on Viola's shoulder. The velvety fur of her coat seemed to caress him back. "According to Perdita, he was never sick. It was just some ridiculous test."

"When did you see your sister?" demanded the baroness. "I might have known you'd follow us to Sussex! You have no regard for your father or me or anyone else."

"I didn't see my sister. She wrote to me. Perhaps she did not realize you meant to tell me the good news yourself when you returned to London," he added sarcastically.

The baroness sniffed. "Don't worry, Julian. I explained to your father that you were too busy at present to answer a deathbed summons. Indeed, I had no idea how busy you *were*," she added with another scathing glance at Viola.

"Julian works too hard," said Viola. "If he didn't have to eat, I'd never see him."

Julian kissed her hand. "That is not true, Mary. If I did not have to work, I would spend every waking moment with you. And, when we are married . . ." He leaned and murmured something in her ear, causing his mother to clear her throat frantically. Viola giggled.

"Julian has never mentioned you before, Miss Anderson," she said piercingly. "How long have you been engaged to my son?"

"Oh, I don't believe in long engagements," Viola replied.

"Why not?" the baroness demanded. "Do you feel some special need for haste, Miss Anderson? And your parents approve, do they? Most curious."

Viola eyed her frostily.

"Miss Andrews," Julian corrected his mother sternly. "Her name is Andrews, not Anderson, Mother. But, then, you know that already, don't you? Mary's parents are both dead," he went on quietly. "Naturally, I wish to provide her with a home as soon as possible. Is that not an excuse for haste?"

"You must have a guardian, Miss Andrews," the duchess remarked shrewdly.

"Not at all, Duchess," Viola replied. "I am twenty-one."

The duchess's eyes narrowed. "But you cannot live alone, girl," she snapped. "Especially not in London. Where *are* you in London? Who is your chaperone? What is your direction?"

"Let me think," said Viola.

"Yes, let me think, too," Julian muttered.

"You don't know your direction?" cried the baroness.

"I'm afraid London is a bit of a mare's nest to me," Viola apologized. "It's my first time here, you see. When I first saw—what was it—Fleet Street, I think, I thought the people were rioting! I quite expected the soldiers to come out to suppress them."

"You must know where you live, gel," the baroness insisted.

"Let me help you," the duchess offered. "Now, which is your park, Miss Andrews? Hyde Park? Green Park? St James's Park? Regent's Park?"

"I don't think there *is* a park," said Viola. "Is there, Dev?"

"No park!" the two older ladies squawked in unison.

"That cannot be," said the baroness. "Not unless you are in the City, or Cheapside, or . . . or I know not what!"

"I wish I knew London better," said Viola with a pretty little shrug.

"If you cannot remember *where*, then you must recall *with whom*," said the duchess. "Come now, Miss Andrews. You must live with *someone*. Who is it?"

"Well recently I have been visiting Lady Viola Gambol," said Viola, seeking refuge in some version of the truth. "Her brother, the Duke of Fanshawe, has a small house here in London. It's nothing to Fanshawe, of course."

"Lady Viola is in London, is she?" the duchess said thoughtfully. "There was not a drop about it in the newspapers. Has she been presented at Court? No, of course she hasn't—I would have heard," she muttered irritably. "And what is your connection to the Gambol family, Miss Andrews?"

"My connection?" Viola echoed blankly. "Well . . . I'm from Yorkshire. So are they."

"Yes. And?" said the duchess.

"Mary's father was the Vicar of Gambolthwaite," Julian intervened. "The Duke of Fanshawe gave him the living. Lady Viola has always been very kind to Mary."

"We were inseparable as children, and we are still very good friends," said Viola.

"I see," said the baroness. "And did Lady Viola give you that coat? I must say, I'm surprised. Personally, I hate to see persons of low rank giving themselves an air of fashion."

"Well, she didn't get it in London," the duchess grumbled. "It would have been offered to me first. I never saw it in any of the shops."

"But I *did* get it in London," said Viola, her eyes twinkling. "I found it in a pawnshop."

The baroness looked nauseous. "A what?"

"Pawnshop. It once belonged to a Russian prince who committed suicide. The coat, not the shop, of course," she added.

If the duchess was repulsed, she made no sign of it. "And the hat?"

"From Lady Viola. I believe it was her mother's."

"The duchess died ten years ago," the baroness protested.

"Really, Miss Andrews, a ten-year-old hat?" She tittered derisively. "No one wears a hat like that any more."

"A good hat never goes out of fashion," Viola said firmly. "Did you know the late Duchess of Fanshawe?" she asked curiously.

The baroness snorted. "Fortunately, no. I was attending the Queen at Frogmore during Miss Lyon's season. Miss Lyon was never invited to Frogmore."

"I was at the wedding," said the duchess, looking at Viola with hooded eyes. "Fanshawe and Berkshire were old friends. She was a vision in white satin and French lace. She had the most alluring walk, I remember. Everyone was in love with her, including your George, Baroness," she added dryly.

"Really?" Viola said faintly.

"May I see your ring?" the duchess asked her.

"My ring?" Viola repeated blankly.

"Your engagement ring, Miss Andrews. May I see it?"

"I've not yet bought it, Duchess," Julian said defensively. "I've been busy."

"You're not busy now," the duchess told him. "Why don't you run along and buy it for the girl now? She seems to be worthy of such a token."

"Yes, why not, Dev?" said Viola. "You're so decisive, I know you won't take long, and I shall be quite safe here with these two dear ladies."

"I cannot leave you," Julian objected, astonished that such a thing had even been suggested. "They may *look* harmless, but, believe me, they will rip you to shreds the moment I'm gone," he murmured in her ear.

"Of course you can leave her," said the duchess. "Your mother and I will look after Miss Andrews very well, young man. It's only three o'clock. You've plenty of time to buy a ring. We will wait for you."

"That's very kind of you, Your Grace," said Julian. "But Mary and I can choose her ring *after* we have enjoyed our ices. We'll go together. And here is the waiter," he added enthusiastically as the young man returned with Viola's bichon.

"Look how tired she is!" Viola exclaimed in dismay, cuddling the contented puppy. "Oh, Dev! We couldn't ask her to walk another step. Indeed, to confess the truth, I'm rather tired myself. Couldn't I sit here and rest while you get my ring?"

"Don't you want to choose it?" he said sharply.

"Surprise me."

"Julian," his mother said shrilly, "you will go at once and buy this dear child her engagement ring. I insist."

"Really, Dev," Viola said gently. "We're just going to talk about the latest fashions. You'd be bored as wood. I'm afraid if you stay," she continued ominously, "you will be forced to know more about ladies' hats, shoes, and dresses than is strictly good for a man."

Faced with the ultimate threat to masculinity, Julian began to waver. If there was anything more excruciatingly dull than listening to a group of ladies discuss their frills and furbelows, he, mercifully, had never discovered it. "Heaven forbid," he murmured. "But I don't like leaving you. Are you quite sure you'll be all right?" he asked, searching her face for some secret signal begging him to stay at her side and defend her from these two scaly dragons.

"I shall be perfectly all right," she assured him with a brilliant smile. "I always find the society of my own sex quite invigorating. When one talks to a man one scarcely exercises the brain at all."

"Take my card to Mr Grey in Bond Street," the duchess said decisively. Whipping out her silver pencil, she scrawled a brief message on the back of her card. "He will wait on you personally *and* work within your budget," she added.

Julian felt as though he were throwing an innocent lamb to the wolves, but, with all three ladies determined to be rid of him, he could not contrive a way to stay without creating embarrassment. "I shall be back as soon as I possibly can," he assured Viola.

"Darling!" she said, caressing him with her voice. "If you bring me back a perfect, emerald-cut, six-carat diamond, I won't even know you're gone."

As he paused in the doorway, she kissed her fingertips and waved.

Immediately upon his departure, the baroness opened the hostilities. "I am not accustomed to sharing my table with dogs, Miss Andrews," she said severely.

"I find it hard to believe," Viola replied sweetly, arranging the little white dog on her lap, "that this is your first bitch. However, if it is so, what can I say? I am honored." Bijou wagged her curly white plume of a tail, radiating unconditional love to everyone in the room, whether they deserved it or not. Viola scratched her gently under her diamond collar as the baroness slowly turned a dangerous shade of reddish purple.

"I believe we are ready to order," the duchess said to the waiter, who had been standing at the ready for quite some time. "Miss Andrews?"

In a gesture borrowed from Julian, Viola kept her eyes on the menu while lifting an index finger. "I'll have a small crème de menthe," she told the waiter at length. "And you, Duchess?"

The duchess looked sour. She had wanted to order the crème de menthe, but now, of course, she could not. "One small black currant," she snapped.

"And you, Baroness?" Viola inquired, mediating quite unnecessarily.

"One small licorice," said Julian's mother. "And you will kindly stop addressing me as 'Baroness,' Miss Andrews. I am properly addressed as 'my lady.' And, for your information, the Duchess of Berkshire is properly addressed as 'Your Grace.' I suppose such niceties are not in play in the wilds of Yorkshire, but you are in civilization now."

"If *I* were a duchess, I should want to be called Duchess as much as possible," Viola replied. "Do unto others, and all that sort of thing. That's in the Bible, Baroness."

"I wouldn't know," Lady Devize said sweetly. "*My* father was not a vicar."

"Your son nearly was," Viola pointed out calmly. "You must have been so relieved when Julian refused to take holy orders."

The baroness stiffened. "That was his father's idea. *I* wanted Julian to make a brilliant marriage. But that's all ruined now, so you might as well take him, my dear."

"I'm so pleased to have your blessing, Baroness," Viola laughed. "I was beginning to think you did not approve of me!"

"You should have put your younger son in the army," interrupted the duchess. "That is what I did with *mine*." Her green eyes drilled into Viola. "Simon looks very handsome in his uniform, too. He's a lieutenant-colonel in the Royal Horse Guards, you know."

"Never heard of it," Viola sniffed.

"But you have not been in Town long, Miss Andrews," the baroness pointed out. "That much is obvious by the way that you dress."

"Thank you for the compliment," Viola replied.

"Oh? You do not think much of our London fashions?" the duchess demanded.

"Are you qualified to judge?" the baroness wanted to know.

"I know what I like," Viola replied, "and I know what I don't like. In this room there is a great deal of the latter and very little of the former. Take the lady over my left shoulder. Could she not benefit from a well-constructed foundation garment?"

The duchess gave a startled laugh, which she quickly disguised as a violent cough. The lady over Viola's left shoulder let out an indignant squawk.

"I vow, it's like the sand without the hourglass," Viola went on loudly.

"Lady Jersey is one of my oldest and dearest friends," the duchess said severely.

"Yes, I see you trying not to laugh. For myself, I never laugh at a tragedy."

The baroness glared at Viola. "Lady Jersey is one of the Patronesses of Almack's. She is . . . Lady Jersey *is* Society!"

Viola snorted. "In that case, Society needs a corset. Now, what are those lines from Shelley?" she continued, oblivious to the gasps from every corner of the room. "I never quote poetry, but I'm afraid I can't resist. 'Round the decay of that colossal wreck, boundless and bare, the lone and level sands stretch far away.'" Bijou yapped appreciatively, but Viola wrinkled her nose. "No, that doesn't quite fit, does it? *Those* sands are not level. They are shifting sands, and, when she walks—Oh! a sandstorm."

The duchess's face was almost as purple as the black-currant ice the waiter placed before her. The baroness was ashen. "Miss Andrews, she is sitting right behind you!"

"Someone should tell the poor thing she looks like an anatomy lesson." Viola shrugged. "Nobody wants to see a lady's bosom go for a walk without her. I vow, the waist of her dress is directly under her armpits!"

The baroness sneered. "That happens to be the very latest fashion from Paris, Miss Andrews. But I don't suppose you see much of Parisian sophistication in the wilds of Yorkshire."

Viola laughed gently. "I want my waist where God put it, not Paris. We won the war, ladies. Of course the French are bitter. Of course they want us to look as ridiculous as possible. There is a place for chaos, ladies, but it is not between a woman's neck and knees."

"Is your figure as bad as that, Miss Andrews?" the Baroness inquired solicitously.

Viola smiled. "How is your ice, baroness?"

"Delicious," said the baroness, and, to the duchess's acute

disappointment, the young woman seemed content to leave it at that.

"You are a young woman of decided opinion, I see," she said. "You do not like this Season's silhouette. What do you think of the hats?"

"One can only assume they must be ugly by design," Viola replied carelessly. "There can't be so many unhappy accidents in one place at one time."

"Young woman, I am known for my hats," the duchess said coldly.

Viola studied the older woman's bonnet with a grave expression. "This one *just* misses the mark for me, I'm afraid."

The duchess bristled. "What is the matter with my hat, Miss Andrews? Do tell."

"It's a very minor flaw, Duchess," Viola assured her. "Hardly worth mentioning. But since you ask, I would not have lined your bonnet in the same fabric as your dress. I'm afraid it looks as though you scrimped a little leftover fabric from your seamstress, waste not, want not."

The duchess noisily set down her spoon. "I have lost my appetite," she announced.

"Who can eat with this mongrel staring at us with its greedy little eyes," the baroness agreed.

Viola hugged her dog protectively. "You're not a mongrel, are you, Bijou?"

"Well, it's not a poodle or a Pomeranian," the duchess said grumpily. "What is it?"

"She's a bichon, of course," Viola said. "Isn't she adorable? Julian gave her to me."

The baroness sniffed. "No one carries a bichon anymore, Miss Andrews. I'm sorry to inform you, but that breed fell out of favor around the time of the French Revolution. Nowadays, they run wild in the gutters of Europe. Though I understand they are becoming quite popular in circuses and county fairs. You are sadly passé, my dear."

Shocked, Viola could do nothing more than raise a brow. In any civilized discussion, one's dogs and one's children were understood to be off-limits.

The baroness smiled. "Miss Andrews, you are not eating your ice," she said smugly. "Is it not to your liking? Shall I call the waiter for you?"

"I'll do it myself," said Viola.

Viola spoke gently, so as not to hurt the waiter. He was, after all, an innocent bystander. "I'm sure it's my fault for having such a sensitive palate," she apologized, "but I'm afraid this is *not* what I ordered. Why, my bichon wouldn't touch it, and she absolutely adores crème de menthe. *This*," she went on, nudging her glass toward the waiter, "has a flavor one doesn't care to describe. Would you be good enough to taste it?"

The waiter did so, and his face flushed with mortification. "I beg your pardon, madam!" he cried. "It seems you have received the licorice by mistake. It is also green, you understand."

"It nearly made *me* green," said Viola. "Please take it away."

"Good heavens, Baroness," the duchess said contemptuously. "Can't you tell the difference between licorice and crème de menthe? The dog can."

Viola gasped. "Oh! You mean the baroness got *my* crème de menthe, and I got *her* licorice? How awkward!"

"Nonsense," said the baroness, turning bright pink. "I thoroughly enjoyed my licorice!"

Impatiently, the duchess tasted the dish. "Crème de menthe," she declared. "Baroness, you owe this young lady an apology. You ate her ice."

"I beg your pardon, Miss Andrews," the baroness spat through her teeth.

"I will return immediately with madam's crème de menthe," the waiter said.

"Never mind," said Viola, a smile spreading across her face. "Here is Julian with my diamond. Lord, isn't he handsome!" she couldn't help adding.

Julian approached the table with caution. His mother looked as though she had a lemon permanently wedged between her lips, but Mary was smiling, and that was all he cared about.

"Is everything all right?" he asked her.

"If I were a cat, I'd purr," Viola assured him. "May I see my ring, please?"

Julian was quite pleased with himself as he place the beautiful emerald ring on her finger, but nothing could exceed Viola's pleasure upon seeing that unquestionably green stone. "Julian! I absolutely adore it!" she cried, hiding her hand behind her back.

Julian smiled at her fondly. "Quite reasonably priced, too."

"Do let us see," said the duchess. "Ah! An *emerald*. How charming."

"Yes. Dev! How did you secretly know what I wanted?" Viola marveled.

"You told me to get you an emerald, my heart, and I got you an emerald," he replied. "Have you quite finished your ice, my love? It's time I got you home. Er . . . Lady Viola will think you've been kidnapped."

Viola instantly handed him the dog and quickly put on her gloves.

When they had departed, the duchess turned to the baroness and said imperiously, "That is a perfectly insufferable young woman. Rarely have I ever encountered so much arrogance and conceit, so much insolence, so much disdain for the opinions of others. Not in a female, anyway. I shall never forget what she said about poor Lady Jersey—and poor Sally within earshot, too!"

"The audacity!" the baroness agreed vehemently. "I shall never forgive her for criticizing your excellent hat, Duchess."

The duchess bristled. "She did not even *mention* your hat, Alexandra," she reminded the other woman. "And what she did n*ot* say spoke volumes."

"As you say, she is insufferable, Your Grace."

"Under no circumstances are you to allow your son to marry that vixen," the duchess commanded. "I forbid it. I don't care if he *has* been disowned. If he marries that girl, I shall be extremely angry with you."

"Let me assure Your Grace," cried the baroness, "Julian will never marry that impudent female! You have my word."

"If I am not mistaken," sniffed the duchess, "they will need a special license if they are to wed. You had better take steps to see that they do not get one, and, as I do not expect that young man to drag his feet, you had better take those steps sooner rather than later. *Now*, in fact."

The baroness jumped to her feet. "Yes, Your Grace."

The duchess left Gunter's at a pace more befitting a woman of her rank, and was fortunate enough to meet Lady Jersey on the way out. "What interesting company you keep, Olivia," sneered the countess. "And what an *economical* hat."

"I wish you could have joined me at my empty table, my dear," replied the duchess. "Were you able to follow the conversation at all?"

Two bright spots of color appeared in Lady Jersey's cheeks. "Certainly not," she snapped.

"Pity," said the duchess.

# Chapter Fourteen

Lord Simon Ascot did not often entertain women overnight in his rooms at the Albany, but Miss Rogers was an extremely talented young actress; for her he set aside his principles and made an exception. It was simply sheer bad luck that his mother should choose to visit him on this particular morning. Neither his lordship nor Miss Rogers stirred when the bed curtains were unceremoniously swept aside, but when the windows were laid bare, and white April light shot into the room, the desired effect was achieved.

Simon sat up and roared, his hair in disarray. "Hawkins!" he bawled at his manservant. "What the devil are you about?"

"Is that any way to greet your mother?" the duchess said in her dry voice.

As wise as she was talented, Miss Rogers unobtrusively seized the bedsheet and silently crawled out of the room. Naturally, the duchess chose not to see the actress; her grace had seated herself decorously near the fire and was busily arranging the skirts of her smartly striped costume.

Hawkins, meanwhile, had brought his lordship's dressing gown, and all Simon had to do was slip into it. "Mother," he said genially, coming to kiss her powdered cheek. "You look absolutely radiant. To what do I owe this unexpected pleasure?"

"I have met the girl you are going to marry," the duchess replied without preamble. "I thought you'd like to know."

Simon frowned as he leaned against the mantelpiece. "The Arbogast is too presumptuous. I have not proposed to her pretty little daughter, nor is a trick like this likely to compel me."

"I do not refer to the Arbogast," his mother retorted. "I never take your flirtations seriously. I am talking about the girl who will lead you to the altar and make a man of you."

"Am I not a man?" Simon wondered.

"You are a child," said his mother. "A spoiled, wilful child. You lack ambition, Simon. The British Empire doesn't run itself, you know. We need *men* to run it. The old breed are dying off. There are places of power opening up every day. I want you to sell out and stand for Parliament. Your brother can give you one of his pocket boroughs."

"Politics?" Simon shook his head mockingly. "You know I faint at the sight of blood."

"That must have made Waterloo very tiresome for you!" the duchess snapped, then instantly apologized. "I'm sorry,

Simon. I know you don't like to talk about the war. But if you marry this girl, you will be Prime Minister within five years. I give you my word."

"I'd rather be a dentist. Less gruesome."

The duchess sighed. "When you meet her, you will understand. She's beautiful, of course, but I wouldn't waste your time if she were only that. By this time next year, with or without you, *she* will be running Society. She will set the fashions. She will choose the entertainments. She will determine who is in and who is out. The plays and assemblies she goes to will be counted as successes—all the rest will fail. As for *her* assemblies, the competition for invitations will be as bloodbaths. I am talking revolution, Simon. A complete regime change!"

"She sounds like a story to frighten small children," Simon observed, shuddering.

"You are not a child," she told him, inexplicably reversing her former position.

"I'm *your* child," he insisted.

"Have I ever asked you to marry anyone?" his mother said, exasperated. "Have I?"

"No," he admitted. "But it sets a very worrying precedent! Besides, I'm half-engaged to the Arbogast. She adores me. It's very comforting."

"You don't need or deserve adoration," his mother told him brutally. "You need discipline. You need a woman who will not put up with any nonsense."

"I already have one of those," he countered, grinning. "I call her Mother."

To his astonishment, the duchess's face suddenly crumpled. "I'm lonely, Simon," she confessed. "I need a companion."

"You have a companion," he reminded her. "How is good old Shrimpy?"

"Hortensia Shrimpton is a crashing bore," his mother

scoffed. "I want *this* girl, Simon. More than I've ever wanted anything in my life. I'll double your allowance if you marry her."

Simon scratched his unshaven chin. "You have my attention," he said dryly. "Would the house in Green Park be out of the question?"

"I'll turn the Bamphs out tomorrow," the duchess promised. "I never liked them anyway."

"I'm not promising anything," he cautioned. "Naturally, I will have to meet Mademoiselle Guillotine before I sacrifice myself on the altar of marriage."

"Fair enough. We can leave as soon as you are dressed." Suddenly spry as a young gazelle, the duchess jumped up and scampered to the door, where she paused. "There is just one tiny little thing you should know about her . . ."

"I knew there had to be a catch," Simon chuckled.

"At present, she is engaged to someone else. That will not be a problem for you, will it?"

Simon yawned. "I shouldn't think so."

"I assure you, he is *the* most infamous, unworthy little *tick* you can imagine. His mother is that ghastly Devize woman who is always trying to cultivate me. How I loathe her!"

Simon's expression changed abruptly. His green eyes sharpened, and his harsh features were more hawklike than ever. "Did you say Devize?"

The duchess sighed. "I can only suppose she's been dazzled by his blue eyes, for he has nothing else to recommend him. When she meets *you*, my love, she will forget she ever knew *him*. I expect nothing less than love at first sight."

"This girl," Simon said, frowning. "She wouldn't . . . No, it couldn't be. Is she . . . ? No, it's quite impossible," he declared. "Engaged to Devize? I don't believe it."

"Simon, you are incoherent," his mother observed.

"No, it's too ridiculous," Simon muttered. "Her name is not by any chance *Andrews*?"

The duchess was thunderstruck. "You know her?"

"I knew it," Simon said savagely, smashing his fist into his open palm. "I knew he wanted her for himself. That lying bastard!"

"I don't understand," said the duchess. "If you know her, what is she doing engaged to *him*? He's nothing compared to you!"

"Too right he isn't," Simon agreed. "But, Mama, as charming as Miss Andrews undoubtedly is, I don't see her taking the reins from Sally Jersey. Why, she's only some country vicar's daughter."

"Don't be nonsensical, Simon. That girl is Lady Viola Gambol. She has a fortune of some half a million pounds. I recognized her almost at once—she's the image of her mother."

Simon was silent for a moment, adjusting his thoughts. "Does Devize know about this?"

The duchess shrugged. "That worries me, too. You may have to kill him—in a duel, of course," she quickly added as he raised a brow. "Don't do anything foolish."

Simon chuckled. "Don't worry about Devize," he assured her. "I know exactly how to deal with a man of his stripe. Just you leave him to me."

The morning was a busy one for Viola. She barely made it to Gambol House in time to meet the dressmaker at the appointed time, and the fitting was almost immediately interrupted. "Yes, Lover? What is it?" she asked as the butler entered her mother's boudoir.

For a long moment, Lover could only stare. Perched atop the dressmaker's stool like a goddess on a pedestal, Lady Viola was a vision in white satin. On her head was a diamond tiara figured with York roses. She was the image of her late mother, and, if Lover was not mistaken, the dress had been her mother's wedding dress. For him, it was like traveling back in time. Even the modiste on her knees, her mouth full of pins, seemed remarkably the same.

"Lover?" Concern marred Viola's face. "Is there some difficulty with the wedding breakfast? Don't tell me we cannot get enough white roses? Oh, Lover, I told you, we *must* have white roses in every room, or my wedding cake will not make sense!"

"Everything is going very smoothly on that front, my lady," Lover hastened to assure her. "Gambol House will be looking its best for the auspicious occasion. I hope you will be very proud of us on Friday morning."

"I'm sure I will be," Viola said complacently, studying her reflection in the cheval glass. "Did you need me for something?"

"I know your ladyship has said you are not at home to visitors," said Lover, "but the Duchess of Berkshire has called to see Miss Andrews."

Viola sighed. "Convey the duchess here to me, Lover," she added, climbing back up on her pedestal. "If she wishes to see me, she must do so without interrupting my busy day."

"Very good, my lady."

Viola got down from her stool to greet the duchess, extending both hands to her and offering a cheek to be kissed. "Duchess! Lover, some tea for the duchess."

Aware that she was going to be scrutinized by an expert, the duchess had dressed for this visit with extraordinary care. Her superbly tailored blue-gray ensemble was tastefully ornamented with yellow and white striped ribbons. Her gray silk bonnet was daringly asymmetrical, folded up over one ear almost in the Cavalier style and held in place with artificial tiger lilies. At the center of each lily was a spray of trembling yellow diamonds.

"Now *that*," said Viola, after a thorough survey, "is a hat worthy of a woman who is known for her hats."

The duchess sighed happily. "This old thing? You flatter me, Lady Viola."

Viola calmly turned the other cheek to be kissed. "Do you know you're the first to puzzle it out?" she chuckled. "Yes, I'm Lady Viola. What gave it away?"

"I was a little acquainted with your mother," the duchess replied, seating herself at the escritoire while Viola resumed her place on the dressmaker's stool. "However, I was not one of those ladies who despised her for taking the last duke off the market," she went on, unabashedly examining the correspondence on the desk. "But, then, I'd already gotten *my* duke. It was your walk that first got me thinking. Your mama was famous for her alluring sway."

"There's a secret to it, you know. Look at my shoes," Viola instructed, lifting her skirts a little. "Notice anything different about them?"

Up went the duchess's pince-nez. "Very clever!" she exclaimed softly. "One heel is slightly higher than the other."

"My mother was a genius," Viola said proudly.

The duchess smiled benevolently. "And so Louisa Lyon's daughter has come to London at last. Why the deception, may I ask? Why pretend to be what you are not?"

Viola explained how and why she had come to London originally.

The duchess shook her head. "Very foolish, my child."

"I'm glad I did it," Viola said defensively. "The real Mary Andrews is a timid little mouse. She would never have survived the journey, let alone Mrs Dean and her . . . friends."

"Oh, I don't fault your instincts, my dear girl," the duchess went on quickly. "But you should not have placed yourself in jeopardy. You ought to have had the Dean woman thoroughly investigated by professionals. There are people who do that sort of thing discreetly, you know."

"People behave differently when they know they are being watched," said Viola, "and Mrs Dean is perfectly capable of bribing a spy. Besides, I *wanted* to come to London. It suited me to take Mary's place . . . for a time. And, of course, I met Dev, so there can be no regretting it."

"Dev," the duchess sniffed. "Does that young man know who you are?"

Viola smiled. "He hasn't a clue. He loves me for myself alone. It will be a lovely surprise for him, don't you think?"

The duchess wrinkled her aquiline nose. "You're not *really* going to marry that infamous young man, are you, my dear? I understand that he was very useful to you in a time of need, but, really, that's no excuse for such a degrading match."

Viola stiffened. "You've had a full report from your son, then. I suppose Lord Simon mentioned his own disgraceful conduct?"

"Yes, Simon was disgraceful," said the duchess. "Most men are, you know, when it comes to beautiful women. I don't make excuses for him, but, you must know, he could never have made an offer of marriage to a Miss Andrews. Simon is too sensible to the duty he owes his family. He's come here today to apologize to you."

"I suppose you've told him who I am," Viola said crossly. "Well, he'd better not spoil my surprise by telling Dev."

"Are you *quite* sure Mr Devize does not know who you are?"

Viola removed her diamond tiara and placed it in her jewel box. "He thinks I am but a poor, simple country girl from Yorkshire," she insisted. "He thinks nothing of titles and fortune."

The duchess laughed dryly. "If he thinks that *you* are a simple country girl, my dear, then he is an imbecile," she said. "Do you really want to marry an imbecile?"

Viola's eyes flashed. "Dev is the cleverest man in London," she snapped. "He topples banks for amusement. When he lifts his little finger, the Stock Exchange jumps to do his will. The Bank of England has spies following his every move."

"Clever?" sneered the duchess. "Did he buy you the diamond you wanted?"

"Yes, he did," Viola snapped. Stretching out her hand, she silently dared the duchess to say anything. The cold white diamond looked as though it had always been on the third finger of her left hand.

The duchess snorted. "Bah! It was an emerald yesterday."

"Yesterday the light was bad," Viola explained. "As you can see, it is a perfect six-carat emerald-cut diamond."

With a grim smile, the duchess opened Viola's jewelry box. With her eyes fixed on Viola, she plucked the emerald ring from its velvet nest and held it up. "*This* is the ring he got you," she said. "An emerald."

Viola took it from her and walked over to the window. "Please believe me when I tell you there are no emeralds in this house," she said coldly, opening the window briefly to throw the ring out. "Anyway, Julian doesn't care about jewelry. He just wants me to be happy."

"I've no doubt," said the duchess as Lover brought in the tea tray, "that Mr Devize is well equipped to make a Miss Andrews happy . . . but Lady Viola? No, my dear. He is not your equal. He will never be your equal. He will drag you down like a millstone around your neck."

Lover cast the duchess a grateful look. The dowager had expressed his own feelings perfectly. He only hoped that Lady Viola would listen. "Thank you, Lover," Viola said sweetly.

"Naturally, you wish to reward the young man for his service to you," the duchess went on harshly. "There's nothing wrong with that. By all means, send Mr Devize a nice hamper from Fortnum & Mason. Buy him a gold watch, if you must. But I'm afraid I see absolutely no reason for you to *marry* him. You should marry someone closer to you in rank, someone worthy of you."

Viola scowled. "Lord Bamph, you mean? I have no intention of marrying a stranger, Duchess, particularly a stranger chosen for me by my beastly father."

"Rupert Bamph!" cried the duchess. "Heavens, no. That preening popinjay will never do for *you*. The thought of him touching you makes me ill. No, it is my son I mean. It is Simon."

Viola recoiled in astonishment. "Madam! Your son is a hound."

"He likes women," the duchess admitted. "He always has. But he is not a predator. He takes his pleasure with the appropriate class of female, and he compensates his paramours accordingly. I have never had any trouble on *that* score. No weeping victims on my doorstep. The moment he saw you, he wanted you. Who can blame him? Can you not forgive him for trying to obtain you in the only way he knew how?"

"Your son mistook me for a harlot, a common money creature. *That* I cannot forgive. Mr Devize knew I was innocent. *And*," she added triumphantly, "he bid for me in *guineas*."

"I wonder *how* Mr Devize knew you were innocent," mused the duchess.

"I *beg* your pardon," Viola said quietly.

"You are a confident young woman, to put it mildly. Who would ever guess that *you* had fallen into such a trap of deception? Depend upon it, if my Simon had known you were in need of a rescue, he would have rescued you."

"Out of the frying pan into the fire!" said Viola.

"Oh, pooh! He would have married you, and you know it, as soon as he found out who you were. The match is perfect. You are a duke's daughter. Simon is a duke's son. If my elder son were not married, you could have *him*, but, as it is, Simon is all I have to offer."

Viola shook her head, smiling. "But what are his qualifications? Apart from his pedigree? What has Lieutenant-Colonel Lord Simon Ascot ever done to make the world sit up and take notice? *Dev* is the most hated man in London. He's made them all sick with rage and envy."

"He's the most hated man in London," the duchess agreed. "This appeals to you?"

"The man I marry must have accomplishments," Viola said.

"I can see you are besotted with this nonentity," the duchess said crankily. "Clever he may be, my dear. But what if he *does* know who you are? Have you considered the possibility that he might be a very clever and accomplished fortune hunter?"

"Not once. He believes that I am Mary Andrews."

"Poor *simple* Miss Andrews from the country," murmured the duchess, sipping her tea. "You will admit it is an odd choice of a wife for such a clever young man. Are you *quite* sure he intends to marry you, my dear? Has he secured the special license?"

"He is doing so today," Viola declared. "Even as we speak."

The duchess raised a brow. "Really? I'm surprised it wasn't done yesterday."

Viola blushed faintly. "It was not possible yesterday. We were . . . too much in the moment, if you see what I mean. I did not want him to leave me."

"I see. Well, perhaps I've misjudged him. If he has taken the trouble to secure the license, then I must believe he means to marry you. I was deathly afraid he might have seduced you merely for sport."

"I do not know what you mean, Duchess," Viola said stiffly. "Mr Devize has not seduced me. He has always treated me with the utmost respect."

"I am relieved to hear it," the duchess said warmly.

"You may come to the wedding breakfast, if you like," Viola said kindly. "Lover assures me it will be quite special. Wear something fabulous."

"Thank you," said the duchess. "I shall. I wish you the best of luck, my dear, but I fear you will be disappointed. For myself, I do not trust Mr Devize. He is too good-looking and far too clever. I suspect he is using you."

"I trust Dev completely," Viola said fiercely.

"The question is, does he deserve your trust?" Leaving Viola to ponder her cautionary advice, the duchess took her leave.

"Has she followed me?" the duchess whispered to her son as they crossed the hall downstairs.

"Yes, but only to the top of the stairs," Simon replied, giving Viola a grave bow.

In response, Viola merely raised a brow.

"That is a good sign," the duchess said happily as she pulled on her gloves. "She is thinking with her *head* now, and not her heart."

In this assertion, the duchess was too optimistic. Viola liked the Duchess of Berkshire personally. She was flattered that her grace desired her for a daughter-in-law. She even trusted that the duchess's interference had been kindly meant. However, she dismissed all of the duchess's advice with scarcely any thought at all. The duchess did not know Dev. The duchess had antiquated notions about duty and rank. It did not matter what *she* thought of the match.

By the time Viola left Gambol House that evening, the duchess was long forgotten. She rushed back to the house in Lombard Street, her mind and heart full of Dev.

"You're home!" she cried happily as Julian came down the stairs to greet her.

"You're out very late," he complained. "Were you with Lady Viola all day?"

"Yes, all day," Viola answered, her eyes twinkling.

Joining arms, they walked up the stairs together. Julian nuzzled her neck. "Dinner is not quite ready," he murmured, kissing her ear.

"It's only just nine o'clock," Viola said defensively. "I think

Cork is doing very well as a cook. You liked her stew yesterday, didn't you?"

"You miss my point," he growled, catching her roughly in his arms at the top of the stairs.

Viola giggled. "What is your point, sir?"

Her pulled her hips against him so that she could feel the hard length of his member. "My point is that dinner is not ready, and we have a little time on our hands. I know what I'd like to do with that time, my sweet."

"What?" she asked innocently.

"You know what," he said curtly. Walking her backward into the bedroom, he threw her none too gently onto the bed. Climbing over her, he unfastened his trousers and released his straining length.

"Dev," she protested as he pushed up her skirts and pried her legs apart. It was not like him to be so rough with her. He was passionate, of course, but never crude. Usually, he kissed and caressed and teased her body until she lost her senses. She hardly knew what to think about the sudden change in him.

"Are you drunk?" she asked, bewildered.

He only laughed. "Help me," he said, his voice low and strangled. "If I cannot have you right now, I shall die. I need you."

Although her body was still tensing as if it was under attack, Viola's heart melted. Without thinking, she took him in hand and guided him to the soft spot between her legs. At the first violent thrust, her body arched in pain and she cried out. The pain was almost as great as it had been the first time. Julian, himself groaning with pleasure, mistook her cries for passion. He took her furiously, firm in the belief that she was with him. Gradually the pain lessened for Viola, but she was too shocked to find any pleasure. He had assured her it would only hurt the first time, but here was pain. And, just as he had been the first time, he was oblivious to her pain.

On the positive side, it was over fairly quickly. "I have been thinking about this all day," he gasped, collapsing at her side.

For Viola, these words added insult to injury. Had he said "I've been thinking about *you* all day," she would have forgiven him instantly. His behavior might have been excused as that of a man in the throes of overwhelming passion. But he had not been thinking of *her* all day. He had been thinking of *this*. That was an entirely different matter. Feeling abused rather than desired, she got up and began straightening her clothes. He had not even bothered to undress her, or himself, and somehow that made it all worse. Suddenly, she felt his hand on her back. It was all she could do not to lash out at him like an angry cat.

"Did you go off?" he asked, still breathless from his exertions.

Viola looked at him incredulously. Still flat on his back, he was doing up his trousers. "No," she said angrily. "How could I? It was beastly! You didn't even kiss me."

"Easily mended." Chuckling, Julian pulled her down to him. For some reason, she let herself be pulled. For some reason, she allowed him to kiss her. For some reason, her breasts began to tingle as his tongue unfurled in her mouth. For some reason, she found herself kissing him back, the beast. Her traitorous woman's body didn't seem to care how badly it had just been treated. She still wanted him. The pleasure that had been denied her in this encounter remained tantalizingly beyond her reach, his to give or not give. Irrationally, she felt he had denied her on purpose, to assert his mastery over her. Her soul rebelled, even as her body responded.

"Don't tell me you didn't enjoy that," he said in her ear. "You're the most passionate lover I've ever known. Your body might have been made for me. I do believe I'm becoming obsessed. I want you morning, noon, and night."

"Is that all I am to you?" she demanded indignantly. "One of your lovers?"

"Of course not," he said sharply. "Don't be silly."

"Silly!" she flashed. "I suppose I should be flattered to know that you've been thinking about *this* all day!"

"Haven't *you*?" he said coolly, sitting up.

"No!"

"Yes, you have," he snorted. "You're just too embarrassed to admit it."

"I have not been thinking about *this*," she insisted virtuously. "I have been thinking about *you*. About us. Our life together. Our future, Julian. I have been planning our wedding. Everything on my end is ready for Friday. Did you get the special license?" she asked. She knew instantly by the change in his face that he hadn't. "You didn't, did you?" she said, appalled.

Julian rubbed the back of his neck. "About the license . . ."

Viola sprang to her feet. "You might have told me *before*," she said bitterly, folding her arms across her breasts protectively. She felt now that he had used her body under false pretenses. The betrayal stung. "I suppose you were too *busy* to get the special license?"

"I went to Doctor's Commons," Julian answered, "but the clerk gave me a barge-load of nonsense about a waiting period."

"You never said anything about a waiting period!"

"That's because there's no such thing," he said irritably.

"So you gave up?"

"No. I went to see my colonel, to ask for his help. Unfortunately, my mother had already been to see him."

"Your mother!" Viola exclaimed.

"Apparently, she doesn't approve of you," he said dryly.

"I can't imagine why," Viola said indignantly.

"Because you're poor," he said bitterly. "My mother has always desired a Society wife for me, God knows why."

"Your colonel was not able to help?"

"My mother's uncle is a very influential man in military

circles," he explained. "I would not want Colonel Fairfax to jeopardize the future of his sons for my sake."

"Or mine?" she said bitterly. "What are we going to do?"

"I don't know," he confessed. "I'll think of something."

Without a word, Viola sat down at the makeshift dining table, her mind suddenly full of all the cavils she had dismissed so easily earlier in the day. Could the duchess be right? Naturally, Viola wanted the duchess to be wrong, but had her feelings for this man clouded her judgment?

"If he has taken the trouble to secure the license, then I know he means to marry you," the duchess had said. "I was afraid he might have seduced you merely for sport."

While hardly a seduction, the feverish coupling he had just subjected her to might well be described as "sport."

"I suspect he is using you," the duchess had said.

Viola felt quite used at the moment.

"Does he deserve your trust?" the duchess had asked.

Suddenly, Viola was not sure.

When the food arrived, she could not look at Julian as he sat down to his meal. "It's a matter of influence, Mary," he told her gently. "Somehow my mother has used her influence to stop me from getting a special license. But I'm not giving up."

"I see," Viola said quietly. "Before, it was a matter of money. Now that I have arranged for you to get the money you need, it has become a matter of influence."

Julian put down his fork. He had only been toying with his food anyway. "What do you mean you arranged it?" he demanded. "You persuaded Lady Viola to send me money! Is that it?"

His blue eyes glowed with fury, but Viola did not care. "I want to marry you," she said, "and I *thought* you wanted to marry me. Have I made a mistake, Julian?"

He looked at her coldly. "Only you can answer that, madam," he said curtly.

Viola stared at him. The enormity of the risk she had taken with him sudden struck her full force. She was no longer a virgin. If, as it turned out, her trust in this man had been stupidly misplaced, what was she to do? How could she go on?

*If he knew who I really was, he would marry me in an instant.* The thought cut her to the quick.

"I think perhaps I *have* made a mistake," she said coldly.

His face flushed with anger. "Perhaps you'd be happier if Lord Simon had bought you!"

"What?" said Viola, stung.

"Think about it, my dear. *You* would be happily situated in the West End, and *I* would not owe the Duke of Fanshawe seventeen thousand guineas. Perhaps it's not too late," he went on brutally. "Perhaps I could sell you to Lord Simon *now*. That would solve all my problems, wouldn't it? God knows I haven't had a moment's peace since I met you. Where are you going?" he demanded as she rose from the table.

"I don't know who you think you're talking to," Viola retorted, "but I am leaving. Good-bye, Mr Devize!"

Julian groaned. "You can't leave," he said, catching her hand. "Don't leave me."

Viola gasped, not with outrage, but because the touch of his hand sent a strong current of foolish desire through her whole body. It was madness to want him now, in the midst of an argument. She had to remind herself that he had done nothing but insult her that evening. First, he had used her body quite selfishly. Then he had revealed that he couldn't be bothered to get the special license. And he had capped it off by threatening to sell her to Lord Simon. Only a complete idiot would still want him after that. "Do you think you own me?" she asked angrily.

He tugged her hand until she landed all at once in his lap. Viola hated to be so weak, but there was no helping it. In his arms she instantly felt better. "If you do not mean to marry me, Dev, you should let me go," she whispered as he began stroking her hair and neck with sure, possessive hands. "I cannot go on like this. I will not be your mistress. If I must give you up for a scoundrel, I will," she added with more conviction than she actually felt.

"I am not a scoundrel, Mary," Julian said firmly. "You should have more faith in me."

"I suppose we've gone too far to turn back now," she murmured, allowing herself to be swept up in the sound of his voice, the feel of his hands, the taste of his mouth.

This time when he took her to bed, he was like a completely different lover. He undressed her slowly. He wanted to take his time with her, going over the firm lines of her body with his mouth and hands, and demanded the same attention from her in return. He wound her up by tiny degrees, until desire mounted almost to mindless desperation, until she was ready to do anything he wanted, however depraved. A single moan of pleasure from his lips filled her with pride and eagerness. She no longer cared about her own pleasure; she wanted only to feel his. Even if the result was pain, she longed to feel him inside her because it was from the final act that he seemed to derive the most pleasure. Long before he even entered her, she was a mumbling fool. She scarcely recognized the person she became as they began to move together.

"Come with me, love," he gasped, pulling her hard against him as he felt himself give way. "Come with me," he urged, and she did, sobbing in his arms, her womb open and tender.

Julian threw himself down beside her, pleased with his achievement. "We went off together that time," he said, yawning.

Viola had never felt so unsure of herself, or so vulnerable. She felt almost as if she were disappearing. Viola was gone, and in her place was a cringing, needy creature that Viola would have scorned to be.

"Yes," she said miserably.

# Chapter Fifteen

Number 32, Lombard Street, was just the sort of dilapidated hole-in-the-wall that Lord Simon expected a conniving weasel like Julian Devize *would* inhabit. He was surprised by the respectable-looking manservant who answered the door.

"Captain Devize is not at home, my lord," Hudson informed him politely.

"I will wait," Lord Simon announced, striding into the hall. "Unless of course there are rats," he added, looking around doubtfully.

Viola, who was eavesdropping on the landing, ran back to the bedroom, her heart pounding. *What in God's name is he doing here?* she wondered. A thousand unhappy notions entered her head.

Hudson, meanwhile, had assured his lordship that there were no rats. "If the matter is urgent, my lord, you will find Captain Devize at the Exchange."

"I can't be seen in public with the man," Lord Simon said irritably.

"I'm afraid the captain keeps rather long hours," Hudson apologized.

Lord Simon was disgusted by the inconvenience to himself. "Have you pen and paper? I'll leave a note for your master. If I'd known he wasn't here," he went on as Hudson obliged him, "I should not have bothered to come in person."

Hudson watched impassively as Lord Simon marred the page with heavy black scrawl.

His lordship saw an opportunity for greater mischief as he was taking his leave. "You seem like a good sort of fellow," he told Hudson. "I'm soon to be married. Why not come and work for me at my house in Green Park? I'll pay you twice what Devize pays."

"Your lordship is very kind," Hudson replied frostily, "but I could never leave the captain. I have been with him since he was a boy."

Lord Simon shrugged; taking Devize's man had only been an afterthought. Stealing Lady Viola was the important thing.

Hudson had scarcely closed the door upon the unexpected visitor before Viola had taken possession of the note Lord Simon left behind. "That is for the captain!" he told her sharply.

Viola looked up from the letter. Hudson had been prepared to snatch the page from her hands, but the expression on her face halted him. In fact, he stumbled back. Her large, dark eyes, in which he had never seen anything but mischief, appeared almost haunted by shock and pain. Her face was white. She looked younger than he had ever seen her look, almost like a bereaved child. In spite of himself, he was moved to feel compassion.

"Are you quite all right, madam?" he asked, concerned.

Instantly, Viola was herself again. Hudson decided it must have been a trick of the light. No one looked less like a bereaved child than the young woman his master had so unwisely married. "I'm quite all right, thank you," she said sharply. "Would you be good enough to summon a hack for me?"

Hudson was happy to do so, and even more delighted to

help bring down the lady's trunk. This time, when Mrs Devize said good-bye, he had high hopes that she really meant it.

In less than twenty minutes, Viola was on her way to Gambol House with Cork and Bijou. She arrived there still in the strong grip of the desire to throw things. Resplendent in correct morning dress, Lover greeted her at the front door. "Good morning, my lady. There are some letters for you on the tray in the morning room."

Viola frowned. "Letters? No one knows I'm here."

"There is a letter from the duke."

Viola sighed. "I daresay he's annoyed with me for leaving Yorkshire."

"His grace is on his way back to London, my lady. Miss Mary Andrews is traveling with him." He paused to study the effect of this information on the lady, but Viola merely shrugged, so he continued. "I believe the Willow Room would be most suitable for her. Would that be satisfactory, my lady?"

"I suppose so," Viola said listlessly. "When does my brother arrive?"

"Friday afternoon, my lady. Alas, not in time for the wedding breakfast."

Viola looked grim. "Never mind the wedding breakfast, Lover. The wedding has been canceled."

"My lady?"

"I'm not going to marry Mr Devize, after all," she explained. "That's all finished." Handing off Bijou to Cork, Viola went into the sunny yellow morning room, pulling off her gloves. "I'm sorry to have put you to so much bother for nothing."

Lover could scarcely contain his joy. Silently, he blessed the Duchess of Berkshire. Her excellent advice seemed to have done the trick. "Very good, my lady."

Viola rounded on him furiously. "In what way is it good, Lover?" she wanted to know. "Have you ever been jilted? Did you enjoy the experience? Because, personally, I find it rather less than good. One might even say it was bad!" To her horror, she felt tears gathering behind the bridge of her arrogant little nose. To stop the humiliating flow, she pressed her fingers to her eyes and flung herself onto the nearest sofa.

Lover was flabbergasted. "*He* has jilted *you*?"

He did not mean to say it aloud. It just slipped out.

"That is right, Lover. *He* has jilted *me*."

At that moment, the front doorbell sounded. Viola groaned. "I'm not at home, Lover," she said piteously. "Whoever it is, tell them to go jump in the river."

Lover hesitated. "If it is the Duchess of Berkshire?"

Viola shuddered. "*Especially* her. She will want to gloat! I don't want to see *anyone*, Lover. All I want is a large box of chocolates and the latest issues of all the ladies' publications."

"Very good, my lady." With a bow, Lover withdrew.

When he returned a few moments later bearing sweets and magazines, Viola had not stirred from the sofa, but she tore into the box of chocolates with renewed vigor. "Who was at the door?" she asked idly as Lover went to adjust the curtains. "The duchess? Her odious son?"

"No, my lady," Lover replied. "It was only Sir Arthur Huffington-Effington, his wife, Mrs Huffington-Effington, and their daughter, Miss Huffington-Effington. They left cards. Sir Arthur is one of our Yorkshire M.P.s, my lady."

"I know who he is, Lover. I put him in Parliament. How did he know I was here? I was never here before. One begins to feel like a fox trapped in a covert." Now quite out of sorts, Viola took a bite out of a chocolate, abandoned it, and selected another.

"I believe your ladyship was kind enough to send Sir Arthur the benefit of your political advice. I posted several letters for your ladyship yesterday."

"Of course," Viola said bitterly. "My letters were in the

twopenny post. Therefore, I must be in London. Oh, I hate London! Everyone is *soooo* clever!"

"Many of the recipients have already sent a reply," Lover went on pleasantly, bringing her the tray piled with envelopes.

The Duke of Fanshawe's letter was on top. Viola set aside her brother's letter, assuming correctly that it contained no information which Lover had not already imparted to her, and examined the rest of the letters. "These all appear to be invitations," she said incredulously. "Why, there must be over *thirty* of the beastly things."

"Thirty-six, my lady. Your ladyship might consider hiring a social secretary. When one is as popular as your ladyship, scheduling conflicts are all too apt to take place."

"But I don't want to go out into Society," said Viola. "Lover, I've just been jilted. The last thing I want," she went on, ripping open an envelope, "is a *ridotto*, whatever that is."

"I believe it is a musical entertainment, my lady," Lover said helpfully. "It begins with a small concert, and finishes with dancing."

Viola shuddered. "Ugh."

"Are the chocolates not to your liking, my lady?" asked Lover, noting that she had not taken a second bite out of any.

"I seem to have lost my appetite," Viola sighed. "I'm glad you sent the Huffy-Effies away, Lover. They fawn over me in the most sickening manner."

There was a slight pause.

"Then again," Viola said thoughtfully, "a little fawning might cheer me up."

"It is possible, my lady."

"And I really ought to make time for our Yorkshire delegates," said Viola, sitting up straight. "One must smile though one's heart is breaking, after all."

"Yes, my lady."

"I am at home to Parliament, then," Viola decided, "but no one else is to be admitted under any circumstances."

The next two hours passed in a blur as Viola entertained the wives and daughters of the many M.P.s representing the various districts of Yorkshire. Occasionally, the ladies were accompanied by their husbands, but more often than not, the ladies assured Viola that their husbands were much too busy vigorously representing her interests in Parliament to be at leisure on a Wednesday morning. Viola generously gave them the benefit of her advice on a variety of subjects. In return, they paid her the most extravagant compliments they could. At first, Viola basked in the respectful obeisance of her visitors, and she kindly forgave them all for being so dull, so insipid, so mindless, and so badly dressed. But soon the endless bowing and scraping ceased to be delightful, and she was left feeling rather hollow.

"What am I to do, Lover?" she asked petulantly when the butler returned after showing the last of her visitors out. "If I go out, I may meet someone I don't like, but if I stay in, I'm certain of it! And these ridiculous invitations! I don't want to go to Mrs Briggs's candlelight supper, and I couldn't be driven at knifepoint to Mrs Shaw's ridotto. I adore politics, but why must all politicians' wives be such deadly bores?"

"You have one more visitor, my lady," Lover said apologetically. "But it is perhaps too late for a morning call. Shall I tell Mr Rampling to come back tomorrow?"

"Heavens, no," said Viola, working out a desperate kink in her neck. "Let us get it over with. He has brought his badly dressed wife with him, I suppose?"

"I believe Mr Rampling to be unmarried, my lady."

"What?" Viola said sharply. "I distinctly recall telling him to marry as soon as possible! What's he been doing with his time? Send him in."

At twenty-five, Mr Rampling was something of a protégé. Viola had chosen him for Parliament primarily because he looked the part, and secondarily because he possessed a remarkable, booming voice perfect for drowning out the opposition. He had the necessary air of gravity and consequence. Blue-eyed and angelically fair, he was tall and good-looking. He had not expected to be ushered into the Presence—he had thought only of leaving his card—and his gratitude for Lady Viola's condescension was immense and voluble.

Viola greeted him cordially and gave him two fingers to shake.

"Do you like Parliament, Mr Rampling?" she asked him pleasantly as he took his seat.

Cornelius Rampling hated Parliament, but he could hardly say so. "I like Parliament excessively, Lady Viola," he boomed. "These are exciting times in which we live. I—"

Viola interrupted him. "Who put you there, Mr Rampling?"

Cornelius blinked rapidly. "Beg pardon, my lady? Who put me . . . ?"

"In Parliament. Who put you in Parliament, Mr Rampling? It's a simple question."

"You did, Lady Viola," he said gravely. "That is, your ladyship's brother did, upon your advice. Indeed, I am most exceedingly grateful to your—"

"Who writes all your speeches for you, Mr Rampling?"

"You do, Lady Viola."

"Who tells you how to vote?"

"You do, Lady Viola."

"As a result, you are known as one of our most promising Members," said Viola. "You would be quite lost without me to guide you."

"I am eternally grateful to your ladyship for the opportunity—"

"And yet you do not take my advice, Mr Rampling," she said coolly.

Cornelius's eyes widened. "I would not, for the world," he

said carefully, "argue with your ladyship, but there can be nothing more precious to me than your ladyship's advice!"

Viola sighed impatiently. "Did I not tell you to marry? Nobody trusts a bachelor in politics—it looks so eccentric. Are you married, Mr Rampling? Are you engaged?"

The young man's cheeks reddened. Occasionally, it was brought home to him that his tyrannical patroness was four years his junior and a stunning beauty besides, but most of the time he was scared witless that she would snatch away all she had given. "I am . . . looking for a wife, my lady. Most diligently. I spend at least three hours of every day in the park, looking."

Viola was frowning. "What do you mean, *looking*?" she said indignantly. "They are young ladies, Mr Rampling. They are not pictures at an exhibition."

"No, your ladyship," he humbly agreed. "But there are so many of them. Of course, it is difficult to know what sort of female would be most pleasing to your ladyship."

"For shame, Mr Rampling! Has your mother not introduced you to any young ladies this Season? Has your sister no friends with whom you might consort?"

"My mother and my sister are in Hampshire, Lady Viola."

"What? Not in Town? How does Lady Caroline expect to get you a wife, if she does not put any effort into the process? Does she have no interest in her future daughter-in-law?"

Cornelius looked uncomfortable. "I'm sorry to say, my mother's health prevents her from coming to Town, Lady Viola. Else she would certainly have come to pay her respects to you."

"Oh," said Viola, relenting. "Well, if your mother is ill, you should take a leave of absence, Mr Rampling. You should be at her side. You can leave directly after lunch."

Cornelius hesitated. A reprieve from the tedium of Whitehall? A holiday in the country? He could see himself fishing in the streams and tearing across the fields on his big black hunter. It sounded too good to be true. "Are you quite sure, my lady?" he said tentatively. "Indeed, the doctors do not seem to think my poor mother is likely to recover quickly. I could be gone for quite some time."

"All the more reason you should go! You only have one mother," Viola replied. "You must go to her at once, Mr Rampling. In fact, I will take you. You may sit on the barouche box. Whereabouts in Hampshire are you?"

Cornelius was taken aback. "I could not ask your ladyship to go to so much trouble," he cried. "I would not dream—"

Viola waved her hand. "It's no trouble. My brother owns some property in Hampshire, and, as I am tired of London at the moment, it suits me very well to escape to the country. Are you anywhere near the charming village of Little Gambol?"

Cornelius laughed awkwardly. "Your ladyship must know that my mother has taken Gambol Hall, Lady Viola."

"Really?" Viola said, pleased. "Then the house is already open. The rooms have been aired, and the staff is all in place. Excellent. Your mother won't object if I pay her a little visit, surely? And your sister . . . What's her name?"

"Lucy, my lady."

"Lucy, of course," Viola said, signaling for the butler. "Have the barouche prepared for the journey to Hampshire, Lover. Tell Cork to pack for a month in the country. Mr Rampling will want to send word to his man as well. We shall leave directly after lunch. Mr Rampling will be staying to lunch with me," she added, smiling at the young man. "There! It's all arranged."

Cornelius's head was spinning. "Your ladyship is too kind," he murmured.

Lover cleared his throat. "My lady? What shall I tell his grace when he returns to London on Friday?"

Viola shrugged. "Tell him I have gone to the country to visit a sick friend. I shall be gone at least a month."

"Very good, my lady." Lover was stiff with disapproval, but Viola took no note of that.


Garraway's tavern in Change Alley was always noisy and crowded, but at the noon hour it resembled one of the fuller circles of hell. Julian pushed his way to the battered oak bar to order his sandwiches, digging his elbows into his fellow brokers, stepping on their feet and shouting to be heard over the din. As he was leaving, a man hailed him from a table at the back of the room. The man wore his hat low over his eyes, the collar of his greatcoat obscuring the lower half of his face, but Julian was just able to recognize the beaklike nose of his former colonel.

"I'm surprised to see you, sir," he said, joining Colonel Fairfax at his table. "Have you changed your mind about helping me?"

Colonel Fairfax was distressed. "I cannot risk helping you get the special license," he apologized. "What can I say? Your mother is a gorgon."

"She is, isn't she?"

"However, I *do* want to help you. After you left, it occurred to me . . . You could take the young lady to Calais and marry her there."

Julian frowned. "Would that be legal?"

"Of course," the colonel replied. "We're no longer at war with France. Britain and France are allies. The marriage would have to be recognized. It's a hell of a lot better than hauling your bride off to Scotland, you will admit. You could honeymoon in Paris. I've arranged passage for you and the lady on the next mail packet," he went on, taking the printed tickets from inside his coat. "It's the least I can do."

Julian accepted the boarding passes gratefully. "This will make her very happy. Thank you, sir. I will pay you back, of course," he added, shaking the other man's hand.

"I know," the colonel replied. "If you don't mind, I think I'll go out the back."

Julian took a moment to put the tickets safely away in his pocket.

"Going somewhere?" said a chilly voice at his elbow.

Julian turned to look at the speaker, a tall, thin, clean-shaven man with the unmistakable mien of a London bureaucrat. "Who are you?"

"We're from the government," the man replied, smiling.

"We?"

"We," said a voice at his other elbow. The tall man's friend was a stout, heavyset man in a rough-looking frieze coat. Without further ado, he seized Julian by the arms.

"There's a pistol in my pocket," the thin man said pleasantly. "It is aimed at your gut, Mr Devize. Shall we sit down?"

Julian had no choice.

"Now put the contents of your pockets onto the table." While the thin man seemed particularly interested in the tickets to Calais, his colleague helped himself to Julian's sandwiches. "You are thinking of visiting France?" the thin man asked politely.

"Obviously," Julian replied.

The thin man smiled thinly. "Yes, obviously. For what purpose?"

"Why is the government interested?" Julian demanded.

"I'm just making conversation," said the thin man. "Who is the other ticket for? Why are you going to France? Who are you working for? What are you up to?"

"This is ridiculous," said Julian. "I refuse to answer your impertinent questions."

"We've already rounded up two of your co-conspirators," said the thin man. "Dolly Dean, the panderess. Mr Harman from the Bank of England. Mr Harman, in particular, seems very eager to cooperate with our investigation."

Julian laughed shortly. "Am I under arrest?"

"Yes," said the thin man. "Yes, I rather think you are."

As Julian was brought out of Garraway's with his hands tied behind his back, a cheer went up and down the room, and the news that the law had finally caught up with the most hated man in London spread like wildfire through the City.

The journey to Hampshire passed with an ease that surprised Mr Rampling, who was used to traveling in the public stagecoach, but, despite all the comforts of Lady Viola's barouche, it became necessary to stop at a roadside inn for tea. Viola was always distressed by headache if she did not have her tea promptly at half-past four, and her mood was already turning unpleasant when she looked out of the window and beheld the Sussex Arms. Sussex, of course, was Julian's county. It had no other associations for the lady.

"Are we in Sussex?" she demanded coldly as the servant opened the carriage door.

Cornelius confirmed the awful truth, and not even the fact that they were less than twenty miles from Little Gambol, Hampshire, could lessen the blow.

"I hate Sussex," she announced. "I despise Sussex. I loathe Sussex with all my heart."

As ever, she spoke with the clearest authority, in a voice that carried and penetrated every corner of the yard. The hostlers could not help but hear her. The innkeeper, who had come out to greet the gentry, heard it very well, too. Cornelius could not help but notice that they were all freakishly large men with angry red faces. He began to tremble with fear. "I wish you would not say such things, my lady," he whispered frantically. "I wish you would not say such things so loudly. You'll get us all killed."

"Are you afraid of Sussex, Mr Rampling?" Viola asked scornfully. "I am not. I hate Sussex, but I do not fear it. Now go and fetch my tea, if you please."

Cornelius swallowed hard as the carriage door banged shut behind him.

The landlord was surprisingly sympathetic. "That's a terrible stutter your wife has, sir," he said, clapping Cornelius on the back.

"Oh, she's not my w—" Cornelius began. "Stutter?"

"My wife was the same way," the landlord went on companionably. "I believe all women hate it at first. Just give her time—she'll get used to it. If she still hates it after a week, buy her a present," he added slyly, laying a finger against the side of his nose.

"Sussex?" said Cornelius, confused.

"Oh, you've got a stutter, too," the landlord said compassionately.

Cornelius slowly caught the landlord's drift. "Stutter!" he said, seizing gratefully on the idea. "Yes, landlord. We both stutter quite awfully."


Evenings at Gambol Hall fell into a timeworn pattern. After dinner, Lady Caroline Rampling drank herself into a stupor while her daughter Lucy darned stockings. If there was no mending to do, Lucy waited for her mother to drift off, then read a book. Lady Caroline did not approve of her daughter reading too much.

At a little past seven, on this particular evening, they were surprised to hear a vehicle pulling across the cobbled drive. Lady Caroline was too drunk to stand, but she roused herself enough to send Lucy to the window. "It is a carriage," Lucy reported, hastily hiding her book.

"Of course it's a carriage," Lady Caroline slurred angrily. "I know it's a carriage, you imbecile. Who is in it?"

"It is a barouche," Lucy clarified. She was quite used to being ill-treated by her mother, and hardly took offense at being called an imbecile. "There is a device on the door. A coat of arms. Three towers, I think."

Lady Caroline launched herself from her chair. "'Tis the Duke of Fanshawe himself!" Overwhelmed by dizziness, she fell back in her chair, retching.

"It's Cornelius!" Lucy exclaimed happily. "It is my brother!"

"Cornelius?" Lady Caroline repeated in astonishment. "Traveling with the duke?"

Lucy left the window and ran out to meet her brother, disregarding her mother's angry reminder that it was unladylike to run. While he was hardly the most affectionate brother in the world, compared to her mother, Cornelius was kind and thoughtful. "Corny!" she cried, flinging her arms around him almost before his feet touched the ground. "What are you doing here?"

Cornelius pushed her away quickly in order to help a lady from the carriage. Lucy stared at Viola in dismay. Although the Ramplings were deeply in Lady Viola's debt, Lucy did not like her brother's patroness. Lady Viola was one of those perfect, beautiful people who have never suffered a toothache or had a pimple in the whole course of their existence. At present, she was wearing a leopard-skin coat and carrying a small white dog. She made Lucy feel old and dowdy.

"You remember Lady Viola, of course," Cornelius said pointedly, and Lucy hastily gave the duke's sister her best curtsey.

Viola signaled for Cork to take Bijou. "Take her down to the garden and make sure she does her business," she instructed, before turning to Lucy. "Hello again, Miss Rampling. Now, mind, I'm incognito in Hampshire. Or is it *incognita*?" she laughed. "In any case, I don't want to call attention to my presence here, you understand," she went on, dusting off her spotted coat. "So you must remember to call me Miss Andrews. How is your mama? I hope she is better."

"Mama?" Lucy echoed stupidly.

"Yes, Mama," Cornelius said quickly and firmly. "I told her ladysh—Miss Andrews, that is—how *ill* Mama has been. She's so ill that she cannot leave her bed, let alone go to London for the Season," Cornelius shouted as Lucy continued to blink in confusion. "We're all very worried about her. Why don't you go and tell her, Lucy—I mean, check on her, of course. Make sure she's not dying, ha ha. I'll look after Lady—er, Miss Andrews."

"I won't be any trouble," Viola promised. "All I need is a good dinner and a warm fire."

Saving her questions for later, Lucy ran back into the house. Removing her mother from the drawing room, however, was easier said than done. "I am not shick, you fool," Lady Caroline bellowed, slapping her daughter's hands away.

"But Lady Viola thinks you are, Mama," Lucy patiently explained.

"I never felt better," snarled Lady Caroline.

"You do not want Lady Viola to see you like this, do you, Mama?" cried Lucy, ringing for the maid.

"Like what?" Lady Caroline demanded. "Leave me alone, you stupid cow. And bring me another bottle from the cellar! Lady Viola will be thirsty."

Viola walked into the room and surveyed the two ladies for a moment. "Mr Rampling! A little water for Lady Caroline, please."

"Water!" Lady Caroline snarled. Infuriated by the suggestion that she drink plain water, she slapped away the glass her son offered her. "I'd rather drink piss!" she screamed.

"Extraordinary," Viola murmured.

Cornelius tried to laugh it off. "She doesn't know what she's saying, Lady Viola. You should be in bed, Mama. Sleepwalking again, ha ha. Lucy, dammit, I told you she must be watched at all times," he said through his teeth. "Where is the nurse?"

"What nurse?" Lucy cried resentfully.

"You know," Cornelius snarled. "*The nurse*."

"Oh, that nurse!" cried Lucy. "I'm afraid we had to dismiss that nurse, Cornelius. She—she drank!" Lucy's face was bright red with embarrassment. "Excessively!"

Lady Caroline suddenly leaned over the arm of her chair. Clinging to it with white hands, she vomited into Lucy's sewing basket. An appalling odor emanated from the lady's ejecta.

Viola found the bell and pulled it. "Send for the doctor at once," she instructed the servant who appeared. "Lady Caroline is violently ill. Did you snort?" she demanded angrily.

She had wronged the servant; he had only guffawed. "Perhaps you had better go and get the doctor yourself, Mr Rampling," said Viola. "You may use my carriage. Miss Rampling and I will look after your mama."

Although he was fairly certain Dr Chadwick would not be pleased to come out to Gambol Hall in the middle of the night to tend to a drunken lady, Mr Rampling obediently departed.

Viola had the servants carry Lady Caroline up to her bedroom. Bramwell, her ladyship's maid, started up in surprise as the footman tossed her mistress onto the bed.

"This is Bramwell," Lucy said quickly. "Bramwell, this is Miss Andrews. Miss Andrews has come all the way from London for a visit."

"I'm the new nurse," Viola announced abruptly. "I shall be managing Lady Caroline's treatment from now on."

Lady Caroline lifted her head and moaned. "I'm seeing spots," she whined piteously. "Hundreds of them. Thousands of them. Spots floating everywhere like eyes."

Bramwell eyed Viola with dislike. "Your coat is making my lady sick," she accused.

Viola only smiled. "Mr Rampling has gone to fetch the doctor. Get her ladyship undressed, and clean her up as best you can. We don't want to embarrass the doctor, after all."

"Who are you to give me orders?" Bramwell demanded.

"You'd better do as she says," Lucy fretted. "Indeed, you had."

"You're the nurse, Miss Andrews," Bramwell glowered. "Why don't *you* clean her up?"

"Because I'm not a servant, I'm a professional woman," Viola replied, crossing the room to open the door. "Miss Rampling, would you be good enough to show me to my room? I'm quite fagged from my journey."

"Sorry, Brams," Lucy whispered, following Viola from the room. "I'll explain later!"

# Chapter Sixteen

Hudson arrived the next morning at Newgate Prison to attend his master. Apart from a few bumps and bruises, Julian was none the worse for wear. "I apologize for the delay, Captain," said Hudson. "They would not let me see you last night."

"Hudson, thank God!" Julian exclaimed, embracing his servant. "It's all a mistake, of course. I'm not plotting against the government. The whole thing is ridiculous."

"Of course not, Captain! Now, I've scraped together enough money to have you transferred from the common area to a private cell. I'll be allowed to stay and attend you."

"No, you must stay and look after Mary," Julian said firmly. "My poor darling! She must be out of her mind with worry. Tell her it's all a mistake. Tell her I'll be home in a few days."

"I'm afraid Mrs Devize has gone." Out of respect for his master's feelings, Hudson tried not to sound pleased. "She took her maid and her dog with her. She's left you, Captain."

Julian stared at him. "Mary would never leave me," he said slowly.

"I know it's difficult to accept such betrayal," said Hudson. "Lord Simon Ascot called yesterday, and . . . and Mrs Devize allowed herself to be persuaded to leave. I'm sorry, Captain."

"Ascot! I don't believe it."

"Here is his lordship's card," Hudson replied, glad that he had brought the proof of Mrs Devize's perfidy.

Julian felt sick to his stomach, and a feeling of bleak desolation came into his heart as he looked at the raised letters on Lord Simon's card. "But she doesn't even like him," he muttered.

"She seems to have overcome her dislike."

Julian sank to the bench that served as his bed. "I'll kill him. I'll bloody well kill him!"

"Perhaps," Hudson said gently, "it is for the best, Captain. If Mrs Devize would rather be his lordship's mistress than your wife, then we are better off without her."

Julian sighed. "I'll probably hang, you know," he said grimly. "Mr Harman of the Bank of England is giving evidence against me. God only knows what Mrs Dean is saying. At least with—with *him*, she will be assured of a roof over her head."

"Come, Captain," Hudson said gently. "Your private cell awaits."


Lady Caroline awoke the next day with a splitting headache. Otherwise, she was quite her usual nasty self. She snarled at the servant who brought in the breakfast tray. She threw a china shepherdess across the room and broke it to bits. She accused her daughter of stealing her peridot ear bobs. When the ear bobs were found on her dressing table, she lambasted Bramwell for her carelessness. All this she accomplished without leaving her bed.

Lucy arranged the pillows and helped her mother sit up. "Do you remember last night at all, Mama?" she asked gently, when the servants had gone.

"No," Lady Caroline snapped, lifting the silver cover of her breakfast. "Should I?" Scowling, she poked at her food with her spoon. "What the devil is this beastly muck?"

"It's porridge, Mama," Lucy answered. "Lady Viola says it is very healthful."

"Oh?" Lady Caroline sneered. "Does she? Does she indeed? Well, I may have to lick Lady Viola's boots when I see her, but she ain't here now! I'll be damned if I eat porridge."

"But Lady Viola *is* here, Mama," Lucy said quickly. "She arrived last night. Don't you remember? She's taken over the house, more or less. The servants are all in terror."

Lady Caroline was stunned. "Does she know we're behind on our rent?" she shrieked. "Is she here to evict us?"

"I don't think so," said Lucy. "She wants us to call her Miss Andrews."

"What on earth for?" Lady Caroline demanded.

Lucy shrugged helplessly. "She says she is incognito. She does not want to call attention to herself. She told Brams she's your new nurse."

"Nurse? Why do I need a nurse? I'm fit as a fiddle."

"I'm afraid Cornelius told her ladyship that you were ill," Lucy answered. "He had to explain to her ladyship why we were not in London for the Season. He was quite surprised when Lady Viola declared her intention of coming for a visit."

"Why did he make *me* sick?" Picking up her spoon, Lady Caroline watched gray porridge fall from it in unappetizing, drippy lumps. "Why couldn't *you* be the sick one? With your long face, you'd made a perfect patient. I hate porridge! Where is her ladyship now?"

Lucy looked out of the window almost fearfully. "She's gone riding with Cornelius. Thank goodness the head groom wouldn't allow us to sell the duke's horses."

Lady Caroline wrinkled her nose. "Cornelius? Is he here, too?"

"Yes, Mama. He accompanied Lady Viola from London."

Lady Caroline gasped. "Are they engaged?" she demanded. "Oh, Lucy! If Cornelius could catch a wife like Lady Viola . . . !" Cured of her headache, she flung off the bedclothes and jumped out of bed. Her brain commenced scheming at once. "Oh, I knew he was not so handsome for nothing! Call Brams! Help me get dressed. Hurry!"

"But Mama," Lucy protested. "Remember Lady Viola thinks you are ill, and your . . . your behavior last night seemed to confirm it. You must not leave your bed."

Lady Caroline scowled. "My behavior? There's nothing wrong with my behavior, Miss Lucy! I'm the eldest daughter of the Earl of Southwood. I am above reproach. And if Cornelius doesn't ruin his chances with Lady Viola, I will take my rightful place in Society again. I will make those bitches rue the day they ever snubbed me! See if I don't!"

The door opened at that moment, and Viola walked in, resplendent in a scarlet riding habit. She pointed at Lucy's mother with her riding crop. "You should be in bed, Lady Caroline. The doctor was most explicit in his instructions. You are a very sick woman. You must have complete bed rest, plain food, and nothing but fresh water to drink. It's the only way you're going to get well."

Lucy's eyes widened in amazement. The doctor had said quite plainly that the only thing wrong with Lady Caroline was a superfluity of strong liquor in her blood.

Lady Caroline blinked rapidly. "How sick am I?" she cried in terror.

"I don't want to alarm you, ma'am," said Viola, leading Lady Caroline back to bed, "but you could die at any time. So, please, don't get out of bed."

"I don't want to die!" cried Lady Caroline, clutching at Viola's arm.

"I'm quite sure you're not going to die, Mama," Lucy hastened to assure her.

"No, indeed," said Viola, moving to inspect the breakfast tray. "Not if you do as you're told. Lady Caroline, you naughty thing, you haven't eaten your porridge!" she scolded.

Lady Caroline forced a smile. She forced herself to pick up her spoon. She forced herself to take a bite. The porridge was cold and drab, but she forced herself to swallow it. "Delicious," she forced herself to say. "May I have just a little treacle, Lady Viola?" she pleaded.

Viola smiled. "Tomorrow," she promised sweetly. "*If* you are feeling better."

"I'm feeling quite well now," Lady Caroline said pathetically.

"Don't try to talk, dear," Viola replied. "You must conserve your strength. Your recovery depends on it." Walking about the room, she opened all the curtains, admitting volumes of bright sunlight. Lady Caroline cried out in pain. "What a beautiful morning!" said Viola, striding for the door. "I'll be back to check on you in a few minutes, dear Lady Caroline, and if you do not eat every bite of your porridge, I shall be very, very angry with you. Come, Miss Rampling," she said imperiously.

Lucy jumped nervously. "Yes?"

"It's time you were dressed, dear. You and I must make something of this glorious day."

Lucy looked down at her gown in confusion. "But I *am* dressed, Lady Viola!"

"No, you're not," Viola informed her firmly. "You're merely clothed, and that's something very different. And you really must remember to call me Miss Andrews," she added. "Come. Your poor mama needs her rest."

Nothing in Miss Rampling's humble wardrobe escaped Viola's wrath. "Rags!" she snarled in disgust as she tore through Lucy's dresses. "How long has it been since you had anything new?" she demanded. "Everything you own looks like it got caught in the rain, then dragged through the mud. I never saw so much brown and gray in my life."

Lucy summoned her dignity. "I have no need of fancy clothes, Lady Viola. I live quietly in the country, and I'm too old to keep up with fashions."

"One is never too old to be fashionable," Viola objected. "Besides, you're only thirty. *I* shall be thirty in nine years. I certainly don't intend to be *old* in nine years!"

"What I mean is I'm a confirmed spinster," Lucy explained. "I shall never marry. So, you see, there's really no point in my dressing like a young girl in the market for a husband."

Viola was appalled. "We do not dress for men, Miss Rampling," she said sternly. "Most men cannot tell one dress from another. The point is always to look one's best. It has nothing to do with finding a husband or being young. Now, then," she went on, taking a position at the open clothespress. "Which of these appalling gray things do you wear in the morning, when you are writing letters? What do you wear to receive visitors?"

"This, I suppose," Lucy replied, indicating the striped gown currently enveloping her thin frame. "But we rarely receive visitors, Lady Viola, and, surely, it does not matter what one wears when one is writing one's letters," she added, chuckling.

"Doesn't matter?" Viola repeated angrily. "Doesn't matter? My dear Lucy, even if you do not receive visitors, you must receive your housekeeper, and your butler. You must discuss the menu with Cook."

"The servants do not care what I wear. In any case, Mama meets with them."

"Well, now that your mother is confined to her room, you must assume the role of mistress of the house," Viola said firmly. "If you continue to dress like a dishrag, the servants will never respect you. This certainly explains the dust I discovered on the mantelpiece!"

"What does my dress have to do with dust on the mantel-piece?" cried Lucy.

Viola turned Lucy to face the mirror. "If I were a servant, I wouldn't dust the mantelpiece for somebody who looked like you," she said brutally. "Now, look at *me*!" she went on, taking Lucy's place at the mirror. "Who wouldn't want to dust *my* mantelpiece?" she asked, preening. "There's nothing else to do, Miss Rampling. You must have all new clothes."

"We cannot possibly afford it," Lucy protested breathlessly.

"My dear girl, you can't afford not to," Viola said briskly. "You must keep up appearances. You are the granddaughter of an earl, not the scullery maid. Come to my room. I've got heaps of idea books from London. You can look at them while I change."

Lucy had no idea what an idea book was. She was doubt-ful, but Viola prevailed, as always. Viola's room was next to Lucy's, separated by a shared dressing room.

Cork, who was just beginning to unpack Viola's trunks, curtseyed as her mistress came in. "Your bath is ready, madam, but I can't find your dressing gown!" she wailed.

Viola went to the correct trunk and put her hands on the dressing gown instantly. "This is Miss Rampling, Cork. She wants to look at my magazines."

Cork obligingly placed Viola's collection of magazines on the worktable near the window. Lucy reluctantly sat down to look at them while Viola went into the dressing room.

The magazines had names like *Le Bon Ton, Les Modes de Paris* and *Le Petit Courier des Dames*. They all featured drawings of beautiful ladies in fantastic costumes. Lucy tried to imagine herself wearing "a half-dress of geranium jaconet muslin with a demi-train; body of Imperial purple and white shot sarsenet, richly embroidered in heliotrope, made in the same manner as last month, except that the waist is a little shorter; the sleeve, which is of delicate pink jaconet muslin, is very full, and is looped up with a scarlet floss silk ornament in the shape of a heart." In such a garment, Lucy felt sure she would look ridiculous.

Twenty minutes later, Viola emerged from the dressing room clad in a peacock blue gown that might have come straight from Paris. Worn over an almost transparent high-necked chemise, it had a deep, square neckline, elbow-length sleeves, and a skirt that was flat across the front but gathered at the back. The waist was longer than the prevailing fashions, almost at the natural waist. On impulse, Viola had pinned a small diamond brooch at her décolleté, and the tiny stones caught fire with the rise and fall of her breasts.

"*This*," Viola announced, joining Lucy at the worktable, "is the perfect morning costume for the country. With the shorter sleeve one need not worry about ink-stained cuffs. I despise an ink-stained cuff. You, my dear," she went on seamlessly as Lucy tried in vain to hide her ink-stained cuffs, "are blessed with a thin, slight figure. That means you can wear the minimum. Something like this, perhaps. Is it not a charming ensemble?"

As Viola held out the fashion plate for inspection, Lucy's eyes widened in alarm. The lady in the picture seemed to be wearing a dress made not of fabric but of flowing water. "I don't think I care to wear the minimum, Lady Viola!"

Viola paid no attention to Lucy's objections. Taking out her pencil and paper, she began to sketch gowns on a pad of paper, talking all the while. Lucy's head began to spin. Resignation succeeded her initial panic. It seemed she was doomed to be the recipient of an entire new wardrobe which she could not afford and certainly could not wear with any confidence. Her only hope was that Viola would lose interest in her latest project and find something else to occupy her time before any of these outrageous costumes were ever realized.

"Have you seen the garden, Lady Viola?" she asked desperately.

"You have reminded me," Viola said gratefully. "One needs

at least three garden costumes in the country—there are *so* many flowers to cut."

Lucy sighed. "Shouldn't we check on Mama?" she pleaded.

"We will check on her when she is feeling a little better," Viola answered serenely, completely absorbed in her work.

"When will that be?"

Viola smiled. "After luncheon, I should think. I've ordered a delightful gruel for her midday repast. She's to have it in her room on a tray. You and Mr Rampling and I will dine alfresco, under the pavilion."

"What pavilion?" Lucy asked nervously.

"The servants are erecting it as we speak," Viola replied. "When one is in the country, it is a crime to stay indoors when the weather is fine. Do you mean to tell me you've never had luncheon on the grass?"

"We often go on picnics in summer," Lucy replied.

"Then we must definitely order a few picnic costumes for you," Viola murmured. "And, of course, we mustn't forget God."

Lucy was startled. "God?"

"One cannot go to church looking like a church mouse," Viola explained.


As Viola had predicted, Lady Caroline was perfectly well after luncheon. She was so much better, in fact, that Viola allowed her to have one glass of watered claret with her dinner. During the night, however, Lady Caroline suffered a relapse. In the morning, she was discovered in the wine cellar, quite unconscious, surrounded by empty bottles. Viola seized the keys to the cellar from the butler, and Cornelius carried Lady Caroline up to bed.

"She must have slipped on the empty bottles," Lucy insisted tearfully.

"Indeed!" Cornelius agreed bitterly. "After she guzzled the contents!"

Only Lucy objected when Viola took the unusual step of locking Lady Caroline in her room. "Can we really do that?" she asked. "I mean, must we?" she corrected herself.

"It is for her own good," Viola said grimly. "We don't want her slipping on any more empty bottles, now, do we?"

Cornelius spent the afternoon attempting to make sense of his mother's accounts, while Viola and Lucy met with the local dressmaker. Feeling rather like a pincushion, Lucy stood in her petticoats for what seemed like hours while Viola argued with the woman. After the dressmaker's departure, boredom ensued, and, to relieve it, Viola threatened to "do something" with Lucy's mousy hair.

Lucy was spared this indignity, however, by the unexpected arrival of two visitors. Mr Rampling received them in the drawing room while the upstairs maid was dispatched to inform the ladies that Lady Cheviot of Cross Mere, and her brother, Mr Devize, had called.

Lucy turned bright pink. Impulsively, she rushed to the mirror and ineffectively fussed with her hair. Her own plainness, reflected back to her in the unforgiving mirror, soon brought her back to her senses, however. Sheepishly, she turned to face Lady Viola, certain that the other girl must be laughing at her ridiculous display of vanity.

Viola was not laughing. To Lucy's surprise, she had turned as pale as death. With white fingers, she gripped the arms of her chair. "Oh, Lucy!" she gasped. "I cannot see him!" Releasing the arms of the chair, she clutched her belly as if in physical pain. "I am still in love with him. I thought it was all finished, but evidently it is not. Though he has hurt me—though he has broken my heart—I still love him, fool that I am."

Lucy sank slowly into her chair, her heart pounding with dread. "You are in love with Mr Devize?" she whispered.

"I am," Viola moaned. "I thought we would be married, but I was wrong."

"Did he promise you marriage?" Lucy asked, astonished.

"Yes. Every day! But he has betrayed me."

Lucy struggled to keep her composure. "I cannot believe it. Mr Devize is an honorable man. He would not betray you. I am sure of it."

Viola blinked at her. "You know him?"

"Yes, I know him very well," Lucy replied. "If Mr Devize has promised to marry you, then marry you he will."

Viola grasped her hand. "Do you really think so, Lucy?"

"Yes," Lucy said simply.

Viola ran to the mirror. "Will you go down first, Lucy?" she asked, adjusting the ribbon in her hair. "I want to look perfect for him."

Lucy felt a stab of violent jealousy. Lady Viola had everything: beauty, wealth, and rank. She even had cleverness and charm. Now, it seemed, she had Alex, too.

"Of course, Lady Viola," she heard her own voice say.

"Miss Andrews!" Viola corrected, dabbing on perfume. "He does not know I am Lady Viola. I thought—I still hope—that he loves me for myself alone."

Lucy went down like a sleepwalker and greeted her guests with determined politeness.

Lady Cheviot was looking especially charming in her emerald green riding habit. "My dear Lucy," she said, eyeing the girl's lifeless gray gown, "how elegant you look."

Alexander Devize was standing at the recently dusted mantelpiece, looking very gentlemanlike in his riding coat and breeches. "Good morning, Miss Rampling," he greeted her cheerfully. "You did not visit us at Cross Mere yesterday, or this morning. The twins were quite sure their auxiliary governess had been murdered!" He smiled. "My sister and I have been dispatched to kidnap you and bring you to the tree house without delay."

Lucy stared at him in agony. His dark eyes were twinkling.

His smile was warm and charming. In spite of his pockmarks, she had always thought him handsome. She had always loved him. It had given her great pain to refuse his offer of marriage. She did not begrudge him the right to marry someone else. But could he not have chosen a plain, ordinary woman, preferably a woman completely unknown to herself? Did he have to punish her by choosing Lady Viola Gambol as his wife?

"I have been very busy, Mr Devize," Lucy said stiffly. "Do please convey my regrets to Henry and Elizabeth. It is a warm afternoon," she went on. "Shall we have lemonade?"

"I have already ordered it," said Cornelius. "Is Miss Andrews not coming down?" he asked Lucy when they were all seated. "Is there a problem with . . . *you know who?*"

He spoke in an undertone, but Lady Cheviot had excellent hearing. Her brows rose. "Miss Andrews?" she repeated politely. "Have you a visitor, Miss Rampling?"

Lucy's reply was hardly attended as Viola entered the room, regal in peacock blue, her small white dog in her arms. Alex Devize and Cornelius sprang to their feet. Perdita stared at Viola in astonishment. Everything and everyone in the room paled in comparison to the new arrival. Perdita felt fat and sweaty, and Lucy simply faded into obscurity.

Cornelius hastily performed the introductions. Lucy watched obliquely as Alex Devize bent over Viola's hand. How they both dissembled! Why, they might have been strangers.

"Your friend is very young, Miss Rampling," Perdita remarked coldly, looking down her nose at the overdressed beauty. "Does she mean to stay long in Hampshire?"

"With Lady Caroline so ill, I am come to help poor Lucy manage," Viola explained. "I shall stay as long as I am needed, Lady Cheviot."

"But, Lucy, my dear!" cried Perdita. "I did not know your mama was ill."

"It was immensely sudden," Viola explained before Lucy could say a word. "The house was in the most shocking state when I arrived, but I believe I am making progress. Poor Lucy doesn't know the first thing about running a household of this size," she added kindly, patting Lucy's hand. "The servants have been taking full advantage of the situation, of course, but I will soon have everything set to rights."

"Have you had the doctor?" Alex inquired of Lucy, but, again, Viola answered.

"Oh, yes, Mr Devize. Dr Chadwick was very helpful. Lady Caroline is to be confined to her room until she is quite well again."

"What a pity," Perdita murmured. "I was hoping Miss Rampling might attend a little assembly I am giving at Cross Mere on Wednesday."

"Oh?" said Viola.

"I'm sure my sister will postpone her ball until Miss Rampling can attend," said Alex.

Perdita looked startled. "Postpone! Impossible, I'm afraid."

"Is it a ball?" Viola inquired. "Or a little assembly?"

"It's really just a small party to introduce my brother to the neighborhood," said Perdita, annoyed. "There will be dancing, of course, and supper."

Viola chuckled. "Are you having a Come-Out Ball, Mr Devize?" she teased him.

Alex smiled back. "Something like that, Miss Andrews."

"What a pity Miss Rampling cannot go," sighed Perdita. "She will be missed."

"Nonsense," said Viola. "An evening of good food, good exercise, and good society would do Lucy a world of good, I am persuaded. *I'm afraid,*" she added in a stage whisper, "*that Lady Caroline has been a difficult patient. So hard on Lucy, you know.*"

Lady Cheviot forced a smile. "Yes, do come, Miss Rampling. Miss Andrews, you are very welcome, too," she added reluctantly.

"Oh, heavens, no," Viola said carelessly. "I must stay here with poor Lady Caroline."

"Oh, no," Lucy said. "*I* will stay with Mama. *You* should go, Miss Andrews."

"Dear Lucy, I'm your mother's nurse," Viola replied. "I'm not here to go to balls or assemblies or whatever. I'm here so that *you* can go to balls and assemblies and whatever."

Lady Cheviot eyed Viola's diamond ornaments suspiciously. "Nurse? You?"

"Your brother can escort you, Lucy," Viola went on. "I daresay Lady Cheviot will be glad of an extra gentleman. There are never enough men to go around at these small country gatherings. Lady Cheviot, you must promise to get Lucy partners. That is my one condition."

"I should be very glad to dance with Miss Rampling," Alex said warmly.

Lucy looked at him, startled. How could he ask her to dance, when he was betrothed to Viola? It was cruel to both Viola and to herself. At the same time, she could not help but admire Viola's ability to hide her feelings. No one would ever suspect that she was in love with Mr Devize. She seemed supremely indifferent to his very existence.

Alex looked at Lucy, puzzled by the look she gave him. "I thought perhaps we could open the ball, Miss Rampling. As old friends, you know."

"Alex," Perdita said reproachfully, "you forget you are engaged already for the first dance. And for the supper dance, too. But I see no reason why Miss Rampling cannot have you for the two-third, or the two-fifth."

"Let us put him down for the two-third," Viola said shrewdly. "And, of course, you will give Lucy your husband for the supper dance."

Perdita stiffened. "I've half promised Lord Cheviot to Mrs Chisholm, I'm afraid."

Viola waved her hand. "Oh, a married lady can always take herself to supper."

"Mrs Chisholm is extremely nearsighted," Perdita snapped. "She requires the arm of a gentleman."

Viola sighed. "Oh, that *is* unfortunate for Lucy. Who else have you got?"

As Viola and Lady Cheviot haggled over available gentlemen, Alex turned to Lucy and said quietly, "I should a thousand times prefer to dance with *you*."

Lucy stiffened at this pleasantry, and Alex was left wondering what he had done to offend her.

The servant brought the lemonade. "Begging your pardon, miss," she addressed Viola. "The cook would like a word with you."

Viola stood up, relegating Lucy to serve the lemonade to her guests. "I daresay it's about the fish," she sighed. "Is there no salmon to be had in Hampshire?"

Lady Cheviot positively smirked. "I'm afraid that's *my* fault, Miss Andrews. *My* cook always gets the salmon—why, she must get up before the dawn! There's plenty of haddock, however. I myself do not care for haddock, but other people seem to find it edible. I'll have my cook send your cook her receipt for white sauce."

"It's very civil of you to offer, Lady Cheviot," Viola said coolly, "but I am hoping we need not resort to white sauce! Please excuse me."

Lady Cheviot and her brother did not stay long after that. After the departure of her guests, Lucy had no more than a few moments alone in her room before Viola descended upon her with a selection of gowns for the ball. "We haven't much time," said Viola. "Lady Cheviot should be shot for inviting you on such short notice. Under the circumstances, I think the best we can do is take one of my dresses and cut it down for you. The question is which one."

The rest of the afternoon was taken up with this momentous decision. Viola pinned and scrutinized each gown in turn, finally selecting a sapphire blue silk. "This will do," she said with an air of resignation. "I have a set of amethysts that should bring out the blue in your eyes."

"My eyes are gray," Lucy said doubtfully.

Viola ignored her. "And the velvet cloak will go very well with golden ringlets."

"My hair is brown, Lady Viola. And it will not hold a curl, I'm sorry to say."

"I can't decide if I want to give you a bosom or not," Viola said, frowning as she studied Lucy's small, thin frame. "I've never needed to wear shapes myself—obviously—but a little padding might be just what *you* need."

"Certainly not!" said Lucy, blushing furiously.

"That settles it," Viola said. "I'm for anything that puts a little color in your cheeks!"

It was left to Lucy to bring up the subject of Mr Devize. "He should not have asked me to dance," she apologized. "He only did so because we are old friends. I hope you were not hurt by this meaningless gesture."

Viola looked at her in amazement. "What are you talking about? Why should I care?"

Lucy blinked in confusion.

Viola laughed suddenly. "That was not *my* Mr Devize! Why, I'd completely forgotten that Julian has an elder brother. Mr Alexander Devize is nothing to me. He's not very handsome, is he?" she added, wrinkling her nose. "What's the matter?" she cried, catching sight of Lucy's pale face.

Forgetting that her dress was pinned all over, Lucy sat down hard on the bed and instantly jumped up again. "Nothing," she said.

"You're white as death," Viola said. "You're in love with him yourself!" she accused.

"No!"

"Oh, and he doesn't even know you're alive. Poor Lucy!" Viola clucked her tongue sympathetically. "How very sad."

Lucy was provoked. "He *does* know I'm alive! Indeed, he asked me to marry him."

"Oh?" said Viola, interested.

"It was a long time ago, and I refused him, of course," Lucy said quickly.

"Because he's not handsome?" said Viola. "That's rather shallow, don't you think?"

"I refused him because the match would not suit," Lucy said indignantly. "My father's suicide . . . My lack of a fortune . . . His family did not approve the match."

"Presumably, he knew all that when he asked you?"

"Well, yes, but . . . I could not accept him. I could not condemn him to a lifetime of regret, even though he was willing to condemn himself."

"Hardly a lifetime," Viola pointed out. "Your lives are half over already."

"I vowed never to regret my decision," Lucy said stiffly. "I know I was right. Sooner or later, he would have come to regret his folly."

Viola sighed. "In my case, I have nothing *but* regret, and I know I was wrong."

"In your case, there is still hope," Lucy said kindly.

Viola shook her head. Taking a scrap of paper from her pocket, she gave it to Lucy, saying, "Read this and tell me to hope, if you can!"

The handwriting was not the best, but Lucy managed to decipher it.

*Dear Sir—*

*Let us be direct and come to terms. I will give you 20,000 guineas for Miss A—. This will yield you an immediate profit of 3,000 guineas. If you are amenable to my offer—as I am sure you will be—you may find me in my rooms at the Albany.*

It was signed simply, Simon Ascot.

"Who," cried Lucy, bewildered, "or what, is 'Miss A'?"

"I am!" Viola told her. "I am Miss A. You see? Julian Devize lured me into his web with a promise of marriage, then he tried to sell me to another man—a man I don't even like!"

Twisting her hands together, she began to stalk the room. "He filled my head with nonsense. That is what they do, you know. They promise you marriage, the moon, and the stars. Then they take advantage of your innocence and trust. When they are quite finished with you, they simply abandon you or pass you on to the next man."

Lucy was pale with horror. "Good heavens, Lady Viola! You didn't let him—you didn't let him *kiss* you?"

Viola stopped dead in her tracks. She did not approve of lying, of course, but occasionally it was absolutely essential to do so. This was one of those occasions.

"Lord, no," she declared vehemently. "Are you mad? You must know I'd never permit such a thing. I'm not a complete fool, you know. I was speaking hypothetically."

"Of course," Lucy said quickly, although she was now quite convinced that Viola *had* been kissed. "I–I never thought otherwise!"

# Chapter Seventeen

A Great Dane and a Dalmatian greeted the Duchess of Berkshire as she walked up the steps to Gambol House on Friday morning. Looking very smart in a lilac costume overlaid with black lace, she fended them off as best she could with her parasol until her footman rescued her.

One of the duke's footmen emerged from the house in what can only be described as a lackadaisical manner and rounded up the dogs. "Is the wedding to take place today?" the duchess demanded of him, handing her shredded parasol to her own footman. "There was no notice in the *Post*. I received no invitation."

This particular footman had traveled with the duke from Yorkshire. "I don't know nothing about no wedding, ma'am," he said, holding on to the dogs' collars with both fists.

The duchess beamed at him. "Excellent! In that case, I'd like to see Miss Andrews."

The footman followed her inside, dragging the dogs. As he closed the door, the dogs flashed off in the direction of the morning room. "Whom shall I say is calling, ma'am?"

The duchess glared at him, but he merely looked back at her. "You know perfectly well who I am," she snapped. "I was here two days ago. Lady Viola will hear of this impudence. You are Jem, are you not?"

He grinned at her. "Jem's my twin brother. I've just come down from Yorkshire with his grace. I'm also called Jem, for ease of use, ma'am. *You* might have been here two days ago, but *I* weren't."

"Oh, I see," said the duchess, slightly mollified. "The duke's back, is he? Good! You may announce the Duchess of Berkshire."

Dickon was delighted to receive her. He even remembered to stand up for the duchess, although he couldn't be bothered to bow. Instead, he pounced on her, seizing her by the hand. "I love duchesses," he said effusively. "My mother was a duchess, you know."

"I know," she answered dryly, her attention caught by a small, pretty, genteel sort of girl. She was not precisely seated on a sofa; rather, she was pinned down to it by a pair of Dalmatians. A third dog, the Dane, was standing with his front paws on the young lady's knees. The girl stared at the duchess with big, innocent brown eyes. When she realized that the duchess was looking back at her, she blushed hotly and hastily turned her attention to the duke's dogs.

The duchess picked up a pug from a chair and sat down with it in her lap.

As every other seat in the room was occupied by some type of canine, the duke contented himself with leaning his portly frame over the back of the sofa occupied by the girl. The duchess waited in vain for an introduction. Finally, she said, "How do you do, my dear? I am the Duchess of Berkshire. Who might you be?"

Looking rather terrified, the young lady tried to get to her feet, but it was impossible.

"Tell her who you are, Mary," the duke encouraged her.

"Please, ma'am! My name is Mary Andrews."

"Little Mary," the duke said fondly, patting her on the head. "When I got to Fanshawe, Viola was gone, but there was little Mary, all alone. I thought I might as well bring her with me to London."

"And here she is!" the duchess said with shamelessly false gaiety. "You must find London very different from Gambolthwaite, Miss Andrews."

Mary's eyes widened in surprise. "Does your ladyship know Gambolthwaite?"

"I'm a duchess, dear, not a ladyship," the duchess corrected her gently.

"Yes, Duchess," Mary said meekly.

"Of course I know all about you, Miss Andrews. Lady Viola told me. She took a great risk coming to London to meet your dreadful aunt. You must be very grateful to her."

"Oh, I am, to be sure, Duchess," Mary assured her.

"Mary's aunt is a Very Bad Woman," said Dickon, shaking his head. "On no account is Mary to see her. Viola absolutely forbids it."

"Yes, she is a bad woman. Have you thought of what you're

going to do next, my dear?" the duchess asked Mary. "I could help you find a position. I know simply everyone."

The duke looked angry. "*Do*, madam? Mary's not going to *do* anything. She's going to stay right with the people who love her."

The duchess's brows rose. "The people who love her!"

"Viola and me," the duke explained. "I've decided to give Mary the protection of my name, you see." Rescuing Mary's hand from the dogs, he kissed it fervently.

"Only if Lady Viola approves, of course," Mary said anxiously.

"Well, she's not likely to, is she?" the duchess snorted. "Any attachment between a Miss Andrews and the Duke of Fanshawe must be considered reprehensible. Miss Andrews, if you had any sense of propriety, you would not be so eager to advance yourself by such artful means! Presumptuous, ambitious creature! Shame on you!"

Mary burst into tears. "Now look what you've done, you old bat!" Dickon said angrily. "Viola won't object—indeed, she won't, Mary! Why, Viola and Mary are dear friends!" Taking out his handkerchief, he dried Mary's tears.

"I would rather die," Mary gasped, "than upset her ladyship!"

"I'm sure you would," the duchess said incredulously. "Where *is* Lady Viola?" she demanded. "I collect she is not at home? Else she would have put an end to this nonsense!"

"Viola's gone to the country to visit a sick friend," Dickon coldly replied.

"Oh?" said the duchess, frowning. "Which sick friend? Which part of the country?"

The duke scowled. "Why does everyone keep asking me that?" he snapped. "Am I my sister's keeper?"

"Of course you're not," the duchess said soothingly. "But poor Viola! She must be so upset, what with her wedding being canceled and all. I'm most anxious to condole with her."

Dickon shrugged. "She doesn't know the wedding's been canceled. Not yet. But I doubt she'll be upset at all. She never liked Bamph, you know, and, as it turns out, she was right!"

"Bamph!" said the duchess.

"Marquis of," Dickon clarified. "A very fine fellow I thought him at first, but, as it turns out, he doesn't wear well. I'm a tolerant man, Duchess. I could have overlooked a fault here and there, but when he practically assaulted poor Mary in St Albans . . . ! He's lucky I didn't kill him!"

"Assaulted?" said the duchess, looking sharply at the girl on the sofa.

"He tried to kiss the poor girl!" said Dickon. "No better than an animal!"

"You must have encouraged him, Miss Andrews," the duchess accused. "Perhaps you didn't mean to," she added generously. "But there it is. You allowed Lord Bamph to compromise you, and now you must marry him or be lost to all good society forever!"

"That's just what *I* said," said the duke. "But *he* flatly refused to marry her, the scoundrel! He said he was only seducing her to keep *her* from seducing *me*! Apparently, they was all afraid I was going to *marry* the gel. What nonsense! As though I could be arsed to marry a vicar's child! I'm a duke, for God's sake."

"You mean . . . You are *not* going to marry Miss Andrews?" the duchess said slowly.

"Of course not!" said Dickon, quite shocked. "Marry Miss Andrews? You're as mad as the Bamphs. Viola would have my guts for garters."

"I beg your pardon," said the duchess, experiencing a thaw. "But when you alluded to giving Miss Andrews the protection of your name, I naturally assumed . . ."

"I'm going to adopt her, of course," Dickon said proudly.

"Oh!" cried the duchess, clapping her hands. "Oh, how delightful! In that case, I daresay Lady Viola will have no objection. No objection at all."

"Of course she won't," said Dickon.

"I do hope her ladyship won't be angry with me," Mary fretted.

"She will not be angry," Dickon assured her. "She never liked Bamph. I saw through him at once—well, almost at once. Good riddance, I say! I don't want the father of my nephew and heir to be a man of such low character."

"Your heir?" said the duchess, her ears pricking up. "You do not plan to marry at all, then, Your Grace? Ever?"

Dickon shuddered. "Lord, no!" he said forcefully. "Viola's always been the strong one. It's up to her to carry on the bloodline. I'm just too squeamish for such exercise. I admit I had high hopes for Bamph," he continued, sighing. "Who am I going to get for her now? I don't know the first thing about arranging marriages—my father arranged the match with Bamph."

"I certainly am not one for arranging marriages," the duchess said modestly, "but this *is* a special case. The siring of a future Duke of Fanshawe is serious business, and must not be left to chance. Fortunately, I have a son I can give you."

The duke blinked at her. "Madam! That is most generous of you."

The duchess shrugged magnanimously. "The match is perfect. His father was a duke, and so was hers. He's thirty-two, which is a good age for a man."

"What about breeding?" Dickon asked suspiciously. "Can he do the job?"

"Would I offer him if there was any doubt?" she returned feistily. "And money is no object, of course. We *are* the Ascots, after all."

"Money's no object for us, either," Dickon said belligerently. "We're the Gambols."

The duchess smiled. "What could be more natural than an alliance between two such rich, noble families of ancient lineage? They will breed."

Dickon's eyes narrowed. "Is your son good-looking, madam? I don't want an ugly nephew!"

"Simon is devastatingly attractive," said Simon's mother. "He is tall, broad-shouldered . . . The pain of his birth was excruciating. But he looks a treat in his uniform, so I don't complain."

"Uniform?" the duke echoed.

"Simon currently holds the rank of lieutenant-colonel in the Horse Guards."

"Regimentals!" Dickon sighed happily.

"He's on parade this afternoon," said she. "Why not come and take a look at him?"

"Oh, I love parades!" cried Dickon. "Don't you, Mary?"

"I've never seen a parade," Mary confessed.

Dickon gaped at her. "Never seen a parade!"

"Then it's all settled," the duchess said happily, climbing to her feet. "I'll call for you at three o'clock. We'll go in my barouche."

"Oh no! I forgot to offer you tea!" cried Miss Andrews, struggling in vain to get up.

The duchess was now so well-disposed toward Miss Andrews that she stooped down to kiss her cheek. "That's quite all right, my dear. We're practically family now. We need not stand on ceremony."


Cold, damp air poured through the bars of the tiny open window of Julian's cell, along with a little gloomy gray light. While stuffing the opening with his coat, the young man had an excellent view of the gallows in the yard below. With the opening blocked, the room was black as pitch and no warmer. With a sigh, he pulled his coat on again. Rats had the run of the place, only bothering to scurry when Julian threw his shoe at them. The air was thick and foul with disease. In such unpleasant surroundings, it was not difficult to imagine the end was near.

The key scraped in the lock and the cell door swung open. Julian looked up, half-expecting to be dragged off to the magistrate, but it was only Hudson.

"I've written a letter to my father," he greeted his servant. "I've asked him to look after you when I'm dead. He'll do it, I expect."

"Captain, they will not hang you," Hudson said tremulously.

"Of course they'll hang me," Julian replied. "They hang a child for stealing a loaf of bread. Why wouldn't they hang me?" He sighed heavily. "Any letters?"

"No, Captain. Just this bill from a Mr Grey, a jeweler."

Hudson held it out to his master, but Julian merely shrugged. "He'll have to get in line for his ten pounds, I'm afraid."

"Ten *thousand* pounds, Captain," Hudson corrected him.

"There must be some mistake," Julian muttered, snatching the bill from his servant.

Hudson began unpacking the basket. "Did I say pounds? I meant guineas. In pounds that would be ten thousand, five hundred, I should think."

"I thought it was *ten pounds*," Julian said indignantly. "Where the devil am I supposed to get *ten thousand guineas*?"

"Try to eat something, Captain," Hudson pleaded with him. "It's only bread and cheese, but I think you'll find it nourishing."

Julian began pacing the tiny cell. Abruptly, he stopped at the window. "This is the end of me, Hudson," he said, looking at the gallows. "I'll die on those gallows. I'm finished. I'm beginning to think I made a mistake," he added dryly.

"Beauty is a snare, Captain. I knew that woman would be your ruination."

"You might have mentioned it sooner," Julian said, trying to smile. "No word from her, then? Nothing at all? No? She might at least have sent me my ring back!" He sat down at the table and tore off a hunk of bread. "Do you know what the worst part of it is?"

Hudson shuddered. "When the neck fails to break. Death by strangulation can very slow and painful, or so I understand."

"I miss her." Julian laughed harshly. "She's left me for another man, and still I miss her. I lie here at night on my cold slab of a cot, and I remember the short, sweet time we had together. I wonder what she's doing right now."

"She is with Lord Simon. You know what she's doing," Hudson said brutally. "Don't torment yourself, Captain. She isn't worth the salt of your tears."

Jumping up, Julian stalked the room. "I've got to get out of here, Hudson," he said wildly. "Couldn't we bribe the guards? I just want to see her one last time."

"I've already pawned everything we had in order to get you into a private cell," Hudson said apologetically. "She's gone, Captain."

Julian picked up the table and threw it against the wall. "I want out of here!" he roared.

"That can be arranged," said a cold, familiar voice from the vicinity of the cell door.

"Mother!" Julian exclaimed, jumping to his feet.

The door creaked open. The baroness came in and threw back her veil. Walking up to Julian, she slapped his face. "*That* is for making me come to Newgate," she explained as Hudson quickly set the table back on its legs. "And *this* is for calling me Mother," she said, slapping Julian again. "Do you think I want people to know that I am here, visiting my son in prison?" she hissed.

"I'm sorry," Julian said stiffly. "I was so surprised that I fear I became exuberant."

"See that it doesn't happen again," she said, seating herself.

Julian remained standing. "Why are you here, madam? Have you come to gloat?"

"I've come to help you, of course," she said. "How will it look if my son is hanged like a common criminal, after all? *That* would not be good for my social standing."

"You're getting me a lawyer?"

She smirked. "People like us don't need lawyers, Julian. I can have the charges against you thrown out like that," she said, snapping her gloved fingers. "My uncle is very well placed in government, as you know, and I'm his favorite niece. I know where all the bodies are buried, so he has little choice in the matter."

"What do you want in return?" Julian asked, his fingers laced together behind his head.

"I want only what is best for you," she replied. "You will not, of course, be marrying Miss Andrews. That is my first condition."

"There is not the least possibility of my marrying Miss Andrews," said Julian, shrugging. "She has left me to become Lord Simon Ascot's mistress."

"The Duchess of Berkshire's son?" The baroness chuckled in unfeigned delight. "Why, that scheming little slut! How did she manage that little trick?"

"We'd be married now if you hadn't used your influence to prevent me from obtaining the special license," Julian said bitterly. "I've seen Colonel Fairfax. Madam, how could you?"

"It was for your own good, Julian," she said smugly. "If Miss Andrews would rather be Lord Simon's mistress than your wife—"

"Quite," he interrupted sharply. "You will secure my freedom if I do not marry Miss Andrews. What else?"

"You will like this," she promised. "I've had a visit from

Lady Bamph. She is come back from Yorkshire. Apparently, the match between her daughter and the Duke of Fanshawe failed to materialize, and the match between Lord Bamph and Lady Viola is in a very precarious position. In fact, the duke has called the whole thing off!"

"The duke is back in London?" Julian asked with fresh interest.

"He is. Lady Bamph is quite desperate. She is willing to let you have Belinda, if you can bring about the marriage of Lady Viola and her son. And so my second condition is that you marry Lady Belinda."

"Marry Belinda?" Julian said dully. "You must be joking."

"She has a dowry of some thirty thousand pounds, Julian," the baroness said, her blue eyes glinting greedily. "This marriage would be our ticket back into Society."

"A pox on Society," he said violently.

"You will marry her, Julian," Lady Devize said coldly. "If you do, you will live to be a very rich man. If you don't, you will hang. The choice is simple."

"Yes," Julian agreed, smiling. "The choice *is* very simple. I'm afraid I can't accept your conditions. Sorry."

"What?" she cried, frightened by his smile. "Are you mad? Hudson, is he mad?"

Hudson's face was white. "He cannot marry Lady Belinda because he is already married—to Miss Andrews," he explained sadly.

"Married already?" she whispered. "Then you will surely hang. Guard!"

She left his cell without another word.

"If only you hadn't married that deceitful strumpet!" Hudson mourned.

"I didn't," said Julian. "Sorry, Hudson. I lied to you. I *wanted* to marry Miss Andrews very much, but I never had the chance. She is not my wife."

Hudson did not know whether to laugh or cry. He settled

for something in between. "But sir! Lady Belinda! You could be free!"

"Free is the last thing I'd be," Julian replied with a snort. "I'd be better off selling my soul to the devil than to my mother. Cheer up, Hudson! The duke is back in town. Let us hope he is in a forgiving mood."

It seemed to Julian that Hudson had scarcely departed for Gambol House when the duke himself appeared at the cell door, demanding admittance. Julian was laying down on his bench with his eyes closed. Before he could sit up, a Great Dane was licking his face, and the duke was peering down at him.

"Dev!" he cried, flinging up his arms. "Guess my surprise when I heard you was in prison! They're saying terrible things about you—worse than usual!"

Julian sat up, despite the best efforts of the Dane to keep him down. "Is Hudson not with you?" he asked, puzzled.

"Hudson? Who is he?"

"My man," said Julian. "I just sent him to Gambol House with a note for you."

"I wasn't there," Dickon said. "I've been out looking for *you*, Dev. I even went to the Exchange. They told me you were incarcerated. I couldn't believe it!"

"Neither could I at first," Julian said ruefully, petting the dog.

"Don't say the law's caught up with you, Dev!" the duke pleaded.

"I'm afraid so."

"But . . . you're not guilty!"

"I suppose that depends on one's point of view."

"They're saying you took some money," the duke said gravely. "I don't believe a word of it, of course. Why would you steal, when you have access to all my accounts? It makes no sense, and so I shall tell them at your trial."

"I did take some money," Julian confessed. "Seventeen thousand guineas, to be exact."

The duke stared. "But why? I've got plenty of money."

"I know. I took it from you."

The duke was taken aback for a moment. "Did you? Oh, I see," he murmured, frowning. "Well . . . You must have had a good reason," he said, after a moment.

"I had a very good reason," Julian assured him. "There was a young lady in trouble. I believe you know her. Her name is Mary Andrews."

The duke's voice was hushed. "Mary? *My* little Mary?"

"Her father was the Vicar of Gambolthwaite," Julian prompted him. "You gave him the living. She's an orphan now."

"I know all that," Dickon said impatiently. "You said Mary was in trouble! What sort of trouble?"

"Her aunt, Mrs Dean—"

"A Very Bad Woman," Dickon interrupted.

"Yes, a very bad woman, indeed," Julian agreed. "She was going to sell Mary."

"Sell Mary? She can't do that, can she? Aren't there laws against that sort of thing?"

"I told you she was a bad woman."

The duke jumped up from the table. "Well, don't just sit there! We've got to stop her!"

"I've already done so, Duke. I *bought* Mary from her . . . with your money, of course. I made Mrs Dean sign a paper relinquishing all claims to her brother's child. Mary is free."

The duke sat back down, heaving a huge sigh of relief. "And this is what they arrested you for?" he said in disbelief. "What a pile of manure! They should be presenting you with the Order of Knighthood. Instead, they treat you like a criminal."

"It's only a crime, Duke, if you say it's a crime," Julian said mildly.

"Of course it's not a crime," the duke said. "Is that all they have on you?"

"As far as I can tell."

"In that case, let's go to dinner," said the duke. "I've a very important matter I want to discuss with you, and I can hardly do that on an empty stomach."

Four hours later, they were still in prison, waiting for Julian's release and the duke was getting hungry. "What did you want to talk to me about?" Julian asked him.

"Hmmm?" asked the duke, searching for crumbs in Julian's food basket.

"You said there was something important you wanted to discuss with me."

"Well, not *very* important. Viola's getting married," said the duke, giving up his search in disgust. He had eaten every scrap of food in the place and was now looking hungrily at the straw on the floor. The Great Dane had fallen asleep.

"But your sister has decided not to marry Lord Bamph," said Julian. "She sent me a note."

"Who said anything about Bamph?" Dickon shrugged. "No, I've found her a better man. You should see him on parade, Dev. You would not believe your eyes. He's like a centaur, if a centaur could be arsed with regimentals and parades, which he probably couldn't. Anyway, he's like a god among men. Viola will be pleased."

"Oh, she doesn't know yet?"

"She's in the country visiting a sick friend. But she likes Lord Simon. His mother tells me they get on very well indeed. And *he* adores her."

"Lord Simon *Ascot*?" Julian said coldly.

"You know him?" Dickon said eagerly.

Julian laughed shortly. "*He's* going to marry your sister?"

"Yes! Isn't it nuts for us?"

"No," said Julian. "No, it isn't nuts for us! Lord Simon is

the shameless home-wrecking rake who took Mary from me. Do you understand?" he shouted as the duke goggled at him.

"Dev, you're not making any sense," the duke complained. "Lord Simon hasn't taken Mary anywhere."

"Yes, he has. He—"

"No, Dev," the duke said firmly. "You've just gone mad from the solitude of prison life, that's all. Mary is with me, safe and sound."

Julian scowled at him. "What do you mean?"

"Well, she's not with me *now*, obviously," the duke conceded. "I couldn't bring a nice girl like that to a place like this! She's at Gambol House, perfectly safe."

"Mary is at Gambol House?" Julian repeated. "You're sure?"

"Of course I'm sure. I'm going to adopt her."

"No, you're not. I'm going to marry her," said Julian.

"I don't think so," said the duke, beginning to frown. "Mary wants me to adopt her."

"No. Mary wants *me* to marry her," Julian retorted.

"She never mentioned it. I'm sorry, Dev. But, as her father, I couldn't allow it. You're just not good enough to marry a duke's daughter. I hate to be a snob about it, but, damn it! You're only a stockjobber!"

"Why don't we let Mary decide for herself?" Julian snapped.

Dickon shrugged. "You're just going to get your heart broken."

"We'll see."

"Yes, we will," said the duke, determined to have the last word.

Eventually, the tall, thin man who had arrested Julian came in person. "Milord Duke," he said, bowing to Dickon. "I understand you wish to withdraw the complaint against Mr Devize?"

"I never made any complaint," Dickon said, thrusting out his chin belligerently. "Who says I made a complaint?"

"The Crown lodged the complaint on Your Grace's behalf," the bureaucrat explained.

"The Crown should mind its own business," the duke observed.

The man smiled thinly. "If Your Grace insists that the money was taken from your account with your full knowledge and permission, then there is nothing I can do."

"Knowledge and permission? Dev, what's the man going on about?"

"Permission was understood, and knowledge . . . unnecessary," said Julian. "I was acting well within the scope of my duties as the duke's agent. I served his interest."

"Ha!" said the duke. "I hope that answers your nasty little questions, my good man!"

"Not quite. What about Calais?"

"What about it?" demanded the duke.

"Didn't he tell you, Your Grace? Two tickets for Calais were discovered on his person."

"I'm not bloody surprised," the duke retorted. "Why, this place must be full of fleas as well. Come, Samson!" he called to his dog. "Let's get you out of here before you're infested."

"The government would like to know *why* Mr Devize was going to Calais, and with whom," smiled the thin man.

"Then you should have let me go," said Julian, smiling back. "You could have followed me. Who knows what you might have seen? Now you'll never know."

Dickon guffawed. "Good answer, Dev!"

The bureaucrat's smile disappeared. "I'll get you next time, Devize," he threatened.

"Don't bet on it," said the duke, clapping his hat on his head.

* * *

It was well after nine o'clock when the duke returned to Gambol House with Julian. A bevy of housemaids were scrubbing the grand staircase, but, undeterred, the butler and two footmen came slipping down to meet their master and his guest. Shedding his coat and hat as he went, Dickon took the door under the stairs, leading Julian through the servants' quarters to the drawing room, where a pile of dogs lay sleeping in front of the fireplace. Yawning, they got up reluctantly to greet the newcomers.

"Lazy buggers," the duke said affectionately. "Where's Mary?" he asked the butler. "She usually reads in here after dinner."

"I believe Miss Andrews has already retired for the evening, Your Grace," Lover answered, unable to look at Julian at all. "It is quite late."

"Wake her up," said Julian. "Tell her Dev is here."

"Well, go and get her, man," said the duke. "Tell her *Papa* is here."

"Very good, Your Grace," said Lover, withdrawing.

Dickon kindly brought Julian a brandy. "Now we'll see what's what with our Mary," he said confidently, pouring out a drink for himself.

Julian was equally confident. "Cheers," he said, knocking back the brandy.

A footman passed by the open doors. "Jem," the duke hailed him. "Go and find out what's keeping Miss Andrews. This young man is waiting to propose to her. He's very nervous, and if she doesn't get here soon, he may run away."

"No, indeed," said Julian.

The footman shook his head. "You're too late, sir," he told Julian. "I've just heard it from the cook. You could have knocked me over with the proverbial. Miss Andrews, if you please, has run off to Hampshire with Mr Rampling, cool as you please! Eloped!"

The duke frowned. "What!" he cried. "That doesn't sound like Mary."

"Aye! She had me fooled, too, Your Grace," the footman said angrily. "I thought she was mild as milk, and I pride myself on my ability to spot a bad 'un. I almost can't believe it!"

"I *don't* believe it," declared the duke. "This is a girl who knows the Bible by heart! At least, I take it on faith she knows the Bible by heart. We've only gotten as far as Job."

"Who is Mr Rampling?" Julian demanded, cutting in. "I know that name, don't I?"

At that moment, Lover returned to report that Miss Andrews was not in her bed.

Julian was on his feet. *"Who is Mr Rampling?"* he shouted

"He's one of our clergymen," the duke replied. "Or is he an M.P.? I always get them confused. Viola picks all my M.P.s and all my vicars. She likes good-looking young men for Parliament, and venerable old farts for the Church."

"I believe Mr Rampling is a Member of Parliament," said Lover. "However—"

"*Where* did you say he took her?" Julian demanded of the footman.

"Hampshire."

"His mother lives there," said Dickon, his memory improving. "Rent-free, in one of my houses, as a matter of fact. I remember my agent brought it to my attention a few months ago, but Viola said it was quite all right, because poor Lady Caroline's husband had left her with nothing, and there but for the grace of God go I, and all that sort of thing. Well, Dev! It rather looks as though she doesn't want either one of us. More brandy, Lover," he commanded. "My friend has lost a wife, and I have lost a daughter. We must commiserate. Already, I miss the pitter-patter of her little feet."

"So do I," Julian said grimly, on his way out the door.

"Where are you going?" the duke asked in astonishment.

"I'm going to Hampshire, of course," Julian replied.

\* \* \*

When Miss Andrews appeared at breakfast the next morning, Dickon was surprised but delighted. "Mary!" he cried, jumping up to hold her chair. "I heard you'd run off to Hants with an M.P."

Mary's brown eyes widened. "No, indeed, Your Grace!" she exclaimed, horrified.

"We seem to have some practical jokers below stairs," the duke said sternly, giving Jem a hard stare of ducal displeasure. "But you were not in your bed, Mary," he chided her.

Mary blushed. "I'm afraid I fell asleep in the library. There are so many fascinating books here. May I—may I alphabetize them for you? Am I too presumptuous?"

"My dear Mary, you may burn them for all I care! Now then," he went on, flourishing his napkin as he resumed his seat, "since you have *not* eloped, are we still on for the adoption? Or would you rather be married?" he asked, scowling.

"Adopted, please," Mary replied instantly. "But only if Lady Viola approves, of course. We could not possibly go against her ladyship's wishes."

"Of course not," the duke said quickly. "It's too bad about Dev, isn't it?"

"Who?" Mary asked innocently.

"Oh, nobody," the duke said happily. "Nobody at all!"

# Chapter Eighteen

Dressing Lucy for Lady Cheviot's little assembly was far too important a task to be relegated to servants. Viola did the work herself, and on Thursday evening, Lucy stood meekly in her bedroom as Viola studied her with a hypercritical eye. Once brown and flat, Lucy's hair was now golden and expertly curled. The slender gown of transparent, shimmering violet gauze with its slip of sapphire blue underneath suited Lucy's tender complexion perfectly and made her gray eyes look blue. Rather unusually, the dress had no sleeves, just a little beaded fringe where the sleeves ought to have been, but, as Viola pointed out, one should always do something a little shocking for a ball. Looking at herself in the mirror, Lucy hardly dared to breathe.

Meanwhile, Viola pawed through Lucy's jewelry. "Where are Miss Lucy's *good* pieces?" she demanded of Bramwell.

"I'm afraid that's all there is," Lucy apologized. Her jewelry had been sold long ago to pay her father's gambling debts.

Viola sent for her own jewel case and, with Bramwell's assistance, scattered tiny diamond pins all over Lucy's gown, with a concentration on the bodice. Then, as Bramwell knelt down to adorn Lucy's skirts, Viola stepped back to study the effect. "A little more random, if you please," she instructed the maid. "I want her gown should resemble the evening sky."

Lucy could not suppress a nervous giggle. "It's not a masquerade, Lady Viola."

"It never hurts to have a theme," Viola replied firmly, taking out a glittering diamond tiara fashioned as a series of stars, with the largest star in the center. This she carefully placed in Lucy's hair. "There are earrings as well," she said, frowning, "but your ears are not pierced. It's very vexing, because it's much too late to pierce them now!"

Lucy was relieved. The thought of hot needles being driven through her flesh was enough to make her feel light-headed.

Long silver satin gloves and a silver fan set with peacock eye feathers completed the ensemble. As a final touch, Viola sprinkled a light dusting of gold powder over her friend's face and shoulders.

"If you please, Miss Lucy," said Bramwell, "I've told Lady

Cheviot I'd be at Cross Mere early to help attend to her female guests. The others are leaving now, in the wagon. . . ."

"Go, go," Lucy assented. A ball represented an opportunity for all the servants in the vicinity to make extra money, and Lucy would not dream of interfering in the time-honored tradition of lending one's servants to one's neighbors for such an event.

"I feel like an imposter," Lucy breathed when Bramwell had gone.

"Then you are well-prepared to meet your future husband," Viola laughed.

Lucy paled. "Do I look like I'm thinking of marriage? I do, don't I?" Full-blown panic seized hold of her. "I'm far too old to be thinking about marriage. I look like an aging spinster pretending to be a young girl! I'm not going! Lady Viola, I can't!"

"Of course you're going," Viola said sharply. "I've worked too hard to be disappointed now. Besides, you've accepted the invitation. You must go."

"Lady Cheviot only invited me as a courtesy. She won't care if I'm there or not. I'm not going," Lucy repeated, beginning to hyperventilate.

Viola brought her a glass of water. "Would you feel better if I gave you a bosom?" she asked kindly. "I found some shapes in your mother's dressing room. You'd be amazed what a large chest can do for a lady's self-confidence."

"I think," Lucy said, summoning her dignity, "that you have done enough to me. You have turned my hair yellow and covered me with diamonds. . . . My dress has no sleeves! There is a crown on my head! I don't even recognize myself!"

"You needn't thank me, dear. I've enjoyed myself."

Lucy's cheeks reddened. "I don't mean to sound ungrateful, Lady Viola," she began, horrified by her outburst. "But please believe me when I tell you I cannot go!"

Unmoved, Viola dragged her out of the room. Cornelius

was waiting at the bottom of the stairs. "About time, too," he grumbled, hardly glancing at his nervous sister. "We'll be late, and I promised Lady Cheviot I'd dance the first dance with Miss Brandon."

"It is customary," Viola said frostily, "for a gentleman to compliment a lady's appearance when she first enters a room."

"I b-beg your pardon, Lady Viola," Cornelius stammered. "Your ladyship's appearance is . . . is . . . very good. Very good, indeed! I compliment you on it. Indeed, I do."

"I see now why you are not married, Mr Rampling," Viola said dryly.

Lucy licked her lips nervously. "Corny, would you be terribly upset if I don't go?"

Cornelius gaped at Lucy. "Not go to the ball? When Lady Viola has spent the last four hours dressing you? Don't be daft. Of course you're going. Do you want me to lose my seat in Parliament?" he added in a harsh undertone.

Thirty minutes later, the Ramplings arrived at Cross Mere in Viola's barouche. The dancing had already begun, with at least half the couples already formed. Always glad of an extra man, Lady Cheviot instantly seized Mr Rampling and put him to work amongst the wallflowers. A superfluous female, Lucy was left to fend for herself.

Lucy at once began to look for Lady Cheviot's children. She caught sight of the six-year-old twins watching the ball from the gallery, their feet dangling between the spindles of the ballustrade. She started toward them, making her way through the hot, crowded ballroom.

A young man in a scarlet coat, crossing the room in a different direction, accidentally collided with Lucy. Fortunately, there was no punch involved.

"I beg your pardon, miss!" he said, stopping to stare at her. "Miss . . . ?"

Lucy smiled at him. "Why, Arthur Bourne! It is I, Miss Rampling. *Lieutenant* Bourne, I should say," she corrected herself after looking more closely at his regimentals. "I did not know you were back from France."

"And I leave for India next week," he replied, devouring her with his eyes. "This is my last chance to see my parents, Miss Rampling. I shall be gone ten years. You are not dancing?"

"I arrived late," Lucy explained.

"So did I," Arthur said, sighing. "My hostess has commanded me to dance with one of her wallflowers. I see Miss Garner there. . . . Duty calls," he groaned.

"Off you go, then," Lucy said cheerfully.

"Are you looking for *your* partner?" he asked her suddenly. "He should be looking for *you*. May I find him for you? Confidentially," he added, "I'd much rather find your partner for you than have to dance with Miss Garner. She flutters her eyelashes at me, you see."

"I'm afraid there's no escaping your duty, Lieutenant," Lucy answered, laughing. "I have no partner for you to fetch. I was just going to sit in the gallery with the children."

As Lucy pointed the twins out to Lieutenant Bourne, Elizabeth caught sight of her. "Look!" she cried, elbowing Henry in the ribs. "There's Lucy!"

Henry scowled at the beautiful golden-haired lady with the tall, handsome officer. "It doesn't look like Lucy," he complained.

"Ladies and gentlemen look different at a ball," Elizabeth explained. "Isn't it exciting?"

"You wicked girl!" Arthur Bourne teased Lucy. "You mean to tell me you don't have a partner, and you were going to let me throw myself away on Miss Garner? I'd much rather dance with you, and you know it. What a lucky thing for me you arrived late, or there would have been no room for me. Shall we join the set? It's not too late."

Lucy was startled by the onslaught of masculine attention. "It's very k-kind of you to offer," she stammered, blushing, "but I think you should dance with Miss Garner. She's only just come out, you know."

"Someone should put her back in," said Arthur. "I'm going to dance with the prettiest girl in the place. Now, stop teasing me," he added, grabbing her hand.

"Oh, Arthur, really," she chided him. She barely had time to wave to the twins before being swept off to join the line.

"Who is she, do you know?" the girl next to her hissed angrily.

Lucy looked around and discovered, to her astonishment, that the girl was making inquiries about *her*. "Good evening, Miss Figgis," she said. "It is I, Miss Rampling."

Eleanor Figgis stared. "It is!" she whispered vehemently to the girl next to her. "It's Lucy Rampling!"

"Why is Lucy dancing with *him*?" Henry howled in the gallery.

"Because he asked her," Elizabeth explained.

"Why doesn't she dance with Uncle Alex?"

"Uncle Alex is dancing with Miss Chisholm."

"Why?" Henry demanded. "Look at Papa, dancing with that wrinkled old lady, instead of Mama. None of this makes any sense! Grown-ups are stupid," he decided.

As Lucy was still waiting to dance, Alex Devize came down the set with his partner, Miss Chisholm, the acknowledged beauty of the neighborhood. His eyes widened in surprise when he saw Lucy, and, for a moment, she was afraid he did not approve of her transformation. Then a smile twitched at the corner of his mouth, and Lucy was relieved.

Miranda Chisholm dug her nails into Alex's arm. "Was that Lucy Rampling? Poor thing. She's quite thirty, you know. Doesn't she look desperate?"

"I think she looks charming," Alex replied. "Who's her partner?"

"Poor Arthur Bourne! He cannot know how *old* she is. Someone should tell him."

"I have often noticed," Alex replied, "that some women are handsomer at thirty than they are at twenty. Miss Rampling would seem to be one of those."

Feeling quite ill-used by her partner, Miss Chisholm began to sulk.

As the evening progressed, the ladies became increasingly vexed by Lucy Rampling's popularity. Lady Cheviot, perhaps, was the most vexed of all. It was very selfish of Lucy to monopolize the attention of all the eligible bachelors, she decided. There simply were not enough men to go around. Two mamas pleaded headaches before the supper dance and left with their daughters. Perdita's party was in danger of imminent collapse, and it was all Lucy's fault. She must have known what would happen when she put on that *sleeveless* purply blue dress sprinkled all over with crystals. (It never occurred to Lady Cheviot they might be diamonds.)

Perdita frowned as she fanned herself rapidly. She could think of nothing constructive to do to save her ball, and her resentment flared. Where had Lucy gotten a dress like that anyway? she wondered. Perdita knew the work of all the local seamstresses, and Lucy's gown far exceeded their provincial skills.

"Hello, Perdita," said a voice directly behind her.

Perdita nearly jumped out of her skin. "Julian!" she cried in shock as her youngest brother kissed her cheek. He was in correct evening dress, she was astounded to see, including gloves. "What are you doing here? No, never mind!" she cried in the same breath, grasping his arm firmly. "You *must* help me. No one is dancing. Tony has disappeared! Alex has disappeared! I am demented!"

"There's your problem," Julian said helpfully. "All the men are fawning over that flat-chested little blond girl in the corner. They're completely ignoring the other girls."

"I know that, Julian," Perdita said impatiently. "But what am I supposed to do about it?"

Julian chuckled. "Leave it to me, of course. What's the girl's name?"

"Rampling," Perdita said eagerly. "Lucy Rampling. What are you going to do?"

"Did you say Rampling?" Julian asked sharply. "Any relation to Lady Caroline?"

"Her daughter. Are you going to make a scene?" Perdita asked anxiously.

"She has a brother, I think. Cornelius Rampling, a member of Parliament?"

"Yes. That is he, dancing with the girl in yellow." She caught her brother's arm. "If you *do* make a scene, Julian, make it a good one, please. Then my ball will be remembered for all the *right* reasons."

Julian glared at the young man dancing with the girl in yellow. "Do you think he's better looking than I am?" he asked irritably.

"What?" Perdita asked, confused. "Who?"

"Where is his new wife?" Julian asked coldly. "I wish to congratulate the happy couple."

"Whose wife?" she cried.

"Mr Rampling's, of course."

"Mr Rampling! He has no wife."

"How strange. I heard he eloped."

Perdita snorted. "He wouldn't dare marry without Lady Viola Gambol's permission. She's his patroness, you know. He doesn't *sneeze* without her permission."

"Are you sure he's not married?" Julian persisted. "His wife would be a tall young woman with masses of black hair, big, dark eyes, and a very good figure?"

Perdita looked at him in surprise. "You mean Miss Andrews?"

Julian's eyes glinted. "You've met her?"

"Yes, but *they* are not married." Sensing a scandal close at hand, she pulled at his arm. "Are they? Lady Viola will not approve of such a wife for one of her M.P.s, I promise you. The girl gives herself such airs!"

"Is she here?" he demanded.

"At my ball? Certainly not. She is nurse-companion to Lady Caroline, and she could not leave her charge alone. Now that I think of it, I'm quite sure *she* had a hand in Miss Rampling's shocking attire this evening."

"Well, I'm damned," Julian muttered. "She's taken a job!"

"Look here, Julian, whatever you're going to do, do it quick," Perdita begged. "Mrs Chisholm is looking at me with a gimlet eye. If she takes Miranda home now, I'm finished!"

Julian made his way to Lucy without delay. "There you are, Miss Rampling," he said smartly, shoving a few men aside. "You promised me this dance, I believe."

Never having been the center of attention before, Lucy was having a difficult time managing her bevy of admirers. In her confusion, she had overcommitted, agreeing to dance with more men than there were dances. It had seemed to her that the only fair thing to do was not to dance at all, but this had led to a bewildering flurry of alternative offers. Everyone wanted to fetch her lemonade and cookies. Everyone wanted to take her for a stroll in the garden. Everyone wanted to fetch her shawl. Lucy was drowning in compliments and propositions.

She stared at Julian, her heart sinking. She did not remember promising to dance with this young man, which was surprising because he was one of the handsomest men she had ever seen. His eyes were a piercing, irresistible blue. He looked like a young god.

"Did I do so, sir?" she asked, embarrassed. "I beg your pardon! My head is whirling . . ."

"You need air, Miss Rampling!" cried one of her admirers.

"I'm afraid I've been very stupid," Lucy said to Julian. "I've promised to dance with too many gentlemen. I'm so sorry, sir, but there are many other ladies—"

"This dance you promised to *me*," Julian insisted, holding

out his hand. "And, as you can have only one husband, Miss Rampling, so you can have only one partner. Come! Give these gentlemen time to find their own partners."

His air of command would allow for no further resistance. His brilliant blue eyes caused her to shiver. As if in a trance, Lucy placed her hand in his and allowed herself to be conducted to the floor. "I'm so sorry, sir," she said nervously. "I seem to have forgotten your name."

"Julian Devize," he said as they took their places in line.

Lucy drew back instinctively. "You did not ask me to dance," she gasped. "I would have remembered that name."

"I lied," he explained. "My sister sent me over to rescue you from your admirers," he added dryly, as, two by two, a dozen or more couples took to the floor.

"I did not know what to do with them," Lucy confessed.

Julian did not reply. He seemed to be staring at Miss Figgis.

"When . . . when did you arrive in Hampshire, Mr Julian?" she asked timidly.

"Just now. Guess my surprise when I discovered my sister was giving a ball. She didn't even invite me. I had to borrow evening dress from my brother-in-law. Who is that girl dancing with your brother?"

Lucy's eyelids fluttered. "Miss Figgis? What do you want with Miss Figgis?"

"Is Miss Figgis engaged to be married?" Julian inquired.

"I don't believe so," said Lucy, startled by the question. "Why do you ask?"

"Good," said Julian. "Mr Rampling should confine his attention to young ladies who are *not* engaged. Meddling with young ladies who *are* engaged can be a very dangerous activity."

"I d-don't know what you mean," Lucy stammered, turning quite pale.

"I think you know *whom* I mean," he countered. "Yes, you know very well whom I mean. Miss Rampling, if your brother has any designs on Miss Andrews, he would do well to abandon them now. I understand she has taken a position in your mother's house. If he tries to take advantage of her, he will have to deal with me."

"Take advantage!" Color flooded into Lucy's face. "Isn't that a trifle rich, coming from you, Mr Julian?" she hissed, mindful of not being overhead by the other couples. "If anyone has taken advantage of my friend, I believe it is *you*. You and this Lord Simon person!" she added, shuddering. "How dare you accuse my poor brother! You judge everyone by yourself."

"I see Mary has told you everything," Julian said grimly. "But she has not told *me* everything! Why did she run away from me? I thought she had eloped with your brother, but now I don't know what to think. She left me to become your mother's nurse! Why?"

Lucy stared at him, aghast. "How can you ask me that, after what you did to her?"

"What I did to her?" Julian repeated angrily. "You believe her to be my victim? You have been deceived, Miss Rampling, as I was deceived."

"How were you deceived?" she scoffed. "You led her to believe you were to be married."

"I can hardly marry someone who ain't there," he pointed out dryly.

"You must excuse me, Mr Julian," Lucy said coldly, sinking into a curtsey. "I have the headache. I am no longer inclined to dance."

With her head high, she swept off the floor.

Abandoned by his partner, Julian left the ballroom.

As Lucy's admirers now all had partners of their own, whom they could not abandon, she was free to step outside for a breath of air. She meant only to go to the edge of the terrace, but somehow she found herself wandering in the garden. She walked until she could no longer hear the orchestra playing.

The air was cool and clean. The night was still. The moonlight was soothing. She felt more like herself than she had all evening. Unlike her newfound admirers, the moon and the stars could be relied upon not to pay her compliments so ridiculously extravagant that she felt mocked rather than flattered.

"Good evening, Lucy," said Elizabeth Cheviot, popping out of the bushes.

"Good evening, Lucy," said Henry Cheviot, popping out of the bushes on the other side.

Between them, the twins gave Lucy the two biggest frights of her life, and nothing delighted them more than making a grown up jump.

"Henry! Lizzie!" Lucy said severely, when she had recovered. "You should be in bed."

"I'm never going to bed," Henry informed her.

"Where is your governess?" Lucy demanded.

"We don't like Miss Shipley," Elizabeth replied.

"That is a wicked thing to say, Eliza," Lucy chided her.

"No, it isn't," the child replied. "It would be wicked to tell lies."

"Oh dear," said Lucy. "Henry, have you locked Miss Shipley in a cupboard again?"

The boy swelled with pride. "I have."

"I helped," Elizabeth said indignantly.

Lucy grasped each child by one hand. "Come along," she said briskly.

There was no sign of Miss Shipley in the nursery. The baby, Hannah, was asleep in her nurse's arms, and the nurse was asleep, too. As the twins watched, amused, Lucy made a thorough search of the schoolroom.

"Elizabeth, do *you* know where Miss Shipley is?"

"Yes, but I gave my word of honor I wouldn't tell," Elizabeth apologized.

"Henry, I shall find your mama and tell her what a naughty

boy you've been," Lucy threatened. "You little devil!" she screamed in pain as the boy bit her on the hand.

"*Now* you're going to get it!" Elizabeth chirped gleefully.

The chase encompassed much of the attics. Henry had the decided advantage of both familiarity with his surroundings and native cunning, in addition to which Lucy was hampered by her skirts and high-heeled slippers. Henry led them up two short flights of stairs. Lucy could see the stars through the open doorway at the top. Suddenly, a head appeared silhouetted against the stars, so suddenly that they all screamed in fright. Henry fell backward into Lucy, Lucy fell backward into Elizabeth, and they all landed together in a heap at the bottom of the stairs.

"Who goes there?" Alex Devize inquired, tossing aside his cheroot.

"Uncle Alex!" Elizabeth darted up the steps, panting. "Oh, Uncle Alex! We went down to the garden, and gave Lucy a fright—no, two frights—and then Lucy took us upstairs, and then we looked for Miss Shipley but Miss Shipley wasn't there, and then Lucy said she would tell Mama, and then Henry *bit* her, and then Lucy said 'You little devil!' and chased him all over the attics, and then you jumped out, and then Henry fell down, and then Lucy fell down, and then *I* fell down, and do you know what? You're the only one of us who didn't fall down!"

"Please continue," said Alex pleasantly. "What happened next?"

"I can't! I'm out of breath."

"I will wait," Alex said magnanimously.

"Then I got up and ran up the stairs to you!" Elizabeth finished presently.

Frowning, Alex took Lucy's hand. "Miss Rampling, you are bleeding!"

"It will hardly incarnadine the sea," Lucy protested, but Alex was black with fury.

"You little devil!" he barked at Henry.

"That is what Lucy said!" Elizabeth volunteered.

Alex took Lucy's hand in his own and proceeded to wrap her microscopic wound in his handkerchief, ignoring her protests.

"I didn't mean to bite her, Uncle Alex!" cried Henry. "It was an accident."

Alex ignored the boy. "Where the devil is Shipley? I suppose the poor woman has come to her senses and found herself a new situation. I'd run away, too, if I could."

"Henry tells me he's locked her in a cupboard, but he won't tell me which cupboard," said Lucy. "I've already searched the nursery and the schoolroom."

"That's peaching!" Henry accused. "You peached on me, Lucy!"

Alex hunkered down and gazed steely eyed into his nephew's face. "Is there no end to your depravity, miserable Henry? Tell me this instant where you've put Miss Shipley!"

Henry's bottom lip quivered. "It's a little hard to explain. . . ."

"Right!" Alex grasped the boy's hand firmly. "Show me. Elizabeth, go to bed! Miss Rampling . . ." Lucy jumped at the authority in his voice. "Will you please accompany me? When found, Miss Shipley may require the good offices of a sensible young lady."

The hallway Henry led them to was excessively dark, and Alex paused on the landing to light a taper, taking a match from his cheroot case. He tried the door handle, but it was firmly locked. "The key, if you please, Master Henry."

Henry obligingly produced a large, black key.

Lucy, meanwhile, had knocked upon the locked door, calling softly, "Miss Shipley? She doesn't answer! Henry, darling, you didn't put anything over Miss Shipley's head, did you? You didn't tie her up? Oh, Mr Devize, do please give me the key!" Alex held the candle close as she fitted the key into the lock.

"It is a very large cupboard," Lucy observed as they advanced into the room.

"It looks like a sort of"—Alex paused as the door slammed shut behind them, followed by Henry's gleeful, retreating laughter—"trap, actually. I ought to have suspected as much. Henry!" he roared, stretching out the name in chagrin.

Lucy spun around. "Oh no!" She rushed to the door, crying, "Henry! Henry, darling!" as she tried the handle. She knelt down and looked through the keyhole. "Darling Henry?" she called, without much hope.

"Darling Henry, if he has an ounce of intelligence," Alex said furiously, "is halfway to France, the little traitor. You *do* have the key, Miss Rampling?"

"Oh, Mr Devize! I'm afraid . . ."

"In your haste to rescue Miss Shipley, you left the key in the lock. Of course!" He held up the candle to survey the room. "There are worst places to die, I suppose," he said cheerfully.

The disused bedchamber in which they found themselves was furnished with indescribably ugly antiquities and musty Jacobean crewelwork. "The children have been playing here," Lucy observed as she stumbled over a toy horse on wheels.

The candle had just revealed to Alex several jars containing frogs and insects, variously decomposed. "Poor Miss Shipley! How she has withered in captivity."

Despite the seriousness of her predicament, Lucy giggled. "I believe that is a bullfrog, sir, and quite a handsome specimen, I might add!"

"Are a you a zoologist, Miss Rampling?" Alex said lightly as he continued to scan the room. "Is there no end to your accomplishments?"

"I have no accomplishments, sir," she replied, "but it is my very great pleasure to study the accomplishments of others."

"That seems to me the most admirable accomplishment of all," he returned. "Personally, I envy and despise the accomplishments of others. In fact, I quite loathe accomplished people. I prefer the company of those creatures who, like ourselves, have no accomplishments at all."

"Oh no!" Lucy cried softly.

"Then you admit you have a few accomplishments, after all?"

"No, sir. I just realized Miss Shipley is not here."

Alex smiled. "You would wish her to be imprisoned with us?"

"Of course not. But if Miss Shipley is not with us, then we are . . ."

"Alone. Yes." Alex's smile widened. "I hope you are not frightened, Miss Rampling?"

"Of course not," Lucy said quickly. "I *would* be afraid to be alone with your brother, but I could never be afraid of you. You are nothing like him, I know."

"My brother?" Alex said sharply. "I did not know you were acquainted with Julian."

"I was just dancing with him," said Lucy, shuddering.

"I did not know he was here. Has he done something to offend you?"

Lucy shook her head rapidly. To her relief, Alex did not press her for a better answer.

"But you are not afraid of *me*?"

"Oh, no," she assured him.

"Because we are such good friends?"

"Yes," she said gratefully.

Alex found a door in one corner of the room. It too was locked. "If I were to tell you that you look amazingly well tonight, would we still be friends?"

Lucy sighed. "Please don't tease me! You know perfectly well my hair was not this color last week, or even three days ago. To confess the truth, Miss Andrews did this to me."

"Did it hurt?" he inquired gravely.

"No," she answered seriously. "She squeezed lemons over my head and locked me on the roof for four hours in the hot sun. It *did* hurt a bit when she plucked my eyebrows," she added, frowning in remembrance. "*And* she threatened to give me a false bosom and pierce my ears! Once she gets going, she's rather like the Mongol Horde."

Alex hooted with laughter. "You absolutely should not *ever* tell your beauty secrets to a prospective suitor, Miss Rampling," he told her.

Lucy laughed. "I believe I can safely promise you that I won't, Mr Devize."

"I'm afraid you just did, Miss Rampling," he said, standing before her.

Lucy stared at him in dismay. "Mr Devize . . ."

"If I were to kiss you now, would we still be friends, do you think?" he asked softly.

Lucy was stiff as a board as he took her in his arms and kissed her. His lips were warm and demanding, but Lucy was too shocked to respond. Her lack of response only seemed to encourage him. Groaning deep in the back of his throat, he tried to coax her lips apart with his devilish tongue. Lucy pushed him away, saying, "Please, don't! I told you I could not marry you. We are in your sister's house, for heaven's sake! There are people downstairs dancing!"

"I could not help it, Lucy," he said. "The thought of you marrying anyone else is enough to drive me mad."

"Mr Devize, we must find a way out of here," Lucy said firmly.

Alex sighed. After a moment, he pushed open the window and looked out. "The drainpipe looks sturdy. Shall I try it?"

"Wait! I have an idea," said Lucy, taking out her handkerchief. Unfolding it, she slid it under the door beneath the keyhole. "Have you got a pencil?"

"Of course," Alex answered, giving her his pencil. "How else would I scribble my name on the dance cards of eager young ladies?"

He watched as Lucy used the pencil to push the key out of

the lock. As she had hoped, the key landed neatly on her handkerchief, and she was able to drag it under the door and into the room. "There!" she said triumphantly, picking it up.

"Where did you learn that neat little trick?" he asked admiringly.

"At school in London," Lucy answered, unlocking the door. "Some of the girls would sneak out at night to meet their beaux."

"I remember." Stepping out into the hall, he signaled that the coast was clear.

"You were not my beau," Lucy protested as they tiptoed toward the stairs.

"You went to Vauxhall Gardens to meet me," he insisted.

"To meet you! No, indeed! Miss Archer was engaged to your friend Mr Brooks, if you recall. When I agreed to go with her, I didn't even know you would be there."

"Nonsense. It was completely by design—my design."

Lucy bit her lip. "Do you think we should tell Lady Cheviot?" she asked him abruptly. "About Miss Shipley, I mean? She must be found."

"I'll find Miss Shipley," he said. "Don't bother Perdita in the middle of a ball—she'll go frantic. You'd better get back to the dancing, before you are missed," he added. "Lucy?"

"Yes, Mr Devize?"

"We are still friends, I hope?"

For a moment, he thought she might refuse. He held his breath.

"Of course," she said. "But I do not want our friendship to change. I should hate to lose you, Mr Devize. As a friend, I mean."

"You won't," he promised.

Upon returning to the ballroom, Lucy was instantly pounced upon by her partner for the supper dance. "There you are!" cried Mr Ambrose. "I knew you'd gone to the ladies' retiring room, but every girl I asked said you weren't there. Jealous cats!"

\* \* \*

"Have you seen Lord Cheviot?" Perdita demanded of every servant she passed in the hall. "Have you seen Mr Devize? Have you seen Mr Julian?"

No one, it seemed, had seen anyone. The supper dance was beginning, and neither Mrs Chisholm nor Miss Chisholm had a partner. Lucy Rampling, of course, had a partner.

Finally, one of the footman offered her a tidbit of information. He had seen Lord Cheviot depart the ballroom to speak to Miss Shipley in the hall. "Something must have happened with the children," Perdita breathed.

Panicking, she ran up to the nursery, equally prepared for either tragedy or vexation.

But all was peaceful in the nursery. Henry and Elizabeth were snug in their beds, sleeping like angels. Even Hannah, who had been teething, was sound asleep in her cradle, snuggling her favorite toy rabbit. The nurse was snoring in her rocking chair, and Perdita did not have the heart to wake her.

Miss Shipley's bedroom was nearby. Perdita knocked on it softly. "Miss Shipley?" she called through the door as she tried the knob.

In response, she heard an odd, secretive rustling sound.

"Miss Shipley!" she called rattling the doorknob.

"Perdita!"

Behind the door, Perdita's husband was on his knees, speaking into the keyhole. "Oh, thank God! I was afraid it might be one of the servants. You know how they like to talk."

Perdita was shocked. Lord Cheviot had never before given her a reason to worry about him. Never before had he made secretive, rustling sounds at her from behind a locked door. "What are you doing in Miss Shipley's room?" she asked coldly.

"That beast Henry locked us in," he explained. "Darling, can you find the key and let us out? It should be on the floor.

I'm afraid poor Miss Shipley knocked it out of the lock before I could get my handkerchief underneath it."

Like an automaton, Perdita found the key and unlocked the door. Lord Cheviot got up from his knees to embrace his wife. Over his shoulder, Perdita had an excellent view of Miss Shipley's bed. Miss Shipley was reclining on it like an odalisque, patting the yawn on her thin lips. Her brown bombazine gown was open at the neck, and, as Perdita watched, she calmly sat up and tied her garter. Even with her hair down and her spectacles off, Miss Shipley was not an attractive woman, and the smug satisfaction on her plain, sallow face did not help matters.

"Tony, how could you?" Perdita cried, pushing him away.

Lord Cheviot gaped at his wife in confusion. Well past forty, he was a tall, spare, plain-looking man with just a touch of gray in his hair. A look of horror slowly spread across his face. "Perdy! You can't possibly think that I . . . That Miss Shipley . . . Look here, damn it!"

Perdita's duty was clear. She was first and foremost on this evening a hostess. Without hesitation, she disentangled herself from her scoundrel of a husband and locked him back in the room with the governess. Then, with a clear conscience, she went back down to her guests, a brilliant smile on her handsome face.

The supper dance was nearly over when a servant tapped Lucy on the shoulder.

"I beg your pardon, miss, but there's a messenger for you from Gambol Hall."

"Something must have happened to Mama," cried Lucy. Quickly, she apologized to her partner and followed the servant out of the house and down the steps to the lone horseman waiting on the drive.

"Mr Julian!" Lucy exclaimed in surprise.

"Your mother's had a bit of an accident," said Julian. "Come. I'll take you to her."

Without another word, he reached down and hauled her in front of him across the saddle.

Turning his mount, he rode off into the night.

Watching from the front steps, Alex could not believe his eyes.

# Chapter Nineteen

Only after Cornelius and Lucy had departed for Cross Mere did Viola judge it safe to unlock Lady Caroline's door. Lady Caroline was sitting in the window seat, dour and silent. It has been days since she had a drink. She eyed Viola warily as the latter brought in the supper tray and set it down on the table. Bijou trailed into the room after her and made a bee-line for Lady Caroline's skirts, her tail wagging in a silent plea for attention.

"Good evening, Lady Caroline," Viola said brightly.

"Lucy should not go to a ball without her mama," Lady Caroline sulked, nudging the bichon away with her foot. "It is most improper."

"Nonsense," Viola laughed sunnily. "There is nothing improper in a lady attending a ball in the company of her brother. I do it quite often, and, I can assure you, Lady Caroline, that I never, ever do anything improper. Shall we dine together?" she went on pleasantly. "Cook has left us a little cold chicken and a plum tart."

Seating herself, she took Bijou onto her lap and began to make the tea.

After supper, the two ladies played cards. Lady Caroline insisted on playing deep, and, by the time she fell asleep, she owed Viola almost seventy pounds. Viola put her to bed gently, then locked her in for the night. She called to Bijou, but the little dog scampered down the hall and disappeared into Lucy's room. As Viola passed her own room, she saw that the long windows that opened onto the balcony were standing wide. The curtains floated on air, and a chill breeze sent shivers down her spine.

The full moon hung like a disc of silver in the night sky, and Viola stopped to look at it, wondering how Lucy was faring at the ball.

*If she fails, it will not be my fault*, she thought virtuously as she closed the window.

Julian watched her from the shadows. She was so absorbed in her thoughts that she did not notice him sitting in a chair beside the fire. She turned to leave, calling to Bijou.

"I don't think she knows her name," he said, making her jump.

For a long moment they stared at each other. The look in his eyes made Viola shiver, and she ran for the door. Instantly, he sprang from the chair to catch her.

"Where do you think you're going, my girl?" he said roughly.

There was possession in his tone. Viola's knees went weak, and she struggled to keep her mind from falling under the spell of physical attraction.

"What are you d-doing here?" she stammered, hardly able to speak.

"I came to congratulate you, of course," he answered, his lips almost touching her ear.

"What for?" Viola asked warily.

"I heard you eloped with Mr Rampling," he answered.

Viola's eyes opened wide. "What?"

"Are you married or not?" he demanded. "I want to hear it from your own lips, traitor."

"What?" she breathed, anger giving her a false sense of strength. "You know perfectly well I can never marry, thanks to you. What would I tell the poor fool?" she added bitterly. "No man would ever marry me knowing the truth, and I would not lie for the sake of getting a husband. You've ruined me, Mr Devize. Perhaps I should be congratulating *you*."

"At least you understand that, my love," he said, pulling her sharply against him. The endearment was like a savage bite rather than a caress. "A man has a right to expect chastity in his bride and loyalty in his wife. *You* are not fit to be married."

"I am unfit," she agreed, trembling, "and it was y*our* doing."

"I remember," he said, turning her around to unfasten her gown. Viola tensed as his hand brushed aside her hair, but to her shame, she seemed helpless to stop him, or even to protest. "I enjoyed ruining you," he whispered against her neck.

Her breath caught in her throat as he pulled the strings of her gown.

"I didn't do it alone," he added.

"No," she admitted brokenly.

"Tell me," he said conversationally as he slowly caressed her shoulders and throat, "if you don't have another fool waiting in the wings, why did you leave me? Satisfy my curiosity."

His lips touched the nape of her neck. He had used their time together well, learning exactly how to caress her to achieve the most passionate response. As he kissed her neck, his hands expertly kneaded the soft flesh at the very base of her spine. Viola bit her lip savagely, but a whimper betrayed her.

"You know perfectly well why I left you!" she snapped, humiliated that, in spite of everything, her body still responded to him. "You promised me marriage, but, instead, you made me your mistress. I don't take kindly to being deceived!"

"I tried to get the license," he growled. "You should have had more faith in me."

"On the contrary," she answered, "I had too much! But no matter! I am better off now."

"Indeed! Do you like your new position as a nurse-companion?"

"Obviously, I do," she snapped.

"I don't believe you," he said.

Turning her to face him, he bent his face to hers.

In the next moment, she was kissing him back hungrily, in the grip of senseless, wild longing. With a groan, he bore her unresisting to the bed, and they fell on it together, clasped in each other's arms. Viola surrendered completely as his mouth burned its way down the length of her body. She had dressed simply, knowing that she would have no maid to help her, and he had little difficulty with her clothing. In a trice, she was naked. Mutely, she offered herself to him, guiding his hand to her loins, her head thrown back, her eyes squeezed shut as she willed him to drive her mad. His slightest touch caused her to murmur helplessly. She cried out as violent pleasure overtook her, arching her back as his fingers worked their magic.

It was not enough. She wanted more. Whether pleasurable or painful, she wanted him inside her. That alone was proof that he still desired her beyond all reason. With her body, she could make him realize that he was not tired of her, that he had been a fool to ever think of getting rid of her. A shared passion could make everything right.

Julian's instinct was to take his own pleasure at once, to use her quickly and brutally. To that end, he swiftly unbuttoned his trousers. His desire for her could not have been more evident. Viola looked up at him, her face flushed with triumph. "It is not over between us, Dev," she panted, twining her legs around him. "You cannot live without me. It will be over when I say it's over. You are powerless. Admit it."

"Don't flatter yourself," he advised her. Standing up, he

forced his erection back into his trousers. "May I remind you, madam, you're the one who is naked, not I?"

Viola raised herself on her elbows, frowning. "What are you doing?" she demanded.

Fully dressed, he leaned across her naked body, planting his hands on either side of her. "I'm not doing anything," he said, smiling. "You don't deserve it."

Viola hastily snatched her dress and used it to cover herself. "I hate you," she snapped, trying to escape from the bed.

Julian chuckled. "That explains why you keep throwing yourself at me."

Wrath kindled in her eyes. "It is *you* who pursued me here," she pointed out coldly. "It is *you* who broke into this house. It is *you* who stripped me."

"I was only looking for my ring," he explained, moving away from the bed. "I assumed you must have it concealed on your person somewhere. As it turns out, you do not."

Too proud to ask him to turn around, Viola stood up defiantly and dressed in front of him.

"Your ring?" she said, frowning as she struggled to tighten the laces of her gown. "What ring?"

"How quickly we forget," Julian scoffed. "You may recall, madam, I bought an engagement ring. As we are no longer engaged, naturally I want it back."

"I threw it away," she informed him. "It reminded me of you."

His eyes narrowed. "You expect me to believe that you threw away a ring worth ten thousand guineas?"

"It was ugly," Viola explained.

"Ugly?" he roared. "I got the exact ring you wanted! A six-carat bloody emerald!"

"*Cut!*" Viola shrieked. "I wanted an emerald *cut*, not an *emerald*. I *hate* emeralds. You have to listen all the way to the end of the sentence, you know," she added scathingly. "Otherwise, you might miss some essential information."

"Why, you ungrateful little baggage!" he said.

"Should I be grateful to you? You used me. You seduced me!" she accused him.

"I seduced you?" he repeated incredulously. "If anything, *you* seduced *me*. You were more than willing to grant me a preview of my wedding night, as I recall."

"I was deceived," Viola spat.

"No," he argued. "*I* was deceived. You made me believe that you loved me."

"No! *You* made *me* believe that *you* loved *me*." Her loosened dress slipped down over her full breasts, and angrily she pulled it back up.

"I think it is *you* who cannot live without *me*, madam," he declared. "*You* are powerless. It will be over when *I* say it's over!"

"No! It will be over when I say it is over."

"Well?" he snapped. "Is it over?"

"It certainly is!" said Viola.

"No, it isn't," he said harshly. Taking hold of her dress, he yanked it down to her knees.

"Yes, it is," Viola shouted, pulling up her dress. "I just said so!"

"Well, I'm starting it up again!" he yelled. Plunging both hands into her hair, he kissed her hard on the mouth. They ended up in a tangle on the rug.

Viola responded wildly as he feverishly sought every possible means of exciting her. She did not care that her gown was in an unsightly bunch around her waist. She did not care that her hair was a riot of tangled curls, or that tears were streaming from her eyes. "You must have missed me very much indeed to come all this way," she observed gleefully as he paused briefly to pull his coat, waistcoat, and coat over his head all in one piece.

"Not at all, I assure you," he replied, watching her dark

eyes for that answering glint as his hand slipped between her thighs. "Did you miss me?"

"Mr Devize, I haven't thought of you in years," she answered, her eyes half-closed as she melted again beneath his touch.

Julian laughed softly. "Liar," he breathed, stretching out beside her. "You think of nothing else. You think of me constantly. Admit it."

She stretched languorously. "No, never."

"You missed me," he insisted, excited by the half smile playing on her lips. "Look at you. You want me even now."

She sighed, wriggling her hips as his hand continued to pleasure her. Reclining next to her, he claimed her breast with his mouth, suckling and nuzzling.

"Did you imagine me touching you like this?" he asked.

Viola could only gasp as she edged closer to climax.

"Show me," he commanded, withdrawing his hand. "Show me how you missed me," he explained, as she looked at him in confusion. "You touch yourself, don't you?"

Viola's eyes widened in shock. "Of course not."

"I think you do. You think of me, and you touch yourself. Admit it."

Viola blushed hotly.

"Show me," he insisted, guiding her hand to the spot. "Show me, and I'll let you have it," he added, unbuttoning his trousers. He watched, amused by her embarrassment as she struggled with the choice he had given her.

"I can't," she finally whispered.

"Why not, my sweet?" he asked gently, stroking her hair from her eyes.

"It's private."

He laughed softly. "It doesn't get much more private than this, my love. Close your eyes and pretend you are alone if that helps. You want me, don't you?"

"Not very much," she said weakly.

"I'll help you," he murmured, taking her hand and placing it on the spot. "That's it," he whispered against her skin as, tentatively, she began caressing herself. Her hand was so unsure that he could almost believe she had never done so before. But, as he began to murmur encouragement and stroke her breasts, she became more efficient. With soft cries, she reached her crisis, and, at the same moment, he kept his promise. He let her have it, driving into her body with one exultant stroke.

Brief and brutal as the final act was, Viola stole another climax just before he collapsed in her arms. Julian heard the heavens clash. Thunder rolled. The earth shattered into a million pieces. He damn near died.

"What was that?" cried Viola, panting.

"I told you it wasn't over," he said, sucking the taste of her kiss from his lips.

"No, Dev," she cried, jumping out of bed and making a frantic search for her clothes. "I heard a noise. It sounded like glass breaking. Lady Caroline!"

"It is not as bad as I thought," a surprisingly well-groomed Viola greeted Lucy in the hall when Julian returned with the latter from Cross Mere. "There was an awful lot of blood at first, but it was only the tiniest little cut, as it turns out. I've cleaned it and bandaged it. I don't think we need trouble Dr Chadwick again."

Distraught, Lucy pushed past her and ran upstairs. There was an earsplitting scream as she discovered her mother's condition. Shocked, Viola and Julian flashed up the stairs after her. Lady Caroline was seated on the floor of her room, cradling a whisky jug in her arms like a baby. Completely untroubled by her bandaged hand, she was suckling vigorously.

"Drunk as a wheelbarrow," said Julian.

"I only left her alone for two minutes while I combed my hair!" Viola said incredulously.

"Let's face it, Miss Andrews," said Julian, squeezing her waist. "As a nurse-companion, you're a complete failure. Miss Rampling, I recommend you turn her off without a character. She's very ill-suited for her present position. I've a much better place for her in London."

Viola was white with anger. "Never!" she said, moving away from him.

Julian scowled. "What do you mean, never? Go and pack your things. I've been away from London too long as it is."

"I will never go to London with you!" Viola declared.

"Indeed, sir!" Lucy said, rounding on him angrily. "You have imposed on my friend enough. She does not wish to see you."

"Is that so?" he drawled.

"I am aware," Lucy said coldly, "of the position you have in mind for her, and, I tell you, Mr Julian, it will not do! My friend deserves better. I must beg you to leave this house and never return. Go, sir!"

Below them, voices reverberated in the hall. "What the devil is going on?" Cornelius Rampling demanded, starting up the stairs with his cloak still around his shoulders. "Mr Devize said you left Cross Mere very suddenly, Lucy. Well? What is the matter?"

"Lady Caroline is perfectly all right," Viola hastened to assure him. "She was trying to escape out of the window, and she had a little accident and cut herself. Oh, only a nick," she added quickly. "In fact, her ladyship is in *very high spirits* at the moment. I daresay, she won't remember any of this in the morning."

"Oh, I see," said Cornelius, taking the hint. "In spite of her injury, her spirits are good. Wonderful! Well, Mr Julian, I am obliged to you for seeing Lucy home. Would you be good enough to find your way out? This is a private, family matter."

"Perhaps Miss Andrews will see me out?" Julian suggested.

"Good night, Mr Julian," Lucy said firmly, drawing Viola into her mother's bedroom.

"I'll call in the morning, then, shall I?"

"Don't bother!" Viola said sharply. "You should go back to London, Mr Julian. There is nothing for you here." So saying, she closed the door in his face.

Slowly, the cheeky grin left Julian's face. For the life of him he could not understand how a woman could run hot one moment, then cold the next. One day, she was promising to be his forever, come what may; the next she had abandoned him to take the perfectly ludicrous position of nurse-companion to the mother of all lushes. One moment they were making love on the rug. Next, she was giving him the brush-off. Women!

As he made his way back downstairs, Bijou suddenly skidded across the marble floor. Julian was glad to see her, but not half as glad as she was to see him. Being a dog, she saw no reason to deny her unconditional love for him. Wagging her tail joyously, she scrambled madly across the floor to get to him.

"Hullo!" he said, smiling at her.

"Well, Perdita!" cried Lord Cheviot, entering his wife's boudoir without knocking. He seemed not to know that he was taking his life into his hands. "Perhaps you would care to explain why you chose to lock me back in Miss Shipley's room? The poor woman was hysterical. I think you owe her an apology."

Perdita's blood boiled as she thought of the smug look on Miss Shipley's face. "Who let you out?" she demanded.

"No one let me out," he said angrily. "I had to break the door. How am I going to explain that to the duke's agent? Madam, you and your children have done at least twenty-five

ounds in damage to this house in the past two years. Don't
lame me when we are evicted!"

"How long has Miss Shipley been your mistress?" Perdita
demanded.

"My what? Don't be ridiculous."

Perdita's hairbrush flew out of her hand and sailed across
he room. "What am I supposed to think? She was in bed with
er clothes half off, smirking at me."

"She has a facial tic!" Tony said indignantly. "Have you no
ompassion?"

"A facial tic that pops her buttons?"

"No, *I* popped her buttons," he explained. "That is, I unbut-
oned them. She fainted. I simply loosened her constrictive
lothing. Constrictive clothing is very bad, I think."

"You have an explanation for everything," she glowered.
"But why, my lord, were you in her room in the first place? I
mean, I know very well *why* you were there, but I'd love to
ear you invent an excuse. I daresay it will make me laugh!"

Tony sighed. "You won't believe me," he said tightly, "but
he baby lost her velveteen rabbit, and Miss Shipley and I
vere looking for it. Hannah can't sleep without her rabbit.
You know that."

"You're right," said his lady. "I *don't* believe you! I saw
Hannah, and she had her rabbit with her. His name is Rollo,
by the way. You'd know that if you were any kind of a father."

"Faugh!" said Tony.

Perdita glared at him. "*What* did you say to me?"

Tony glared back at her. "I said, I'm going out to the
garden for a smoke!"

"*That*," said Perdita, "is what I thought you said. And don't
other coming to my bed tonight! Your services will *not* be
equired, my lord."

"There's no need," Tony said caustically, "to state the obvious."

Turning on his heel, he walked out, letting the door slam
ehind him.

"I never trusted the Shipley woman," declared Lady
Cheviot's maid, coming out of the closet in which she had
been eavesdropping. "These governesses are all alike, slipping into bed with the master every chance they get."

"She's not even pretty!" cried Perdita.

"Of course not, milady. You'd never be so foolish as to hire
a *pretty* governess."

The door opened, and Perdita flung her face cream at the
man who entered. The jar struck the doorjamb, leaving an
ugly mark.

"Shall I come back when it's safe?" Alex asked gravely.

Perdita covered her eyes with her hands. "Oh, I'm sorry,
Alex. I thought you were Tony, my faithless, philandering,
soon-to-be *former* husband!"

Alex wasn't listening. "Did you know Julian would be here
tonight?" he asked abruptly.

Perdita glared at him, exasperated. "Julian? No. I was completely surprised. Why?"

"How does Julian know Miss Rampling?" Alex demanded.
"What exactly is the relationship there?"

"I neither know nor care!" Perdita snapped. "My husband
has taken a mistress, and she is my governess! I just found out."

"What?" he said, grimacing in confusion.

"I caught them together in her room. It completely ruined
my ball."

"Tony and the governess?" he repeated incredulously.
"She's not even pretty!"

"I know! He might at least have the decency to keep his
mistress in London. How long do you think this has been
going on right under my nose?"

Alex sat down. "This is incredible. He's admitted to it?"

"No, of course not," said his sister. "He claims that Henry,
of all people, locked him in! His own son! He *says* he was
only looking for Rollo—you know, the bunny Hannah cud-
dles at night—in Miss Shipley's room. A likely story."

"What does Henry say?" Alex asked sharply.

Perdita stared. "I am *not* going to accuse my son without evidence," she said. "Henry's obviously innocent! He was sound asleep when I checked on him. He couldn't have done it."

"Oh, couldn't he?" Alex said grimly.

# Chapter Twenty

Lucy's sleep was filled with strange dreams that night. She dreamed that Alex kissed her on the deck of a great ship traveling to exotic lands. Then he kissed her at the top of Mount Vesuvius. The pyramids of Egypt whirled by as he kissed her in a golden sandstorm. She was kissed on tropical islands and sparkling white beaches. She was kissed in the Hanging Gardens of Babylon. She was kissed locally, too, in the New Forest, on the village green, in a punt on the river, and, rather shockingly, behind the baptismal font in the village church.

She woke up, trembling. Viola, dressed in her scarlet riding habit, was opening the curtains. Outside the sky was brilliant. "Did you enjoy your ride?" Lucy said, sitting up and stretching her arms over her head.

"I haven't been riding," Viola said, wringing her hands. "Oh, Lucy!" she cried, flinging herself on the bed. "Bijou has been kidnapped!"

"Viola, calm yourself," Lucy urged. "It's quite a big house, you know. She must be here somewhere. You cannot really imagine that someone has *kidnapped* your dog."

"Oh, but he has, the low-down, dirty buccaneer!" Viola insisted.

There was no need for her to tell Lucy who "he" was.

"This came for me at dawn from Cross Mere," said Viola, handing Lucy a scrap of brown paper. "It is a ransom note."

"It is a laundry list," Lucy corrected her gently.

"The other side!" cried Viola, turning the paper over.

"Oh, I see," Lucy murmured. "'If you ever want to see Mop again,'" she began to read.

"That is what he calls Bijou," Viola said bitterly. Springing up from the bed, she stalked the room, whipping her riding crop against her skirts. "Oh, how I hate him!"

"'If you ever want to see Mop again, you will bring my ring to me at Cross Mere,'" Lucy read with growing horror. "'I will be waiting for you at the Italian Fountain at ten o'-clock. If you are late, I will take her to London in your stead, and you will never see her again.'"

She dropped the note in astonishment. "It *is* a ransom note!"

"Oh, my poor Bijou! He would not hurt her, do you think?"

"Mr Julian seems to be capable of anything," Lucy said grimly.

"He is," said Viola. "I confess it is what attracted me to him in the first place."

"Do you have his ring?" Lucy asked sensibly. "He seems to want it back rather badly."

Viola shuddered. "That ghastly emerald he bought me in London! *The* most hideous jewel man ever inflicted upon woman! Green is the color of jealousy, for heaven's sake!"

"Then you do have it? Viola, you must give it back."

Viola scowled at her. "Are you on *his* side now?"

"Of course not," Lucy said quickly. "What he has done is unforgivable—obviously. But if you give him his ring back, perhaps he will stop tormenting you. It *does* seem to be the simplest way to get your dog back. And she *is* the most important thing, is she not?"

Viola drew herself up to her full height. "I do not negotiate with dog thieves!"

"You needn't negotiate," Lucy said soothingly. "Just give him his ring back."

"I can't," said Viola. "I don't have it. I threw it away."

Lucy stared. "You threw it away?"

"It was ugly," Viola explained. "I wanted a diamond. I was very clear on that point. I should have known *then* that he was no good. You know what my trouble is, Lucy? I can't admit when I'm wrong. There is a part of me that—even now—still wants to believe in him." She snatched up the ransom note. "When I found this, I actually thought it might contain some satisfactory explanation of his behavior. Yes! I thought that some beastly note, scrawled on the back of a laundry list, might actually make everything all right! I'm such a fool."

"What are you going to do?"

"Well, I'm going to get my dog back," Viola declared. "I shall have to meet the bastard, of course. You and I will ride over to Cross Mere together. You have to visit Lady Cheviot anyway, to thank her for the glorious time you had at the ball. You did have a glorious time, didn't you?"

"Yes, of course," Lucy fibbed.

"Good. While I distract Julian at the fountain, you will sneak into the house and rescue Bijou. Hurry up and get dressed."

"What!" cried Lucy. "You expect *me* to search Lady Cheviot's house?"

"Not to split hairs, but it's actually my brother's house," said Viola.

"What about Mama?"

"Lucy! I can't ask your mother to search Lady Cheviot's house."

"I mean we cannot leave my mother alone."

"Cornelius can sit with her. It's high time he took more responsibility for Lady Caroline anyway. Please, Lucy! She's only a puppy. He's probably pulling her ears right now."

Lucy paled. "He wouldn't!"

"You said yourself he's capable of anything!"

"What am I supposed to *say* if someone sees me poking around Cross Mere?"

"You attended a ball there last night," Viola reminded her. "Say you left your fan or your handkerchief or something. They'll let you look for it."

"In the *bachelors' quarters?*"

"Lucy, I need you," Viola said seriously. *"Bijou* needs you. Don't go wobbly on us!"

"Oh, all right!" Lucy said crossly, climbing out of bed. "I'll do it."

Lucy was not an accomplished horsewoman, which made it necessary for the two ladies to travel to Cross Mere by road, rather than by taking the shortcut across the meadow; Lucy could no more jump a fence than she could fly.

"You must learn to ride properly, Lucy," Viola said irritably. "We'd be there by now if we could cut across the fields. If I am late, I may lose Bijou forever!"

"I suppose I could try jumping," Lucy offered, eyeing the hedges doubtfully.

"If you broke your neck, then I really *would* be late," Viola pointed out.

Condemned to the narrow lanes between the hedgerows, Lucy and Viola picked their way through gaggles of geese and herds of cattle and sheep before arriving at Cross Mere. The boundary between the two estates was marked by the Folly. As they rode between the two towers, Viola could reach up and just touch the underside of the parapet with her riding crop.

The house at Cross Mere was a large red brick structure of the Queen Anne variety, completely unremarkable. It was so unappetizing, architecturally speaking, that Viola marveled that tenants had been found for it. Lucy led her around to the stables.

"Good morning, Miss Lucy," said the groom as he came forward to take charge of the horses. "You're here early, and

hank goodness, too, with Miss Shipley on her way out and
no one to mind Master Henry and Miss Elizabeth."

"Miss Shipley is leaving? Oh dear," said Lucy. "I'm not
surprised! I'd better go up to the house at once. You don't
mind, do you, Viola?"

Almost without waiting to hear Viola's answer, Lucy
picked up her skirts and ran into the house. Left alone with
the groom, Viola gave him a bright smile. "Good morning,"
she said. "I am Miss Andrews. Would you mind showing me
the way to the Italian Fountain?"

In the previous century, a small wilderness, confined by a
crumbling brick wall, had been established between the stables and the gardens at Cross Mere. The groom led Viola to
it and showed her the path that led through the wilderness to
the garden.

Viola had not gone far when she saw a man and a woman
standing in the shadowy embrace of an oak tree. Recognizing
the gentleman, Viola crept up to them.

"It is a handsome offer, my lord," the woman was saying.

"I can do no less as a gentleman," Lord Cheviot replied. "I
wish I could do more."

"You are very good, my lord," said she, blushing rosily.

"If I were not married, it would be different, of course,"
said Lord Cheviot. "But I cannot subject my wife and children
to ugly gossip. I only hope you can forgive me."

"Indeed, my lord," said Miss Shipley, in a treacly voice that
made Viola's skin crawl, "there is nothing to forgive. These
have been the happiest days of my life."

"Oh, Miss Shipley! Dash it all," said Tony.

"Oh, my lord!" sobbed Miss Shipley, burying her face in
his chest.

"There, there," said Tony, patting her here and there.

Viola could endure no more. She stepped on a twig, breaking it with a sharp crack.

"Oh, I beg your pardon!" she said as the pair whirled

around to stare at her. Miss Shipley stood white-faced, cling
ing to Lord Cheviot's arm.

"Good God!" said Tony Cheviot, gaping at Viola in disbe
lief. "What are *you* doing here?"

"Good morning, Lord Cheviot," Viola said, smiling pleas
antly. "I am Miss Andrews. I have come to see your Italian
Fountain. Would you be good enough to take me to it?"

Miss Shipley she ignored completely. She simply did not
see her.

Lord Cheviot stared at her helplessly. "What did you say
your name was?"

"Andrews," Viola repeated firmly.

"Oh, yes, of course," he murmured. "Miss Andrews."

"My lord?" Viola said, clearing her throat. "The Italian
Fountain, if you please."

"Of course!" Tony said quickly. "This way, Miss Andrews.
This way."

Recovering as best he could from the nasty shock of seeing
his landlord's sister on the grounds of Cross Mere, he offered
her his arm. Leaving Miss Shipley to fend for herself, he led
Viola away from the gate. "I think you will find that the Ital
ian Fountain has been quite beautifully maintained while I
have held the lease here at Cross Mere," he babbled. "Indeed,
I have made many improvements over the past three years."

"I don't doubt it for a second," Viola said warmly.

"Now, my son Henry *did* carve his initials in the banister,"
Tony admitted, "but I'm fairly confident that it can be refin
ished to everybody's satisfaction. Then, of course there's Miss
Shipley's door."

"Her door?"

"Well, I had to break it, of course."

"Of course you did," Viola agreed. "You had to get in."

Tony frowned. "Don't be ridiculous! I had to get *out*."

"Completely understandable," said Viola.

"I suppose, after you've inspected the fountain, you'll wan

o see the house," he said gloomily. "About the crack in the
dining-room chimneypiece—"

"Is there a crack in the dining-room chimneypiece?" she
asked politely.

"It was there when we took the place," he said fiercely.
"You cannot blame me for *that*. You can tell your brother that
I, naturally, will be responsible for all damages. But I'm not
responsible for the crack in the dining room chimneypiece."

"Oh, so you *do* remember me," Viola said smugly. "Have I
changed *very* much since the age of seventeen?"

"No, not at all," he replied unflatteringly. "You are, perhaps, a little taller."

"Aren't you going to ask me why I call myself Miss Andrews?" Viola snapped, vexed that he had not taken the opportunity to pay her a compliment.

"I assume you are incognito," he answered with a shrug.
"It's really none of my business what you call yourself. I hope
your brother is in good health?"

"My brother is perfectly robust, thank you. And your
wife?"

Tony jumped nervously. "Perdita? What about her?"

"Is her ladyship in good health?"

"Perdita is in excellent health," he said quickly. "There, you
see," he went on, spiriting her out of the wilderness into the
formal garden. "Behold, the Italian Garden, with the fountain
at the center. I put a new drain in last spring. Now it works
a treat."

Julian was sitting on the terrace wall. Dressed for riding,
he looked even more handsome than usual. As they approached, he jumped down, frowning as he dusted off the seat
of his riding breeches. There was no sign of Bijou.

Viola confined her attention to the fountain. It was a big
one, hewn of marble, with classical figures representing the
nine Muses crowning the god Apollo at the top of Mt Parnas-
us. Apollo looked as smug as any mortal man surrounded by

nine half-naked damsels could possibly look. Nine sprays o water, meant to represent the wellsprings of the imagination no doubt, babbled merrily into the reflecting pond.

"As you can see," Tony said fussily, "it is in perfect work ing order."

"Erato's nose is missing," Viola said critically.

"It was like that when we took the place," Tony said auto matically.

"Perhaps she cut it off to spite her face," Julian suggested strolling over.

"Oh, hullo, Julian. This is my brother-in-law Mr Devize," Tony murmured. "Julian, this is Miss . . . I'm sorry. What di you say your name was again?" he asked Viola.

"Miss Andrews," Viola said. "How do you do, Mr Devize?" She sank into a beautiful curtsey. Her lips smiled, but he eyes were stormy. Julian answered with a formal bow.

"Are those *my* riding breeches you are wearing?" Tony sud denly demanded of his brother-in-law. "And my new, wine colored coat!" he added savagely.

"Yes," Julian answered coolly. "Your valet was ver obliging. Miss Andrews, I see, is dressed for riding, too Perhaps she would care to go for a gallop with me?"

"Not even a trot, Mr Julian," Viola answered, smiling a Lord Cheviot. "I'm very thirsty, my lord. Would you be goo enough to offer me a lemonade?"

"You're perfectly welcome to come into the house," he sai grudgingly, "but mind the step at the back door. It was loose when we moved in," he added quickly.

"I've just come from the stables," Viola averred. "I'm really not fit to enter the house. Would you send it out to me' I will drink it here with Mr Julian."

"Right-o!" Relieved, Tony bounded up the steps to th terrace.

"You're late," Julian told Viola, almost before Lord Chevio was out of earshot.

"How would *you* know?" she said belligerently. "You awned your watch."

"There are clocks in the house."

"But who sets them?" Viola countered. "Anyway, you waited for me, so you can't complain. Where is my dog?"

"Mop is perfectly safe, I assure you. For now," he added ominously.

"Her name is Bijou!"

"What can I tell you? She answers to Mop now," he said smugly.

"Monster!"

He merely smiled. "Where is my ring?"

Viola squared her shoulders. "I told you. I don't have it. I threw it away."

He laughed mirthlessly. "Then you'd better find the dustman and get it back, my dear."

"I threw it out of a window at Gambol House. It's probably in the river!"

"Swim," he advised her.

Viola stamped her foot. "I want my dog!"

He took a step toward her. "Actually," he said, "I think you'll find she's *my* dog. I paid for her, after all. I found her all alone at Gambol Hall as I was leaving. She came with me quite willingly. Such an affectionate little creature. *You* came with me quite willingly, too, as I recall," he added cheekily. "You went off like a Roman candle."

"Here is your lemonade, miss," said the servant, who had crept up on them.

"Thank you," said Viola. Snatching the glass from the tray, she flung the contents into Julian's face. "Would you be good enough to bring me another?" she asked the servant politely, returning the glass to the tray. "The gentleman drank mine."

Julian calmly took out his handkerchief and wiped his face. "You will regret that, Miss Andrews," he said in a still, quiet voice that for some reason made her tremble.

"I think I will go into the house, after all," she said quickly, hurrying after the servant.

Julian fell into step beside her. "I owe Mr Grey ten thousand guineas for that ring."

"I tell you, I cannot give you what I do not have!" she hissed.

"Then you must bring me something of equal value, my sweet," he said.

"Fine!" Viola snapped. At the same time, she stumbled over the loose step at the back door of the house. If Julian had not caught her in his arms, she would have been sent sprawling across the polished marble floor within.

"Are you all right?" he asked, holding her so close she could hear his heart beating.

"Perfectly all right," she snapped, humiliated. "Thank you. Will you let me go, please?"

He released her so abruptly, she nearly fell again. "You will meet me at dusk, at the Folly," he commanded. "Do you know where it is?"

"No," she said sulkily.

"You'll find it," he said confidently. "I will be waiting for you with Bijou."

So saying, he turned on his heel and left her.

"Miss Rampling!"

Lucy jumped, hitting her head on the underside of Julian's bed. Scrambling to her feet, she turned to find Alex Devize standing in the doorway with a look of shock seared onto his face. Lucy turned beet-red.

"Oh, Mr Devize," she breathed. "You frightened me!"

"What are you doing in my brother's room?" Alex blurted out.

"Oh! Is this your b-brother's room?" Lucy stammered, beads of sweat pricking her brow.

"I beg your pardon, Miss Rampling," Alex said stiffly. "I

s, of course, none of my business. You need not explain your
movements to me."

"There's really nothing to explain. I was simply looking for
my handkerchief," Lucy said quickly. "I must have left it here
last night."

"In my brother's bed?" Alex almost snarled.

Lucy turned white. "Of course not! I didn't even know this
was his room," she added unconvincingly.

"Did you find it?" Alex asked politely.

Lucy went blank. "Find what?"

"Your handkerchief."

"Oh, yes, thank you!" Lucy said, producing her handkerchief from her pocket. In the next instant, she cringed. "I
mean, no! Of course not! What would *my* handkerchief be
doing in Mr Julian's room?" She laughed nervously and
scooted to the door. "Please excuse me, Mr Devize! I must go
and congratulate Lady Cheviot on the success of her ball."

"Didn't you get my note?" he said sharply.

Lucy blinked at him. "Did you send a note, Mr Devize?"

"Yes, I did. Didn't you get it?"

"No, I'm sorry. Your brother's note caused such an uproar
at the Hall that I'm afraid I didn't even look to see if there
were any other letters."

"I see," he said grimly.

"Was it important?" she asked him.

"Yes. About last night . . ."

Lucy's face broke out in hives as she recalled his kiss.
"Please don't mention it, Mr Devize," she pleaded. "Pray, let
us never mention the unfortunate incident again."

"I would like nothing better than to forget it," he said rather
sharply.

"There's no need to be rude," said Lucy.

Alex sighed. "I don't mean to be rude, Miss Rampling," he
said. "The thing is, I think I must tell my sister."

Lucy blinked at him. "Tell your sister! Tell Lady Chevio that you kissed me?"

"No," he said quickly. "I must tell her what Henry did that's all. You see, you and I were not Henry's only victim last night. He locked my brother-in-law in the governess' bedroom—*with the governess*. Most unfortunately, my siste discovered them. I'm afraid Perdita jumped to all the wrong conclusions. She is determined to dismiss Miss Shipley."

"Oh, poor Miss Shipley!" cried Lucy. "What will she d if she's turned off?"

"Poor Tony!" Alex retorted. "Perdita's threatening to leave him."

"Well, he *was* in Miss Shipley's room," Lucy pointed out.

"Lured there by the infamous Henry, and locked in!"

"Henry wouldn't do that to his father, surely," Lucy protested

"Why not? He did it to *us*," Alex pointed out gruffly, "hi favorite uncle and his auxiliary governess. Why wouldn't h do it to his father and his primary governess? This is a bad be ginning. If I can't convince *you*, how will I convince Perdita She thinks Henry is an angel!"

"She can't possibly think *that*," said Lucy. "I suppose you' better tell her what he did to *us*, even if it helps Lord Cheviot Indeed, you should have done so already. Why didn't you?"

"I wanted to talk to you first," he explained. "I will leave your name out of it, of course. There could be some harm to your reputation, after all."

"I think it's a little late to worry about my reputation, M Devize," Lucy said wryly. "Now, *where* could that little dog be?" she murmured in frustration.

"Dog?"

"Small, white, looks rather like a powder puff?" Lucy said hopefully.

"If you're looking for a dog, the twins were playing with a puppy this morning at breakfast," Alex offered helpfully.

"Did it look like a powderpuff?" Lucy asked eagerly.

"Not anymore," he said dryly.

Lucy gasped. "Where is she now?"

"The dog? I have no idea. The twins are playing croquet on the south lawn. You can see them from the window."

"Thank you!" Lucy breathed, running from the room as if her skirts were on fire.

Alex stood at the window, watching as Lucy joined the two children on the lawn below. He didn't know what to think. Lucy and Julian? Julian and Lucy?

Yesterday, he would have thought such an attachment impossible.

"Women!" Julian complained, breezing into the room. "Was it Alexander Pope who said we can't live with them or without them?" he asked his brother, tearing off his coat.

"Erasmus," Alex replied without thinking. "Although Ovid has some remarkably similar lines in his *Amores*."

Julian began to remove his wet clothing.

"What happened to you?" Alex asked him listlessly.

"Too much lemonade," Julian explained. He went to the washbasin, and, stripping to the waist, poured cold water from the jug over his head. "Hand me a clean shirt, will you? What are you doing in my room?" he asked curiously as Alex tossed him a fresh shirt from the wardrobe.

"I was just admiring the view from your window," Alex said, thinking quickly. To give credence to his story, he looked out onto the lawn. It was a brilliant spring day. The grass was emerald, and the sky was robin's egg blue. Miss Andrews, in scarlet, had joined Lucy and the twins on the south lawn. In her quiet gray habit, Lucy looked dull and insignificant. Why then could Alex not take his eyes off of her?

"Now, now, old man," said Julian, joining him at the window. "I saw her first."

"Did you?" Alex wondered.

"I met her in London," Julian explained. "My life has been

upside down ever since. Troublesome creature, but I can'
seem to do without her."

"If that's how you feel about it," Alex said sharply, "yo
should marry her."

Julian flashed him a look of surprise. "I intend to."

"What's stopping you?" Alex snapped. "Go to the cour
and get yourself a special license. You can be married by an
clergyman in the country."

"I went to Doctor's Commons," Julian said irritably. "Trou
ble is, our mother got there before me. Apparently, she doe
not approve of my fiancée. She's used her connections t
make it impossible for me to get a special license."

Alex's lip curled. "So you just gave up?"

"Don't I always?" Julian said sarcastically. "I didn't giv
up, thank you. *She* gave up. She left London, without so muc
as a word to me. I thought she'd married someone else.
came here hating her."

Alex's heart skipped a beat. "Then . . . you are no longe
engaged?"

"Oh, we're engaged," Julian said grimly. "Was it Pope wh
said the course of true love never did run smooth?"

"No. Shakespeare."

"What did Pope say?" Julian said irritably. "I'm beginnin
to think he doesn't deserve his reputation as a man of wit."

"Pope said that women fall when men are weak."

"Ouch," Julian said ruefully.

"He also said fools rush in where angels fear to tread."

"Another good one." Julian grinned suddenly. "Don't loo
so unhappy, Alex! Your day will come. Someone will tak
pity on you one of these days. She might even be pretty."

"I can but hope," Alex said, fixing a smile on his face.

"You will find yourself doing the strangest things," Julia
predicted. "I kidnapped her dog, just so she'd have to talk t
me again! I'm not proud of it, but it worked. I was arreste
and thrown in Newgate Prison because of her. I just got out."

Alex was shocked. "I can't believe you *took* her dog! That's just sick, Julian."

"I know."

"I told her I saw her dog with the twins this morning."

"Why would you do such a thing?" Julian demanded angrily. "That dog's the only leverage I have."

"Leverage! Will you listen to yourself?"

"I don't care," said Julian. "Where are the twins now?"

"I don't know," said Alex.

Julian's eyes narrowed with suspicion. "Why are you blocking the window? What are you hiding?"

"Nothing."

"Move," Julian commanded.

"No. Why should I?"

"Have you ever heard the story of Cain and Abel?" Julian asked.

"Yes," Alex answered. "The elder brother killed the younger."

"Are you going to kill me, Alex?" Julian laughed.

Alex sighed. "The twins are on the south lawn with Miss Rampling and Miss Andrews," he said, resigned.

Julian chuckled. To Alex's ears, it was a foul, lecherous sound. "There she is," he said, looking out the window. "It looks like she's giving young Henry a very large dose of what he's in for. Shall we go down and rescue the boy?"

"Excuse me," Alex said coldly. "I must speak to my sister."

# Chapter Twenty-One

Henry and Elizabeth had never seen anything quite as splendid as Viola.

"Who is she?" Elizabeth whispered, staring in helpless

admiration as Viola strode across the grass in her beautiful scarlet riding habit.

"Who is she?" Henry scoffed at her ignorance. "She's only our new governess!"

"She doesn't look like a governess," Elizabeth said doubtfully. "She looks like a queen."

"Times are hard," Henry shrugged. "Even queens must have something to live on. She probably lost her kingdom in the war."

Viola took no notice of the twins. "I see you did not find my poor Bijou," she said irritably to Lucy. "How I'd like to murder that man!" she added furiously.

"What man?" Henry and Elizabeth wanted to know.

Viola wrinkled her nose at the children. "Who are you?" she demanded, her riding crop at her hip.

"Viola, this is Miss Elizabeth Cheviot, and this is Mr. Henry Cheviot," Lucy said, shouldering her mallet to make the introduction. "Children, this is . . . well . . . You may call her Miss Andrews."

Inspired by Viola's noble appearance, Henry planted his mallet on the ground and made a sweeping bow. Not to be outdone, Elizabeth sank all the way to the grass in a solemn curtsey.

"Master Henry knows where Bijou is," Lucy told Viola quickly. "He's promised to give her back . . . *if* I can beat him at croquet."

Suddenly Viola was very interested in Master Henry. Like most naughty little boys, he was unduly attractive, with big blue eyes and a crop of thick chestnut hair. "This handsome young man here? You know where my dog is?" she asked, tickling Henry's nose with her crop.

"Is it *your* dog?" cried Henry. "Uncle Julian said it was *his* dog."

"Your Uncle Julian is a very bad man," Viola told him

"She's *my* dog, and he knows it. Her name is Bijou. I want her back, Master Henry. Will you help me?"

Henry grinned at her, his blue eyes glinting with admiration. "I never heard of a governess with a dog," he said.

"My goodness," said Viola. "Aren't they adorable when they're small? How old are you, Master Henry?"

"Almost seven," lied Henry. "You're beautiful!"

Viola was amused. "Thank you, Master Henry."

Elizabeth plucked at Viola's skirts. Like her brother, she had big blue eyes. Her chestnut hair hung down her back in ringlets. "Did you lose your kingdom?" she asked timidly.

"I suppose I have, in a way," Viola answered. "You see, I wouldn't marry the nasty, old nobleman my father picked out for me, so I've been disinherited."

"I knew it was something like that," cried Henry, delighted. "Would *you* like to play croquet with us?"

"Now, Henry," she scolded him. "Aren't you playing with Miss Rampling just now?"

"Oh, Lucy's no good," he said. "She'll never get your dog back. I'll let *you* win."

Viola smiled. "You don't have to let me win, Master Henry," she said, taking the mallet from Lucy. "You just have to let me go first."

By the time Julian had found his way to the south lawn, Viola had run all thirteen hoops and struck the peg in a single turn. Seated on a nearby bench, Lucy and Elizabeth applauded. Even Henry was impressed.

"My turn, I think," said Julian, striding onto the circuit. Stripping off his coat, he rolled up his sleeves and plucked the mallet from Henry's hands. Henry, naturally, objected. "Sorry, Harry," Julian told him without a shred of remorse. "But I'm afraid you're way out of your depth with Miss Andrews. She'll eat you alive. Better leave her to me."

"Don't call me Harry," Henry snarled, retreating to the bench to pout.

"That is *my* ball, Mr Julian," Viola said sharply as Julian approached her yellow ball.

"No. *That* is your ball, Miss Andrews," he argued, indicating the red ball that had just struck the peg. "You can't possibly have *two* balls."

"We *each* have two balls, Mr Julian," she said with asperity. "Mine are red and yellow. Yours are black and blue. Do you even know how to play the game?"

"Of course I know how to play the game," he scoffed, moving on to the black ball. "I invented croquet. I was simply testing you. Now, if you don't mind, Miss Andrews, I'll have absolute silence while I take my first stroke. In life as in bed," he added for her ears alone.

With consummate skill, he put his ball through the nearest hoop. "Ha!"

"I really must ask you to be quiet while I take my turn," Viola said coldly.

Julian scowled. "It's still *my* turn," he objected. "I ran the hoop!"

"You ran the wrong hoop at the wrong time," she explained sadly. "In life, as in bed."

"No, I didn't. What do you mean *as in bed*?" he demanded roughly.

"You're not that good," Viola explained. With a sharp swing of her mallet, she sent her yellow ball rolling toward his black ball. The two balls clicked and came to rest side by side.

"You *hit* my ball," he complained, enraged. "Foul play, madam!"

Ignoring him, Viola walked over to the two balls, placed her foot firmly on her own ball, and gave it an excellent whack. Julian's ball flew across the lawn and disappeared into the hedges.

"That's cheating, you baggage," he complained.

"That's croquet," she sweetly replied, using her last stroke to return her ball back to its original position. "*Now* it's your turn. Ah-ah-ah," she chided him as he went to his blue ball. "You cannot play your blue ball until your black ball is finished. Your black ball is somewhere in the hedges," she reminded him helpfully.

"Harry!" Julian called to his nephew. "Go and find my ball, would you? There's a lad."

"I won't," said Henry. He seemed to be holding a grudge against his uncle. "And don't call me Harry!" he shrieked.

"This is a stupid game," Julian declared as he plunged into the hedges after his ball.

"You invented it," Viola reminded him, even as she found his ball with her foot and nudged it under her skirt.

"No," he retorted. "The game I invented is much better. It's called sexual intercourse."

"I suppose the man who invented the pianoforte wasn't much of a pianist, either," she mused. "One never hears of him, at any rate. *His* music must have been quite forgettable."

Julian poked his head out of the hedge to glare at her. "You were singing a different tune last night, as I recall, madam. You went off three times, at least."

"I'm heartily sorry if I gave you that impression," she apologized. "I didn't want to hurt your feelings, so I may have fudged a little."

Julian stood nose to nose with her. "Your foot is on my ball, madam."

"So it is," she admitted.

In the next moment, the black ball shot across the lawn and struck the yellow ball, knocking it out of place.

"You *threw* that ball," Viola accused him, striding after him back onto the circuit. "You picked it up and threw it."

"Prove it," he invited her. With his next stroke, he hit her ball again.

"What are you doing?" she demanded. "You can't win like this."

"Neither can you," he retorted, hitting her ball again.

"This is stupid," she said, tossing down her mallet. "I forfeit. Congratulations on your splendid victory, Mr Julian! Well done."

Julian caught her arm. "You can't blame me for wanting to postpone the inevitable, Miss Andrews," he said. "Nobody likes a broken heart."

"If you had a heart," she said, glaring at him, "you would not have taken my dog."

His expression hardened. "Well, you know what you must do to get her back!"

Viola laughed. "I certainly do. Oh, Master Henry!" she called. Picking up her skirts, she ran lightly to the boy and knelt down to look him in the eye. "Master Henry," she said, her eyes pleading, "may I have my dog back, please?"

"Don't do it, Harry!" Julian shouted.

"She's in the tree house," said Henry, hopping up from the bench to seize Viola's hand. "I'll take you to her."

"Judas," Julian growled.

Lucy caught his arm. "I must ask you again to leave my friend alone, Mr Julian. You have a remarkable ability to discompose her!"

"Really?" Julian said, flattered. "What does she say about me?"

"Nothing of a complimentary nature, I assure you. Where are you going?" she cried as he disentangled himself from her.

"To the tree house, of course," he answered, laughing. "To discompose your friend."

"Oh, he is a scoundrel," Lucy groaned, stamping her foot.

"Uncle Alex?" Elizabeth exclaimed.

"No, dear. Your Uncle Julian," Lucy said absently before she realized that the elder of Elizabeth's uncles was upon them.

Alex caught Elizabeth in his arms and easily swung her up to rest on his shoulder. "Who's a scoundrel?" he asked cheerfully.

Lucy blushed. "Forgive me. I should not speak so of your brother."

"He should not give you reason to speak so," Alex replied. "Now, where is young Henry? His mother would speak to him of a very serious matter."

Lucy was eager for some good news. "Were you successful, Mr Devize? Is Miss Shipley to be allowed to stay?"

"I think so."

"Oh no!" cried Elizabeth. "We don't want Miss Shipley. We like our *new* governess."

"Elizabeth!" Alex rebuked her. "Miss Rampling is not your governess."

"Not Lucy," Elizabeth said scornfully. "Her!"

Viola was coming toward them from the far side of the lawn, a squirming bundle in her arms. Clearly, she was trying to outstrip Julian and young Henry, but, as she was hampered by the heavy skirts of her riding costume, they had no difficulty keeping up with her.

"You can't leave!" wailed Henry. "You're the new governess. You can have any room you want in the whole house," he promised wildly. Then, even more wildly: "I'll be good!"

"I am not your governess, you beastly boy," Viola stopped to hiss at him.

"I'm afraid she's had a better offer, Harry," said Julian. "She's going to be your aunt."

"How?" Henry demanded suspiciously.

"Your uncle is making a joke," Viola said coldly.

"No, I'm not," said Julian. "You see, Harry, I'm going to marry Miss Andrews. That will make her your Aunt Mary."

"We're no longer engaged!" Viola shouted at him.

"It's a very big secret, Harry," Julian went on calmly. "I wanted *you* to be the first to know, but you mustn't tell anyone until after we are married. *Then* you can tell everyone that *you* knew it *first*."

"Mr Devize, this is unpardonable!" Turning on her heel,

Viola crossed the lawn, calling to Lucy. "Look what they've done to her," she cried, showing Lucy the bundle in her arms.

Lucy gasped. As Alex had predicted, the little white dog was white no more. She had been caked in black mud and stuck all over with turkey feathers.

"They tarred and feathered her, the little monsters!"

"It's not real tar!" Elizabeth assured her anxiously. "It's only mud."

"It will wash off," said Julian, chuckling as he joined the party. "Look! She's wagging her tail. Look, she's licking my hand."

Viola slapped his hand away angrily. "She's having a spasm," she corrected him.

"I'll give her a bath myself," he offered. "She'll be good as new."

"I think you've done quite enough, Mr Julian," Lucy said coldly. "*We* will look after Bijou. Good afternoon! Good afternoon, Mr Devize," she added in a more civil tone to Alex.

"I'll walk you to the stables," Julian said cheerfully. "I feel like a ride myself."

"I'll go with you," cried Henry.

"No, Henry," said Alex. "Your mother wants to see you."

"The Shipley is staying," Elizabeth whispered to her twin.

Viola and Lucy hurried toward the stable, Henry's howl ringing in their ears. Julian kept up with them easily, announcing his intention to accompany them on horseback all the way back to Gambol Hall. Not even the fact that Lucy did not jump could dissuade him.

"I adore trudging along muddy country lanes," he declared.

Deliverance came in the form of Lord Cheviot himself. As the party neared the stables, his lordship came out of the building and verbally attacked his brother-in-law. "What the devil do you mean by taking Sultan out last night? He's lame this morning."

"He threw a shoe on the way home, but he ain't lame," Julian protested.

"He's got a big knee!" Lord Cheviot cried, red in the face. He was not passionate about many things, but he did love his horses.

"It was like that when I got on," Julian said mulishly.

"Rather like the crack in the dining-room chimneypiece," said Viola.

Tony was taken aback. "Er . . . yes," he said, miffed by the lady's interference. "Look here, Julian, how long do you propose to stay here in my house, spilling lemonade on my best clothes and laming my horses? That's right! I know about the lemonade!"

"Calm yourself, Tony. I'm leaving in the morning."

"You are?" Viola said, startled.

"Yes," Julian said. "I've been away from London too long as it is. It would be folly to stay here another day, would it not?"

"Yes," she agreed. "Folly."

"Good-bye, Mr Julian," Lucy said, pulling Viola away as the groom brought the ladies' mounts.

"Good-bye, Miss Rampling," Julian said cheerfully. "*Au revoir,* Miss Andrews."

"Poor Bijou," Lucy murmured as she pulled the wet, shivering bichon out of her bath some time later. "What sort of a man would kidnap a sweet, devoted little creature like you?"

"A bad man," said Viola, wrapping her now-white puppy up in a rose-colored damask towel. "A very bad man. I will certainly take him to task when I see him at the Folly."

Lucy's mouth fell open. "When you see him at the Folly!" she repeated incredulously. "You have not consented to meet him, surely!"

"I must," Viola said simply.

"Have you taken leave of your senses? Viola, you cannot be serious."

Carrying Bijou to the rug by the fireside, Viola began rubbing her down with the towel. "We have some unfinished business," she said. "That's all."

"You cannot meet him," Lucy insisted. "What unfinished business? You have Bijou."

"You said yourself, I must give him his ring back."

"You don't have his ring," Lucy pointed out.

"Then I must give him something of equal value." Viola shrugged. "I have a lot of rings. I'll just give him another one."

"Send your servant," Lucy exclaimed.

"And have Julian claim he never received it?" Viola shook her head. "No, Lucy. It's my responsibility. I must face him."

"Let me go in your place," Lucy offered.

Viola scowled at her. "Why should *you* go in my place?"

"Because it would be folly for *you* to go!" said Lucy. "Mr Julian is by no means a respectable young man. You would not be safe with him, I am persuaded."

"Oh, but you did not hear what he said to little Henry," Viola protested. "Lucy, he told his nephew that he was going to marry me! It could not have been plainer."

"Oh!" said Lucy, aghast. "That is too much effrontery, even from him! To use his nephew—a mere child—for his own devious ends . . . !"

Viola looked up, frowning. "But, surely, he would not say such a thing to his own nephew if he did not mean it," she said. "He would not tell Henry that I was going to be his aunt if he had no intention of marrying me. That would be unconscionable."

"Mr Julian is the sort of man who will stop at nothing to get what he wants," said Lucy.

"True. But I don't think he would lie to little Henry," Viola protested. "And if what he wants is to marry me, after all—"

"Viola! Have you forgotten that this is the man who tried to sell you to Lord Simon?" Lucy demanded. "Of *course* he would lie to his nephew. He wants you to run away with him to London, doesn't he?"

"Well, yes. But he loves me, Lucy. That is, I believe he loves me."

Lucy sighed. "That is not love, Viola. It is lust."

Viola shrugged. "Is there a difference, really?"

Lucy was shocked. "Of course there is!"

"For men, I mean," Viola clarified. "They're not terribly sophisticated, you know. They want what they love, and they love what they want."

"If he loved you," Lucy said firmly, "if he *truly* loved you, he would not declare his intentions to a six-year-old boy. He would declare them to the world! Not that I believe for an instant that *marriage* is his object," she went on sourly. "Viola, if you throw yourself into his power, what will prevent him from selling you to Lord Simon? He cannot be trusted. I would not see you injured by a rake."

"Julian is not a rake," Viola said firmly. "I promised to meet him at the Folly, and meet him I will. And if he wants to marry me, I will go with him to London. So there!"

"And if he does not mean to marry you?" Lucy said sharply.

"Then I will throw myself in the river to preserve my virtue!" Viola said crossly. "Will that make you happy, Miss Lucy?"

"No, of course not," Lucy said, distressed. "Can I not dissuade you from meeting him? Is there nothing I can say?"

"No, nothing."

Lucy took a deep breath. "Very well, then. I can only wish you luck."

"Thank you," Viola said coolly.

"You would not really drown yourself?" Lucy asked nervously.

"Don't be ridiculous," Viola snapped, fetching Bijou's brush and beginning the long task of brushing out the bichon's matted fur.

"I will leave you then," said Lucy.

"Good-bye," Viola sniffed.

Lucy went out, closed the door of Viola's bedroom, and locked it. Unlike Henry, she was careful to take the key away with her. Viola heard the key turn in the lock and ran to the door.

"Lucy!" she cried, rattling the locked door furiously. "What are you doing?"

"Saving you from yourself," Lucy answered. "I will go to the Folly in your place."

"What!" Viola howled. "Let me out this instant!"

"I will give Mr Julian the diamonds you lent me for the ball," Lucy went on with steely determination. "In the morning he will be gone."

"You let me out of here right now, Lucy Rampling," Viola screamed, stamping her foot. "I am going to murder you!"

"You will thank me for this later," said Lucy.

"Please, Lucy! You don't understand! I must see him."

"Do you know who you sound like?" Lucy said angrily. "You sound just like Mama when she's . . . *thirsty!* Well, you locked *her* in her room. Now I am locking you in yours!"

"You bitch!"

The loud crash from within the room was enough to bring Cornelius to the stairs. "What the devil is going on?" he demanded.

"Lady Viola is having a tantrum," Lucy explained. "She wants us all out of the house."

Cornelius turned pale. "She's evicting us? What about my seat in Parliament? Is she taking it back? Lucy, I am nothing without my seat!"

"I'm sure it's just a tantrum," Lucy assured him, running lightly down the stairs. "You know what these high-strung arisocrats are like. Why don't you take Mama for a nice long drive?" she suggested brightly. "I'll give the servants the afternoon off, and I'll stay here to look after her ladyship. Hopefully, her temper will have improved by the time you get back."

Lucy's optimism proved to be unfounded, however. Viola's temper only seemed to get worse and worse. She screamed until she was hoarse, broke things until Lucy feared for Bijou's safety, then lapsed into an eerie silence. Anxious, Lucy knelt down and peered through the keyhole. A dark, glittering eye glared back at her with palpable hostility.

"Lucy, I hate you!" Viola croaked.

Hastily, Lucy collected the diamonds Viola had lent her and ran out of the house.


Alex reined in his horse as he reached the Folly. His brother was tossing pebbles from the parapet. "Julian!" he called. "What are you doing up there?"

Julian frowned at him. "Nothing," he said irritably. "I'm just enjoying the view from the Folly. Were you looking for me?"

"No," Alex replied. "Miss Rampling left her handkerchief at Cross Mere. I was just going to Gambol Hall to return it to her."

Julian's lip curled. "I see."

"You have some objection to my scheme?" Alex said sharply. "Is there some reason I should *not* return this handkerchief to Miss Rampling?"

Julian's face was impassive. "No, I like your scheme. I think you should return Miss Rampling's handkerchief without delay. Quicker, in fact."

"I will, sir!" Alex snarled, urging his horse straight through the Folly at a gallop.

* * *

Lady Cheviot sat composed on the cream and gold-striped sofa in her drawing room. All day she had been deluged by visits from her neighbors, who all wished to congratulate her on the success of her ball, even as they secretly delighted in its failure. Perdita had dressed accordingly in a morning gown almost as opulent as the ball gown she had worn the night before.

"Ah, Shipley, there you are," she said warmly as the slim sallow governess slipped into the room, her spectacles glinting, her mousy hair scraped back into a knot. "I have spoken to Master Henry. The little angel admits his mistake. You are innocent. I have decided to allow you to remain here in my employ. That is all."

Miss Shipley smiled queerly. "Your ladyship is very kind," she said unctuously. "However, I do not choose to remain."

"Don't be ungrateful, Shipley," Perdita warned her.

"Indeed, I am most exceedingly grateful to my Lord Cheviot for his generosity," Miss Shipley replied, still smiling. "His lordship has provided for us so well, that I shall never have to work again. The child, of course, will want for nothing."

Turning to the side, Miss Shipley showed her ladyship a budding young pregnancy.

"Congratulations," Perdita said coolly. "How soon do you leave?"

Viola opened her bedroom window and walked out onto the small balcony. The big oak tree was too far away to touch, but so close that squirrels routinely jumped onto her balcony. She was not a squirrel, of course, but she was a fine, healthy girl. She could jump.

She climbed on top of the stone balustrade, took a deep breath, and jumped.

# Chapter Twenty-Two

Skirts billowing, Viola fell through the smaller branches of
the tree, sustaining numerous scratches on the way down.
Finally, she struck a branch heavy enough to hold her weight.
The impact knocked the breath from her body. She fell again,
tearing her fingernails on the branch just before she fell to the
hard ground.

For a moment she lay gasping like a fish. Then she picked
herself up and trudged, limping, toward the lane. She made it
as far as the garden, where she collapsed in pain.

Alex could not believe his eyes. Miss Andrews's scarlet
riding costume was torn and dirty. Her black hair was matted
with blood. There was blood on her cheek. She looked as if
she had been through a mangle. As he came up the drive, she
climbed laboriously to her feet, then collapsed again when
her left leg gave out from under her.

Alex dismounted, calling loudly for help, and ran to her
side. "Good God!" he exclaimed as she fell into his arms.
"What has happened?"

Blinking back tears of pain, Viola seized hold of his lapels.
"I must get to the Folly," she said, gritting her teeth.

"You can't even walk," he said, lifting her up in his arms as

if she weighed nothing. "I'm taking you inside to Miss Ram
pling. Hello there!" he called again, as he began carrying he
back up to the house.

"Lucy," Viola spat bitterly. "Lucy has gone to the Folly t
meet Julian!"

"Has she?" Alex muttered. "Where the devil are the se
vants?" he snapped they reached the door.

"Lucy gave them the afternoon off," Viola explained.

With a roar of disgust, Alex kicked the door open an
carried Viola inside. Depositing her on a sofa in the drawin
room, he leaned over her. "Where are you hurt, Miss A
drews?"

Viola struggled to get up. "I must get to the Folly. I mu
stop Lucy!"

"Never mind all that!" he said sharply. "Have you broke
anything?"

"Everything in my room," she said. "How could Lucy be s
beastly cruel as to lock me in? I had to go out of the windov
Mr Devize. Squirrels do it all the time. Why can't I?"

"Don't try to talk," Alex said sternly. "You've obviously i
jured your brain. Also, I think your ankle might be broke
It's swelling up. I don't like to leave you alone, but I think I
better get the doctor."

"No!" Viola protested, catching his arm. "You must go t
the Folly, Mr Devize. Stop her, before it's too late. Please!
you do not," she went on, wincing in pain, "I shall. I'll *craw*
to the Folly if I have to."

"Don't be a fool," he said sharply. "I will go to the Folly.
will tell Miss Rampling what has happened. Then I will fetc
the doctor."

"Tell her it's her fault if I die," Viola said, falling back o
the sofa. "That should fix her."

Alex rode hard to the Folly.

* * *

"What are you doing here?" Julian demanded as Lucy approached.

Lucy looked up, startled by his voice, to find Julian watching her from the parapet. Grim and determined, she picked up her skirts and began climbing up the stairs to him.

"Where is Miss Andrews?" he demanded.

"She isn't coming," Lucy said quietly. "I am here in her place."

"No, thank you," he scoffed.

Flushing, Lucy presented him with the diamonds. Julian looked at the velvet bag with contempt. "What is that?"

"Something of equal value, Mr Julian," she answered. "My friend no longer has your ring. Take these diamonds and go."

"You take them and go," he retorted. "Where's Mary? Why isn't she here?"

"She doesn't want to see you," Lucy lied. "She wants nothing more to do with you. Go back to London, Mr Julian," she pleaded. "Leave my friend in peace."

Julian's eyes narrowed. "You've poisoned her against me," he accused.

"You have no one to blame but yourself, Mr Julian," she told him harshly. "You made the bargain to sell her. You betrayed her trust. You broke her heart."

"What the devil are you talking about?" he growled. "*I* bought her."

"Indeed," Lucy said, revolted. "And when you were tired of her, you arranged to sell her to another man! It is despicable."

Julian's face was gray. "You've been telling lies, Miss Rampling."

"Is it a lie?" cried Lucy. "I saw your letter, sir! The poor girl carries it with her, to remind her of your perfidy."

"What letter, you lying cat? I never wrote any letter."

"The letter I saw was written by Lord Simon," Lucy replied. "It laid out the whole disgusting transaction in plain

English. You were to sell her to him for a profit of three tho
sand guineas. Can you deny it?"

"This is what Mary thinks?" Julian said, after a long paus
"How could you tell her something so beastly?"

"I didn't! *She* told *me.*"

"I don't believe you. Where is she? Is she at the house?"

As he started down the stairs, Lucy darted after hi
pulling at his arm. "Leave her alone, sir! Haven't you do
enough to her?"

A flash of movement across the meadow caught Julia
eye. It was not Mary, however, as he had hoped. It was h
brother, riding Tony Cheviot's black hunter. "You have ruin
my happiness, Miss Rampling," he said coldly, pulling Lu
into his arms. "Now I shall ruin yours." With that, he clamp
his lips down on hers in a fierce, bruising kiss.

"I'm sorry to interrupt," Alex called up to them, his mou
twitching in agitation.

Shocked, Lucy disentangled herself from Julian ar
dragged the back of her hand across her lips.

"We were just finishing up," Julian said pleasantly.

"Miss Andrews has been injured," Alex informed the
curtly. "I'm just going for the doctor now."

"Oh no!" cried Lucy, running down the steps. "What h
happened?"

Alex could not bring himself to look at her. "Julian, wou
you be good enough to escort Miss Rampling to her frien
I was forced to leave Miss Andrews alone, Miss Rampli
having dismissed all her servants. I will send the doctor," I
added. "I will not return."

Without another word, he tore off in the direction of t
village.

"What have I done?" Lucy whispered, running blind
back toward the house. She could not outrun Julian, howeve
and by the time she reached the house, gasping for breath, th
reunion had taken place.

Viola's face was pale but serene as Julian brought her a glass of wine. "I want you to know, Lucy," she said, stretching out her hands, "that I forgive your interference. I know you meant well. Indeed, I'm so happy at this moment that I could not possibly hold a grudge!"

"I could," Julian said darkly. "You might have been killed. What possessed you to jump out of the window?"

Lucy gasped in horror. "I'm so sorry! I'm so sorry you were hurt!"

"It doesn't matter now," Viola said, smiling into Julian's eyes. "Anyway, Julian doesn't think anything is broken."

"It's still a very bad sprain," said Julian.

"Lucy was only trying to protect me," said Viola.

Julian's eyes snapped angrily. "She has been filling your head with nonsense! *You* may forgive her, but I don't."

"Is it nonsense?" Viola asked.

"Of course it is," he said. "What? You didn't really believe that I was going to *sell* you to Lord Simon, did you?"

"What was I supposed to think?" Viola said. "He came to Lombard Street to buy me. He left you a note with a fixed price!"

"My God," said Julian. "You must know I would never do such a thing!"

"You said you would," Viola reminded him.

"No, I didn't," he said angrily.

"You said it would make your life easier!"

"I-I was angry," he stammered.

"You gave the condesa to your colonel," she reminded him.

"That was a long time ago," he said. "And I never loved her. You couldn't possibly have believed . . . ! My God, when Hudson told me you'd run off with Lord Simon, I nearly lost my mind!"

"And why would I run off with Lord Simon, a man I despise?" she demanded.

"Well, you wouldn't, would you?"

"No."

Lucy threw up her hands. "Please! You cannot allow your self to trust this man again! He kissed *me* at the Folly, fo heaven's sake! He must be a fiend of lust or something. H obviously cannot control his base male urges."

"You're lying!" Viola gasped.

"She's a desperate spinster," said Julian. "Of course she' lying, darling. *She* kissed *me* at the Folly."

"Lies, Viola, lies!" Lucy gasped.

"You're right, Miss Rampling," said Julian. "These *are* vil lies. Let us forget they were ever spoken."

"You think you're so clever!" Lucy snapped. "How d you propose to marry in London without a special license Mr Julian?"

"I don't," Julian replied. "Not that it's any of your busines Miss Rampling."

"We'll elope, of course," said Viola.

"Gretna Green? If he loved you, he wouldn't dream of suc a thing," said Lucy. "Besides, he said he was taking you t London."

Viola frowned. "Dev?"

"Don't listen to her, sweetheart. She's jealous."

Lucy glared at him. "If you love her, sir, you would no even think of eloping. You would go to Sussex at once an reconcile with your father. The banns would be called from the pulpit, as is proper. Then you would marry her in th church where you were baptized. That is how a gentleman i love behaves."

"This has nothing to do with my father," Julian said angrily "Miss Andrews and I will be married in London. I *will* get th license."

"How?" Viola demanded. "Has your mother relented?"

"No, but I've spoken to the Duke of Fanshawe."

"Dickon knows?" Viola said, a little startled.

"Yes. He only wants you to be happy. He'll get the special license for us."

"Of course he will," Viola said, laughing with relief. "Who better?"

"He certainly has more influence than my mother," said Julian. "I'll leave for London tomorrow at first light. With any luck, I'll be back the following day with the license. We'll be married when I return, and you won't even have to leave your sofa."

"I want to go with you."

"Nonsense," he said firmly. "You can't even walk."

"Oh, very well," Viola said sulkily.

Presently Dr Chadwick arrived to dress Viola's cuts and scrapes and to confirm Julian's assertion that her ankle was not broken, but had sustained a bad sprain. By the time Julian returned to Cross Mere, it was well after dark. Dinner having already ended, he strolled down to the kitchen for emergency provisions. There he found his brother deep in a bottle of port.

"Does Tony know you're drinking his Cockburn?" Julian asked, helping himself to a steak pie from the larder.

"Does he know you're eating his pie?" Alex retorted as his brother found a bottle of beer.

"I think he'd rather not know," Julian replied, joining Alex at the table.

"You're probably right. How is Miss Andrews?"

"I'm glad you asked," Julian said cheerfully. "Nasty sprain, of course, but she's a strong, healthy girl. She'll be right as rain in a few days."

"You needn't sound so pleased," Alex grumbled.

"Why shouldn't I be pleased? I'm getting married."

Alex set down his glass. "Are you, by God?" he asked in a hollow voice.

"By God, I am. I told you that already, didn't I?"

"I'm sure you'll be very happy together," Alex said stiffly.

"So am I. I leave for London at first light," said Julian. " shall return with the license and marry her here."

"While you are in London, you should insert a notice in the papers," said Alex.

Julian sighed. "I've no time for such niceties."

"You need a best man," Alex observed.

"Well, you're my best man, of course," Julian said instantl "I wouldn't have it any other way."

"Certainly," Alex said wearily. "Do you want me to go London for you?"

"No. I need the duke's help if I'm to get the special l cense," Julian replied. "You might talk to the vicar for m arrange the service. I suppose we can do it at Gambol Hall. daresay Miss Rampling can manage the wedding breakfast

"Of course, Julian," Alex said quietly. "I'll help in any wa I can."

"Thanks, old man."

"Don't anybody move," Tony Cheviot commanded, lea ing into the room with a pistol in his hand. "Oh, it's you," h said morosely, placing the pistol in the pocket of his purpl satin dressing gown. "I thought you were burglars."

"What have *you* got worth stealing?" Julian asked rudely

"You're eating my pie," Tony complained. "*And* you'r drinking my vintage port!" he added, glaring at Alex. "Yo *are* burglars!"

Angrily, he grabbed the pie from Julian. For good measur he took the port from Alex.

"You call this hospitality?" said Julian. "I am going t bed."

"So am I," said Alex.

"Good night!" Tony said indignantly.

And so it was that, through no fault of his own, his lad found him alone in the kitchen holding half a steak an kidney pie in one hand and a bottle of port in the other. Sh was wearing her pink quilted dressing gown and her hai

as in curl papers, but that was not what made Tony's blood
curdle in fear. Rather, it was the cold, deadly look in her
blue eyes.

"I might have known," Perdita said scathingly, "you'd be
down here in the middle of the night eating and drinking your
head off. I myself have lost my appetite."

"I wasn't eating!" Tony cried. "Julian ate the pie, and Alex
opened the port."

"Are you quite sure it wasn't little Henry?" his wife asked
coldly. "You seem to blame my son for everything!"

"Not everything," Tony mumbled.

"Well, you can't blame him for *this*," said Perdita. "Tony,
I've decided to divorce you."

Tony stared at her blankly. "No, you can't!" he protested.
"I won't let you. Think of the children, Perdita."

"I have thought of them," she replied. "They will come
with me, of course."

"You can't take my children from me," Tony said.

"You don't need *my* children," she told him. "You have a
new family now. I expect you to marry Miss Shipley as soon
as our divorce is granted by the House of Lords."

Tony guffawed. "Marry Shipley? You're mad!"

"Miss Shipley is with child," Perdita told him. "I expect
you to do the decent thing, Tony, for the child's sake."

Tony was stunned into silence.

"Didn't she tell you?" Perdita asked. "I assure you, she is
quite gloriously pregnant!"

"Well, it ain't mine!" Tony sputtered.

"Of course it is," Perdita snapped. "While I was in London
begging my mother for a little money to pay Georgie's school
fees, you couldn't think of anything better to do than bed the
governess! She isn't even pretty!"

"I never touched her," said Tony.

"She didn't get pregnant by herself," Perdita snarled.
"I'm leaving you, Tony. I'm going back to my father in

Sussex. I'm taking my children with me. Don't you dare t
to stop me!"

Tony became angry. "I can't believe you would take h
word over mine," he said. "You'll never get a bill of divor
through! I'll fight you. My father will vote against you."

"My father will beat your father," Perdita sneered. "Lo
Devize is vastly more popular in Lords than Lord Snowde
I *will* get my divorce."

Lady Cheviot swept out of the room.

In the morning, she was enraged to discover that her lo
had beaten her to the punch. She did not mind that Tony ha
left Hamphsire—she was glad not to see him at breakfa
Her complaint was more substantial: Tony had taken the ca
riage, the couple's only vehicle, and the only chaise for hi
in the village had already been taken by the odious Mi
Shipley. Until the chaise returned from London, Perdita w
stranded in Hampshire.

After breakfast, Alex rode over to Gambol Hall.

Lucy appeared pale and worried.

"How is the patient?" Alex asked her. "My brother assur
me it was only a sprain."

"Oh, the patient is much better," Lucy assured him. "She
sitting up in the garden. I will take you to her. I know she w
be delighted to see you. She regards you as quite the hero
she added with a strained smile. "She thinks of you alread
as her brother."

"Brother!" Alex said, startled.

"Oh dear," Lucy said, wringing her hands. "I have sa
too much."

"Indeed, you have said too little!" said Alex, detaining h
when she would have sped off. "Why should Miss Andrev
think of me as a *brother*?"

Lucy's eyes filled with tears. "Your brother has convince

y friend that he loves her! That he means to marry her. You
w him kiss me at the Folly. You know what a scoundrel he
! I am sorry to pain you—I know he is your brother—but he
such a man. I do not care that he has injured me. I suppose,
my age, I should be flattered by a young man's attentions!
t any rate, he can do *me* no real harm. But my friend truly
·lieves in his love. She is completely taken in by him. I think
ɪe would believe the moon is made of green cheese upon his
ɪthority."

"Julian . . . and Miss Andrews," Alex murmured, his voice
ɪghted by astonishment.

"He did not tell you? It is as I suspected! He is not sincere.
·e declared himself to little Henry, but to no one else in his
ɪmily! Mr Devize, I have tried to warn her—he clearly does
ɔt mean to marry her—but she will not listen to a word
say!"

"But he *does* mean to marry her," Alex said quickly. "I
.d not understand him, but now I do. He is determined to
arry her. You must accept it, Miss Rampling."

Lucy blinked in surprise. "I . . . I am glad," she stammered.

"Are you, Lucy?" he asked her gently.

Lucy blushed. "Of course I am. I did not want to see my
iend break her heart. But do you believe that he loves her?"
ɪe asked tentatively.

"Why else would he want to marry her?" Alex asked. "It
ɪust be love."

Lucy bit her lip. "Perhaps my suspicions are unworthy," she
ɪltered.

"Tell me," he said curtly.

"I daresay you have long suspected that Miss Andrews is
ɔt truly my mother's nurse."

"I have always thought her a most unusual choice for that
ɔsition," he said wryly.

"She is in fact a very rich young lady," Lucy blurted out.
ɪe is your brother," she went on, biting her lip. "You know

him better than I. Can it be he is after her fortune? Do yo
think it possible that he loves her? Does he seem like a ma
in love?"

"I don't wish to pain you, Miss Rampling, but he does."

Lucy looked down in embarrassment. "You do not pain m
sir. I did not want to be right! I want my friend to be happ
You have relieved my mind of all anxiety. I just wish . . ."

"Yes?" he said gently. "What is it you wish?"

"I suppose I am old-fashioned, Mr Devize," Lucy sa
sheepishly. "But *I* think the banns should be called out
church three Sundays in a row. *Then* let the marriage tal
place. What is three weeks, after all, if two people are tru
in love?"

"An eternity," said Alex.

As Lucy had predicted, Viola was indeed delighted to se
her future brother-in-law. A sofa had been placed outside fo
her in the rose garden. Wrapped in a luxuriant cashme
shawl, she reclined upon it like a queen, offering Alex he
hand, which he kissed politely.

"I am pleased to find you looking so well," he said.

Despite a few scratches, and a swollen ankle, Viola looke
radiantly beautiful. "Never mind about me," she said impa
tiently. "I am tolerably well. What about Julian? Has he gor
off to London as planned?"

"No," Alex said crisply. "There's been a change in plan
Julian wants you to go to our family home in Sussex with ou
sister, Perdita."

"Sussex?" Viola repeated in astonishment.

"Yes. The marriage will take place in Sussex."

"There, you see, Lucy!" Viola crowed in triumph. "Julian ha
gone to Sussex to reconcile with his father. He *does* love me."

"So it would seem," Lucy said, looking at Alex uneasily.

"My sister is to hire a chaise for the journey," Alex bega
but Viola interrupted him.

"No need," she assured him. "We can go in my carriage. We can leave as soon as you like, Mr Devize."

"My dear! Your ankle," Lucy protested.

"Nonsense!" Viola said angrily. "I scarcely notice the pain."

"You will in a jostling carriage," Lucy retorted.

"No, I won't," she argued.

"Ordinarily, I would agree with you, Miss Rampling," said Alex. "But, in this case, the young people are so eager, any delay would seem cruel."

"I knew I liked you," Viola said happily.

"I shall be your outrider, of course, so you need not fear anything on the road to Devizes," Alex went on. "My brother also asked that Miss Rampling come along."

"Lucy? Why?" Viola asked. "She is against the marriage."

"I am not against it," Lucy protested. "I've had doubts about the groom's intentions, that's all."

"Perhaps that is why Julian wants you there, Miss Rampling," Alex replied.

"You should be there," said Viola, "to apologize for your hateful suspicions."

"But I cannot go," said Lucy. "I cannot leave my mother."

"Oh, Cornelius can look after *her*," Viola said carelessly. "You can be my maid of honor. You would not refuse me, surely?"

Lucy became flustered. "Of course not," she whispered.

"Then it's all settled," said Alex.

# Chapter Twenty-Three

"Come and sit next to me, Master Henry," Viola invited as Perdita and her three youngest children climbed into the car-

riage. Lady Cheviot, Miss Elizabeth, and Baby Hannah, th
latter safely ensconced in her nursemaid's arms, took up on
side of the carriage, while Viola, Lucy, and Henry took th
other. Perdita was vexed to be facing the horses, but, as it wa
not her carriage, there was nothing she could do. The footma
stepped up behind her, and the carriage shot smoothly dow
the drive.

"Is Miss Shipley not coming with us?" Lucy asked in su
prise.

Perdita stiffened. "Miss Shipley," she repeated coolly
"Why, no. Miss Shipley has left us to take a new position i
London."

Lucy's mouth fell open. "But why, Lady Cheviot? I though
you had reinstated her. Did your brother not tell you wha
Henry did to him the night of the ball?"

"Peaching again," Henry grumbled, snuggling up to Viola

"Yes, he did," Perdita answered. Her tone was that of on
bored beyond endurance. "But Miss Shipley did not wish t
be reinstated. She has done very well for herself," she adde
with a contemptuous sniff. "She is happy."

"Why, what did you do, Master Henry?" Viola asked
nudging the boy playfully.

"Henry was very naughty," said Perdita. "He locked peopl
up. My husband and our former governess. My brothe
Alexander and an unknown lady. I cannot make out who sh
was, and Alex refuses to say."

"Well, who was she, Henry?" Viola demanded. "Hmm?"

"Can't tell," Henry said, luxuriating in Viola's attention
"Word of honor."

"Uncle Alex would murder him if he told," Eliza informe
them.

"That is as it should be," Viola pronounced, petting Henry
"A gentleman must always protect a lady from any harm t
her reputation. But I'll wager that Miss Elizabeth knows. Sh
can tell us."

Elizabeth did know, but she had also been sworn to secrecy.

Viola laughed. "But you are a girl, Eliza. We females are never bound by our word the way men are. Why, if *I* was obliged to keep my word, I should have to marry my pony, Gypsy, instead of your charming Uncle Julian. I wouldn't like *that* at all."

Elizabeth's eyes were enormous. "Am I really allowed to break my word?" she cried.

"Of course you are, my love," said her mother. "If I had to keep my word, I should have to give Colonel Brandon the ten shillings I lost to him at cards. I certainly shan't be doing that!"

"There is no need for you to break your word, Eliza," Lucy said quickly. "*I* was the lady. Mr Devize and I were merely looking for poor Miss Shipley when Henry locked us in a room."

"You, Lucy?" said Perdita. "Henry! Why would you do such a wicked thing to poor Miss Rampling?"

Henry shrugged.

"Because Uncle Alex is in love with her," Elizabeth peached. "We heard them talking at the Folly. He asked her to marry him."

"Eliza!" cried Perdita as Lucy's face flamed. "You mustn't tell such ridiculous lies. You're embarrassing Miss Rampling."

"It's true, Mama," clamored Elizabeth. "We thought if we locked her in with Uncle Alex, he might kiss her or something."

"But I don't suppose he did," Henry added resentfully.

"Certainly not," Lucy lied stoutly.

"Of course not," Perdita scoffed. "Uncle Alex is a gentleman."

"*Uncle Julian* would have kissed her. I bet he kisses *you* a lot," Henry said to Viola.

"Don't be silly," Viola replied. "Only *married* people kiss.

Your Uncle Julian is always mindful of my honor. He wouldn't dream of compromising me. What you did was very wrong, Henry. You have done great harm to Lucy's reputation. Now she will have to marry Uncle Alex, or disappear from all good society."

Lucy did not realize she was being teased. "We were scarcely alone for three minutes before we managed to get out!" she protested vehemently.

"Three minutes is *quite* long enough," said Perdita. "A lot can happen in three minutes. You will find that out when you are married."

"Nothing happened," said Lucy, panicking.

"It's not a bad match, Lucy," Viola said thoughtfully, looking out of the window. Alex was riding alongside the carriage on his brother-in-law's best hunter. "And it *does* explain why you were kissing Julian at the Folly. You wanted to make Alex jealous. I suppose I can forgive you for that," she added charitably. "It's the sort of thing *I* would do."

"I did *not* kiss Mr Julian," Lucy said furiously. "*He* kissed *me.*"

Viola bristled. "Julian wouldn't do that."

"He did," Lucy insisted. "He was furious because I took your place at the rendezvous. He said something nonsensical about ruining all my hope of happiness, and then he kissed me. Mr Devize was just coming upon us. The poor man looked so shocked!"

"Of course he was shocked," said Viola. "It must have been very shocking indeed to see the woman he loves kissing his brother! I daresay his heart was broken."

"Oh," said Lucy. "I had not thought of that."

"He probably thinks you're in love with Julian."

"No!" said Lucy.

"He looks sad to me," Viola said, observing Mr Devize from the window.

"Do you think so?" Lucy said, studying Alex.

"I fear I must warn you, Lucy," said Perdita. "I don't think my father will look upon the alliance with a friendly eye. And my mother will be quite livid! They both expect great things from Alex in the way of marriage."

"Lady Cheviot, I assure you, there is to be no alliance!" said Lucy firmly. "May we please talk of something else?"

The ladies relented, and Viola began to question Perdita about her family home. As they drew closer to the barony, Alex rode ahead of the carriage to inform his father of their approach.

Lord Devize was pulling dandelions in his garden when his eldest son arrived. To keep his head cool as he worked, the baron wisely had knotted his handkerchief at the corners and was wearing it as a cap. Otherwise, he looked almost exactly like his gardener as he knelt in the flowerbed. Caught unawares, he could not disguise his delight at the sudden appearance of his son and heir, but, very quickly, as Alex made his way toward him on foot, he remembered to scowl. "What are you doing here, sir?" he snarled, stabbing at a particularly obstreperous colony of dandelions. "Out of money? Again?"

"I've come to my senses, Father," Alex announced abruptly. "I am prepared to marry Miss Peacock, if—"

Overjoyed, the baron surged to his feet. He nearly made it, too. "Give me your hand, sir," he rasped, flailing. "I want to embrace you, my son."

Alex obligingly hauled his father up and allowed himself to be embraced. "I have one condition, Father. It concerns Julian."

The baron withdrew, his eyes hooded. "Who?"

"Don't be childish, Father," Alex said impatiently. "I will marry Miss Peacock, as you wish, if you will make Julian marry Miss Rampling. That is my offer."

The baron scowled. "Who the devil is Miss Rampling? Not Agrippa Rampling's girl?"

"Yes. What of it? You cannot object to her breeding. Her

grandfather was an earl. It is not Lucy's fault her father los
all their money and committed suicide."

"Nor is it my fault," Lord Devize pointed out. "What do
care who Julian marries? I have no son by that name. He ca
marry who he wants. Did he send you to plead for him?" h
jeered contemptuously. "Too cowardly to face me himself?"

"He doesn't know I'm here," Alex admitted. "In point o
fact, he's jilted Miss Rampling for another girl. Her heart i
broken. I know she puts on a brave front, but inside she i
slowly dying. I can see it in her eyes."

Lord Devize did not care if Lucy Rampling slowly died
"What am I to do about it?" he growled. "Surely Julian ha
the right to choose his own wife."

"And I don't?"

"Certainly, if you wish to be disowned," the baron replied

"You can't disown me," Alex said smugly. "I'm your heir
If you allow Julian to jilt Miss Rampling, I will never marry
Miss Peacock. Indeed, I will never marry at all."

The baron flinched. "You can't mean it! Think of th
unbroken line," he pleaded. "The barony has passed from
father to eldest son in an unbroken line for five hundred years!"

"I *do* mean it, sir," Alex assured him.

"But how am I to make Julian do anything? The boy don'
listen to me. He never has!"

"Go to Julian," Alex urged. "Apologize."

The baron reddened with anger. "Apologize! Never! Le
*him* apologize."

"Admit you were wrong, Father," Alex insisted. "Miss An
drews has money. Lucy does not. I believe Julian still love
Miss Rampling. I saw him kiss her. He would marry her, i
you would only give him an allowance."

"I will not apologize," declared the baron. "But if you wil
marry Molly Peacock, I'll agree to bribe the worthless young
man to marry Miss Rampling. But I will never receive then

at the castle," he warned, "and I will never acknowledge the connection."

"You will see Miss Rampling," Alex said firmly. "And you will treat her with every courtesy. The banns will be called in the village church, beginning this Sunday."

The baron stuck out his chin. "For you and Molly?"

Alex nodded curtly. "And for Julian and Lucy. Miss Rampling is on her way here now with Perdita and Miss Andrews. They will be arriving within the hour. I suggest we go inside and make ourselves presentable."

The baron scowled. "Miss Andrews? Why is *she* coming to Devize?"

"She thinks she is going to meet Julian here and marry him," Alex explained. "You will have to tell her the truth. It won't be easy. She fancies herself in love. However—"

"Have you no regard for the poor girl's feelings?" the baron asked in astonishment.

"No, none," Alex replied. "Miss Andrews is of no importance to me whatsoever. I'm sorry if her feelings are hurt, of course, but that's life, isn't it? There must be winners, and there must be losers."

"You're heartless," the baron complained.

"I wish to God that were true," Alex muttered.


"It's quite a small castle, isn't it?" Viola said, wrinkling her nose as the ancestral home of the Devize family came into view.

Perdita smiled at the young woman's pretensions. "Fortunately, Julian will not inherit."

"No," Viola agreed. "But I should like it to be bigger all the same."

Lucy was in awe of the ancient-looking Norman structure. "I think Castle Devize is very grand indeed. It is exactly what a castle should be."

"You don't think it too cold and militaristic?" Viola asked
"All those battlements? All those loopholes for the archers to
shoot out of? It has a moat, for heaven's sake! And a draw
bridge, too! That hardly seems friendly."

"It's a *fortress,* Miss Andrews," Perdita said dryly. "One
can hardly expect a fortress to be warm and inviting."

Viola sniffed. "At any rate, *my* country estate will not be a
castle. I prefer a cozy, pleasant, welcoming place. Something
a bit more like Versailles, perhaps, or the Pavilion at Brighton
one hears so much about. A place where one's friends can
gather and make merry."

Perdita dissolved into laughter. "You're too much, Miss
Andrews! As Julian's wife, you have as much chance of
making merry at *Versailles* as you do of flying to the moon."

"I shall have to build, of course," Viola conceded. "That's
the only way to get exactly what one wants. What do you
think, Lady Cheviot, of pulling down Gambol Hall *and* Cross
Mere and putting up one great, good place instead?"

Perdita stared at her as if she had sprouted a second head
"Pull down Gambol Hall and Cross Mere? Are you mad?
They belong to the Duke of Fanshawe!"

Viola laughed at her astonishment. "Didn't your husband
tell you? I'm sorry, I thought you were in on my little secret
The Duke of Fanshawe is my elder brother. I'm Lady Viola
I daresay I can persuade my brother to give me his Hampshire
properties as a wedding gift."

Perdita choked, causing Viola great concern. "I hope Julian
doesn't choke when I tell him," she fretted as Lucy rapped
Perdita sharply on the back.

Perdita choked again. "Julian doesn't know?"

"I don't want him to know until after we're married," Viola
explained. "I want to be married for myself alone, you see."

"Oh, I see," Perdita said faintly.

"You don't *mind* if I pull down Cross Mere, do you?" Viola
asked. "You can always live somewhere else. My brother

wns houses all over Britain, you know, and we have a devil
f a time finding tenants for them all."

"Indeed, Lady Viola," Perdita said faintly.

"Oh, and you *must* let me put you in touch with my old
overness, Miss Taylor," Viola went on. "I'm afraid I wore her
ut and had to pension her off to a cottage, but she can rec-
mmend somebody for you."

"Indeed, Lady Viola. I'd be most grateful."

"I don't mind telling you, Lady Cheviot, I didn't much care
or your Miss Shipley. Never mind that her clothes hang
unny on her, she was dreary and ugly. That whiny, grating
oice! The tears and hysterics! Frankly, Lady Cheviot, I think
our children deserve better."

"But, Viola, you don't even know Miss Shipley," Lucy
rotested. "How can you say such terrible things about her?"

"Such terrible, *accurate* things," sniffed Perdita.

"I know Miss Shipley as well I like," Viola retorted. "Lord
heviot introduced her to me. I stumbled upon them in that
rettyish little wilderness you have there at Cross Mere, so he
vas obliged to present her."

Perdita froze. "You saw my husband and Miss Shipley? In
he wilderness? Alone?"

"It was quite an emotional performance," Viola said, gri-
nacing in distaste. "Water was pouring out of her face. Cheviot
vas so embarrassed, I believe he had no choice but to take her
n his arms, which, of course, was *exactly* what she wanted. I
hall never forget the way her big Adam's apple was bobbing
p and down as she sobbed. It was too hideous to be forgotten.
This has been the happiest time of my life!' cried she. Ugh! I
onestly thought I was going to vomit. However, I did not," she
dded quickly as she became aware of Perdita's shocked face.

Lucy looked shocked, too.

"You can easily see that you are better off without her,"
aid Viola.

"Quite," Perdita agreed faintly.

* * *

The courtyard of the castle was a big, cobbled square ope
to the sky, with a handsome marble drinking fountain in th
middle. Chiefly it was the province of the baron's dogs an
servants; both species rushed forth to greet the carriag
Lord Devize had not troubled himself to wash or change h
clothes for the occasion, but he did remove the handkerchi
from his head.

Henry did not run to meet his grandfather, as was h
usual habit. Instead, he seemed glued to the skirts of a tal
well-formed female. The female, the baron noted with ap
proval, did not shy away from the big mastiff that amble
over to sniff her and the little white dog she carried in he
arms. As the bichon trembled in terror, Viola stood ab
solutely still.

"Come, Brutus!" the baron commanded as his daughte
came to greet him, and the mastiff turned away reluctantly.

"That's a dreadful name for a mastiff!" Viola rebuked th
baron. "You're not a Brutus, are you?" she asked the big do,
leaning down to scratch his head with a gloved hand.

The baron stared at her, enraptured by a vision that too
him back in time more than twenty years. "Louisa Lyon! /
I live and breathe!"

Viola gave him a dazzling smile. "Did you know m
mother?" she cried.

"You're Louisa's daughter, are you?" he said, coming to h
senses. "I knew your mother very well, child. I was in lov
with her—I admit it. We all were. We called her the Highlan
Dasher, you know. She swooped down on London one Seaso
and married the richest man she could find. I'm sorry, m
dear. I don't know what Louisa called you."

"Viola," she said, curtseying.

He beamed at her. "Yes, of course. Her favorite flower."

"And her favorite sweet," said Viola. "She adored viol

reams. She ate so many during her confinement that I was
uite blue when I was born."

"Papa," Perdita interrupted. "May I introduce Miss Ram-
ling—"

"Not now, Perdita," he said impatiently, taking Viola's arm
nd guiding her into the residential part of the castle. "What
rings you to Castle Devize, Lady Viola?"

She laughed. "Matrimony, of course! I'm going to marry
our son."

"Ah!" he said, eyeing her curves appreciatively. "Now
here will be a great marriage! You look like you'd breed noth-
g but sons."

"Thank you," said Viola, laughing. "Where is my bride-
room? Have you reconciled with him? I shall be very un-
appy with you, Baron, if you have not."

The great doors of the castle opened onto a vast medieval
all hung with dusty heraldic banners. The rest of the furnish-
gs, however, looked comfortable and up-to-date. Perdita
llowed them inside, followed by the nursery maid, followed
y Henry and Elizabeth. Lucy, bedraggled and forgotten,
ntered last.

"Of course we've reconciled," the baron assured Viola.
There was never any serious contention between us. He's
pstairs, making himself presentable. Come in and sit down,
y dear," he invited her.

"I've been sitting for hours," Viola protested, preferring to
tudy the family portraits hung on the paneled walls. "Let me
tretch my legs."

"Of course. Would you care for some refreshment? Or per-
aps you would care to see the garden? Ah, here is my son
ow!"

Viola looked up to see Alex standing in the gallery above
em. He ran lightly down the stairs and went straight to
ucy, his hair damp and freshly combed. "Miss Rampling! I

apologize for not being here when you arrived. I assume m
sister has introduced you?"

Having dispatched her children up to the nursery, Perdi
sank into a chair. "I tried," she said, yawning.

Alex succeeded where his sister had failed. Although irr
tated to be parted from Viola, the baron graciously spare
Lucy a moment. "So this is Miss Rampling, eh?" he sai
gruffly.

Lucy curtseyed. "How do you do, my lord."

Unimpressed, he harumphed. "So you want to marry m
son, do you?" he said gravely, looking at her with a lowere
brow. "Personally, I would rethink the matter."

Perdita sat up in her chair, and even Viola's attention wa
caught.

Lucy began to stammer. "I-I had not thought to . . . I ha
not thought it possible, my lord! I never thought you woul
approve."

"You seem all right to me," said the baron, shrugging.

"It is very possible, I assure you, Miss Rampling," sai
Alex. "My father has consented to have the banns read o
Sunday."

Lucy flushed. "I must say, this rather high-handed of yo
Mr Devize. You haven't asked me yet! I mean, not since th
last time."

Alex frowned. "Asked you what?"

"To marry you, of course," Viola interrupted. "You have t
propose to her, Mr Devize."

"Really, Alex," Perdita murmured. "If I were you, Lucy,
should refuse him again."

"What?" said Alex.

"You can't just have your father do it for you," Lucy sai
angrily. "You can't just have the banns read. Just because I'
thirty and poor doesn't mean you can take me for granted!"

"What are you talking about?" he demanded. "I'm n

asking you to marry *me,* Lucy. You're going to marry Julian.
It's all arranged. You needn't thank me."

"Lucy marry Julian?" Viola howled. "No! *I'm* going to
marry Julian!"

"*You* can't marry Julian," the baron protested at once.
"You're going to marry Alex, for he's to inherit. Julian is
nothing but a disobedient flea!"

"What," said Viola, "is going on?"

"I'm sorry for you, Miss Andrews," Alex said. "But Julian
must marry Miss Rampling. I saw them kissing. There's nothing else to be done."

"That is ridiculous," said Lucy. "That is like saying that I
must marry *you* because you kissed me at the Cross Mere
Ball."

"So you *did* kiss her!" said Perdita.

"That was before I knew about your affair with Julian!"
Alex accused Lucy. "I know you're in love with him!"

"In love with Julian?" Lucy said indignantly. "Affair! I
am not such an idiot as that."

"*I'm* the one who loves Julian," Viola reminded them. "I'm
the idiot."

"No, no, no!" cried the baron. "Julian will marry Miss
Rampling. You, my dear, must marry Alex," he added, taking
Viola by the hand.

"I don't want to marry Julian," said Lucy.

The baron shrugged. "I don't really care if you marry him
or not," he admitted. "As long as Alex marries this magnificent creature, I shall be very well pleased."

"What about Molly Peacock?" Alex demanded.

"Never mind Molly," the baron said impatiently. "Who
can think of a Miss Peacock when Lady Viola is in the
room!"

"Who?" Alex said, bewildered.

"Lady Viola Gambol! This young lady."

"You mean Miss Andrews?" Alex said slowly.

"I'm not really Miss Andrews," Viola said. "I'm Vio Gambol. You're not going to choke, are you, Mr Devize?"

"I don't care who you are," said Alex, not choking at all. have no wish to marry you."

"And I have no wish to marry you! Where is Julian?" Vio demanded to know.

The baron looked sulky. "He's not here."

"What! Where is he? He was supposed to meet me here

The baron shrugged his shoulders. "Says who?"

Viola glared at Alex. "Well?"

"My brother," Alex said sheepishly, "has gone to Londor

Viola looked at him incredulously. "London! You said was on his way to Sussex to reconcile with his father."

"I lied," Alex explained. "He went to London as planne to get the special license."

"Alex!" Lucy protested.

"I'm sorry," said Alex. "I thought Miss Rampling was love with Julian. I wanted her to be happy. So I lied to yo Miss Andrews—Lady Viola, I should say. My father had lor been wanting me to marry his neighbor's daughter. I offere to marry her in exchange for his assistance in persuadir Julian to marry Miss Rampling."

"You lied to me because you wanted Lucy to be happy Viola said angrily. "What about *my* happiness? Your brothe happiness? Didn't that mean anything to you?"

"Not really, no," Alex said.

"Mr Devize!" Lucy protested. "Your brother thinks Lac Viola is waiting for him in Hampshire!"

"I'm going to London at once," Viola announced. "I can married there as easily as anywhere else, and my brother there, too."

"I'm sure you could have the banns called here," said Luc "Mr Devize can go to London and inform Mr Julian—"

"I'm not waiting three weeks," Viola said decisively. "I' wasted enough time already, thanks to you, Mr Devize. We

married at Gambol House. I suppose you are all invited.
▸u too, Alex," she added coolly.

"Fine," said Alex. "Miss Rampling, may I speak to you for
▸moment in private?"

Perdita jumped up. "I'd better go and get the children
▸ady," she said.

"Stay where you are," said the baron. "Alex can have noth-
▸g to say to this girl that anyone cannot hear."

Viola took the baron firmly by the arm. "You mentioned a gar-
▸n," she said, leading him outside. "You may show it to me now."

"He can't marry *her*," said the baron, shaking his fist in
▸stration. "I want him to marry *you*," he told Viola.

"There's no chance of that," she told him frankly. "I'm
▸ing to marry Julian."

"But a girl with no dowry! It's scandalous."

"She's already refused him twice," said Viola. "You can't
▸k her to refuse him a third time, not at her age. And you
▸n't stop them from marrying."

"How old *is* she?" he asked anxiously. "I expect a grandson,
▸u know!"

"She's only thirty," Viola assured him. "You'll get your
▸andson. Of course, if you make her nervous and unhappy,
▸e isn't likely to conceive, is she?"

"No," he agreed.

"Then you'd better be nice to her, hadn't you?"

"Oh, all right," he said gruffly. "Come, let's go in," he said.
▸hey've been in there long enough. Well?" he presently de-
▸anded of his son. "Are you going to marry her or not?"

Alex stood next to Lucy's chair. "I am, sir," he said coldly.
▸he banns will be called on Sunday," he went on as Viola
▸shed to kiss Lucy, "and there's nothing you can do about it."

"The banns?" said Viola. "Don't you want to marry Lucy
▸icker than that? You should come to London with me and
▸t a special license. We can have a double wedding."

"She's not getting any younger, you know," the bar
muttered.

"I suppose I'm old-fashioned," said Alex, "but I think
should do the thing properly."

"You do?" said Lucy.

"Don't you?" he said.

"Of course," she agreed. "But, after all, what is thr
weeks, if two people are in love?"

"An eternity?"

"Exactly," she said, smiling up at him.


# Chapter Twenty-Four


"I'm so sorry, Mr Devize," said the butler at Gaml
House, but Julian could not help but feel that Lover was
sorry at all. "The family are all out. Her ladyship is in t
country visiting a sick friend, and his grace has gone away
the weekend."

"Damn," Julian said savagely. "I need to discuss an urg
matter with the duke. When do you expect him back?"

"Monday, perhaps."

"Monday!"

"Or Tuesday," Lover said serenely. "It is possible that I
grace may not come back at all this Season. Would you c
to leave your card?"

"Of all the damned, bloody, inconvenient . . . !" Julian
his lip in frustration. "No card. Just tell the duke I need to s
him the moment he gets back."

"Very good, sir."

Lord Cheviot received quite a different reception when
called less than an hour later.

Lover was all smiles. "Welcome to Gambol House, my ⸱rd. His grace is away from home at the moment, but we do ⸱xpect him to return within the hour, if your lordship would ⸱re to wait."

The duke did indeed return within the hour. With him was ⸱tiny duchess not his own, a tall, broad-shouldered Horse ⸱uard, and a demure young lady with big, brown eyes. As ⸱ways, the duke was glad to see Lord Cheviot. "Tony and I ⸱ere at school together," he explained, introducing the vis- ⸱ount to his companions. "I've known him a hundred years, ⸱d not once has he touched me for money. Now *that* is what ⸱call a true friend."

The Duchess of Berkshire looked at Tony through her ⸱yeglass. "Lord Snowden's son, of course," she said in her ⸱eep, gravelly voice. "I know your father. This is my son, ⸱imon."

"Simon is engaged to Viola," Dickon said enthusiastically ⸱s Simon and Tony exchanged their formal bows. "Is he not ⸱handsome fellow? Do you think Viola will be pleased with ⸱m? She is in the country visiting a sick friend, or else she ⸱ould be here."

"I had the pleasure of seeing her ladyship in Hampshire," ⸱aid Tony.

The duchess smiled. "Then we may expect her back very ⸱oon. No one would willingly stay in Hampshire for more ⸱an a week, I am sure."

"I believe, ma'am," Tony replied, "it is a great deal like ⸱erkshire."

"And this young lady," said Dickon, his homely face ⸱reathed in smiles as he brought the brown-eyed girl for- ⸱ard, "is Miss Mary Andrews."

"How do you do, Miss Andrews?" Tony said without bat- ⸱ng an eye. "Dickon, may I speak to you?"

"Of course," said the duke, settling down on the sofa with ⸱Mary beside him. "You can tell me anything."

"In private, I mean. I beg your pardon, ma'am. Miss An drews. My lord."

The duke followed him out, dragging his feet. "What's th matter, Tony?" he anxiously inquired. "Have I been naughty Are you angry with me?"

"No, nothing like that," Tony assured him. "Let's go out the garden. I don't even want the servants to overhear what must tell you."

Thanks to the Thames, the garden smelled strongly onions, but Tony scarcely seemed to notice as he sat down o a stone bench. "The thing is, Dickon, I'm having a spot bother with my governess."

Dickon joined him on the bench. "Aren't you a little old f a governess?"

"My children's governess," Tony clarified. "She's havin a baby."

"Don't you like babies?"

"She says it's mine," Tony explained.

The duke's eyes widened. "Don't you like your ow babies?"

"It's not mine!" cried Tony, punching in the crown of h hat. "I never touched the bloody cow!"

"What cow?" Dickon asked, a little startled.

"Miss Shipley!"

"Funny name for a cow," said Dickon.

"Miss Shipley is the governess," Tony said patiently. "She having a baby. She says it's mine, but it isn't. It can't be. never touched her."

"It could have been immaculate conception," Dickon sai helpfully.

"Immaculate conception? No. The thing is, she's convince my wife that her beastly baby *is* mine. Perdita is threatenin to divorce me."

"You're going too fast," Dickon complained. "Who Perdita?"

"Perdita is my wife, of course!"

Dickon was now quite puzzled. "As such, wouldn't *she* be the mother of your children?"

"Exactly!"

"Well, there you are, then," Dickon said happily. "Glad I could help."

"But you haven't helped," Tony pointed out. "Perdita is beside herself. The ungodly woman is taking a house in London, if you please!"

"So your wife is taking a house in London. What's wrong with that? Lots of people take houses in London," the duke pointed out.

"No, Shipley is taking a house in London!" Tony said impatiently. "I gave her too much money, you see."

"They say that money *is* the root of all evil."

"When it all happened, Perdita dismissed Shipley, and I . . . Well, I felt sorry for the old girl. She's so deucedly unattractive, you see. I'm afraid I gave her fifty pounds. Now, of course, she wants more, *and* she has my letter," he added in a frantic whisper.

"You said you gave her too much money. You could ask for some back."

"Did you hear what I said? She has my letter! If I don't find a way to provide Miss Shipley with fifty pounds per annum, she will show it to Perdita. If Perdita sees that letter, I'm finished. Can you help me, Dickon? Could you lend me, say, a thousand pounds?"

Dickon was taken aback. "Sorry, old man. Neither a borrower nor a lender be. Dev is very firm with me on that, and I don't like to cross him."

"Dev?"

"Devize, you know. My stockjobber. You must talk to him about it, I'm afraid."

"I can't talk to *him!*" Tony said savagely. "He's my brother-in-law. He'd tell his sister."

Dickon sighed. "Well, I'm sorry, Tony. I'd like to help, bu it simply can't be done. Dev would have my guts for garters.

"I'm sorry, too," said Tony.

Dickon started in surprise as his friend turned on his heel "You're not leaving?"

"Yes, I must. It's getting late, and I must find a room for th night."

"I've got plenty of rooms," Dickon said quickly. "Just picl one. I can't lend you any money, old man, but I can offer yo a bed for the night. It's the least I can do for an old friend."

"Well, that's very civil of you, Dickon. I'm sorry I aske you for money," Tony said, hanging his head in shame. "I won't happen again. You dropped this, I think," he added picking up something from the ground.

Dickon looked at the emerald ring curiously. "I've neve seen it before in my life."

"It looks like a lady's ring," Tony observed. "It probabl belongs to your sister."

"No, indeed," said Dickon. "Viola hates emeralds, alway has. Even as a baby she shied away from them. You'd bette keep it."

"I couldn't," Tony protested. "It looks expensive. It mus belong to someone."

"Finders keepers, losers weepers," said Dickon. "Take it, he urged his friend. "Give it to your wife."

"Yes, that might work," Tony murmured bleakly, slippin the ring in his pocket.


Gambol House was boiling over with activity when th duke went down for his breakfast the following mornin The carpets were being dragged out to be beaten in the plaz The chandeliers had all been lowered and were being vigor ously polished. Flowers were pouring into the great receptio rooms. Huge arrangements of fruit were being carrie

rough the halls. Musicians were tuning up in the gallery.
he dogs were nowhere in evidence.

More hungry than curious, Dickon proceeded to the break-
st room.

Viola was at the sideboard helping herself to eggs and
con. "Close the door!" she shouted. "Don't let the dogs out."

"Viola!" he cried as the dogs overwhelmed him. "At last!
ou're home."

"I am home," Viola agreed warmly, tossing bacon to the
amoring dogs. Seating herself at the table, she drew Bijou
to her lap. "You remember Miss Rampling, of course," she
ded, drawing her brother's attention to a thin little person
ated at her elbow. "I stayed with Miss Rampling when I was
ely in Hampshire."

"How-de-do, Miss Rampling," Dickon said civilly before
urning to his sister. "Is that a bichon?" he asked incredu-
sly.

"Yes. Her name is Bijou. Would you like to hold her?"

"Would I?" he said eagerly, snatching the puppy from his
ter's lap. "I haven't had a bichon in decades! Where did you
d her?"

"Gently!" Viola admonished him.

With the puppy snugged under one arm, Dickon skipped
er to the sideboard. "When did you get back?" he asked his
ter. "No one told me."

At Viola's elbow was a silk-covered notebook and a silver
ncil. Setting down her fork, she picked up the pencil and
ote something down. "It was very late. You'd already gone
bed," she explained. "How was your trip to Yorkshire?"
e asked, setting down her pencil. "Did you enjoy the
mphs?"

Dickon's face fell. "No, I did not," he said as he piled steak
d kippers onto his plate. "I'm afraid I have bad news for
u, Viola. You can't marry Lord Bamph, after all."

He stole a look at his sister's face and was relieved to s
her quite unexcited.

"What is the bad news?" she asked calmly.

"You don't mind about Bamph, then?"

"Why should I mind? I never wanted to marry him at al
Picking up her pencil, Viola made another hasty note.

"In that case, I have even more good news," Dickon sa
joining them at table. "I've found the most wonderful you
man to take his place!"

"Yes, I know," said Viola, laughing. "He told me all about
"He did, did he?"

"Yes. He said you'd get the special license for us?"

"Oh, you're pleased, then?" Dickon cried, relieved.

"Ecstatic," said Viola. "No. No, it wouldn't be proper to
perience ecstasy before marriage, would it, Lucy? At prese
I am merely delighted."

"Then it's all settled," said her brother. "We can leave
York at any time you like."

"York! Heavens, no," said Viola. "York is much too
away. We shall be married here, tomorrow morning at ni
o'clock. Good heavens! I've so much to do!"

"But you said you wanted to be married at York Minste
the duke reminded his sister.

"I did," Viola conceded. "However, York Minster is not
London, and *I* am not in York. We shall have to have a spec
license."

"Oh, I see," Dickon murmured.

The door opened, and Mary Andrews came into the brea
fast parlor.

"Don't let the dogs out!" cried Viola, and the footm
jumped to close the door.

"My lady!" Mary cried in astonishment.

"My dear Miss Andrews," said Viola, giving the girl
hand. "What a pleasure it is to see you again. This my frie
Miss Rampling."

Lucy greeted the young lady cordially.

"You're looking very well," Viola complimented Miss
Andrews.

Miss Andrews was indeed in very good looks. Her hair was
simply but elegantly dressed, and her dove gray gown was
fashionable while still appropriate for a young lady in half-
mourning. "Thank you, my lady," she breathed. "I believe
Miss Dobbins has smartened me up."

"Dobbins is with you? Excellent," said Viola, crossing
something off her list. "She's really the only one who understands my hair. And now, Miss Andrews, we must decide
what is to become of you," she went on presently. "Living
with your aunt is completely out of the question, I'm afraid.
I have met her, and she will not do, to put it mildly. Have
you given the matter any thought?"

"Yes, my lady," said Mary, looking hopefully at the duke.

"I've been thinking about it, Viola," said Dickon. "I've decided to adopt Miss Andrews. Only if you approve, of
course," he added quickly.

Viola considered the matter. "That's not a bad idea," she
decided. "Once I am married, my duty to my husband will
take me away from you a great deal of the time. I would not
want you to be lonely."

"I would not be lonely if I had a daughter," said Dickon.

"No, indeed. I think you should adopt Miss Andrews."

Mary burst into tears of relief. Viola was so moved that
she embraced Mary. Then she ran down the room to her
brother and kissed the top of his bald head. "You've managed
everything so well, Dickon. I'm quite proud of you. Do you
know, I think that some of Dev's cleverness may have rubbed
off on you."

Dickon blushed at the compliment.

Viola picked up her list. "Come, Lucy," she commanded
from the doorway. "You're getting married tomorrow, and you
have nothing to wear!"

"Is Miss Rampling getting married, too?" cried Dickor

"Yes, a double wedding," Viola called over her shoulde

When they had gone, the duke reached for Mary's hand
am glad you are here, my dear," he said. "I should be v
lonely without you. Very lonely indeed."

"Thank you, Your Grace," Mary said, drying her eyes.

"Please, call me Papa."

"Yes, Papa," said Mary.

At half past eight, Perdita stepped into the breakfast roc
then immediately stepped back out, her heart pounding. "T
is ridiculous," she told herself. "Tony isn't here. Why wo
Tony be here? I am imagining things, horrible things."

Taking a deep breath, she reentered the room. Contrary
all common sense, she saw her husband again. He was s
holding silver tongs and scavenging amongst the chaf
dishes.

"Perdita!" Tony cried, dropping the tongs.

"What are you doing here?" she demanded. "Are y
following me?"

"I was here first," he pointed out. "You know the duke a
I were at school together."

Perdita scowled. "You're not staying here!"

"Why shouldn't I?" he said belligerently.

"Because *I* am staying here—with Lady Viola."

"Well, I am staying here—with Dickon."

Perdita debated sweeping from the room, but she was
hungry to stand on principles. "Are there any muffins lef
she asked coldly.

"No."

"I suppose you ate them all," she accused him.

"No!" he protested. "There's plenty of toast and marmalad

Somewhat mollified, Perdita sat down and began slath
ing her toast with butter.

"Where are the children?" he asked her.

"George and William are at Eton. Philip and Arthur are at Harrow," replied his wife. "I'm surprised you've forgotten where you send the cheques."

"I meant the younger children, of course," he snapped. "Henry, Elizabeth, and Hannah."

"You remember their names! How nice. They're upstairs in the nursery, quite content."

"I suppose," he said presently, "you have come to London to sue me for divorce?"

"I have not yet spoken to my father about the matter," she replied primly. "My brothers are to be married tomorrow. I did not want to spoil their day. But rest assured, Tony Cheviot, I *will* divorce you."

"How?" he said, sticking out his chin. "You can't prove anything."

Perdita laughed at him. "She's pregnant, you fool!"

"It's not mine," Tony said angrily. "Perdita, I am prepared to admit that you were right about Miss Shipley's character, but you are *not* right about *mine*. I am innocent."

"I have a witness!" she said fiercely.

"You have a witness," he repeated blankly. "A witness to what? I did not have relations with that woman!"

"No? Lady Viola saw you with *that woman* in the wilderness!"

"Yes. And?"

"You were engaged in criminal conversation. *And* you were embracing her!"

Tony stared at her. His face slowly turned red. "That's a damned lie!"

Flinging down her napkin, she ran from the room before he could see that her eyes were filled with tears.

Dressed to go out, Viola and Lucy were just coming down the stairs. Viola was drawing on her gloves. "There you are, Perdita. Would you mind going over the music with the maestro? I want

everything—" She broke off abruptly as she caught sight o
Lady Cheviot's face. "Why, Perdita!" she cried in concern
"What on earth is the matter?"

"Nothing," said Perdita. "Of course I will go over th
music with the maestro."

"I'd do it myself, but I've so much to do before the wed
ding," Viola said. "And, of course, I have a tin ear, whic
don't help matters."

"I'm very happy to do it," Perdita said. "You girls run alon
and do your shopping."

"What a pity Cheviot isn't here," Viola sighed. "He's ver
musical, and I trust his taste."

"You!" said Tony Cheviot, coming out of the breakfas
parlor.

Perdita turned to stare at him. She had never seen Tony s
angry. He was positively livid, almost blue in the face.

"Ah, Cheviot!" said Viola, her face lighting up. "There yo
are. You'll speak to the musicians for me, won't you?"

"How *dare* you show your face here?" he snarled at her.

Viola looked around in startled confusion. "Who is he talk
ing to?" she wondered. "Cheviot?" she called to him. "T
whom are you speaking?"

"You may well ask," Tony growled, striding over to her.

"Me?" cried Viola, truly astonished.

"You!" he retorted, sticking out his jaw. "What do yo
mean by telling my wife you saw me in the wilderness wit
Miss Shipley?"

Viola looked blank. "I did see you in the wilderness wit
Miss Shipley," she pointed out. "You introduced her to m
Was it a secret?"

"Well, of course you saw me in the wilderness with Mi
Shipley," Tony said angrily. "That's because I *was* in t
wilderness with Miss Shipley! But I was not embracing her

"I never said you were," Viola said indignantly.

Perdita's eyes widened. "You did!" she cried.

"I'm sure I didn't," said Viola. "Miss Shipley was crying, or pretending to, at any rate. She threw herself at Cheviot and wept all over him. It was repulsive. If I hadn't come along when I did, there's no telling how much money he would have given the conniving woman."

"I gave her too much as it is," Tony said bitterly.

"You gave her money!" cried Perdita, furious. "How much?"

"Fifty pounds."

"What is fifty pounds, if it rids you of a Miss Shipley?" Viola said, shuddering. "I shall never forget the insufferable, smug look she gave me."

Perdita gasped. "I know that look! She gave me the same look the night of the ball, when I first found them together. She was in bed with her skirts up."

Viola snorted. "Of course she was," she said tartly.

"I never touched her skirts," Tony said stoutly. "I only popped her buttons."

"Oh!" said Perdita.

"Perdita," Viola said gently. "You can't possibly think that Cheviot and Miss Shipley . . . ! Why, the woman's not even attractive. She has a mustache!"

"For God's sake, Perdita. Listen to Lady Viola. I am innocent!"

"I want to believe you, Tony. I really do. But I—"

"Shall I tell her about you and me, Tony?" Viola offered.

"Only," Tony said grimly, "if you think it will help!"

"What about you and my husband?" Perdita demanded.

"Oh, it's nothing bad," Viola assured her. "About four or five years ago, when I was sixteen, Dickon invited him to come to Lyons for the shooting."

"Yes, I know," Perdita said impatiently.

"Well, I'm afraid I got the most ridiculous idea in my head that I was violently in love with—with your husband," Viola confessed.

"With Tony?" Perdita said incredulously.

"Of course I wasn't really," Viola said quickly. "It was only calf-love. But I didn't know it was calf-love at the time, so naturally, I put everything I had into winning his affections. Of course, he ignored me. But that only made me bolder. I'm not proud of it, but I . . . Well, I . . ." Viola approached Perdita and whispered in her ear.

Perdita's blue eyes started from their sockets. Her cheek turned white. "No!" she said.

"Oh, yes," said Viola.

"And he—he rejected you?"

"Most cruelly," said Viola. "Believe me, if Tony was going to betray you, it would have been that night with me. Not in the wilderness with some beastly, ugly governess."

"Viola!" Lucy protested, scandalized.

"What?" Viola said innocently. "I was young and foolish. Of course, I never looked at another man after that until Julian, because, you see, after Tony, I had standards. I hope that helps?" she added, turning to Perdita.

"Oh, Tony!" said Perdita.

"Perdy!" said Tony, taking her in his arms.

"Come, Lucy," Viola said quickly.


Baroness Devize rose late, as was her habit when in London. Whilst drinking her tea, she scanned the society columns, hoping in vain to find some mention of herself. Disappointed yet again, she completed her morning toilette and went down to see what gifts the post had brought.

She was reading a most exciting letter when the butler came in and announced Lord Devize. "Good morning, madam," said her husband.

Lady Devize held up one finger and continued to read her letter.

"The Honorable Mr Alexander Devize," announced
e butler.

This was too much. Reluctantly, the baroness set aside her
ter. "You idiot!" she snarled. "No! No! No!"

"For God's sake, madam," the baron complained. "Is that
y way to talk to your son?"

"I am not addressing my son," she snapped. "I am ad-
essing the new butler. The 'Honorable' is never to be
oken aloud, Bentley. One sees it in writing, of course, but
speech it is considered to be understood. Such errors are
inful to me. If it is ever repeated, I will turn you off with-
t a character. You will never work in this town again.
ow, get out."

The butler practically ran away.

The baroness smiled coldly. "Well, Alexander! Have you
me to your senses?" she inquired. "Have you come to
ndon to find a suitable wife?"

"Not quite," said Alex. "I have found a suitable wife, and
ave brought her to London."

"The wedding's tomorrow morning," the baron informed
s lady. "Nine o'clock sharp."

The baroness sniffed. "You are with your father. Does that
ean you have decided to marry Miss Peacock, after all?"

Alex took a deep breath. "The bride is Miss Lucy
ampling," he said simply.

"What! That penniless little nobody?" The baroness glared
her husband. "The girl has no beauty, no fortune, no con-
ctions. Nothing to recommend the match!"

"I take a different view," Alex said quietly.

"George? Are you going to allow this?"

The baron shrugged. "His mind is made up."

"It would be a great compliment to my bride, Mama, if you
uld attend the wedding."

The baroness sniffed. "I'm afraid you must excuse me,

Alexander. I have a very important engagement tomorro
morning. I cannot disappoint my friend."

"Engagement! Damn it, madam! What could be more i
portant than your son's wedding day?" Lord Devize 
manded angrily.

The baroness picked up her letter fondly. "Lady Vi
Gambol," she said reverently. "Her ladyship writes to inv
me to a breakfast tomorrow morning at Gambol House. I
her ladyship's first time in London, you know. The event
sure to be attended by the most illustrious members of Socie
I shall be among my peers, at last."

The baron began to laugh. "Gambol House!"

Alex quickly laid a hand on his father's arm. "Don't, Fathe
he said. "There's no point, and we have much to do before
morrow." He bowed stiffly. "Good-bye, Mother. I hope 
breakfast tomorrow is to your liking."

The baroness's thoughts were elsewhere. "Now, what sh
I wear?" she murmured almost giddily as she got up to ri
the bell.

# Chapter Twenty-Five

Viola and Lucy returned to Gambol House later th
afternoon, trailing parcels and dressmakers. The doors we
wide open, as flowers were being delivered. Viola just ma
aged to catch the Dalmatian by his collar as he was slippi
out the door. "Where is my brother?" she demanded o
passing footman. "His dogs are menacing my delive
people!"

Lover appeared to take control of the dog.

"I don't mean to complain, Lover," Viola said, waving

cy to go upstairs without her, "but Gambol House is in
aos! Has the ice arrived at least?"

"Yes, my lady," Lover replied, dragging the dog by its
llar. "His grace has been asking for you. He's in his study."

"I'll take the dog," Viola offered. "You must have a hun-
ed things to do."

The duke sprang up nervously as the door to his sanctuary
ened and the Dalmatian bounded in. "Viola! Thank God!"
cried, collapsing in relief when he saw it was his sister.
Vhere have you been?"

"I've been shopping," she answered, surprised by his emo-
nal state.

"Shopping! At a time like this?"

"Lucy needed a dress," Viola said defensively. "Why,
at's happened?"

The duke chewed at his fingers. "Dev's here," he said, his
gers in his mouth.

"Where?" Viola demanded instantly, looking around.

Dickon crossed the room in leaps and bounds and seized
s sister's hands. "He wants Mary," he said, his mouth quiv-
ng. "He is threatening to keep all your money if I don't let
n marry her! Viola, what are we going to do?"

"Oh, my goodness!" said Viola.

"Mary doesn't want to get married," Dickon said
etchedly. "She doesn't even know Dev. I can't very well ask
r to marry a stranger, can I? She's not strong like you,
ola."

"Don't worry, Dickon," Viola assured him. "She won't
ve to marry Dev."

"But your money, Viola!" he cried, panicking. "He's got
ur money, and he's threatening to take mine, too. This is a
le to him I've never seen before. He was always so gentle
th me, so kind and patient. Why, the man is absolutely ruth-
ss. He'd skin his own grandmother, I do believe! You should
ve seen his eyes!" The duke shivered uncontrollably.

Viola smiled. "I have seen his eyes," she said.

"Then you *know!*" he said, clutching her. "Viola, we ca let Mary fall into the hands of such a man. Then again, need our money, don't we?"

Viola patted his hand. "I'll take care of Mr Devize," s promised.

Dickon sighed in relief. "I knew I could count on yo young Viola! You never let me down. But what are you goi to do? You've never met a villain like this, I assure you."

"It's really quite simple," Viola replied. "I'll just marry h myself."

"Who?" the duke asked in confusion.

"Dev, of course."

"You can't marry Dev!" he protested. "Dev is a Very B Man. Besides, it's Mary he wants."

"I'm sure he'd rather have me," said Viola.

Dickon frowned. "What about Lord Simon?"

"What about him?" she asked, surprised.

"Aren't you going to marry Lord Simon?"

"Certainly not."

"You'd really give him up for poor Mary's sake? Y wouldn't mind?"

"Not at all, I assure you. You see, Dickon, I like Dev."

"You *like* him?" Dickon repeated incredulously.

"I love him."

"You LOVE him?" Dickon repeated even more incred lously.

"Yes," she said simply. "I got to know him very well wh I came to London."

"But he's only the younger son of a baron," Dick protested. "He has no money."

"He'll have *our* money," she pointed out.

"You know what I mean. He's only a stockjobber."

Viola shrugged. "He'll be Chancellor of the Exchequer ten years."

"Everyone hates him!"

"I know," said Viola. "Isn't it nice for me? Now, don't
worry," she went on soothingly. "Think of what a handsome,
clever devil your nephew will be."

Kissing his cheek, she slipped from the room.

His face set and grim, Julian paced back and forth in front
of the big marble fireplace in the drawing room. He was so
lost in his thoughts, that he did not hear Viola come in.

"Hello, Dev."

He pounced on her, swinging her up in his arms and claiming her mouth with his. "I thought you were still in Hampshire," he said when he could kiss her no more.

"You've not seen your brother," she guessed. "He was
supposed to tell you."

"I have been out all day," he said. "Then I came here to see
the duke. He seems to think you don't want to marry me."

"He's a little confused," said Viola. "Shall we sit down?"

"Of course! My God, your ankle. I haven't asked you how
is. How is it?"

"It's very good," she assured him, taking his hands as he
sat next to her. "It's only slowed me down a little. Dev, there's
something I have to tell you."

Julian sat next to her. "You don't want to marry me," he
guessed.

"Of course I want to marry you," she said quickly. "You
may not want to marry *me* when I tell you what I have to tell
you."

He shook his head. "There's nothing you could say that
would change how I feel."

"That's good," Viola said, relieved. "I'm not Mary, Dev.
I'm Viola. Viola Gambol."

Julian merely looked at her.

"I'm the duke's sister," she clarified. "Did you hear me?"

"Yes," he answered, pulling his hands away.

"Well, aren't you going to say anything?" she demanded.

"No," he replied shortly. Standing up, he walked to th fireplace, his back to her.

Viola hung her head. "I should have told you before," sh said miserably. "I came to London in Mary's place . . . to mee her aunt." She looked up at him, hoping he would at least loo at her. When he did not, she began to babble. "I wanted to b sure Mrs Dean would be a fit guardian for the child, whicl of course, she isn't. I thought you knew at first who I was. Be cause you work for my brother, I naturally assumed you kne who I was. I thought you were spying on me, to be hones You must have thought me so conceited."

He threw her a quick, unsmiling glance over his shoulde

Viola went on, encouraged by his attention. "Whe realized you didn't know who I was, I was afraid to tell you

"Afraid?"

"Well, you might've held me for ransom or somethin Then I didn't want to tell you because I was afraid, if yc knew, you'd send me away. I didn't want you to send n away."

She paused, but he still said nothing.

"Then, when you couldn't get the license, I thought yc didn't want to marry me. I knew if I told you who I was, th you *would* marry me, but perhaps not because you wanted I didn't want *that*. Then Lord Simon came . . . Then, in Ham shire, I thought . . ."

Here she paused, putting her hand over her eyes. "I do know what I thought in Hampshire. It all happened so fast

He still did not speak.

Viola did not know what else to say. "Dev, I know you angry, but you'll have to talk to me. You must say som thing!"

He turned to face her. "Thank you for being honest w me, madam," he said. "Now I shall be honest with you."

"All right," she said uneasily.

"I know who you are. The first thing I saw when I walked into this house was that gargantuan portrait of your mother. I thought it was *you* at first. She was very beautiful, your mother."

Viola started up angrily. "You knew? And you let me go on, burbling like a frightened child!"

"Yes," he replied, glowering at her. "I let you go on."

"I suppose I deserved that," Viola said grudgingly.

"What happens now?" he demanded.

Viola was bewildered by his anger. "What do you mean? You still want to marry me, don't you?"

He glared at her. "Do you want to marry me?"

"Well, y-yes," she stammered. "If you want to marry me, that is."

He looked suspicious. "What about Lord Simon?"

Viola blinked in surprise. "What about him?"

"Well, aren't you going to marry him?" he wanted to know.

"How could you even imagine such a thing?" she whispered, horrified.

Julian crossed the room to stand in front of her. "Answer the question, madam!"

"No! I'm not going to marry Lord Simon," she said. "I'm going to marry *you,* if you'll stop being an idiot."

"Oh, I'm an idiot, am I? Your brother seems to think you're going to marry Lord Simon."

"I told you he was confused," said Viola. "He's even more confused than I thought. Dev, you of all people should know I never marry Lord Simon. I'd never marry anyone but you."

"Do you mean that?"

"Of course I mean it," she assured him, taking his hand.

Julian fell to his knees. "I thought you were going to marry him and try to keep me on a string—a pet, a lover," he confessed. "I was so angry!"

"Darling!" she cried, throwing her arms around him. "Wh
didn't you say something?"

Julian laughed shakily. "I'm glad I didn't. I wanted to thro
tle you. I wanted to die!"

"You know I don't approve of adultery."

"You know," he said, fingering the silk of her skirt, "it
bad luck for the groom to see the bride before the wedding

"Not if he kisses her," Viola replied.

Miss Shipley entered Gambol House shielded by a delive
of flowers. Swept along, she made her way down the length
the great hall before being stopped by a liveried servant.

"Musician, seamstress, or cook?" he asked, then departe
abruptly when she answered "Governess" out of habit.

Farther along down the hall, she spotted a stout, bald ma
dragging a Great Dane by its collar. "Excuse me, kind si
she called to him sweetly. "Could you help me, please?"

"Who are you?" the Duke of Fanshawe asked, regardin
her with suspicion.

Miss Shipley tried a different approach. "I'm lookin
for Lord Cheviot," she announced haughtily. "I was told h
was here."

"Tony? I suppose he's here somewhere," the duke replie

"Would you mind awfully telling him I'm here?" Mis
Shipley said coldly.

"Is he expecting you?" Dickon wanted to know.

"If he isn't, he should be," she answered, smirking. "Pr
tell his lordship that Miss Shipley desires to see him. He w
know what it is about."

"Oh?" said Dickon, giving her a wink. "You're the go
erness, are you?"

Miss Shipley sniffed indignantly. "I am. And who mig
you be, sir?"

"Me? I'm the Duke of Fanshawe," he replied. "Tony and I
ere at school together."

"Your Grace!" she squawked, growing sweet again. "I'm
 sorry! I didn't recognize you, Your Grace."

"That's because we've never met before," he explained.
Why don't you come in here and sit down?" he suggested
ndly. "You shouldn't be on your feet more than necessary,
u know. You've got to think of the baby."

Miss Shipley preceded him into his study. "Your Grace is
ry kind," she said, fluttering her eyelids at him.

"I'll go and find Tony for you," he offered. "You've got his
tter, I suppose?"

"Oh, yes, Your Grace," she assured him. "I'm prepared to
 quite reasonable."

"Good, good. Now, don't mind Samson," he said, releasing
e Great Dane. "He won't bite you unless you try to leave the
om."

"What?" cried Miss Shipley as the door swung closed.


Lord Cheviot found his wife in the banquet hall directing
e servants as they decorated the room. Feeling lighthearted
d carefree, he came up behind her and covered her eyes
ith his hands. "Guess who?"

Perdita shrieked. The notebook she was writing in flew up
 the air, scattering pages. "What do you think you're
ing?" she demanded savagely. "It's bad enough I'm stuck
re managing this whole wedding by myself without you
eaking up on me and frightening me to death!"

"I'm sorry," said Tony, getting on his knees to retrieve her
pers.

"I'm demented," she said irritably, snatching her checklist
om him. "And all you can think to do is come up behind
ople and say guess who!"

"What can I do to help?"

"I don't know," she said grumpily. "Papa's handling all t
legal mishmash. Viola's dressing Lucy—and herse
obviously. The servants are managing the food. The flow
are here, thank God."

"I thought you were doing it all by yourself," he teased h

She glared at him. "Have you selected the music?"

"Piece of cake," he assured her.

"The cake!" cried Perdita.

"Let the servants manage all that," he said firmly. "Co
and have your tea."

Perdita was astonished to learn that it was almost five o
clock. "I'd love a cup of tea," she confessed.

"There you are, Tony!"

The duke's voice boomed from across the room.

"I've been looking for you everywhere." "I've got her!"

"Got who?" Tony asked, not unreasonably.

"You said you were having a spot of bother with t
governess," Dickon reminded him. "I've got her. She's in
study."

"Miss Shipley!" cried Perdita. "Here?"

The duke glanced at her. "Who are you?" he asked.

"I'm his wife," she told him.

"Whose wife?"

"Tony's wife," she snapped. "For heaven's sake, you we
at our wedding!"

"You were slimmer then," he said defensively. "How d
you like my wedding present?"

"The elephant? It died, I'm very sorry to say," she repli
stiffly.

Dickon guffawed. "Of course it died! But how did it taste

Perdita rounded on her husband furiously. "Tony! *What*
Miss Shipley doing here?"

"I didn't invite her," he protested.

"She has your letter, Tony," Dickon said helpfully.

Perdita's eyes were like shards of blue glass. "What letter?"
e snarled. "Take me to her," she demanded.

Miss Shipley was quite surprised to see her former mis-
ss. "My lady!"

"What are you doing there, Shipley?" Perdita demanded.

"I only want justice for my unborn child," Miss Shipley
ained.

"No, I meant what are you doing *there,* on the duke's
sk?"

Miss Shipley eyed Samson warily. "That dog was growling
me."

"Good dog," Perdita observed, patting the Great Dane on
e head. "You can come down now, Miss Shipley. All I want
the letter."

"Lord Cheviot!" she cried, catching sight of her protector.
'all off the dog! Your wife has gone mad!"

Tony sank into a chair, his head in his hands. "Just give her
e letter, Miss Shipley," he said miserably. "The jig is up."

"Give me the letter," Perdita said more persuasively, "or I'll
ve this dog the command to rip you apart."

There was no such command, of course, but Miss Shipley
d not know that. With trembling hands, she drew his lord-
ip's letter from her bosom.

Perdita took it and read it. It was not, as she had feared, a
ve letter. "Well, Tony?" she said coldly. "Would you care to
.plain this?"

"I couldn't help it," he said. "I felt sorry for her, so I wrote
r a letter of reference. I thought," he added darkly, "she
ight need it to find another job."

"Ha!" said Miss Shipley. "I'll never work again! May I
mind your lordship whose baby I'm carrying? You had your
n, my lord, and now you must pay!"

"It's not true, Perdita!" cried Tony. "You must believe me.
vrote that cursed letter—I admit it! But I never had any fun.
ever!"

"If it's not yours, then whose is it?" Perdita demanded.

"Well, don't look at me," said the duke, taking control his dog. "I've never really been interested in that sort of thi You said she was deucedly unattractive, Tony, but you ne said she was a man," he added. "You could have knocked over with a feather."

"What are you talking about, Dickon?" Tony groaned disgust. "She's not a man. She's just not very pretty."

"She is so a man," Dickon insisted. "I wasn't born yest day, you know. There are some very important anatomical ferences between men and women, you know. What's the thing a man has that woman don't? Hmmm? Three guesse

Tony's face was red. "My wife is in the room," he point out indignantly.

"Pshaw! If you've seen one, you've seen them all. Sh got, what, four sons?"

"Five," Perdita corrected him. "But what makes you think . . How do you know," she began more carefully, "that Miss Sh ley has that thing that men have and women don't?"

Dickon goggled in amazement. "Look at her," he urge "It's quite a large one—plain as the nose on her face, in fa

"You've seen it?" cried Perdita.

"It's right under her chin," said Dickon. "Her Adam's app Lord, woman, it's the size of my fist. Look!"

"So it is," said Perdita, after a moment.

"Women don't have Adam's apples," Dickon told the loftily. "If they did, it would be called Eve's apple."

"Miss Shipley, are you a man?" Perdita demanded.

Miss Shipley glared at them.

"Miss Shipley?" Perdita repeated. "Answer the question and don't lie! There are ways," she added threateningly, ' finding out."

"All right," said Miss Shipley, her pointed chin lifted in fiance. "My name isn't Charlotte. It's Charles."

"But you can't be a man," said Tony. "You cried! Men don't cry."

"Try being a governess," Miss Shipley snarled. "You'd cry, too. I thought it would be an easy job—after all, women do it. That was before I met your Henry."

"I told you she was a man," Dickon said triumphantly. "Now, about the baby . . ."

Miss Shipley's lip curled. "What about it?"

"It's not really Tony's, is it?" he said. "And don't lie! There are ways of finding out."

"It's a pillow," said Miss Shipley.

"Now do you believe me?" Tony demanded of his wife.

"Yes," she answered. "But I'm still quite annoyed with you for writing that letter."

"Give her the ring," Dickon suggested.

Perdita was intrigued. "What ring?"

Tony took it out of his pocket and presented it to her. "It's nothing much," he mumbled.

"An emerald, Tony?" Perdita said, looking at the ring with scorn. "Green is the color of jealousy. Are you trying to say that I'm jealous?"

Tony was taken aback.

"Because I'm not jealous," Perdita said, sweeping to the door. "I never have been."

"There's no pleasing some people," Dickon observed sadly. "Come, Samson."

When the dog had gone, Miss Shipley climbed down from the desk.

"Where do you think you're going?" Tony demanded.

She sniffed. "Am I under arrest?"

"Well, no," he admitted.

"Do you want me to stay?"

"Certainly not," said Tony, and Miss Shipley walked out of Gambol House a free man.

* * *

Armed with her invitation to breakfast, the baroness arrived at Gambol House the following morning. She was nearly twenty minutes late, a condition she blamed alternately on the horrendous traffic and the stupidity of her servants.

In spite of her tardiness, Gambol House opened its doors to her readily. The air inside was cool and sweet, quite different from ordinary air. It smelled of some exquisitely subtle mixture of flowers and precious wood. The ceilings were high, the furnishings opulent. Strains of sublime music floated in the air, almost like another layer of fragrance. To the baroness's finely tuned ear, it sounded quite outrageously expensive.

Her attempts to hurry the footman met with no success, and she had ample time to visit her reflection in each of the beautifully framed mirrors she passed. Her gown was the very latest in color, a manganese blue, worn with a cunningly cut redingote of saffron superfine. Her hat was in the same two colors, double-brimmed and bristling with sprays of tulle. She had been perfectly satisfied of her own magnificence when she had left Portland Place, but, somehow, in the mirrors of Gambol House, she looked a paler, thinner version of herself.

She stopped the footman at the doors and steadied herself with a deep breath.

"I am ready," she told him presently. "You may announce me."

It was too late, however, for any such announcement; the ceremony was well underway.

"Ceremony?" she said, startled. "I was invited to breakfast."

The baroness was obliged to slip into a chair at the very back of the room. The gentleman next to her looked startled and stood up to bow. He looked familiar to the baroness, but she could not place him. The company, she was pleased to see, was a small and exclusive set. They looked quite delightful from the back. The military gentlemen wore their regi-

mentals with distinction, and the lords wore their sashes and
swords ditto. The ladies were universally well-hatted. At the
very front of the room was a mitered bishop.

Immediately before the bishop stood two couples. The
ladies were similarly dressed in white satin, with lace veils
obscuring their hair. The trains of their gowns were heavily
embroidered in silver and gold. The gentlemen were more
varied. One was simply attired in a pearl gray coat and pan-
taloons. The other was a military gentleman in a scarlet coat
with braid upon the shoulders. The baroness recognized at
once, even without attending the bishop's language, that she
was at a wedding.

She glanced at the gentleman on her right. She still did not
recognize him, but he seemed so in awe of her that she did
not scruple to speak. "A double wedding!" she whispered.
"What a clever surprise."

"It was immensely sudden," Hudson agreed, rather startled
that Lady Devize had deigned to speak to him.

"So good of Lady Viola to invite me," she murmured.
"Who is getting married?"

Hudson flashed her a look of surprise. "Your son, my lady."

"What?" she snarled, on her feet. "Julian is marrying that
hussy? Over my dead body! I object!" she added, in a voice
that carried.

The expensive sounds of the string quartet ceased.

The baron turned and scowled at his wife. "Sit down,
woman!"

The baroness stared at him. "What are you doing here,
George?" she demanded. "You should be at Alexander's
wedding!"

"I *am* at Alex's wedding," the baron said indignantly. "I'm
certainly not at Julian's wedding! I don't even have a son by
that name. I'm certainly not here to wish him well, the disobedient wretch."

"No one thinks you are, Baron," Viola assured him.

The bishop held up a hand for silence. "To which union do you object, madam?" he asked the baroness.

The baroness looked at Lucy's frightened face with scorn. "I object to both," she replied stoutly. "*That* woman has no dowry—and *that* woman has no shame."

"Sit down at once," the baron commanded her. "You're making a damn fool of yourself."

"You old fool," she snarled at him. "If you had any sense, you would have put a stop to this yourself!"

"Madam," the bishop interrupted, "if you know of some impediment—"

"She doesn't," said Viola. "Just ignore her."

"Yes, I do," said the baroness.

"A lack of dowry is no impediment in the eyes of God," the bishop said sternly.

"It should be!" she told him angrily.

"As for your complaint against Lady Viola," the bishop began.

The baroness looked blank. "L-Lady V-Viola?" she stammered. "I have no complaint against Lady Viola!"

Perdita hurried over to her mother. There was a quick exchange of ideas. The baroness's face turned red. "I withdraw my objection," she said, hurrying back to her seat.

The Duke of Fanshawe raised his hand tentatively. "This strange female has given me courage," he said. "I, too, have an objection."

"No, you don't," Viola informed him coldly.

Cowed by her frowning eyes, Dickon slumped in defeat. "I withdraw my objection."

"In that case," the bishop said irritably, "those whom God hath joined together, let no man put asunder."

Upon these magic words, the doors were thrown open, and in the next room, where the wedding breakfast had been laid, the string quartet began to play the quiet, stately chords of Pachelbel's *Canon*.

# Epilogue

His sister's marriage was scarcely a day old when the duke began to fear the union might not bear fruit. At breakfast, the bride blushed not at all, and the bichon curled up in her lap seemed to interest her more than the handsome new husband at her elbow. Even more worrying was the behavior of the groom; Julian consumed only the briefest, most perfunctory, unbuttered muffin before pushing back his chair.

"Well, I'm off," he announced calmly, apparently intending to get away.

"Off you go, then," said his lady, apparently content to let him escape.

Dickon was not so complacent. If his sister could not be bothered to cling to her husband, he certainly could. "Off?" he repeated, aghast. "Off where?"

Julian barely raised a brow. "To the Exchange, of course," he answered.

"He missed yesterday because of the wedding," Viola added, blowing gently on her tea to cool it. "It's no telling what the rascals got up to. They're like children."

Dickon gaped at them in disbelief. In his view, they were the most unnatural newlyweds in the historical record. Where was the passion? The billing and cooing? Indeed, these things were markedly absent. "The Exchange!" he spluttered. "At a time like this?"

"Of course," Julian said easily, pausing to wind his watch. "I hope you don't think I'm the sort of man who'd be content to sit in his wife's lap all day."

Viola sniffed. "For one thing, Bijou would never permit it."

"That's a very undutiful attitude, I must say," Dickon angrily complained to his brother-in-law. "My sister may accuse you of neglect! I for one would not blame her if she did."

"He can't neglect me if I'm not here," Viola pointed out with decidedly unbridal indifference. "I myself shall be out all day, I shouldn't wonder."

"Out? Out where?" Dickon demanded.

"I have a hundred things to do," Viola said vaguely.

"You should be *in*, young Viola, not *out*," he told her sternly. "And *he* should be *on*, not *off*. What's the matter with you people? This ought to be the happiest day of my life, and you're spoiling it altogether."

"If *I* don't object to his going out, I don't see how it matters to *you*," Viola returned. "Just because we're married doesn't mean we have to spend every waking moment together."

"That's exactly what it means, young Viola," Dickon argued. "At least until you give me a nephew, it does. After that, you may do what you like. And you, too, Dev," he added generously.

Julian put his hands on the back of his chair and leaned toward his wife. "What's he talking about? Why should we *give* him a nephew?"

Viola came very near to rolling her eyes.

"It's to do with the succession," Dickon explained. "Didn't my sister tell you?"

"Tell me what?" Julian demanded.

Viola frowned at his tone. "You might have noticed a

ready, Mr Devize, that my brother has no children. Obviously, this means that *my* eldest son will inherit. *Ergo*, his nephew."

"Precisely," said Dickon. "Though I'd rethink the name if I were you. I was thinking Richard, perhaps, after his dear old uncle."

"I've decided to call him Lyon, after my mother," Viola announced.

"Don't I have a say?" Julian objected.

"Of course," said Viola. "I thought you might like to contribute the surname. Lyon Devize. Mr Lyon Devize."

"How about Richard Lyon Devize?" Dickon suggested.

"It's a little early to be christening the lad," Viola said hastily.

"Indeed!" said Dickon, returning to his main theme. "Before he can be christened he's got to be born. And before he can be born, he's got to be conceived."

"Really," said Viola. "Who told you that?"

"Tony," Dickon told her proudly. "And he'd know, wouldn't he?"

Julian frowned. "If you're in such a bloody hurry, Duke, why don't you just get married and do it yourself?"

"Because I can't, that's why!" Dickon roared, his ears reddening. "Just you finish your breakfast, young Viola, and get back to bed where you belong—and take this—this *shirker* with you! My nephew ain't going to conceive himself, you know!"

Viola sighed impatiently. "Dickon, we cannot stay in bed all day. That would be . . ."

"Exhausting?" Julian suggested as she paused.

"I was going to say delightful," Viola said dryly. "Unfortunately, it simply isn't possible. Even otters must leave time for other things. Dam-building or whatever. Dev and I have a great deal to do if we are to be presented at Court next week."

These last words seemed to annoy her husband. "We discussed this, madam," he said grimly. "I don't want to be presented at Court, not next week, nor ever."

"It *is* a damned, tedious waste of an evening," Viola conceded. "But if you want to be Chancellor of the Exchequer, we must begin nursing the ground *now*, before we go away on our honeymoon. We cannot begin by insulting the Queen."

Dickon brightened instantly. "Oh, there's to be a honeymoon, is there? Good! Good! I'm glad *someone* is thinking. When do you go?"

"*After* our presentation," Viola said, looking at Julian with defiance.

Julian was staring at his wife. "What in God's name makes you think I want to be Chancellor of the Exchequer? Chancellor of the Exchequer!" he said, beginning to laugh. "Madam, I think you might have me confused with someone else. Even if I *were* ambitious, such a position would never be offered to me. In case you haven't noticed, you just married the most hated man in London. I am a leper, both politically and socially."

"I've never found the animosity of fools to be much of an obstacle," Viola replied. "Neither socially nor politically. Anyway, as my husband, you'll always be acceptable to the Tories, and your father can sort you with the Opposition. Politically, you're perfectly situated. When the time comes, it won't even matter which party is in power."

"Less talk of politics, please," Dickon said severely. "More talk of honeymoon."

"My father!" Julian protested. "He wouldn't lift a finger to help me. He only came to my wedding because it was my brother's wedding, too."

"You're wrong, Dev," said Viola. "The baron and I have discussed the matter at length, and he's all for it. He's still not speaking to you, of course, but he's all for your advancement."

Julian displeasure was growing by the minute. "You've spoken to my father?" he said coldly. "About me?"

"At length. You are our favorite subject, hands down."

"Oh, please don't quarrel," Dickon fretted. "It's very bad for the baby."

"No quarrel," Julian said coolly. "I just realized something—married Lady Macbeth."

"What!" cried Dickon. "Well, sir! This is a most unwelcome complication. You might have said so *before* you married my sister!"

"I didn't know until this moment," said Julian, glaring at his bride.

"Odd sort of marriage," Dickon observed.

"Isn't it?" Julian said darkly, causing Viola to sigh.

"What's to be done?" Dickon wondered, wringing his hands. "Dev, you can't have two wives—there are laws! You'll have to get rid of this Lady Macbeth person. Sad, of course, but there it is."

"Why don't you go and ask Lover to take care of that for us?" Viola suggested to her brother. "I think you'll find him remarkably efficient. Dev, you're being ridiculous," she went on when her brother had left the room. "I'm not asking you to kill anyone. I'm only asking you to seek a position worthy of your talents."

"That's just what Lady Macbeth would say," he insisted.

Viola gathered Bijou to her breast and hugged her. "Well, I was only trying to make you happy. Of course, if you don't *wish* to be Chancellor . . ."

She looked at him inquiringly.

"All right," he said, after a moment. "Let's say I do. What's the plan? First, you drag me to Court—"

"Where you will look absolutely delightful in your silk breeches," she put in eagerly.

"Likewise in your hoop skirt and feathers!" he retaliated. "Then what?"

"Honeymoon," she said innocently. "We mustn't neglect one another."

"Oh, yes? And where are we going?"

"Anywhere you like," she answered warmly.

"Really?" he said suspiciously.

"Certainly. As long as it's Paris."

Julian hid a smile. "I suppose I *could* spend a few days away from London, and, as it happens, I have two tickets for the packet to Calais."

Viola lifted a brow. "You just *happen* to have two tickets to Calais? What an amazing coincidence. Or did I marry Machiavelli?"

"Neither. As it happens, I *had* been planning to elope with you to France, but since you upstaged me . . . Well, we might as well put them to good use. We can leave tonight."

Viola shook her head. "No, Dev. First we must be presented at Court. Then we can go play on the Continent."

"Can't we do the Court thing after the honeymoon?" he suggested. "I shall be in a much better mood after the honeymoon."

"Undoubtedly," Viola agreed, "but *I* shall be too big."

"Nonsense. You'll be getting plenty of exercise. You could eat your way through Paris and still come back light as a feather."

"Of course *I* shall be light as a feather," Viola answered impatiently. "It's the baby that's so disgustingly fat."

Julian drew his breath in sharply, but seemed to forget to exhale. "Good God," he murmured. "You don't mean . . ."

Viola chuckled. "I wish you could see your face. You look absolutely terrified. Here, sit down," she added gently, pushing his chair out with her foot. "It's not all that shocking, I hope, when you consider that we *have* been rather naughty. I won't say we've been going at it like minks, but others might. Given the fact that we are both young and in tip-top form, one might even say that a baby was inevitable. Sort of like the waiter showing up at the end of the meal."

"Are you sure?" he demanded as, white-faced, he sank into his chair.

"No," she admitted, "but I *am* absolutely certain."

He stared at her. "What the devil does that mean?"

"It's early days yet, but I have a strong feeling about it.

he explained. "And, when I was in Hampshire, I had the
strangest dream."

"Feelings! Dreams!" he said, rather contemptuously.
"Have you seen a doctor?"

"I'm not sick," she protested. "Of that I am certain *and*
sure. And I don't want my brother to know—not yet. He has
some very silly ideas about what I ought to eat in order to
breed a masculine child. If a doctor were to visit me now, I'd
be looking at months of eel pie and God knows what else."
She paused as if something had unsettled her stomach. After
a few deep breaths, she went on. "I'll see a doctor in Paris if
it will make you feel better. Incidentally, did you know that
there was a stock exchange of sorts in Paris?"

"The Bourse?"

"Is that what it's called?"

"Yes. It's much older than our Exchange, you know."

"I had no idea. You should definitely go and see it when
we're in Paris. You could stick your head in, couldn't you,
while I'm shopping or whatever?"

Julian snorted. "My God, you're devious," he accused.
"And if I should happen to break a *French* bank while I'm
sticking my head in the Bourse . . . ?"

"So much the better," said Viola. "If you did so, people
here might forget all about what you did to Child's Bank, you
dreadful man."

"It's not that simple," Julian warned her. "Something like that
would take months. I can't leave London for as long as that."

"Of course you can. Hire a man of business to do your will.
Paris is only two days away," she reminded him. "If there's an
emergency, you can always go home. Darling, you really must
learn to delegate."

"I've always secretly wanted to study the Bourse," Julian
admitted.

Walking in upon this remark, the duke naturally was
cheered. "Of course you have, Dev. You're a man, aren't you?

It's perfectly natural. And now you're married, you can study it anytime you like. And no need to worry about the Macbeth situation. I talked to Lover, and, believe me, she's as good as dead. He's going to make it look like a suicide."

"Well done," Viola congratulated him.

Julian scraped back his chair again. "I have to go. I shan't be home for tea."

"Then you won't miss me," Viola told him. "Lucy and I are having tea with your mother. We're going to thrash out once and for all which of us is to be her favorite daughter-in-law. I've a terrible, sinking feeling it's going to be me. I'll walk you out," she offered, gathering up Bijou and climbing to her feet.

"But you *will* be home for dinner, won't you, Dev?" Dickon exclaimed. "It's eel pie. I ordered it special."

Viola hastily pressed the dog into Julian's arms and ran from the room with her hand clapped over her mouth.

"What's the matter with her?" Dickon wanted to know.

"Nothing, Duke," said Julian. "She's just happy, that's all."

## More by Bestselling Author
# Fern Michaels

# Romantic Suspense from
# Lisa Jackson

| | | |
|---|---|---|
| **See How She Dies** | 0-8217-7605-3 | $6.99US/$9.99C |
| **Final Scream** | 0-8217-7712-2 | $7.99US/$10.99 |
| **Wishes** | 0-8217-6309-1 | $5.99US/$7.99C |
| **Whispers** | 0-8217-7603-7 | $6.99US/$9.99C |
| **Twice Kissed** | 0-8217-6038-6 | $5.99US/$7.99C |
| **Unspoken** | 0-8217-6402-0 | $6.50US/$8.50C |
| **If She Only Knew** | 0-8217-6708-9 | $6.50US/$8.50C |
| **Hot Blooded** | 0-8217-6841-7 | $6.99US/$9.99C |
| **Cold Blooded** | 0-8217-6934-0 | $6.99US/$9.99C |
| **The Night Before** | 0-8217-6936-7 | $6.99US/$9.99C |
| **The Morning After** | 0-8217-7295-3 | $6.99US/$9.99C |
| **Deep Freeze** | 0-8217-7296-1 | $7.99US/$10.99 |
| **Fatal Burn** | 0-8217-7577-4 | $7.99US/$10.99 |
| **Shiver** | 0-8217-7578-2 | $7.99US/$10.99 |
| **Most Likely to Die** | 0-8217-7576-6 | $7.99US/$10.99 |
| **Absolute Fear** | 0-8217-7936-2 | $7.99US/$9.49C |
| **Almost Dead** | 0-8217-7579-0 | $7.99US/$10.99 |
| **Lost Souls** | 0-8217-7938-9 | $7.99US/$10.99 |
| **Left to Die** | 1-4201-0276-1 | $7.99US/$10.99 |
| **Wicked Game** | 1-4201-0338-5 | $7.99US/$9.99C |
| **Malice** | 0-8217-7940-0 | $7.99US/$9.49C |

*Available Wherever Books Are Sold!*
Visit our website at www.kensingtonbooks.com